ULAN BATOR

MONGOLIA

HEILONGKIANG

MANCHURIA

KIRIN

MARITIME PROVINCE

Vladivostok

Harbin

Changchun

Ssuping

CHAHAR

LIAONING

Liao R.

JEHOL

Mukden

Sea of Japan

KOREA

38th Parallel

Kalgan

SUIYUAN

PEKING

Shanhaikwan

Tangku

Tientsin

'Po'
Hai
Bay

Dairen
Port Arthur

NINGHSIA

Taiyuan

Yenan

SHANSI

HOPEI

Yellow R.

SHANTUNG

Tsingtao

Yellow Sea

JAPAN

Lanchow

SHENSI

Sian

HONAN

Hsuchow

Suhsien

HUAIPEI
PLAIN

Peng Pu

Nienchuangchi

KIANGSU

Suchou

SZECHWAN

HUPEH

Huai R.

Nanking

Shanghai

Chengtu

Yangtze R.

ANHWEI

Hangchow

East China Sea

Chungking

HUNAN

KIANGSI

CHEKIANG

Kweiyang

KWEICHOW

FUKIEN

Taipei

KWANGTUNG

FORMOSA
(TAIWAN)

Canton

Pacific Ocean

KWANGSI

HAINAN

South China Sea

PHILIPPINES

©1999 A. Karl / J. Kemp

The Peking Letter

ALSO BY SEYMOUR TOPPING

Journey Between Two Chinas

The Peking Letter

A NOVEL OF THE CHINESE CIVIL WAR

SEYMOUR TOPPING

A CORNELIA AND MICHAEL BESSIE BOOK

PublicAffairs • NEW YORK

Photo on page 1 courtesy of CORBIS/Underwood & Underwood.

Photo on page 141 courtesy of China Photos, Peking.

Photo on page 241 courtesy of the Associated Press.

Book design by Victoria Kuskowski and Scott Levine.

Part title translation and calligraphy by Nancy Yang Liu.

Library of Congress Cataloging-in-Publication Data

Topping, Seymour, 1921–

The Peking letter : a novel of the Chinese civil war / Seymour Topping. — 1st ed.

p.   cm.

ISBN 1–891620–35–5 (hardcover)

1. China—History—Civil War, 1945–1949 Fiction.   I. Title.

PS3570.0663P4   1999   99–29834

813'.54—dc21   CIP

FIRST EDITION

1 3 5 7 9 10 8 6 4 2

114710

OCT 2 3 1999

FOR MY FATHER, JOSEPH,
IN MEMORY OF HIS LOVE AND TRUST

The Tao that can be told
is not the eternal Tao.

These words, spoken in China some twenty-five hundred years ago, introduce us to the Tao, translated in the West as "the Way." They make up the first line of the Tao Te Ching, written by the legendary Taoist philosopher, Lao Tsu, and are among the most famous words in all the literature of the world. The Tao Te Ching helps us see how the fundamental forces of the cosmos are mirrored in our own individual, inner structure. And it invites us to try to live in direct relationship to all these forces.*

Better stop short than fill to the brim.
Oversharpen the blade, and the edge will soon blunt.
Amass a store of gold and jade, and no one can protect it.
Claim wealth and titles, and disaster will follow.
Retire when the work is done.
This is the way of heaven.

Lao Tsu, circa 604–c. 531 B.C.

"Well then," said the Lord of the River, "what should I do and what should I not do? How am I to know in the end what to accept and what to reject, what to abide by and what to discard?"

Jo of the North Sea said, "From the point of view of the Way, what is noble or what is mean? These are merely what are called endless changes. Do not hobble your will, or you will be departing from the Way!"

Chuang Tzu, circa 369–c. 531 B.C., in "The Fable of the Autumn Floods"
From the translation by Burton Watson

*From the introduction by Jacob Needleman to *Lao Tsu: Tao Te Ching,* translation by Gia-Fu Feng and Jane English.

Acknowledgments

My deep appreciation for the wise guidance of my editor, Michael Bessie, and my thanks to Kate Darnton of PublicAffairs for her skillful editing of the manuscript. My thanks also to Judith Economos, Professor Lawrence R. Sullivan, and Alexandra Shelley, who read the manuscript and made very helpful suggestions. I am most grateful to my wife, Audrey Ronning Topping, author and photojournalist, for sharing her extensive China experience, and for her encouragement over the years.

For quotations from translations of Taoist writings I am indebted to the works: *Taoism and Chinese Religion* by Henri Maspero, translated from the French by Frank A. Kierman, Jr. (Amherst: University of Massachusetts Press, 1981); *Tao Te Ching, Lao Tsu* by Gia-Fu Feng and Jane English (New York: Alfred A. Knopf, 1972); *Chuang Tzu* by Burton Watson (New York: Columbia University Press, 1964); and *The New Lao Tzu* by Ray Grigg (Boston: C. E. Tuttle Co., 1995).

Author's Note

This novel takes place during the civil war between the forces of Chiang Kai-shek and Mao Tse-tung. I covered the war from 1946 to 1949 as a journalist on the Nationalist and Communist sides, being based in Peking, an intriguing walled city (now replaced by the modern and less appealing Beijing), and in Nanking, then Chiang's capital. My story is fictitious but enacted within the historical framework of that period. At the time, Chinese Communist armies were descending on Peking. Americans were being evacuated from the China mainland, while the Central Intelligence Agency was seeking to install a clandestine network there. In the United States the House Committee on Un-American Activities was hunting alleged Communist sympathizers in the State Department, claiming they had undermined Chiang Kai-shek's armies.

My tale, which revolves about those events, is told through the experiences of Eric Jensen, a young American scholar, who had been researching the inner meaning of the Tao, that mystical dynamic at the center of much of ancient Chinese philosophy. When Jensen falls in love with a Chinese woman revolutionary he becomes entangled in political conspiracy and is sent trekking across remote battlefields. The comments made to him by Chinese leaders and the American ambassador, J. Leighton Stuart, are fictitious, but to my knowledge their substance reflects the actual views of those historic personages. Some of the scenes from Jensen's odyssey—the Communist encirclement of Peking, the fall of Nanking, the decisive Battle of the Huai-Hai, and the conquest of Manchuria—are drawn from my reporting as a journalist.

I offer this novel as an entertainment, yet I dare to hope that its historical perspectives may also help to make China more understandable.

Scarsdale, New York
April 1999

Note: The English renderings of Chinese names are in the Wade-Giles romanization of the period.

Part One

THE TEMPLE OF HEAVEN

天之坛

Chapter One

PEKING, OCTOBER 1948

The massive oaken door of the Peking Language School swung open and a tall, lean man in a soft ranch hat emerged. He paused in the dim light cast by the brass lamp dangling from the arch of the entryway. He was an American, in his mid-twenties, his height accentuated by the black hat pulled down over thick reddish hair that fell to his shoulders. He wore a long black Chinese robe.

Eric Jensen hooked the fur-lined collar of his gown against the October chill and tucked his hands into the broad sleeves. In the school chapel the evening prayer service was ending and he could hear faintly the school hymn being sung by the missionary students:

> *In scattered rural hamlets,*
> *Or where great cities hum,*
> *To China as a Nation*
> *We pray, Thy Kingdom Come.*

Jensen pictured the missionaries before the pulpit holding the hands of their children as they sang. "Innocents and martyrs," he muttered.

Communist armies were advancing on Peking. Other students, from the foreign banks, trading companies, and the military, had already been evacuated. The siege would soon begin. Yet the student missionaries were preparing to go forth into the countryside to preach their gospel.

Although living apart as a scholar-in-residence, Jensen had become friendly with a few of the younger missionaries. They approached him curious about his work. He answered questions freely about his study of Taoist scriptures at the universities, monasteries, and in the archives of secret societies. Pressed, he'd talk about his service with General Joseph Stilwell, the World War II China Theater commander and a graduate of the school: years of hacking through the jungles on the Ledo Road, in combat with the Japanese, opening the Burma Road, the link to China. But he dissembled—hating the need to be devious—when they asked why he had chosen to live in the austere missionary-run school. Jensen shrugged. It no longer mattered very much. Soon they'd hear that the director had thrown him out. Given him two days to leave the school premises.

Jensen rubbed the stubble on his chin and walked quickly down the worn stone steps into the alleyway. The cobbled hutung alley was deserted, murky under the darkening sky. Jensen beckoned, and a three-wheeled pedicab came swiftly out of the shadow of the school's compound wall, guided by a gaunt Chinese holding the handlebars with his left hand and the bicycle seat with the other as he ran alongside. "You are well, Master?" the pedicab man said in the purring Peking dialect, touching the brim of his brown fedora. The fedora was a whimsical accessory to Ying's blue cotton jacket and baggy trousers. At times Jensen would offer to exchange his Australian hat for the battered fedora, much to Ying's amusement.

"To the shop of Wang Li," Jensen said as he mounted the pedicab, not inviting the usual banter. He spoke fluent Mandarin. Only a slight tonal inflection revealed that he was not born to the language. Ying wrapped a frayed blanket around Jensen's legs, leaped onto the bicycle seat, and pedaled rapidly west along the Tou Tiao Hutung toward Hatamen Street. The pedicab bumped over cobblestones through the twilight, past the walled compounds of whitewashed brick houses. Here in Peking's Inner City, the old imperial Tartar City of the Manchus, most of the great houses belonged to Nationalist government officials, wealthy Chinese, or foreigners. Already their gates were barred for the night. Soon the police patrols would pass, and when the thud of their hobnailed boots receded, the peasant refugees would emerge from the shadows to trudge these alleyways, defying the curfew in their unceasing hunt for food. The refugees came from villages devastated in the renewed civil war between the Nationalist forces of Chiang Kai-shek and Mao Tse-tung's Communists, now in its third year. They hammered on the gates, imploring, until scraps of food were thrown over the compound walls: small bribes given to restore the peace of the night. As his pedicab rolled past the compounds, Jensen could hear the shouts of children at play in the courtyards. The smoke of coal stoves curled above the sloping tiled roofs.

Suddenly Jensen noticed shadows cast along the alleyway ahead. Three emaciated dogs were stalking the still form of a beggar woman. Slumped against a red door with shining brass fittings, she held a bundled infant in her arms. Jensen cried out to Ying to halt. The pedicab driver watched uneasily as Jensen jumped out, shook the woman's shoulder, and dropped some bills into her lap. The mongrel curs scampered away. A pedicab man who had been sleeping in the passenger seat of his cycle sat upright. A pair of magpies perched on a compound wall screeched. Jensen returned to the pedicab. He knew the stalking dogs would return. Once he might have done more to help the woman, but he had learned to constrain his compassion and rage at what he witnessed on the streets. Giving of alms was the Taoist way. But doing more to rescue a beggar would mean, by Chinese custom, accepting responsibility for the creature's survival. As the war closed in on Peking, the spectacle of starving refugees dying on the streets was so common as to hardly engage the curiosity of the passerby.

Ying turned south on Hatamen Street, bypassing the Imperial City. Beyond the southern wall, low-hanging clouds were taking on a pink glow, reflecting the lights of Peking's Outer City, the old Chinese quarter. Jensen leaned back, arms folded, eyes half closed, his thoughts tumbling. Everything had come unhinged. The outraged director denouncing him as a violator of Christian trust, ordering him out of the Language School. He'd been reckless. This last affair, the wild night in the school. Someone hearing, someone seeing as he groped, dulled by the Mongol wine, along the corridor wall to the room of the woman from Taiyuan; her strange lusts and cries. This, after those other nights, when, weary of poring over Taoist scriptures, he had ventured into the Chinese wine shops with Chi, his Chinese drinking companion, or made the rounds of company houses with the French lieutenant. The bribes paid the gatekeepers hadn't been enough to cloak his returns after the city curfew. Indeed, the director had already warned him, especially after that one night when the Chinese gendarmes had hauled him back after curfew and threatened severe action against the school.

But in a sense, leaving was a relief after the confining months. Perhaps, unconsciously, he had invited expulsion. But what would the Smith people do when they learned he'd lost his cover as a scholar? The school was supposed to be his safehouse when the Communists occupied the city. Now that he'd botched his mission, would they spirit him out of China? Or dispose of him? Smith had warned that he would be removed if he bolted or was stripped of his cover. Until now he had abided by his contract. And he would never betray their plan. *No!* Whatever the risk, he would not leave Peking. To leave would mean giving up the work on his book; the search for the essence of the universal Tao . . . *the Way* . . . grasping the wisdom of Chuang Tzu and Lao Tsu. If they came for him, they wouldn't find him pliant. But for now he must find a place to live, to take shelter. Wang Li would help.

Ying pedaled the pedicab through the towering Front Gate, which led into the Chinese City. Jensen glanced at his watch. He was too early for his appointment with Wang Li. "Ying," he called out, "take me first to the Wine Shop of the Three Parrots."

The pedicab rolled through bustling marketplaces and crooked hutungs. Jensen looked about him relishing as always the myriad sensations of the city's irrepressible life. Nor did he shrink from the stench of the refuse-filled gutters or the acrid fumes of the coal lumps smoldering in the open stoves of the clamoring sidewalk food peddlers. The crowds were swelled by refugees from the countryside and by disheveled stragglers from the defeated Nationalist armies in the north. The traffic was a clutter of rickshas, two-wheeled wooden carts, overburdened donkeys and camels, and American-made trucks of the Nationalist garrison. Polished limousines of government officials and the foreign consulates nosed through the tangled traffic, their haughty Chinese chauffeurs sounding their horns incessantly.

Shouting for pedestrians to clear the way, Ying drew up before the Wine Shop of the Three Parrots. "Come for me in two hours at the shop of Wang Li," Jensen said. Ying saluted and pedaled off. Jensen entered the tiny wine stall, sat on a wooden stool, and ordered a flask of *shaohsing*, the hot yellow wine, patiently returning the smiles of the Chinese customers who stole shy glances at him. He tossed back several cups of the wine and thought about what Chi had asked him to do.

Chi was a second-year medical student at Yenching, the university on the outskirts of Peking. Jensen had met him in the U.S. Information Library. A moon-faced Cantonese, son of a wealthy rice merchant, Chi had been a rollicking companion, and the two spent many nights over cups of *shaohsing* discussing philosophy and politics. Chi joked that Jensen was a reincarnation of Hsi Kang, a third-century Taoist poet seven foot eight inches in height, who composed verses during drinking bouts with his friends in the fabled Club of the Bamboo Grove. Jensen conceded only that he shared Hsi Kang's addiction to wine. More often, brooding over his entanglement with the Smith people, he thought he was failing, like Hsi Kang, to heed the cautions of the Taoist sage, Chuang Tzu, against being drawn into the affairs of rulers. Might he suffer Hsi Kang's fate? Although innocent of any offense against the people, Hsi Kang was accused of treason and executed by the Emperor. The poet went to his execution strumming his lute.

But lately Chi had changed. He was more and more obsessed with politics. He could argue on until the curfew hour, angrily cataloging the misdeeds of the Chiang Kai-shek government and extolling the promised reforms of the Communists. While Jensen understood Chi's frustration at the corruption and repression of Chiang's political party, the Kuomintang, he saw no point in substituting one dictatorship for another. He would never voice his doubts directly, but preferred to debate with Chi in Taoist terms. But then Chi would grow irritable when Jensen quoted from the Taoist sages: *The people prosper when ruled by those officials who govern least. Look for salvation in the cultivation of the human spirit.* At their last meeting in the wine shop, Jensen had spoken out more directly, shedding the pretense imposed on him by Smith that he appear sympathetic to the Communists. "Accept Mao Tse-tung and you will see the ruin of your culture," Jensen had said. "The Maoists are a reincarnation of the Legalists of two thousand years ago. Yes, the Legalists built the Great Wall, but they also buried philosophers alive."

Chi was furious. "Your Taoist philosophy did not rescue the Chinese people from poverty and war in feudal times. It will do no more for them today. The Way is the means by which gentlemen scholars such as you retreat from the suffering of the people to idle contemplation on the mountaintops."

Jensen mulled over the rebuke for days. Chi was right, he concluded. He was only a spectator to the anguish of the Chinese people. If China descended into chaos, he could always retreat to the comfort of his home in Webster, Missouri. For Chi and his people, there was no escape. Chi had made the hard choice between the Communists and the Nationalists. There was no middle ground . . . no democratic party able to silence the guns and feed the people. The Communists were promising more. And here am I, Jensen berated himself, professing love for the Chinese people, yet aloof from their struggle.

Jensen was still feeling the sting of the rebuke when Chi unexpectedly knocked at the door of his room in the Language School. He was accompanied by a woman student, Li-nan, whom Jensen recognized immediately. He had first noticed her in the American Library and, thereafter, looked for her.

Jensen seated his visitors on the narrow cot of his sparsely furnished room. Chi was flushed and agitated, but Li-nan appeared composed with a polite smile and still hands folded in her lap.

"Eric, you know about the attack on the Pei-ta University students?" Chi asked, speaking in Chinese, his voice strained.

"Yes, murderous, murderous." Jensen replied. He'd learned of the clash that afternoon. Gendarmes had assaulted a column of Pei-ta University students as they tried to enter the Imperial City, bearing placards demanding an end to the civil war. When the students broke down the barriers at the Tienanmen the gendarmes charged the column with fixed bayonets. Two students had been killed and a dozen others wounded.

"The day after tomorrow," Chi said, "we are planning a great protest demonstration of Yenching, Pei-ta, and Tsinghua University students at the Temple of Heaven. Eric, we want you to be there. The gendarmes are less likely to bayonet us if foreigners are looking on."

"I'll be there," Eric said quietly. He glanced at Li-nan, who was studying him intently. Jensen had watched her in the library on several occasions moving gracefully amid the student throng, fine ivory features tilted up as she examined the book stacks; watching as her gown folded about her slim body when she reached for a volume. Serene, patrician in manner, she was tall for a Chinese woman, five foot six or seven. In reveries after cups of wine he had imagined himself living with a woman like her, spending soft evenings lolling beside a lotus pool in their Ming garden while contemplating the revelations and mysteries in the verses of Lao Tsu's Tao Te Ching. The very presence of Li-nan brought to mind a verse:

> *The mystery of the valley*
> *is female*
> *It is the emptiness in woman*
> *and the fullness of the Great Mother,*
> *The endless source of everything*
> *and the generosity of all that is.*

Chi reclaimed Jensen's attention. "You are a true friend of China," he said, grasping his hand.

Li-nan smiled at Jensen and rose to leave. But Chi paused. In a whisper, he said to Jensen, "There is something else of even greater importance . . . the greatest of importance."

Li-nan became visibly uneasy. She touched Chi's shoulder. "You can discuss that with Mr. Jensen after the demonstration," she said firmly.

Chi glanced at Li-nan and shrugged. "Well then," he said curtly. "Let us meet after the demonstration at the Altar of Heaven in the Temple Park."

Li-nan bowed and extended her hand to Jensen. "Thank you. We are most grateful."

"Until we meet again," Jensen said, bowing as he shook her hand.

Hunched over his porcelain cup in the wine shop, Jensen puzzled over Chi's matter of "greatest importance" and why Li-nan had silenced him. He would go to the demonstration at the Temple of Heaven as he had promised, although he was not persuaded that the presence of foreigners would prevent violence. Chi's demonstration seemed more likely to invite bloodshed. But perhaps he could be of some help, Jensen reasoned, and the prospect of seeing Li-nan enticed him.

As he left the wine stall, Jensen declined the offer of the pot-bellied proprietor to take the waitress, a thin, pigtailed waif, no more than fifteen years of age, to the house in the rear to enjoy her for the night. A cluster of giggling children soon fell in behind him, pointing and shouting "Red foreign devil!" and "See the red monster!" The children gathered round when he paused to buy a bag of hot chestnuts picked from a peddler's caldron. Jensen stooped to give a chestnut to a small boy with his head shaven except for a top knot. Then with a smile he offered his hand. The tot took it shyly and together they walked to the nearby bird shop with the other children trailing behind. In the open shanty shop Jensen inspected the chirping thrushes in cages hanging from the roof beam. He lifted up the tot so that he could inspect a shrieking yellow-crested white cockatoo.

Waving good-bye to the children, Jensen continued along the narrow hutungs toward Wang Li's shop. The bazaar was crowded with frenetic shoppers shouldering up to counters to buy the cheap Shang-hai-made watches and cloth. They paid with tall stacks of yuan, whose worth was dwindling daily in the unbridled inflation. In the jade shops, foreigners examined antique pieces and jewelry that could be bought at bargain prices for dollars. From rooms above the shops came the click-ing of mah-jongg ivories.

Jensen strode along Jade Street to the antiques shop of Wang Li. Shopkeepers hawking precious stones, silks, and silver bowed as the fa-miliar tall figure passed by. The window of Wang's shop was already shuttered for the night. Jensen pulled the bell cord. The carved teak door opened slowly, and Wang welcomed Jensen with a bow. A tall, slightly stooped man in his seventies, Wang's high cheek bones and arched eyebrows revealed his Manchu blood. He made an imposing fig-ure in his blue brocade gown.

Jensen paused to glance at jade ornaments in a display case before walking to the rear of the shop, where he parted red silken curtains and entered a small room hung with calligraphic scrolls. He seated himself on a brocade-covered sofa, stretching his legs beneath a low redwood table. On the table stood a porcelain tea service and a One Thousand Flower dish filled with sliced oranges and sunflower seeds.

Wang closed the curtains. "Before anything else," he said, his eyes alight. He walked over to the German steel safe in the corner of the room, spun the combination, and returned with an exquisitely sculpted terra-cotta figurine, about eighteen inches high, of a Chinese woman dancer in flowing robes. The statue was very old but still retained patches of red glaze. Wang placed the figurine gently on the table.

"Magnificent," Jensen breathed.

"Well?" said Wang.

Jensen studied the figure closely. "Mortuary pottery, Southern Tang, about the year 900."

"Correct, of course," Wang said, as he picked up the figurine and returned it to the safe. ·

Jensen smiled. "You have been a good teacher. Is it for sale?"

"No, not yet," Wang said laughing. "Not to the speculators. It deserves a museum. It will go into the vault with the other special things. And how are you progressing with your research?" He offered Jensen a cigarette from a black lacquer box. Reaching inside his gown, Jensen took out a carved ivory cigarette holder, inserted the cigarette, lit it with an army Zippo, and drew heavily.

"I am leaving the Language School," Jensen said quietly.

Wang's eyebrows lifted slightly. He poured green tea into the porcelain cups. "The book? It is finished?"

Jensen sipped his tea. He was unhappy about not being entirely open with Wang, his friend and benefactor. When he entered the Language School he had told Wang his purpose was to do research for his book in the Taoist archives and that the school would be his sanctuary when the Communists occupied Peking. They might accept his residence as a scholar, especially if he offered to become a teacher of English at one of the universities. He had not misled Wang as far as these aspects of his plan were concerned. He simply did not tell Wang everything. He did not tell him of the Smith people. He did not explain that his part-time job in the U.S. Information Library was really a means to engage with left-wing Chinese students, like Chi, who came there hungry for books unobtainable elsewhere.

"No," Jensen said. "I displeased the director. My behavior was not to his liking. I need another place to live."

"As always, my house is yours," Wang said, bowing slightly. He paused, tucking his fine-boned hands into the sleeves of his gown. "It will not be difficult to obtain a residence permit for you in the Chinese City. The palms of the police are always outstretched for squeeze."

"And later?" Jensen asked, looking steadily into Wang's eyes.

"More difficult," Wang said. "The Communists are suspicious. Their radio speaks constantly of American spies. They would want to know why are you living in the Chinese quarter." He hesitated. "They might interrogate your Chinese acquaintances. The Communists may not take bribes like the Kuomintang officials."

Jensen, knowing he had his answer, stubbed out his cigarette and rose. "I understand," he said.

Wang nodded. "Your precious things will be safe. Only you and I know the location of the vault. Return when you can."

As Jensen left the shop, he thought of a last resort. He would go to his friend, the French lieutenant, to ask for shelter. Like all the consular residences, the lieutenant's compound enjoyed diplomatic immunity. The Communists—when they came—might not challenge his presence there. But there was no telling how the Smith people would react.

Chapter Two

His entrapment had begun well over a year ago, on January 29, 1947. It was early morning and Jensen sat on his rolled mattress in the Marine barracks in Peking waiting for the order to go. The barracks were empty except for him and eight other U.S. Army enlisted men. The Marines were long gone, having left after the evacuation of the defeated Japanese Army. Jensen and the eight others were the only remaining members of the American branch of Executive Headquarters, a group that had been set up by General George Marshall to curb the fighting between the Nationalist and Communist armies. Jensen had served on several of its truce teams. But now, after Marshall failed to bring Chiang Kai-shek and Mao Tse-tung into a coalition government, the headquarters was ordered disbanded.

Jensen didn't join in the lively chatter and laughter of the others, who were thinking only of making it home for Christmas. There was no joy in that for him. From childhood, entranced by the tales told by his missionary parents, Jensen's goal had been to get to China. Through the war years, and before at the University of Michigan, he had planned for a life in Peking where he would continue his research into Taoism. His fluent Chinese brought him a transfer, as he had requested, from Army duty in Burma to Peking as an interpreter with the truce teams. Now, after only a captivating taste of Peking, he was being forced to leave China. Inexplicably, although his academic credentials were excellent, his application to take his discharge and remain in the city as a scholar had been denied.

"Attention!" An Army colonel in a trench coat entered the barracks. "We're flying to Shanghai," the colonel said briskly. "Sergeant Jensen, you'll leave with a second group in about fifteen minutes. The rest of you . . . follow me."

Jensen was alone when a Marine major, wearing a leather flight jacket and a green overseas cap, appeared. "You're to come with me, Sergeant Jensen," the major said. Jensen put on his cap. Why a Marine escort? Who was this major? He was obviously of Chinese ancestry but spoke with the accent of a well-educated American. Jensen followed the major into the courtyard, where a staff car was waiting. "Put your duffel in," the major said, climbing behind the wheel.

Jensen felt a growing unease as the car sped not to the South Field, which the army transports used, but to the West Field and directly onto the tarmac alongside a C-47 marked with U.S. Navy insignia. "Get aboard," the major said. Bewildered, Jensen heaved his duffel through the open door of the plane and climbed up the ladder. He and the major were the only passengers.

As the plane took off and banked, Jensen saw it was headed east into the rising sun rather than south toward Shanghai. Turning to the major, who sat beside him in the bucket seats, he began, "I don't understand . . ."

The major looked straight ahead, expressionless. "You will."

When the plane began its descent after less than two hours, Jensen could see through breaks in the cloud cover that they were coming into Tsingtao, the U.S. Navy and Marine base. The plane landed and taxied back past parked C-46 transports and Mustang fighter planes to a Navy staff car. Jensen and the major were driven to a dock where a small canopied launch was tied up, manned by a petty officer and two sailors wearing sidearms. One sailor took Jensen's duffel as the major motioned him into the launch. The launch moved through a light mist past two destroyers anchored side by side in the deep-water basin. It pitched as it left the shelter of the breakwater, headed into Kiaochow Bay, and came alongside a Navy transport topheavy with communications and radar gear. The transport's pilot ladder was down. A petty officer at the gangway saluted as the major and Jensen came aboard and led them below to a small stateroom.

"Drop your duffel," the major said. "You'll be here for several days." Jensen followed the major up a winding ladder to a deck where he knocked on an unmarked door. "Go in," the major said, and closed the door behind Jensen.

Jensen entered a spacious wardroom. Seated behind a bare steel desk was a gray-haired man who looked to be in his fifties. "Welcome, Sergeant Jensen," the man said in a cultured southern drawl. He motioned Jensen to a leather couch and surveyed him with a tight smile. "I apologize for the rather theatrical manner in which you were brought here. It was necessary. Like a cup of tea? It'll be an hour or so before lunch."

Jensen, sitting with his arms folded, his combat boots crossed before him, nodded. His host rose, leaning on a cane and limping slightly, and brought a cup of green tea from a porcelain service. He placed it on the chow table before the couch. Jensen sipped his tea, looking over his cup at his host. The southerner was tall and thin, elegantly turned out in a white turtleneck shirt and a blue blazer with a silk handkerchief in the pocket. His gray hair was carefully combed back, and his dark eyes under black beetle eyebrows studied Jensen carefully.

"My name is Smith," the gray-haired man said, as he poured another cup of tea and eased into a chair beside the couch. "I'm an employee of the Central Intelligence Agency. It's a rather new government organization. I'm sure you're familiar with it." Without waiting for a reply, he continued in a soft voice: "You've been brought here because we have a proposal, which, I trust, you'll find appealing. Before giving you the details, I'd like to check some facts." He went to the desk, fetched a green file folder that he opened on his lap.

Reading quickly, he said: "'Eric Jensen was born on December 11, 1920, in Webster, Missouri, the son of Neil Jensen, a pastor of the Norwegian Lutheran Church, who served as a missionary in China for four years.'"

As he flipped over pages, Smith looked up, amused. "While both you and your elder brother, Rolf, were obsessively attracted to China, it appears you disappointed your father by showing no interest, unlike Rolf, in becoming a missionary. In fact, your father disciplined you for skipping church. At seventeen you shocked the town. Jonathan Berry found you in bed with his daughter, Doris, at two in the morning. Accusing you of climbing a drainpipe to get into her room, he threatened to have you jailed."

Jensen ran a hand through his thick hair and didn't return Smith's playful smile. He wasn't surprised by the detail in the file. It was simple enough to obtain. He had worked with Army intelligence. But why this exercise? Evidently Smith wanted to impress upon him that the government knew all. He was trying to discourage him from concealing anything.

"Cigarette?" Smith inquired, picking up a package of Chesterfields from the side table.

"I'll have one of these," Jensen replied, taking out a packet from his shirt pocket. Smith scratched a match and lit Jensen's cigarette.

"Ruby cigarettes, made in Tientsin," he remarked. "You prefer everything Chinese." Jensen shrugged and inhaled deeply. Smith placed an ashtray on the chow table and turned back to read aloud from the file.

"'Jensen attended the University of Michigan. Professor Parkinson, chairman of the Department of Far Eastern Studies, described Jensen as his most talented student in Chinese language and philosophy. Jensen's research on Chuang Tzu, the early Taoist philosopher, was deemed exceptional. His paper on Chuang Tzu's thesis that man must realize personal freedom to become consonant with the cosmic God Force was published in the *British Eastern Review*. When Jensen was asked to expand the monograph into a book, he agreed to do so upon completion of original research in Peking. Parkinson also recalled Jensen's intense interest in Chinese art.

"'As Jensen's studies progressed, particularly in the period when he focused on the alchemy and sorcery practiced by the Neo-Taoists, he led an almost monastic life. On occasion, he wore a Chinese gown. He practiced Taoist meditative breathing exercises, becoming so adept that he could contain his inhalation for one hundred twenty heartbeats. His concentration was extraordinary.'"

Smith looked up from the file. "Satisfy my curiosity, Sergeant Jensen. Why the Chinese gown?"

"Why not?" Jensen replied with a trace of a smile, glancing over Smith's garb, which looked more suited to the veranda of a Virginia mansion than the wardroom of a warship in the China seas. "The Chinese . . . for thousands of years . . . have found the gown to be most comfortable."

Smith coughed. "I see," he said, and resumed reading. "'Upon graduation, Jensen was drafted and sent to the Army language school, where he perfected his Chinese. He stood at the head of his class. After basic training he was assigned to General Stilwell's headquarters in Burma as an interpreter with Chinese army divisions. He was awarded the Silver Star in January 1945 for valor in the battle for Mount Huilungshan during the reopening of the Burma Road . When his Chinese battalion commander and the American military adviser were killed, Jensen led the unit in the final bayonet assault, which took the Japanese-held crest of the mountain.'"

"Admirable," Smith said. "Your sense of duty . . . one of the reasons we're interested in you."

Jensen nodded, and Smith went back to the file: "'Jensen was offered a battlefield commission, but he declined it and later volunteered for duty as an interpreter with Executive Headquarters in Peking. As an interpreter with the truce teams he earned the highest efficiency ratings. When Executive Headquarters closed, Jensen applied for a discharge in Peking, stating he intended to research the Taoist archives and complete a book. His application was circulated to the CIA. On the recommendation of the director of the agency, the Army denied it.'"

Jensen glared, but said nothing as Smith closed the file.

"Correct?" Smith asked.

"Your research is flawed," Jensen said, stubbing out his cigarette. "I didn't climb up the drainpipe. Doris let me in the back door."

Smith smiled appreciatively. "Enough for now," he said, standing up. "It's been a long morning, Sergeant Jensen. There'll be lunch on a tray in your cabin. We'll meet this afternoon."

But in his cabin Jensen kicked off his combat boots and sat cross-legged on the floor ignoring the lunch tray on the table. Arms folded, he closed his eyes, thinking over the morning's events. Why had he been selected for whatever task Smith had in mind? Was it his application to remain in Peking that triggered the CIA's interest? What more did they know about what he had done in China and how did they intend to use the information? Rising, he nibbled a sandwich. The afternoon would surely be a more trying session.

Smith began without introductory pleasantries. "Why did you apply to remain in China?"

"Finish my book on Taoism. Also, I like the life . . . "

"Yes, enjoy the lotus life in China, as many foreigners do," Smith interjected contemptuously. "Privilege without responsibility. As for the war, you don't seem supportive of the Nationalist cause. Twice in combat zones on behalf of the Communists you protested decisions made by your truce team commanders. The Communist members of the team thanked you and were seen recording your favorable interventions."

"I care about the Chinese people, not politics. In both cases, I felt the truce lines should be redrawn to make sure villagers were out of the possible line of fire."

"Your affection for the Chinese extends to collecting their art objects. Many objects, in fact," Smith said sharply.

Jensen knew at that moment he was in trouble. He breathed heavily, took a Zippo lighter out of his pants pocket, and lit a cigarette before replying in a casual tone. "Yes. I collect Chinese things. As your file shows, Chinese art has always fascinated me."

"What's your relationship to Wang Li, the antiques dealer?"

"He's a friend. He's taught me a lot about Chinese art."

"In fact, Sergeant Jensen, you've been in business with him," Smith said, pouncing.

"While on truce team missions in isolated localities you covertly acquired rare antiques. You carried them concealed in your duffel back to Peking on truce planes. You bought extremely valuable art at very low prices from families in desperate straits. How does that speak to your affection for the Chinese?"

No sense withholding, Jensen thought. "I paid the families prices far above what they'd have gotten otherwise," he said. "They were happy to sell. And I've preserved priceless art from destruction in the war."

"Oh yes, yes. And you kept some art objects for yourself. And others you sold to Wang Li to finance more purchases. What kind of a Taoist are you? I recall a line from Lao Tsu's Tao Te Ching: 'Refrain from prizing rare possessions.' Correct?"

"Lao Tsu was also tolerant of man's imperfections," Jensen said coolly. "As for the art objects . . . it's never been my intention to take them out of China. One day they'll go to a museum."

Smith handed Jensen a sheaf of papers. "You've been indiscreet, Sergeant. Naïve, at best. These are photostats of checks endorsed by Wang Li. You illegally sent them to his account in the Bank of California through the Army Post Office. These are incriminating documents. They prove you guilty of black-marketing and fraud under the federal regulations governing the APO."

"None of that money went into any account of mine," Jensen said firmly. "All of it was forwarded to Wang Li's son and daughter at the University of Michigan. It paid for their education. You know that."

"You'd have trouble convincing a court martial," Smith said, rising from his chair. "In fact, I'm sure you'd get years of jail time in Leavenworth. However, my dear Jensen, there's no need for such unpleasantness." Smith's features relaxed into a smile, and his drawl became more pronounced. "I have a proposal that'll serve us all very well. We'll talk more about it in the morning. Have an enjoyable evening. If you like, the major will accompany you to the movie being shown to the crew. I'm told it's a Betty Grable film," he said, as he opened the door and signaled to the major in the corridor. "Not really to my taste. I prefer Hitchcock."

Jensen felt tense as he entered the wardroom the next morning, but he tried to appear outwardly relaxed. He had discarded his combat jacket. His wool shirt was open at the neck, revealing a turquoise-studded silver amulet on a thong. Smith was standing near the desk, leafing through a file. "Make yourself comfortable," he said.

As Jensen sprawled on the couch, legs outstretched, hands in his pockets, Smith approached and peered at the amulet. "Tibetan talisman," Jensen said. "To ward off evil spirits."

Smith smiled: "I hope you'll not find me such a spirit."

Jensen looked at his interlocutor with grudging respect.

"Jensen, there is a way out," Smith began deliberately, his features hardening. "This proposal will allow you to remain in China, finish your book, and retain your antiques. Wang Li would be left undisturbed. So listen well." Smith leaned against the desk.

"What I am about to tell you is top secret. If you repeat any of it, I wouldn't vouch for your well-being. However, no need for threats. We think you can be trusted. Your war record speaks to that. If you give me your word you'll not betray our confidence, that'll be sufficient."

"You have it," Jensen said.

"Good," Smith said, smiling. "This is our situation. We estimate the Communists will be in full control of the China mainland within three years. At that time the White House will be pressured by the powerful China lobby into breaking all ties with the mainland. In response, Mao will ally himself more closely with the Soviet Union. But some of us in

the agency, the State Department, and in the White House do not believe the Chinese-Soviet relationship will remain stable." Smith began
to walk about the room, leaning heavily on his cane, speaking as if he
were addressing a large audience.

"The ideological differences run too deep. There are territorial dis-
putes . . . resentment about Stalin's deals with Chiang Kai-shek for
leases on Port Arthur and Dairen in Manchuria. We have reports of a
clique within the politburo, led by Chou En-lai, which favors an independent foreign policy line. All that will make for an opening to wean
China away from the Soviet Union."

Smith dropped into a chair beside the couch. "Unfortunately," he
said with a sigh, "this assessment is a minority view. There's panic
about the Soviet takeover of Eastern Europe. There's no tolerance for
dealing with any brand of Communists. The House Committee on Un-
American Activities is hunting Communists in the government, in the
unions, even in Hollywood. Although there are people in the White
House who agree with our assessment, the President has not been
brought in. Too risky. His political advisers think if it becomes known
there's any leaning toward a link with the Chinese Communists the political effect would be catastrophic. Republicans already are blaming the
President for the setbacks of Chiang Kai-shek's armies. Even General
Marshall and General Stilwell are being accused of being soft on the
Communists."

Smith went to a porthole and looked out. Then he turned, with a
thumb in his belt, and said, "Despite all that . . . some of us—call us
what you will—believe we cannot turn our backs on China. We believe
that when the time is propitious, we should reach out to the Chinese
Communists for an understanding. If we're successful, it could tilt the
world balance of power in our favor." Fixing his gaze on Jensen, he continued: "To do that we need people who know the Chinese . . . people

trusted by them . . . people in a position to keep us informed and tell us when and how we should make our move. Not ordinary agents, but advisers deep in Chinese society."

Leaning forward, his brow knitted, Smith said, "You understand?"

"If you're asking me to become a spy," Jensen said evenly, "the answer is no. I . . ."

Smith's features suddenly contorted, and with a sweep of his hand he gestured Jensen into silence. "We're not simply asking you to become a spy. We're asking you to keep open a channel to the Chinese people. We're asking you to help your country and the China you profess to love." Smith snorted impatiently. "You can't spend the rest of your life munching lotus leaves."

Jensen leaped to his feet and glared at Smith. "I did my bit in Burma and other places. I knew what that was all about. I'm not sure of your game." He hesitated and then dropped back onto the couch, bit his lip, reached for a cigarette, lit it, and stared for several moments into the flame of the lighter before snapping it shut. "What would you have me do?" he said quietly.

Smith clasped his hands and flexed them. "This would be the plan. You'd return to Peking. The Army will grant you a local discharge. You'll enter the Language School, where you'll continue your study of the Taoist classics. You shouldn't have a problem getting admitted. The director, John Scott, is a clergyman of your father's church. Not only missionaries study there. Stilwell himself as a young officer attended in the twenties, when the warlords were fighting over control of the city. We'll arrange for you to work part time in the U.S. Information Agency library. You're certain to meet intellectuals and students there who lean to the Communists. After the occupation they are likely to be recruited into the Party, if they are not already members. You'll be sympathetic to their views. You'll remain in the Language School as a scholar-in-residence and, when the Communists come, offer to become a teacher of English at one of the universities. They'll need foreign specialists for a time. We think they'll be receptive to you. They'll remember your work on the truce teams. Finally, you'll wait until we call on you."

Frowning, Jensen searched Smith's features without attempting a reply.

"Come back in the morning with your answer," Smith said. He paused with his hand on the doorknob: "I assume you understand now why we can't afford any leak. Perhaps I've told you too much. I've risked that because I believe you need to know what we're up to if you're to work loyally with us."

Jensen went back to his cabin. He paced the narrow space and then seated himself on the floor in the Lotus Position, his hands cupped. Through his nostrils he began inhaling the Breath of the Nine Heavens, and in total concentration guided *ch'i*, his breath, through the passages of his body, bringing energy to the Palace of the Brain before expelling *ch'i* after more than one hundred heartbeats. Cleansed, free of all tensions, and in a state of heightened awareness, he meditated.

Are these people really working to keep a line open between Washington and Mao? If so, he'd be more than happy to help. But what if it's all a trick? He knew these intelligence types. What if they simply wanted him to spy on the Chinese? He recoiled at the thought of manipulating his Chinese friends. He recalled the Taoist discipline: *Being without entanglements, one can be upright and calm. Being upright and calm, one can be born again.* After years of Army barracks life, the thought of living in a missionary-run school appalled him. He longed for a free life in Peking. Writing his book. Seeking the wisdom of Chuang Tzu and the other Taoist philosophers. And that dream: sharing his explorations with a cultured Chinese woman in a house and garden surrounded by his precious things. Yes, Smith detected his weakness: his greed for Chinese art. He should heed the caution of Lao Tsu: *He who is obsessed with desire will not see what is most significant.* Smith had indeed quoted accurately from the Tao Te Ching. No eluding this guy, this Smith. The fraud charge would always be held as a gun to his head. Smith was offering him a comfortable way out. If he said no, Smith's people would find some way to dispose of him. Likely kill him before he left the ship. They'd never allow him to go free with what he now knew. If he escaped, eventually they'd find him. No choice. He had to go with the flow of events.

In the morning when Jensen rejoined him, Smith was once again in his blue blazer, waiting, leaning on his cane. They faced each other in the center of the wardroom. Jensen said: "Okay."

"There are conditions," Smith said. "You'll write to your father through the Chinese mail. It's read by the Nationalist secret police. You'll tell your father you have a scholarship. You intend to enter the Language School to complete your study of the Taoist classics. The Roberts Educational Foundation will award you a scholarship with a monthly stipend of fifteen hundred dollars. It will be deposited into an account in the Peking branch of the Hong Kong and Shanghai Bank. Expect no further assistance. The State Department, including the consulate in Peking, are unaware of our operation.

"If the operation is uncovered, the director of the CIA will testify that he knows nothing of our activities. When my people contact you, the introduction will be the code phrase: 'the rarest rose quartz.' Your reply: 'in my Suchou garden.' The code name for the operation is Wagging Pipit.

Smith handed over a sheet of paper and commanded: "Memorize."

Once Jensen had scanned it, Smith retrieved the paper, tore it into shreds, and put a match to it in an ashtray, before continuing: "You must remain in the Language School. We must always know where to find you quickly. When the Communists close on Peking, the school will be the only feasible cover. The Nationalist secret police will be suspicious of any foreigner loose in the city without ties. When the Communists take the city, the school will serve as your safehouse. We've got means of monitoring your activities. If you lose your cover or if you fail to hold to our other conditions . . . we'll have you out of China. There'll be no assurance of your well-being. Or mine," he added with a tight smile. Smith cocked his head, looked intently into Jensen's eyes, and extended his hand. Jensen hesitated, and then took it.

Chapter Three

As Jensen settled into Ying's pedicab outside Wang Li's shop, he tried to shut the meeting with Smith out of his mind. But the echoes persisted: *Wait until we call upon you. . . . We've got means of monitoring your activities.* "Ying, go to the restaurant of the Three Wise Owls," Jensen said.

At the restaurant, Jensen telephoned his friend, Jean Leone, to ask if he could call on him. He was cheered by the Frenchman's warm response. "But of course," the lieutenant said. "Come at once."

As Ying pedaled back from the Chinese City into the Tartar City, Jensen glimpsed an incandescent search flare descending beyond the southern wall. The arc traced from a watchtower atop the wall where sentries were searching for infiltrating Communist guerrillas. Tension was mounting within Peking. "There is great anger in the bazaars over the gendarme attack on the Pei-ta student demonstrators at Tienanmen," Ying had told him. Jensen knew the government had reason to fear the students. Previous regimes had been overthrown by common folk rallied by student demonstrators.

In the Legation Quarter, as Jensen rode past, the diplomatic compounds were agleam with bright lights. These stately missions, whose ambassadors once arrogantly parleyed with the Manchu emperors, now housed only consular officials. The real embassies were located far to the south in Nanking, the gray city on the Yangtze River, which Chiang Kai-shek proclaimed his capital in 1928. In the official Kuomintang gazetteer, Peking, meaning "Northern Capital," had been renamed Peiping, "Northern Peace," but the change was slow to come into the speech of those who lived under the spell of Peking's imperial style. Over the portico of the former Foreign Office there hung a silken banner inscribed: LONG LIVE PRESIDENT CHIANG KAI-SHEK AND THE CHINESE REPUBLIC. A red banner will replace it soon, Jensen thought.

Only two months earlier, Chiang Kai-shek had stopped off in Peking en route to Mukden, the principal city of Manchuria, to assume personal direction of the vast battle raging there. Jensen and the French lieutenant were among the spectators who saw the Generalissimo reviewing troops at a parade before the Forbidden City's Gate of Heavenly Peace. As the Generalissimo took the salute, standing ramrod erect on a reviewing platform before the Tienanmen, the lieutenant growled: "He won't be a help to his generals in Manchuria . . . not with his warlord tactics. Even with all that American equipment, he'll be no match for Lin Piao."

Weeks later, when Chiang passed through Peking again, the government-controlled press was brimming with claims of victories. "Nonsense," Leone exclaimed impatiently, telling Jensen of French intelligence reports: Chiang had grouped his best divisions in the Manchurian cities, leaving the Communist commander, Lin Piao, free to maneuver his Fourth Field Army in the countryside. The blunder was fatal. Lin Piao lay siege in turn to the isolated Nationalist garrisons and ambushed them when they attempted to break out. With some thirty of his best divisions lost, Chiang had returned to Nanking. Lin Piao's army, refitted with captured American equipment, was now moving south to engage the forces of General Fu Tso-yi, who commanded a half million troops along a line from Tientsin near the Po Hai Bay westward through Peking to Inner Mongolia. Fu's forces were falling back into defensive positions.

The pedicab turned into a hutung near the old Foreign Office and drew up before a door freshly painted bright red. Jensen handed Ying forty yuan, twice what a pedicab man might expect to earn in a single day. Still he wondered if it was enough for Ying's family. Jensen had exchanged dollars for yuan that morning with a black-market dealer who traded openly in a stall on Morrison Street. The new gold yuan introduced three months earlier at four to a dollar had already depreciated twentyfold.

"Shall I wait for you tomorrow, Master?" Ying asked.

"I am going to the Temple of Heaven at nine," Jensen said. Ying rubbed the handle of his pedicab and lowered his eyes.

"You are afraid?" Jensen asked.

"The gendarmes will be there. The students fill them with anger. Even foreigners will not be safe." Ying hesitated. "The gendarmes . . . "

"I will go," Jensen interjected impatiently.

Ying moistened his lips. "I will take you, Master." Averting his eyes, Ying pedaled away swiftly. Jensen watched him disappear into the gloom. Ying was right, Jensen thought. A clash between the gendarmes and students was inevitable. But there could be no turning away from his promise to Chi and Li-nan. *Li-nan.* To see her was incentive enough to be there.

Jensen thrust Ying's warning from his mind and pulled the bell chain. He noticed that the door's brass nameplate was new and bore an inscription: LIEUTENANT JEAN LEONE, ASSISTANT MILITARY ATTACHÉ, CONSULATE OF FRANCE. He had not seen Leone for some five weeks, not since the lieutenant completed his studies at the Language School.

A Chinese in a long white servant's gown opened the door and ushered Jensen into a courtyard paved with gray flagstone. Jensen stooped low as he was led through a circular moon gate into a garden shaded by two cypress trees and a huge linden. Beyond a lotus pool at the far end of the garden stood the main house facing south.

Jean Leone was waiting for Jensen in the lounge, whiskey glass in hand, seated beside a crackling fire that cast dancing shadows. The spacious lounge was one of two great rooms in the main house, the other being a bedroom. The walls were hung with Ming scrolls of landscape scenes painted on silk. Draped on the far wall was a small crimson-and-black Chen Lung carpet embossed with a dragon and phoenix; Jensen recognized it as a throne carpet from the Forbidden City. He never asked how it came to be there.

The lieutenant was a lean man with dark, impish eyes behind metal-rimmed spectacles and jet black hair worn straight back. He was a year or two older than Jensen. He wore a German hunting jacket of fine brown leather over a black turtleneck. With upraised glass and a rather sardonic smile on his lips, he watched as Jensen shed his Chinese robe, revealing the worn Army shirt and drab olive trousers with scuffed combat boots. Only once had he chided Jensen about his dress. "Be not a slave to man's conventions," Jensen had replied. He was not disposed to explain any aspect of his behavior.

Leone found Jensen engrossing, a man of bewildering contrasts. He seemed a tender soul, gentle blue eyes set in finely molded Norwegian features, a kind giant to the street children, a generous giver of alms to the beggars. Yet there was the night when thieves set upon them as they emerged from a wine stall in the Chinese City. Jensen warded off the thrusting knives; bodies were hurled through the air, and four Chinese lay still on the cobblestones.

"Drink, buddy?" Leone asked, holding up the scotch bottle. Jensen nodded. The Frenchman habitually amused Jensen by peppering his fluent English with barracks slang acquired when he was a liaison officer with the American forces in North Africa. When irritated Leone would also lapse into Alemannic oaths that he had learned as a boy in his native Alsace.

"There's news tonight," Leone said, as he poured scotch from a pinch bottle and added water from a silver decanter. "Lin Piao's Fourth Field Army has taken the pass at Shanhaikwan where the Great Wall meets the sea. He chose the invasion route from Manchuria . . . the same used by the Manchu tribes in the seventeenth century. Stunning, *n'est-ce pas?* The siege of Peking must begin in a few weeks."

"How long can Fu Tso-yi hold out?" Jensen asked, as he accepted the scotch and settled in a high-backed chair before the fire.

The lieutenant shrugged. "Chiang Kai-shek will order Fu Tso-yi to resist, to delay Lin Piao's march south. But Fu knows it's hopeless. He'll bargain with the Communists." Leone leaned forward, his highball glass tightly clamped between his hands. "And Fu, *mon cher,* is not without something to trade. He'll hold Peking in his grasp like this . . . as if it were a delicate Ming vase. He'll ask for a face-saving surrender that will allow him to escape with his head. And he'll threaten a house-to-house fight that will demolish Peking if the Communists come over the wall. It'll be an interesting game to watch."

Game! Leone saw the civil war as a game of generals and politicians, Jensen thought. But what about the ordinary Chinese? Once, when Jensen had asked the question, Leone had shrugged. "I'm French. I think of what it will mean for Indochina. It will be bad for us if the

Communists win. They'll camp on our frontier. One day they'll join with Ho Chi Minh against us. They've not forgotten that the Indochina kings once sent tribute to the Chinese emperors."

Jensen looked moodily into the fire. "Jean," he said, "I can't stop thinking about what this war may do to Peking and its people. This city . . . heart of China's culture . . . its treasures, all the beautiful byways, temples, and palaces . . . everything could be ruined if there's street fighting." Jensen ran his fist along the arm of his chair. "Power . . . that's all these bloody generals on both sides seem to care about."

"That's the way these warlords—or whatever they call themselves— have played their game all through history," the lieutenant said.

"I may leave Peking before the finale," Jensen said abruptly.

Leone frowned. "But *pourquoi*, buddy? You love it here, you bastard. You've said it so many times . . . there's nothing for you in the States."

"I'm being told to leave the Language School."

"But your book . . . "

Jensen gulped the remainder of his drink. "The truth is, Jean, they've discovered I'm not a suitable boarder. 'Consorting with missionaries by day and consorting with the devil by night,' is the way the director put it."

Leone clasped his hands and doubled over in laughter. "How funny," he gasped as he took Jensen's glass and poured another scotch. "Eric . . . live here," he exclaimed. "Look, *mon cher*. I've finished the language course. I'm now the assistant military attaché. Yes? *Bravo!*" He settled back in his chair, a wry crook to his mouth, and raised his glass. "With the siege about to begin, I don't expect visitors from the embassy in Nanking. Plenty of room here . . . for us and a pair of girls from Madame Loh's house. Why not, my dear string bean? Life will become very dull after the Reds come in."

"You're very generous," Jensen said. He rose, walked over to the mantel, and touched the golden Tibetan Buddha figure sitting there. How much should he tell Leone? He hated to be less than frank, but he felt he must abide by the oath of silence exacted by Smith. He would accept Leone's invitation. As for Smith, there was nothing to do but wait for his next move. As much as he liked Jean and was grateful for his hospitality, he knew he wouldn't be entirely comfortable in the lieutenant's house. Leone lived in the old colonial style. His aloof treatment of Chinese, the way he commanded his servants, irked Jensen. Also, the idea of sharing his bed with a joy girl wasn't entirely entrancing. Once, he had been utterly charmed by the joy girls—birds of paradise chirping in delight as they entertained their guests. But the pleasure dissipated as he became more aware that the girls were caged creatures in borrowed plumage, allowed by their pimps to peck only a few dry crumbs in return for selling themselves.

Jensen looked into his drink as he sloshed it in the glass. "Thanks, Jean," he said. "You're very generous. Of course, I want to stay in Peking. I'll move in. There's work to be done on my book. I have my job at the library. After the takeover I may try teaching English at one of the universities. The Communists will need people like me . . . at least for a while."

Leone frowned. *Mon dieu!* he thought—Always believing because of his goodness he'll be embraced by the Chinese. "Eric, what . . ." Leone began but then stopped short. "Excellent," he said. "It's settled. You'll live here."

Jensen suddenly plucked Leone from his chair, lifting him high into the air. "Thank you, my lord of ten thousand chariots," Jensen rumbled, grinning up at the startled Leone. "I'm host tonight. We'll go to the Mongolian restaurant near the Bell Tower. We shall drink *paikareh* . . . the lava of the gods. Agreed?"

"D'accord, d'accord," Leone said, laughing as he was returned to earth.

The Frenchman's jeep was parked within the compound. Leone undid the chain that locked the wheel, and they climbed in. Leone drove quickly. Swerving into an unlighted hutung, he barely missed a Chinese carrying two buckets of night soil at the ends of a bamboo pole. "*Merde* everywhere," Leone whooped, peering through the windshield. He halted before the oaken door of an old palace compound that once had been the residence of a Manchu family. Under a dim light before the doorway crouched four beggars, one of them a woman with a swaddled infant at her exposed breast. Leone waved the beggars aside and pulled a bell chain.

The door creaked as it was pulled open by a stocky man wearing a peaked fur cap whose wide cheekbones marked him as Mongolian. Cursing at the beggars, the man slammed the door shut behind Leone and Jensen. He led them across a garden courtyard to a one-story house and down stone steps into a large room hung with rubbings of Mongolian warriors on horseback. Large copper hot pots bubbled on the tables. Jensen and Leone were seated at a small table covered with a badly stained white tablecloth. Jensen ordered *paikareh,* and the waiter brought them two small glasses and a goblet of the clear spirits distilled from millet and aged with pigeon droppings.

Looking around the room, Jensen noticed a foreign couple seated at a nearby table. He recognized the woman, a blonde in her late thirties, her handsome features somewhat spoiled by an overabundance of mascara and bright red lipstick. She wore teardrop jade earrings and a flowered Chinese silk jacket over a green dress that looked too tight for her full figure. She was Blanche Heyward, the secretary of the American consul general. Jensen had met her at a Fourth of July cocktail party at the consulate. Sitting with her was a slim man, obviously younger than she, wearing a black leather jacket with the insignia of Claire Chennault's Flying Tigers, the American World War II squadron, now transformed into a commercial airline.

Jensen caught the blond woman's eye, and she smiled. "Hello there," she said. "Come on over. Join us. Plenty of room."

Jensen glanced at Leone, who nodded. "Thank you," Jensen said, as he and Leone picked up their glasses and joined the couple.

The waiter brought plates of vegetables, mutton, and beef to be cooked. "I'm Blanche. This is Johnny," the woman said. She fished a bit of beef out of the hot pot with long serving chopsticks, dropped it in her sauce bowl and, using her smaller chopsticks, offered the morsel to her companion, who seized it between his teeth.

"Johnny is back from Mukden and needs nourishment," Blanche said, as she smiled at the pilot. "He got out just before the Chicoms came in."

Leone leaned forward. "What was it like?" he asked, as he fished for mutton in the hot pot with his chopsticks.

The pilot surveyed Leone's hunting jacket, frowning. "You're kind of fancy," he said, with a belligerent edge to his voice.

"Johnny," Blanche said firmly.

Jensen looked at her gratefully.

The pilot shrugged. "Okay, okay." He motioned to the waiter to re-fill his glass with *paikareh*. "So he wants to know. Well. It was hard . . . fucking hard." He picked up his chopsticks and rapped them on the hot pot. "Yes sir. We flew in enough grain for the Nat troops. But nothing for the three hundred thousand slopies starving on the streets . . . He nodded, then picked up his glass and drained it. "No matter, buster. If you had dollars in the restaurants you could get beer, steak and, yes sir, ice cream. Those Korean hostesses at the good ol' Star Dance Hall kept working as if there was no war."

"You checked them out, Johnny, I'm sure," Blanche said, laughing.

The pilot grimaced. "You should've seen those buggers in the gutters. They went blind . . . eating bark, leaves. But the smell of the place . . . "

"You took people out?" Jensen asked.

"Yup. They fought like hounds in heat to get on until we chopped fingers to get the cargo doors closed. But those Nationalist bastards made the real dough. They let only the rich fuckers get on and then cleaned them out. Their cockpits were so loaded with gold bars, the transports wobbled on takeoff."

"Interesting, very interesting. Thank you," Leone said. He put down his chopsticks. "Eric, we must go. We've got a lot to do before the curfew. *Allez*." He saluted the pilot and Blanche and turned to go.

Jensen rose, embarrassed by Leone's abrupt departure. "Thanks for the hospitality," he said. "We've got some other stops." He rounded the table and offered his hand to Blanche. She obviously had not recalled their earlier encounter at the consulate party. "I'm Eric Jensen, and my friend is Lieutenant Jean Leone of the French mission."

"Eric the Red?" Blanche said, looking up into Jensen's eyes.

Jensen attempted a polite smile, wishing that Blanche's breath, heavy with the rich spices of the hot pot sauce, was less pungent. "Good-night."

"See you around," Blanche called out as Jensen went to the small table and dropped a wad of yuan beside the empty *paikareh* goblet.

As he followed Leone out of the compound, Jensen put some bills into the beggar woman's outstretched hand. Leone saw him and said impatiently, "You've only given her a few extra days of suffering."

When they got into the jeep, Leone revved the engine and pulled away with a roar. "Eric, I have a fantastic idea. Let's go to the house of my friend Madame Loh," he said, turning north without waiting for Jensen's response. "You've not been there. You'll like it."

Jensen settled in his seat without responding. He occasionally made the rounds of company houses with Leone, but he preferred to go alone to the House of Three Pleasures. At times he went there only to take tea and rice cakes with the joy girls and listen to their songs as they plucked the strings of their erhus. His loneliness would dissolve as the girls flocked, laughing and saying, "The Red One is here."

His first visit to the House of Three Pleasures had been months ago during the Moon Festival. Flushed with yellow wine, he had invited Summer Swallow to take him to the upper floor. She led him to a room illuminated by a single flickering kerosene lamp where there was a great round couch piled with silken pillows. Summer Swallow had undressed him and led him to the couch. He enjoyed a night of new delights. When he awoke the next morning, Jensen had looked at Summer Swallow sleeping beside him, admiring the curve of her breasts above the silk-lined coverlet. Another night, he amused the joy girls by experimenting in the sexual practices of the Neo-Taoist philosophers. In a volume containing the scriptures of Liu Ching, carried in his army duffel, Jensen had noted: *He who can perform several tens of copulation in a single day and night without letting his Essence escape will be cured of all diseases, and his longevity will grow. If you change women several times, the benefit increases; if you change women ten times in a night, this is excellent to the highest degree.* As a disciple of the purist Chuang Tzu, Jensen had no faith in these Neo-Taoist alchemists, but the urge to dabble in their sexual mysticism had grown in him since the age of seventeen, when he had found a Taoist history in his father's library and read of the mythical Yellow Emperor who, more than two thousand years before Christ, had bedded twelve hundred women and thus become Immortal. On the night of his experiment, Jensen invited four of the girls to the round couch. As he drank the yellow wine, they disrobed him, stroking and massaging his body while exclaiming at the greatness of his Jade Shaft. Then, seeking through union with *yin* to transform his *ch'ing*—essence—into *shen*—spirit—he mounted each girl in turn, striving to withhold. But he failed at the end and fell asleep exhausted amid the giggles of the joy girls. In the morning he joined in their laughter. Soon after, he gave up dabbling in the practices of the Neo-Taoists, and he also ended his occasional experiments with opium.

A brilliant moon had risen over Peking, silhouetting its splendors. In the Tartar City the purple and golden tile roofs of the palaces and temples of the Forbidden City curved toward the heavens. On a precise axis to the north stood the Bell and Drum Towers where watchmen once rang the bell to greet the morning and at day's end beat the drum.

Leone drove through the deserted streets to the Gate of Fixed Peace in the north wall. The huge iron-bound gate was still open. Floodlights illuminated the gate and reflected dully off the tarnished green-glazed tiles of the three-tiered tower that rose above it. The gate was one of nine that pierced the crenellated forty-foot-high wall encircling the Tartar City. On the south it joined the thirty-foot wall of the Chinese City. Guerrilla bands often roamed this section of the wall at night, attempting to harass the Nationalist defenders.

A soldier wearing an ocher-colored uniform and carrying a Thompson submachine gun signaled for Leone to halt. An officer, pistol strapped to his waist, and two soldiers with bayoneted rifles emerged from a fortified enclosure. The officer peered into the jeep, scanning their faces with a flashlight.

Leone displayed his credentials. "My friend is from the American consulate," he said in Chinese.

The officer shrugged. "You may proceed at your own risk. The gate will not be held open past midnight." He signaled to the sentry, and Leone drove through.

Jensen glanced back at the wall, wondering if it would withstand a Communist assault. Made of earth, concrete, and brick, the wall was some sixty feet thick at its base and reinforced with huge projecting buttresses. Like the emperors of China, the Nationalists were relying on it for the ultimate defense of the city.

◆

The road to Madame Loh's took Jensen and Leone past the Altar of Earth Temple. They stopped in front of a two-story house enclosed by a brick wall topped by barbed wire. It was one of the residences built for Japanese officials during the wartime occupation. Jensen followed Leone to the iron gate, where the gatekeeper, an old man with a wispy beard, let them in. They walked past a pond covered with withered lotus stems. Black-and-amber goldfish darted among the pods. Leone jerked the bell chain impatiently. The door was opened by a white-gowned servant. Behind him stood a middle-aged Chinese woman, her elegantly coiffured hair decked with golden combs, her ample figure clothed in a red brocade *cheongsam*, slit high at the sides Shanghai style.

"Ah, Jean. It is you," the woman said in fluent French. "But it is so late."

"Madame Loh, this is my friend, Eric Jensen. It is never too late for an hour with Silver Cloud."

Madame Loh frowned, a slight wrinkling of the brow and a pursing of her heavily rouged lips. She glanced up at Jensen, at blue eyes that revealed a hint of embarrassment. "If you wish," she said, stepping aside to let them enter.

As they walked along a carpeted hallway, Jensen heard shouts mingled with bursts of laughter and the clicking of mah-jongg tiles. He glanced into a lounge where four Chinese men sat at a mah-jongg table with stacks of currency beside them. A Nationalist Army officer, his tunic open, reclined on one couch, and an elderly Chinese, wearing a black skullcap and a blue silk robe, lay on the other. Slim girls sat beside them, tending to their opium pipes. Another strummed a two-stringed erhu as she sang a popular Shanghai love song. Madame Loh led Leone and Jensen into an adjoining room and seated them on a divan flanked by tall crimson vases. Scrolls depicting misted Kweilin landscapes adorned the wall. "I will bring the girls," Madame Loh said.

Leone lit a cigarette and rose to study a celadon vase on the fireplace mantel. "Sung dynasty; lovely isn't it?"

Jensen glanced at the vase. "A reproduction," he said. Leone sighed and returned to the divan, sinking into the soft satin cushions.

"Madame Loh . . . interesting woman." Leone said. "She was once the concubine of a French merchant in Shanghai. When the Japs took over the French Quarter during the war, he went off. Left her with nothing except her jewels. A Japanese colonel took her to Tsingtao as his mistress. Under his protection she opened a company house. When the Japs surrendered she shifted her business to the American Marines. When that ran out she came here."

Two women entered, slim in *cheongsams* slit to the thighs, their faces white with powder and eyes darkened by heavy mascara. "Ah, my precious Silver Cloud," Leone said in Chinese, embracing the girl in the yellow brocade. Her long shining hair was tied back, setting off high cheekbones suggestive of Manchu ancestors. She accepted his embrace with lowered eyes and a shy smile. She bowed to Jensen and gestured with a delicate hand toward her companion. "This is my friend, Little Flower."

"Speak to Little Flower," Leone said, nudging Jensen. "She'll show you the way." He took Silver Cloud by the arm to lead her away. Silver Cloud hesitated, flushing in embarrassment. She was being treated like a common prostitute, Jensen thought. There'd been none of the ceremony of the tea meeting, no time allowed for the coquettish surrender that was the way of the joy girls in the better company houses. "Jean . . ." Jensen began, but he was interrupted by the lieutenant.

"Come. There's not enough time," Leone said curtly.

Jensen turned to Little Flower uncertainly. Despite the clinging *cheongsam* and the heavy makeup, she didn't look more than sixteen. Her long hair, parted in the middle, fell softly over her shoulders. "Tea, sir?" she said shyly, stooping as she spoke. Her Mandarin was heavily accented, marking her as from a distant province. Jensen nodded. Little Flower looked at him gratefully and pressed a call button. A girl in a blue peasant gown responded, and Little Flower asked for tea. Little Flower and Jensen sat side by side on a couch in silence until the servant returned. Little Flower poured jasmine tea into blue rice-china cups.

"How is it, sir, you speak Mandarin so well?" Little Flower said, sipping her tea, her eyes large and dark over the cup.

"My Chinese is very poor," Jensen said, making the customary polite response. "I learned at school."

"But how did you come here?"

"I came with Executive Headquarters."

Little Flower laughed, a little tinkling laugh. "The officers of Executive Headquarters visited us often. They spoke of the headquarters as the Temple of One Thousand Sleeping Colonels. We were sorry when they departed."

As Little Flower refilled the teacups Jensen looked at her more closely, at her tiny bound feet and her long red-lacquered nails. Only in the interior provinces did some old-fashioned families of the upper classes still bind the feet of girls as a mark of status.

"How did you come to this house?" Jensen asked.

"It is a sad tale."

"Tell me."

"Until two years ago I lived with my family in a village in Shantung. My father was a landlord. More than thirty peasants rented land from him. One day after the militia in our district left to fight against the Communists, three students came into our village. They said they were from the People's Liberation Army. They spoke to the people. After a few days the peasants who rented our land came into our house, tied my father's hands, and led him out with a rope around his neck. My mother, my two younger brothers, and I followed them. They took my father to a Speak Bitterness Meeting. All the poor peasants were there. The students denounced the landlords as evil. Then Old Liu, who had been in our house many times, stepped forward. He said my father beat him and took his daughter as a concubine when he could not pay his rent."

"Did your father do that?"

"I do not know," Little Flower said, her fingertips over her painted lips. "I was young. I know Liu's daughter worked as a servant in our house. At the meeting my father stood with his head bowed when the peasants shouted about his high rents. Old Liu threw the first stone. Then the others. Soon my father was dead."

Little Flower was speaking in the singsong manner of a village storyteller and gazing vacantly across the room. Jensen wondered if she was fabricating a tale to win his sympathy. The joy girls sometimes told tales of woe to entice more generous payment from their patrons. Looking at her quivering lips, he hazarded she was telling the truth. He knew there had been many such peasant trials and executions of landlords and Kuomintang officials in the Liberation Areas.

"We carried the body of my father back to our house. The peasants were there taking away our things. The next morning we left the village, walking with bundles on our backs. Under her jacket Mother carried two hundred silver dollars, which my father had buried. On the third night, outside the town of Tzu-po I was awakened by screams. Robbers were beating my mother. They took our silver. We went into Tzu-po and begged for food. Nationalist soldiers were looting the shops as they evacuated the town. We went to the railway station, fighting to get through the crowds of refugees. When a train came, Mother climbed on top and pulled us up . . . first my youngest brother, then me.

As my oldest brother was climbing up, the train moved. He fell off. We never saw him again.

"When we reached Tsingtao we went to the refugee camp set up by the American Marines. They gave us a little rice each day. One day I saw Mother talking to a woman with beautifully combed hair who was wearing foreign shoes. The woman touched my hair and my breasts. She gave money to my mother. 'Go with her,' my mother said. 'She will be kind to you. It is better for you and for us.'

"It was Madame Loh. She took me into Tsingtao, where she had a company house for Marines. She taught me what I must do. When the Marines left Tsingtao, she brought me here."

Jensen sat wordless as Little Flower poured another cup of tea. When he heard a boisterous cry from Leone on the upper floor he looked uneasily at his watch. It was just past eleven. Leone returned alone. "We must hurry to make the gate," he said.

Jensen looked at Little Flower. "Are you safe here?"

"Yes. Madame Loh pays squeeze to the Kuomintang district commander. The Communist guerrillas do not disturb us."

Jensen thrust money into Little Flower's hands. "You can come to see me if you need help. We live in the Kuan Tou Hutung, near the Foreign Office." Looking into her grateful eyes, Jensen knew that he would meet her again.

Madame Loh was not at the door to say farewell as was customary. The other patrons had gone. Jensen followed Leone out to the jeep. It had begun to rain. They drove swiftly back to the gate, which was barely ajar. The rain was pelting against the lookout towers, where snouts of .50-caliber machine guns protruded from the apertures. The guards waved them through.

Leone drove slowly through the rainstorm. "Why didn't you take Little Flower to bed?" he asked irritably. "She'd have been good."

"I didn't want her," Jensen replied curtly as he stared through the foggy windshield debating whether to chide Leone for his treatment of Silver Cloud. He wiped the windshield with his palm and thought of a line from the Tao Te Ching: *Without desire there is tranquillity.*

"You treat them better than they treat each other," Leone said impatiently.

As the rain slackened, Leone drove more quickly through the nearly deserted streets. They were stopped twice by infantry patrols. Finally the lieutenant brought the jeep to a halt before the Language School. "I'll come in the morning to help move your things to the house," he said.

"Can you come in the afternoon? I'm going to the Temple of Heaven in the morning."

Leone looked at Jensen startled. "The Temple of Heaven? But you know what's happening. You've seen the newspapers. The gendarmes will be out in force. And the leftist students will provoke them. We have intelligence reports that the secret police are sweeping up students here and in Nanking and Shanghai. Stay out of it, Eric," Leone said heatedly.

Jensen climbed from the jeep and turned toward Leone at the wheel. "If foreigners are watching, maybe the gendarmes won't crack skulls. I promised some of the students I'd be there."

Leone shrugged. "Always the missionary," the Frenchman grumbled as he drove off.

Walking up to his room, Jensen thought of Li-nan. He imagined being with her in another world: in his garden, beside the lotus pool, reading the Taoist verses. Cups of wine, laughter. . . . Tomorrow he would see her at the demonstration. Later, they would meet at the Altar of Heaven. And yes, Chi would tell him about that matter of the greatest importance. He must warn Chi to be wary of the police. In his room as he drifted toward sleep, he did not hear the distant wail of a siren that pierced the stillness of the curfew hour.

Chapter Four

The police car, a black Ford sedan with curtained windows, its siren wailing, sped east over the Joyous Pavilion Road toward the Peking prison. The beams of its headlights bored through the darkness of the empty avenue. Less than an hour earlier, the thoroughfare had been a noisy tangle of cars, rickshas, bicycles, and peasant carts trafficking through the Shun Chih Gate of the southern wall. The sedan turned south on Classic Road, running past the machine-gun emplacement, where soldiers peered over sandbags, awaiting its passage. It pulled up with a jerk before the prison gate. The driver honked his horn impatiently and, as the ponderous gates parted, gunned the car into the cobbled floodlit courtyard.

Colonel Liu Chih, chief of the Kuomintang secret police, flung open the door of the sedan and leaped out before the chauffeur could scramble about to help him. Liu, a powerfully built man, some six feet tall, dressed in a black tunic and a black astrakhan cap, ran up the stone steps to the arched entrance of the three-story prison. Two men in the leather-belted uniforms of the gendarmerie were waiting for him. Liu followed them down a corridor lined with iron cell doors, solid except for peepholes. The three descended stairs to a steel-bolted door.

Liu elbowed past the others into a large room, dark except for a spotlight attached to the stone ceiling. The spotlight burned down on a hospital operating table. On it lay a nude man, his head turned to the right, spittle dripping from his bruised mouth. His eyes were open and staring. His arms and legs were manacled to the edges of the table. Medical tongs lay between his spread legs. Beside the table there stood a mobile electric generator, its lead wires attached to copper clamps that lay loose on the moist stone floor. A tub of dirty water had been placed on wooden stilts behind the head of the table, which was hinged so that it could be tilted back to submerge the upper part of the man's body.

A thin-faced civilian in a black tunic stood beside the table. He bowed slightly to Liu, his mouth working nervously. "Chi died a few minutes ago," he said.

"Dead," Liu said softly, his eyes narrowing. Those eyes were a vivid blue, strange in a Chinese and a peculiar contrast to his mahogany complexion. Liu whipped off the astrakhan and smoothed back his closely cropped hair.

"Anything more?"

"No. He only repeated what he said when delirious . . . just before we called you. He said, 'Letter . . . the letter.' That was all."

Liu ran his fingers along the white hairline scar that curved over his right cheek. "You were too quick with him," he said curtly.

The thin-faced one shrugged. "He was on the table for more than ten hours. Our student informant warned us: Among all in the Yenching cell, Chi was the hard one. When we dipped him, he sucked water into his lungs. Tried to die."

Liu studied the corpse's bloated features. "Only one or two more words might have been enough. 'Letter' may have something to do with messages being sent to the Communists."

The thin-faced one nodded.

"And the foreigner?"

"The photograph in Chi's wallet seems to be from last summer. Chi posed with the foreigner in the picnic area on Coal Hill. He is an American ... Eric Jensen. He is even taller than you, Colonel. He is a scholar—lives in the Language School of the Christian Missionary Board. Speaks Mandarin unusually well. He researches the Taoist archives at the universities and in the monasteries. He also works in the American Library ... apparently to help support himself. We have opened letters to his father in which he tells of writing a book on Taoism. Most of his friends are students like Chi. We have seen him in tea houses and company houses with Leone, the young one in the French military atttaché's office. At times he enjoys himself too much. He likes his wine."

Colonel Liu glowered at the thin-faced one, his blue eyes narrowed. "Learn more about him."

The thin-faced one nodded.

Chapter Five

Ying was sitting in his pedicab waiting to go to the Temple of Heaven when the gate of the Language School was swung open for Jensen. The bells were pealing for nine o'clock mass in the Gothic tower of St. Michel's Church in the Legation Quarter. An old peddler, squatting on the lawn bordering the compound wall, hailed the American as he passed. "A five-flavored egg for you, Master," he cried, holding up a porcelain jug. Jensen inspected the mounds of pears, persimmons, and peanuts laid out neatly on the peddler's red cloth. He selected a green pear, rubbed it with his bandanna, and bit into it before getting into Ying's pedicab. Flocks of trained pigeons circled in the placid blue sky, bamboo whistles attached to their tails.

Ying pedaled easily in the morning freshness, and Jensen lowered the pedicab's canvas hood so that he could glance back at Coal Hill. Last summer he and Chi had often hiked up the winding path to the summit to relax in the shade of the graceful Pavilion of Ten Thousand Springs.

They would look down over the Imperial Gardens and the yellow roofs of the palaces of the Forbidden City, where the Ming and Manchu emperors had once reigned. How Chi had raged at Fu Tso-yi, the Nationalist army commander, his impertinence at putting his headquarters in the Forbidden City and quartering his personal guard with their horses in the ceremonial halls.

The pedicab rolled through the Legation Quarter past the diplomatic compounds. The quarter still bore the scars of the antiforeign Boxer Rebellion at the turn of the century, when Christian missionaries and their Chinese converts had been murdered in many regions of China. In Peking, the foreign legations were spared when an allied expedition lifted the fifty-five-day siege by imperial Manchu troops. Only two years had elapsed since the Western powers had relinquished the last of the extraterritorial rights wrested in compensation from the Empress Dowager.

Approaching the walled-in park of the Temple of Heaven, Jensen said, "Ying, take me to the West Gate. I will walk from there to the Hall of Annual Prayer. Wait for my return at the North Gate. Do not be afraid."

The gendarmes at the gate looked with curiosity at the oddly dressed foreigner but made no move to stop him. As he came upon the Hall of Annual Prayer, Jensen was stunned by the scene. Massed on the marble steps and balustrades under the hall's blue spired dome were hundreds of students. They carried placards bearing slogans: PROTEST GOVERNMENT BRUTALITY, PEACE AND DEMOCRACY, NO MORE AMERICAN INTERFERENCE. Gendarmes, wearing bucket helmets, rifles at their hips, stood in the forecourt facing the students.

Jensen hurried through the vast courtyard to the west of the hall, where he found three foreign journalists. One was a heavyset American in a trench coat and snap brim hat, Chris Harris of Universal Press.

With him were Jules Depew of Agence-France Presse and Spencer Morse of the Associated Press. There were no other foreigners about. Why had Chi told him that foreign diplomats would be there?

Harris waved to Jensen, recognizing him as a clerk at the American Library. Jensen headed toward him, feeling a surge of envy. These journalists, by their reporting, could influence what was happening in China.

"Looks like the students won't move," Harris said, fingering an unlit cigar.

The nervous Frenchman stamped his feet to warm them. "If they don't . . . poof . . . heads will be cracked." Depew said. "The government is taking a harder line. They must do something. The BBC this morning, Chris, you heard? *Mon Dieu*! Student demonstrations in all the big cities."

The A.P. man opened his Rolleiflex camera and squinted into the viewer to focus it. "Look at that bunch . . . begging for trouble." The students in the front rank were shaking fists at the gendarmes. Their banners identified them as students of Yenching. Jensen bit his lip as he spotted Li-nan dressed in a blue tunic, her hair in a pigtail, standing in the front rank with fist upraised. He looked vainly for Chi. The students were now spitting in the direction of the gendarmes and shouting obscenities.

A gendarme officer strode toward the hall and called though a megaphone. "Move to the West Gate, or we shall use force."

Angry replies echoed through the courtyard: "Kuomintang fascists!" "Down with Chiang Kai-shek!" The Yenching students were the most provocative. Jensen winced as he heard them shout the worst of insults: "turtle eggs" and "in your mother's cunt."

There was a stirring among the gendarmes. Some of them raised their rifles and fired. Several of the students on the marble steps collapsed while others screamed in pain and fear. In panic, the students began retreating up the steps of the hall, a few of them toppling over the balustrades. Jensen lost sight of Li-nan as the gendarmes surged forward, jabbing with bayonets and swinging rifle butts.

"Li-nan, Li-nan," Jensen cried out. He ran toward the hall.

"Come back," Harris shouted after him. "Come back, you fool!"

Jensen vaulted over the balustrades onto the veranda into the melee of students struggling to escape. Towering above the crowd, he spotted Li-nan within the hall, pinned against one of the red wooden pillars. She was clutching her head, blood streaming down her face. Jensen shouldered toward her and, planting his hands on the pillar above her head, shielded her from the surging crowd.

"Let me help you," he said in Chinese. She nodded. Jensen pulled out his shirt and ripped a strip off the bottom. "Hold this to your forehead."

With his arm about Li-nan's shoulders, Jensen pushed through the mob and guided her out to the veranda and down the side stairs into the garden. They went to a small gate that opened onto a cedar wood and walked quickly toward the North Gate. Frightened students were jostling there before the locked entrance. "Make way for an injured student," Jensen shouted. Students took up the cry, and the crowd parted. Jensen pressed his face between the iron bars of the gate and called out to a young gendarme officer. "I am taking this girl to a hospital." The officer gaped at the foreigner with the bleeding girl and ordered the gate opened. Ying was waiting on East Street at the Bridge of Heaven.

"I'll take you to the Union Medical Hospital," Jensen said, as he helped Li-nan into the pedicab.

"No," Li-nan whispered. "The secret police will find me. Let your pedicab man take me back to Yenching. I'll be safer there. I know a doctor who'll care for me."

Jensen looked at her in surprise. It was the first time she had spoken to him in English. He ripped off the other tail of his shirt and handed it to her. "The bleeding isn't so bad now. I'll take you to my friend's house. We can drive to Yenching in his car.

"Ying," he shouted, "take us to the house of the lieutenant." Li-nan pushed herself up as if to leap from the pedicab.

"Don't be afraid," Jensen said. "My friend is a French military attaché. You can trust him." She settled back carefully, closing her eyes in pain.

At the lieutenant's house Jensen jumped off the pedicab and rang the bell. Leone came to the door in a dressing gown, unshaven and rumpled. He glanced at the girl, frowned, and led them into a bedroom. "Bring water and my medical kit," he said to the servant as he helped Li-nan onto the bed.

Leone brushed back Li-nan's hair, washed the wound, and sprinkled sulfa powder on a crude bandage that he wrapped around her head. "What hit you?" he asked.

"A rifle butt," she said, easing back on the pillow. Her bandaged head and peasant tunic contrasted strangely with the black silk pillow and the bedspread embroidered with an orange-and-blue phoenix. "I'll be well enough in a few minutes. I'll go back to Yenching."

In the lounge Leone confronted Jensen irritably. "I warned you not to get involved. The police may have followed you here. You could lose your residence permit. They could raise hell with my consul general. They could throw me out of Peking."

"I'm sorry, Jean," Jensen said, surprised by his outburst. "The girl was hurt."

Leone tightened the sash of his black silk dressing gown. He leaned on the fireplace mantel and ran his fingers over the Tibetan Buddha figure sitting there. After a few moments he sighed. "No matter. Sorry about lecturing you. The truth is, Eric, I do worry about being thrown out of Peking. I like it here. You don't know how much better it is for me . . . here in Peking instead of a stinking barracks at Marseilles or a post in North Africa . . . like the one where my father drank himself to death." Leone walked from the room.

Jensen, upset by Leone's words, eased his bruised body onto a couch. I ought to leave, he thought. It's not fair to him.

Leone was back in a few minutes, carrying a broad-brimmed peasant hat. "Here. This will cover her bandage." He handed the keys of the jeep to Jensen. "Take her to Yenching. I've looked outside the house. No police. If you're not back before dark I'll go to the garrison headquarters to ask about you." As he turned to leave, Leone cocked his head and smiled. "By the way, I suppose you didn't notice. She's very pretty."

Li-nan was still resting, her eyes closed, when Jensen entered the bedroom. Her bulky tunic was open, revealing a white silk blouse softly molded over the full curve of her breasts. She's lovely, Jensen thought, so lovely. "We can drive to Yenching now," Jensen said, touching her shoulder. Li-nan rose painfully and sat on the edge of the bed.

"Here. You'll need this hat to hide the bandage."

Li-nan smiled feebly, donned the hat, and buttoned her jacket. Jensen helped her into Leone's jeep and dismissed Ying, who pedaled off relieved.

They drove through the West Straight Gate of the Tartar City wall. The guards, accustomed to picnickers going out on Sunday afternoon to the Summer Palace, hardly glanced at Li-nan as they passed.

"You're safe now, Li-nan," Jensen said, as he threaded through the thick traffic.

"In English I'm called Lilian."

"Where did you learn to speak such good English?"

"At the American school in Shanghai."

"What are you studying at Yenching?"

"I'm a second-year medical student."

Jensen glanced at Lilian. "Medicine? Why medicine?"

"There aren't many jobs in China in which a woman can hope to be treated as an equal. Medicine is one of them."

They drove on in silence for a time before Jensen asked: "How did you get to the Temple this morning? It's five or six miles to Yenching."

"We walked. We went into the city when the gate opened at six."

"The guards let you by with those banners?"

Lilian glanced uneasily at Jensen. "We picked up the banners in the city . . . on the Pei-ta University campus."

"You're certainly well-organized."

"Yes. We've had a lot of experience. Students have been fighting for democracy since 1919."

"I'm familiar with the history of the Chinese student movement," Jensen answered stiffly. They drove on again in silence for a time. "I didn't see Chi at the demonstration," Jensen said.

Lilian took off the broad-brimmed hat, placed it in her lap, and looked straight ahead, her features impassive. She said, "He disappeared soon after we spoke to you at the Language School."

"What's happened to him?"

"We believe he was taken by the secret police."

"You say that so calmly, Lilian. Do you know where he is now?"

"No. He's not the first to be taken, and he won't be the last."

They were at Yenching and Jensen drove onto the campus, a walled park known in the time of the Mings as the Villa of Breeze and Mist. Just inside the gate, Lilian said, "Please do not drive any farther. It's better I go on from here alone."

"Can we meet again?"

"If you like. Come next Sunday. I'll meet you at three near the Po Ya Pagoda by the little lake. But please come by bicycle or bus . . . not jeep. You'll attract less attention."

Jensen was surprised by her quick response. There was none of the reserve customary in a Chinese girl of her class. As he helped her from the jeep, Lilian looked straight at him. "You've been very kind," she said. "Please understand. I do worry about Chi. More than I can say. He's my closest friend. But we must be strong if the revolution is to succeed."

"I understand," Jensen said. "But tell me, that night in my room. What did Chi want to talk to me about when he said it was a 'matter of the greatest importance'?"

Lilian hesitated. "I'm not sure," she said firmly. "Oh yes. Your friend, the lieutenant, was very helpful. Please thank him for me." She paused. "It might be better if you did not mention to him what we discussed."

Jensen looked puzzled. "But why?"

"The military attachés talk to the Nationalist intelligence people."

Jensen frowned: "I don't think you need to worry about that." But then he raised both hands reassuringly. "But I'll do as you ask."

"Thank you. Until Sunday," Lilian said. Turning, she walked slowly down the cobbled path toward a dormitory. Jensen watched her go, wondering what she was withholding from him.

Chapter Six

Embarrassed at having scolded him for bringing Lilian to the compound, Leone uncorked a bottle of Dom Perignon as Jensen walked through the door. "Liberated from the cellar of the consulate—the last of the last case," he said, holding it aloft reverently. That night they dined on Beggar's Chicken, which Leone's Chinese cook had been baking in clay since the previous night.

Jensen slept fitfully and in the morning he borrowed Leone's jeep and went to fetch his belongings from the Language School. Before stopping at his dormitory room, he quickly climbed the back staircase to the upper floor and knocked at a door at the end of the hall. Moments passed and then the door was abruptly pulled open. A woman in a black *cheongsam* stood there, her left hand planted defiantly on her hip.

"Well hi, lamb," the woman drawled, her features softening. "I thought it was one of those damn missionaries. Haven't seen you for days." The small room looked more like a monastic cell than a bedroom. Apart from a chair and an iron cot, the only other furniture was a battered chest of drawers. On it stood a silver framed photograph of a young Chinese man in a Mandarin robe. Beside it were two tulip glasses and a bottle of brandy from the winery of Peking's French Benedictine monastery.

Joan Taylor had come to the school two weeks ago from Taiyuan, the besieged Shansi capital of the warlord Yen Hsi-shan, where she had been a teacher at the university. As the Communists were preparing to scale the city's walls, Joan was evacuated on one of Chennault's transports bringing in foodstuffs and taking out refugees.

The first time Jensen saw her, Joan was standing alone outside the school director's office. She was striking: dark flirtatious eyes, black hair pulled back in a large bun, golden hoop earrings. She had just rented the room of a departed student. Jensen offered to carry her two bulging leather suitcases and small pink valise. Depositing her baggage in her new room, he glanced up to find Joan examining him with unconcealed interest.

"Missionary?" she asked, as she took off her shaggy raccoon coat, hitched up her gray woolen *cheongsam,* and seated herself on the cot, crossing her legs. She leaned back, resting on her arms as she looked him over.

Jensen smiled, taking her in, the long silk-clad legs. "I'm not a missionary," he said quietly. "I'm a scholar-in-residence here. My name is Eric Jensen."

"Well, thank the good Lord," she said, taking a cigarette from a silver case. "I'm Joan Taylor." She smiled and rose languidly from the cot. Standing on her toes, she peered out the window. "I'll see you around," she said.

Jensen let his eyes wander over the slim figure, the *cheongsam* that clung to her hips, the incongruous black slippers with the high heels. She had to be in her mid-thirties, but she was a piece of work. He had not seen anything like her since his Army leaves in Shanghai.

Joan did not turn about as Jensen said, "Yes, see you around."

After their first meeting, Joan would seek out Jensen in the dining hall, finding him much more congenial than the missionaries. Unattached foreign women who sashayed about China were usually considered unsavory, slipping from one job to another, some becoming consorts of wealthy Chinese. Joan's flamboyant manner did not help. She seemed to delight in shocking the missionaries with her tight dresses and bright pink lipstick. Jensen, enjoying her company, was impervious to their sniffs and disapproving glances.

Joan's drawl became more prolonged when she spoke of her past. "I'm from Nice, Louisiana. Never want to see that hole again." During the war she escaped Nice by volunteering as a hostess in a Red Cross canteen in Honolulu. "I listened to the boys moan on and on about their wives and sweethearts until they reached for my thigh under the table," she said with a half smile. "After the war, when the American School in Shanghai was reopening, I applied for a job. They okayed my Louisiana teaching certificate. Didn't ask me if I was quadroon or octoroon. I don't look Negro, do I? But my mother is Creole—one-fourth Negro—and it's on my Louisiana birth certificate. In Nice that's enough. I had too much nigger in me to teach in a white school. So I taught Negro kids.

"Shanghai was a pretty exciting place for a Creole from Nice. But they fired me because I was screwing around too much. When I couldn't find another job in Shanghai I took a teaching contract in Taiyuan."

One night Joan and Jensen took a pedicab to the Chinese City. They wandered along Silk Street near the Front Gate, taking in the honky-

tonk bars lit by blinking electric signs. They sampled plump persimmons from a peddler's cart and then strolled down a crooked hutung to
a small restaurant that Jensen claimed served the best meat dumplings
in China. It was only an hour before curfew when they emerged, laughing and flushed with wine.

Swaying slightly, they walked down Silk Street in search of a pedicab. Suddenly a stocky man with a sack over his shoulder crouched before Jensen. Four other peasants surrounded them. "Mister, we are poor
peasants from a village in the north," said the man. "The soldiers
burned our village. We lost everything. Our children are hungry. Give
us, honorable sir, a little money."

Jensen nodded. He peeled one hundred yuan, worth only a few dollars in the raging inflation, from a roll and handed it to the peasant.

"Oh, good sir, so little. There are so many of us."

Jensen handed over two fifty-yuan notes without speaking.

"Wong, take all the money from the foreign devil," said a voice in the
darkness. The stocky peasant took a club from his sack. A bushy-haired
man came up behind him, pulled out a broadsword, and waved it in the
air. "Give us the money," said the stocky one. Jensen reached into his
gown with his right hand but then swiftly swung the other arm about,
knocking the raised club aside. He seized the surprised peasant, lifted
him, and hurled his body at the man with the raised broadsword.
Jensen punched down a third assailant. The other two fled.

Joan watched with frightened eyes. "Let's go," she gasped.

Jensen, standing over the peasants, said softly: "They must be very
hungry. They know the penalty for attacking a foreigner: beheading."
He raised the bushy-haired man to his feet and stuffed a handful of
yuan notes into his shirt. "For your children . . . You have shamed your
ancestors," he said. Dropping the frightened peasant onto the cobblestones, he took Joan by the arm and led her down the hutung.

They reached the Language School just as the city siren sounded the curfew. They headed to Joan's room, where she poured two brandies. Her fright having ebbed away, she seemed intoxicated by their adventure. In animated tones she began again to speak of her past life. Jensen listened, slightly disquieted by Joan's tales of night life in the bars and great houses of Shanghai, by her affair with a Chinese general.

The brandy bottle was almost empty when she began to talk about Taiyuan. "Taiyuan was okay. I taught English at the university. They gave me a bungalow, a cook boy, and a wash amah. The Chennault pilots, nice fellers, kept me supplied with French brandy. After six months I moved in with the head of my department. He was Chinese, a good-looking guy." She gestured to the photograph on the chest of drawers.

"His name was John—John Huang. He got his Ph.D. in comparative literature at Georgetown University. Worked a while in Washington in some government agency. Was I in love with him?" She poured another drink. "Yes, very much. He gave me peace. I married him in the Catholic Church. He wanted it that way. Our happiness didn't last, though. He talked too much to the students about the new China. My poor man . . ." she said, holding her glass up to the lamplight and tilting it as she gazed through the amber liquor. "When the Communists camped outside the walls, the old warlord went berserk. He purged anyone suspected of links to the Communists. One of the teaching assistants denounced John." Joan walked to the chest of drawers, rested her arms on it, and looked at the photograph. "The secret police chief arrested him . . . put him before a people's court. He had befriended some of the left-wing students, but he wasn't a Communist. They beat him to death with sticks." She rested her face on her arms. Jensen waited in silence until she returned to the cot.

Joan lit another cigarette and drew on it deeply. "After that I got drunk more often. When Chennault's planes started taking people out

I left," Joan said. "The town was finished anyway. The students were being drafted to dig trenches. The airlift wasn't bringing in enough food. People were starving."

Jensen, who disliked brandy, had turned to *paikareh,* which he had brought back from the Chinese City in a porcelain goblet. After tossing back shots of straight *paikareh* he rose unsteadily and went out to the hall toilet, leaving the door ajar. As he made his way down the corridor, propping himself on the rough brick wall with one hand, a door opposite opened, squeaking on rusted hinges. A woman looked out and withdrew hastily. Joan was waiting in the doorway when he returned. She was smiling, swaying, her pink lips parted. She had exchanged the gray wool *cheongsam* that she had worn to the city for a black sheath. Jensen lurched into her arms. Joan kicked the door shut. She didn't resist when he pressed her down on the cot. She laughed in a wild, shrill way, and taking hold of his fumbling hands, stilled them.

"What's your hurry," she said. She stood up and shed her dress. As Jensen watched, his throat tightening, she reached back to free her breasts. Her dusky figure bent over him, helping him to unhook his gown. Then she lay down beside him, stroking his bare chest and threading her hands through the tufts below his belly. She began to hum, a strange steady hum. He tensed, his back arching, as he felt her lips flicking down. Jensen groaned. Joan came astride him grasping him with both hands, plunging and rocking. Her humming swelled to a moan. Then suddenly she let out a high-pitched scream like that of a wounded cat. A chill ran through Jensen and he felt the lust go out of him.

"Joan, what is it?" he said. Jensen reached for her hand and pulled her body down beside him. She didn't speak. Soon she was resting quietly.

Jensen awoke as the early morning light filtered through the slit window. Joan was asleep. The blanket had slipped away, exposing her breasts. Jensen kissed her cheek, her throat and breasts. She stirred but did not open her eyes. He caressed her gently, then more searchingly. She parted for him and he mounted her. Later when she was once more asleep, he slipped from the cot, dressed, and went to his room.

In the afternoon Jensen returned to Joan's room, vaguely disturbed and wanting to talk, but he found her cold and distracted. Strands of hair loose from her bun strayed over her cheek, her mascara was streaked, and a button was missing from her white blouse. The bed was undone and the brandy bottle lay beside it empty. "I'm sorry," she said. "I was drunk. Please go. No hard feelings." Her eyes were blank. "I'll see you around."

Jensen had not seen her since that afternoon.

"It's time for a farewell drink," Joan said. She lit a cigarette, perched on the cot, and crossed her legs. "Those sanctimonious bastards asked me to get out of the school by tomorrow. The director sent me a note—said they need the room for missionaries coming down from Manchuria. They don't really need this room now. I guess I'm too much for them. Doesn't make much difference. I was about to move out."

Jensen tossed his hat on the cot as she poured a splash of brandy for him. "I'm leaving too," he said. "Someone saw me going in and out of your room that night."

Joan chuckled, leaned over, and kissed Jensen full on the mouth. "Sorry," she said. The two laughed and raised their glasses.

"What are you going to do, Joan?" Jensen asked, as he accepted a cigarette.

"I've got a secretarial job in the Universal Press office. Peking won't change all that much after the Chicoms come in. Things will settle down after a while. Even the Communists will need the help of foreign devils. Did you ever think of yourself as a foreign devil, Eric?" Joan laughed, put out her cigarette, and lit another. "Maybe they've got us figured just right. Most of us knocking about China are devils escaping some kind of hell."

Eric twisted his glass, disturbed at how distraught she seemed. Hiding her fears. Drinking too much. He wanted to reach out to Joan, to comfort her somehow, protect her. He put down the brandy untouched. "I'm moving in with Jean Leone, the French military attaché." He paused. "We'll stay in touch. Is there anything I can do?"

"I'll be all right. The job in the U.P. office will be good as long as Chris Harris stays around. And he'll hang on as long as he can file stories. I'm going to share a Chinese house with Ted Burke. You know, the ex-Marine, the guy who was the security officer at the consulate. He's sick . . . his liver is shot. Drinks too much. They want to send him home. But he won't go. He's quit the State Department."

She saw the question in Jensen's eyes. "No, lamb, I'm not going to sleep with Burke. There are two bedrooms. He's got a Chinese girlfriend. We'll share a cook boy. It'll be okay as long as he doesn't get drunk too often."

Joan came close to Jensen and reached up to gently rub the red bristle on his jaw with the back of her hand. "You're always so serious. Don't worry. I'll be okay. It's been worse. This is still better than Louisiana." She leaned back, smiling. "I'll call you at Leone's house. Does he have French brandy? This local stuff is terrible." She touched her fingers to her lips and waved as she opened the door.

Jensen went to his room, packed, and carried his suitcase down to the entryway. As he had done so often, he glanced at the patina-aged plaque set into the wall by the door bearing the names of Christian missionaries slain during the Boxer Rebellion, half a century ago. As he looked at the familiar plaque, he decided to say good-bye to John Scott, the director, whom he had not seen since his terse dismissal from the school. In the office, Jensen was told that Scott was conducting a service in the chapel. Jensen entered the chapel just as the missionaries were solemnly filing into the old pine pews, the children hushed by stern glances from their parents. They bowed their heads as Scott, a Lutheran minister, invited them to pray for missionaries fleeing from the fighting in Manchuria. Jensen, in a pew at the rear of the chapel, gazed at Scott, a tall man with austere, craggy features, thinking how much he resembled his own father.

The image returned to him of the white frame church in Webster, the sunlight slanting through the arched windows casting his father in a halo at the pulpit; he was just a boy sitting in the front pew beside his mother, who always wore a black felt hat with a thin red feather. Later, his drift away from the church; rebelling at first against the church's petty denials of beer, dances in town, and the close embrace of a girl. The wrenching breach came later, after he began reading translations of forbidden Taoist literature tucked away in his father's library. Those angry, painful exchanges as he questioned the strictures and catechisms of the church; his father not knowing he had discovered Chuang Tzu and embraced the philosopher's credo: *Let man enjoy the fullness of life, free of the bondage of conventions, seeking wisdom and every earthly sensation and delight, unafraid of death, and at one with the universal God Force.*

The voice of the minister brought him out of his recollections. Arms outstretched, Scott intoned from the pulpit: "We beseech Thee, O Lord, shield our brethren and bring them to safe shelter. We who have been called by Jesus the Savior shall not shrink from our holy mission in China. Inspired by the martyred missionaries who served before us, we shall endure what we must in Your Name."

Amens echoed in the vaulted chapel. Jensen joined in the closing hymn and, as the service ended and the missionaries filed out, he studied the peaceful faces of the ordained ministers, the doctors, the nurses, the teachers; men in white shirts with starched collars and sober ties, the women in freshly pressed dresses shepherding their children from the pews. He envied their spirit of commitment and the comfort they seemed to enjoy in their revelation, something he had not yet attained in his own search. Jensen was replacing his Bible in the rack of the pew when John Scott walked down the aisle, a large Bible clasped under crossed arms. Jensen wanted to cry out to him, this colleague of his father, and ask forgiveness for offending him. But he could not summon the will. Scott disappeared, and Jensen followed the missionaries out of the chapel.

Jensen was loading his bags into the jeep when a thin, stooped Chinese in a black mandarin robe hurried down the steps of the school. It was Professor Wu, who had been a guide in Jensen's study of the Taoist classics. Wu seemed ageless, a teacher of many generations of language students, forever smiling as he peered over horn-rimmed glasses.

Jensen took the professor's hand in both of his own. "Professor Wu, I did mean to say good bye. I have been asked to leave the school."

"Yes, I know," the professor said in the sharply enunciated Chinese he used when talking to foreign students. "Everything is changing. I thought of going back to my village, but the Communists are already there. My brother's grain shop has been confiscated. He was denounced because he dealt with the landlords. It is more than two years, but the Communists still shout about the American Marine who raped a Chinese girl in Peking. There is no place for me in their world. What if they learn I have worked in an American school?"

"At least they're not corrupt like the Kuomintang," Jensen said.

"Corruption is an old disease in China," the professor said, tucking his hands into the sleeves of his gown. "There are worse things. But we shall see. You can always go back to the United States."

"I intend to stay," Jensen answered. "I will come to see you." The professor stood on the steps, his hand raised in farewell, as Jensen drove off toward the American Library.

At the library Jensen noticed there were few Chinese students in the reading room. At that hour the tables were usually crowded. He went to the newspaper rack and lifted out the *Peiping Chronicle*, the government-owned local newspaper. There was no mention of the demonstration at the Temple of Heaven. Jensen looked at the clipboard of the radio file, which included playbacks of news articles about China published in the United States. There was an Associated Press report that four students had been killed and twenty-one others injured in the clash in the Temple park. The Peking garrison commander had issued a statement blaming the violence on Communist subversion. Police had arrested more than thirty students in a sweep of the Yenching campus. A Washington dispatch reported that the American ambassador in Nanking had appealed for release of the students.

Jensen leaned heavily on the newspaper rack. He reread the dispatch. The stillness of the reading room was broken only by the creak of his heavy footsteps as he walked back to his desk. He sat there, face in hands, wondering if Lilian had been seized.

Chapter Seven

On Sunday, Jensen shared lunch with Leone before leaving for Yenching to meet Lilian. The lieutenant, who had donned a fur-lined Chinese gown against the chill in the dining room, was not in his usual chipper form. He toyed with his chopsticks, hardly tasting the braised sliced carp, one of his favorite dishes. Between servings he studied the local press reports about the Battle of the Huai-Hai. One million Nationalist and Communist troops were in combat on the Huapei Plain, northwest of Nanking above the Yangtze River. Leone contemptuously dismissed Nationalist claims of victories. Otherwise he said very little. Jensen watched Leone uneasily over the rim of his bowl as he scooped the last of his rice. Worried that Lilian had been seized by the police, he was determined to resist any suggestion that he not go to Yenching. If she was jailed he must find some way to help her. Leone, however, pointedly refrained from mentioning the turbulence at the university.

After lunch, Jensen borrowed the cook's bicycle. Before setting off for Yenching, he pressed a wad of yuan notes on the cook, whose eager outstretched hand belied his polite protestations against being compensated.

It was a cool, sunny October day. Jensen, wearing his Army jacket, pedaled vigorously through the West Straight Gate and along the tree-lined blacktop road winding out beyond the city wall. Cars and buses crowded with Peking folk drove past him en route to the Summer Palace, possibly for a last outing before the Communists occupied the Peking suburbs. He bypassed two-wheeled Peking carts pulled by oxen and mules, loaded with cabbages and wheat grain, and steered gingerly through herds of pigs and flocks of yellow-billed white ducks being driven to the markets. Double-humped camels trudged by, carrying sacks of coal and bundles of firewood. He laughed when a goat herdsman cracked his long whip after him, and it occurred to Jensen that he had not laughed for days. He was excited at the thought of being with Lilian.

The temple bell sounded as Jensen entered the Yenching compound. He rode onto a stone walk curling around the little lake to the pagoda-shaped water tower. Students were seated on the hillside below the thirteen-tiered tower, and some turned to look at the tall foreigner with the great mop of red hair. Jensen was about to inquire about Lilian when he saw her walking toward him down the steps of the tower. He noticed that she had undone her single braid, allowing her hair to tumble over her slim shoulders. She wore a pink sweater under an open blue jacket and a blue silk kerchief knotted at her throat. There was a patch bandage on her forehead.

"Hello," Lilian said in English, smiling up at him. "Please, now. I don't even know your Christian name." Jensen extended his hand. "Eric." She took his hand in both of hers. "How do you do," she said playfully. The smile melted into earnestness. "I owe you very much."

Jensen gazed at her in delight. He had expected to find Lilian rather withdrawn, not like this spirited creature.

"Put your bicycle in the rack. Let's walk along the lake," Lilian said. "If we don't escape now, my classmates will be upon you to talk politics or practice their English." They strolled along the shore and Lilian buttoned her jacket as the wind rippled the surface of the lake. They paused at a little red arch, all that remained of a Ching dynasty pavilion.

"Have you known your lieutenant friend for a long time?" Lilian asked.

"Yes. We're good friends. I've just moved into his house. I met Jean at the missionary Language School."

Lilian picked up a flat stone and skimmed it across the surface of the lake. "See the pavilion on the little island in the lake? It was given by Henry Luce, the owner of your magazine *Time*. The gift was in memory of his father. He was a missionary in China." She threw another stone into the water and watched it skip across the sun-speckled waters. "In the time of the Mings the island was called Pine Breezes and Moonlit Water."

Lilian looked thoughtfully into Jensen's eyes. "Yenching was founded by American Christian missions. Your ambassador in Nanking was the first president. Missionaries still support the school. But now the students speak against missionaries."

Jensen frowned. "But why? They help your people."

"True. They relieve the people's suffering with rice, schools, and hospitals. But they also suppress the anger of the people. We believe in revolution, not charity, as the way to a better China."

Jensen scrutinized Lilian's features: the imperious profile, the delicate ivory skin, and the touch of pink lipstick that matched her expensive cashmere sweater. Pretty elegant for a revolutionary, he thought.

"I understand what you are saying," Jensen said, wondering why

Lilian had raised the missionary issue. "But the people still must eat. They can't subsist on Communist revolutionary promises."

"I'm not a Communist, if that's what you are suggesting," Lilian said calmly. "My father is an official at the Central Bank. Almost all of us at Yenching are from wealthy or middle-class families. Very few students have become Communists. Most of us have no illusions about what will happen to the wealthy classes when the Communists take power."

Jensen thrust his hands into the pockets of his jacket. "Chi spoke to me the same way. I suppose if I were a Chinese student I might have the same attitude."

"We don't have a choice," Lilian went on firmly. "The democratic parties have no power. There'll be no reform under the Kuomintang . . . only more corruption. Under the Communists at least there'll be hope. That's why we lean to their side."

Jensen searched Lilian's eyes. She hardly knows me, he thought, yet she is speaking so openly. Her boldness with a near stranger was puzzling. It was as if she was drawing him out. He decided to do the same. "Why did you provoke the gendarmes at the Temple?" Jensen asked bluntly. "Four students were killed."

"Sometimes we must pay a price in blood," Lilian said, averting her eyes. "It's the only way we have to arouse the people."

"I see," Jensen said. He hadn't been asked to go to the demonstration to forestall violence. He'd been invited to witness martyrdom. They strolled for a time without speaking before Jensen asked: "How does your family feel about all this?"

"My mother understands. She's from an old Mandarin family. Her father was an enlightened man . . . a scholar. She was the first woman in her family not to have her feet bound. No tottering on Golden Lilies for her. She studied philosophy at Catholic University in Shanghai. My father? He is suspicious of what's happening to me. He wants me to return to Shanghai. To our villa in the Hungjao district. He'd like me to marry a rich man. Or go to school in the States . . . "

Lilian hunted along the shore for another stone and sent it skimming across the water. "I won't do what he asks. I would like to go back home. But only to see my mother . . . walk with her in her garden. Oh! You should see her garden. There's a little pond with lotus blossoms. I used to sit beside it . . . and feed millet to the golden carp."

"It must be exquisite," Jensen said. "I'd like to have a garden like that . . . someday."

Lilian looked up at Jensen with a little sad smile. "It is exquisite. But it belongs to another age. My father also belongs to another age—old China. You wouldn't know it if you met him. Graduated from Princeton . . . travels to New York and Zurich for the bank . . . plays golf at the Hungjao country club."

Lilian seated herself on a flat rock, locked her arms over her knees, and looked out over the lake. "I remember, when I was a child, going with him to shop at the Wing An Department Store on Nanking Road. When our Rolls stopped in traffic, the beggars pressed their faces against the windows. I'd ask about them, and he'd answer, 'It's always been like that. It will always be so.'"

"Your mother and father seem very different."

"I think my father cares for my mother. But in his own way. He's kept one concubine after another in an apartment on Avenue Joffre in the French Quarter. He expects my mother to accept it. She doesn't complain. But she refuses to have his concubines in the house . . . like many wives do. She said to me when I left to go to Yenching: 'Your generation will not live as comfortably as mine. Don't regret it. There are more important things.'"

Lilian tilted up her chin. "I honor my father. It's our custom. But it is my mother who has shown me the way."

"Do you have brothers or sisters?"

"Two brothers. The older one is in America studying business at Harvard. We're like most rich Chinese families. One son must be sent someplace as security against what may happen here. My other brother? My mother encouraged him to study philosophy. I suppose she dreamed of him being like her father . . . a scholar conversing with poets and painters in the Tiger Hill gardens of Suchou. But he was called into the Army. Part of the government price for giving a passport to the elder son."

Lilian turned away from the lake. She ran her fingers over the bark of the tree. "I'm sorry, but I must go now. The police have arrested many students. Chi certainly is among them. There's a protest meeting in the Boyd Gymnasium."

"Let me go with you," Jensen said quickly.

"I thank you, Eric. But it wouldn't be wise for you to come with me. The students are very angry. Many are anti-American. They say Americans prolong the war by giving aid to Chiang Kai-shek."

They walked back to the pagoda, where Jensen retrieved his bicycle. "I'm sorry about making so many speeches," Lilian said.

Jensen shook his head. "I understand how you feel. Can we meet again?"

"If you like. Come on Tuesday, about noon. We can meet here at the pagoda again."

"Wonderful," Jensen said, swinging his leg over his bicycle. He waved to Lilian as he pedaled off. When he glanced back, she was already walking up the hill to the pagoda, where a lone figure stood on the lower tier, waiting for her.

Chapter Eight

From the pagoda atop the hill, an elderly Chinese in a blue Mandarin robe watched as Lilian said good-bye to Jensen. He had observed Jensen's arrival, watched him greet Lilian and walk with her to the lake. Now he waited impatiently as Lilian climbed up the hill to the pagoda.

"Can we trust him, Li-nan?" the old man asked urgently.

"I cannot say, Professor Chang. Not yet."

"Did you test him?"

"Yes. He speaks as if he cares for our people . . . as if he understands our problems," Lilian replied, her brow knitted. "But it troubles me that he lives with the French military attaché. He is no longer a student at the Language School. What is he doing? Why is he in China?"

"Chi was so sure of him," the professor said.

"Yes. Chi was convinced he could be trusted. But perhaps Chi was too hasty. When I first met Jensen at the Language School, Chi already wanted to talk to him about the plan."

"Did he?" the professor exclaimed in alarm.

"No. I dissuaded him."

"Good! If there should be a leak, it would ruin everything. Perhaps cost us our lives." The professor gazed toward the lake and sighed. "The siege will begin soon. We must move quickly." He leaned forward: "We depend on you, Li-nan. Learn everything you can about Jensen. Everything may turn on him. We have not yet found anyone else who can carry the letter. When our friend comes, invite Jensen to my house for tea. He will make the decision after meeting Jensen."

Lilian lowered her eyes. "I will do as you say, Professor. Now, I must go to the meeting in the gymnasium."

The ridges above the professor's brow tightened and he closed his eyes as if he were in pain. "There is danger of violence. The wall newspapers in the dormitories have been inflammatory."

Lilian turned and hurried down the steps. As she walked around the lake toward the gymnasium building she thought of Jensen. She had found him somewhat strange at first . . . so unlike Chinese men . . . so tall . . . the long reddish hair and the deep blue eyes. But there was a grace about him, an eagerness, and a warmth in the way he looked at her. His concern for Chi. . . . As she entered the main hall of the gymnasium she felt glad she would see him again soon.

The mass meeting was already in progress. Several hundred students stood densely packed at the far end of the hall confronting two figures. One was a slender youth in Western clothes, his hair neatly parted and close-cropped at the sides. He was looking into the crowd from face to face and smiling nervously. The other youth, dressed in a gray Chinese gown, was sobbing hysterically. He raised his hand, palm out, waving it side-to-side. The two had already confessed to informing on the students who had been arrested in the police sweep of the campus.

"I was tortured," the student in the Chinese gown said, his voice rising to a scream. "I was forced to speak. They put water through my nose. I was put on the Tiger Bench with my knees tied. My feet were raised until my knees were breaking. Ai ya, the Blue-Eyed One . . ." He backed off in panic as the crowd edged toward him. There were loud cries: "Strike the traitors! Strike them!"

The massed students surged forward. Lilian heard screams. She could not see beyond the backs of the students in front of her. She moved forward with them. She felt softness underfoot and sickened with the realization she was trampling over a body. Pushed by the crowd, she stumbled out the side door of the gymnasium and down the stone steps. She went to the grass plot beside the building, and after the others had tramped past, she leaned heavily against the brick wall.

Chapter Nine

On Tuesday, before the lieutenant's household stirred, Jensen set out once again for Yenching on the cook's bicycle. With each thought of Lilian, he pressed the pedals harder. At the West Straight Gate Jensen paused for breakfast at a food cart. The peddler cackled as he prepared the savory noodles and cold tea, exposing black stumps of teeth. "Ai ya, the number of fools under heaven multiplies more quickly than the sages can count," he said, inclining his head toward a column of civilians marching along the city wall. One carried a blue-and-white Kuomintang flag. Jensen guessed the marchers had been drafted into the Citizens Defense Corps. Only the day before, a government proclamation had ordered all able-bodied residents, "and not excepting nuns, actresses, and prostitutes," inducted into the corps.

"Why 'fools,' Old Uncle?" Jensen asked.

"In the bazaars the people say it does not matter who is master of

Peking. For us, to fight is to lose. We do not share the victory feasts of generals."

"Do you not fear the Communists?"

"I have seen many armies come into Peking. The Communists will be no different. They are Chinese."

As Jensen paid the peddler, he thought the government might have blundered in banning the writings of Mao Tse-tung. Few Chinese living outside the Communist areas understood how the Communists intended to change their lives.

Passing through the gate Jensen saw hundreds of coolies building defense works under military guard. The mud brick houses just beyond the city's outer wall had been leveled to clear fields of fire. Countless trees, among them century-old cypresses, had been felled for timber to reinforce gun emplacements. Bare monarch stumps now dotted the open space. The landscape that Taoist painters had so lovingly depicted was now ravaged.

Less than a mile beyond the gate the road was blocked by an ambling ox. Dismounting, Jensen suddenly became aware that another cyclist, a Chinese wearing a black peaked cap, had also stopped some hundred yards behind him. When Jensen turned into the Yenching campus, he glanced back. The man in the peaked cap was following.

Lilian was sitting on the steps of the pagoda. Her hair was tied back with a blue ribbon and she wore a blue tunic buttoned to the throat. She lifted her bicycle out of the wooden rack, mounted, and waved to Jensen to follow. They sped along the stone walk. Students turned to stare at the foreigner, his knees spread like wings to accommodate his long legs, pedaling furiously to keep up with Lilian, who was laughing and calling encouragement over her shoulder.

Lilian drew up to a stone bench in a pine grove. With a flourish, she produced two bottles of orange soda from the basket latched to her bicycle handlebars. They sat, breathless and smiling at each other. Then Jensen said, "I'm being followed."

The gaiety drained from Lilian's face. "It's to be expected," she said. "It must be one of Chen Li-fu's men. You know Chen Li-fu?"

"Of course. He runs the Kuomintang Party organization."

"Yes . . . and also the gendarme special forces and secret police. His Thought Control Police cover every university campus. Once the police were forbidden to enter any campus . . . but no longer. One of his agents must have seen you last Sunday. If you come again, be careful. The road may be dangerous."

Jensen nodded, secretly pleased by her concern. "I'm more worried about you," he said.

"You're a puzzle, Eric," Lilian said, securing her soda bottle between her feet. "I don't understand why you're in China . . . or why you're here with me."

Eric laughed and, reaching down, plucked at the brown withered grass. He was silent for a moment, as if to gather himself, and when he began to speak he plucked the blades of grass more swiftly. "My father is the pastor of the Lutheran church in Webster, a small town in Missouri . . . only about four thousand people . . . farming country. Before that he was a missionary in China. Why am I in China? Well, on Sundays, when my brother and I were very young, our father often took us by the hand to a wooden box behind the pews. Above the box there was a plaque. On it were the names of missionaries killed during the Boxer Rebellion. He would give us each a penny and tell us to drop it through the slot. 'This is for China,' he would say, 'so the missionaries can feed the hungry people. It's our God-given duty to help them.'"

Jensen glanced at Lilian with a faint smile. "Misguided?"

Lilian shook her head.

"When missionaries came home from China they preached at our church. My brother and I were fascinated by their tales. How they passed through the sky-high Yangtze River gorges . . . of their boats pulled through the torrents by trackers on the shore. We dreamed of going to China. My parents were so happy when my brother decided to become a missionary." Jensen sighed, tossed a handful of grass into the air. "The war interfered. He's now pastor of a church in Kansas."

"And you, Eric?" Lilian asked.

"I was obsessed by China, but for me it was adventure . . . an escape from the dullness of Missouri. My interest, when I listened to the missionaries, was in temples and jade treasures, not in the saving of souls. I used to climb into the attic of our house, open the old trunks, and play with little treasures brought back from China by my father. I read every China book in his library. Once he found me reading a book on Taoism. He snatched it away. 'Read Confucius,' he said. 'It'll be better for your undisciplined soul.' In his sermons my father often spoke of Confucius. It went well with Lutheran morality. Respect for order . . . as decreed by the elders of the church. For me it seemed like a depressing way to live. In any case, after my father tore the Taoist book from my hands I read everything on Taoism I could find. I dreamed I'd go to China and live according to the Way. Foolishly, I thought I was already a Taoist. At the university I did research into Taoist philosophy. What am I doing now? I'm continuing that research. I'm writing a book mainly on the philosophy of Chuang Tzu. How it relates to modern man."

Lilian listened soberly. Then she clasped her hands about her knee and leaned back on the bench, grinning. "Taoism," she exclaimed. "You follow the Way?"

Jensen folded his arms and surveyed her angrily, regretting he had revealed so much of himself. "No." Jensen said firmly. "Living by disciplines laid down by the sages two thousand years ago doesn't fit life today. But I am searching for the essence of the Tao, the Way, because I believe it holds the secret of life, of being at one with the nature of the universe."

"Sorcery, alchemy, and immortality," Lilian said incredulously. "All that hocus-pocus?"

"Lilian . . . please listen to me," Jensen said indignantly, rising from the bench. "Chuang Tzu speaks to the cultivation of the spirit of man. How man can realize himself free of the bondage of transitory conventions. How man can reach out to the God Force of the cosmos. You speak of hocus-pocus—false rites—those are of the Neo-Taoists . . . who came after Chuang Tzu and Lao Tsu. Every faith has been corrupted by false priests. They exploit the name of the first teacher. They concoct ritual and make false promises to consolidate their authority. Taoism is no exception." Jensen ran his fingers through his rumpled hair. "There's no hocus-pocus in the Way of Chuang Tzu and Lao Tsu."

"Even so, it is an egotistical philosophy," Lilian said vehemently. "The Taoist gentleman is concerned only about his immortal spirit . . . the contemplative life . . . not caring for woman or for the masses. *Yin-yang,* and all that nonsense. You are *yang* . . . the sun, heaven, and creation."

"Yes," Jensen said softly, "but you are *yin* . . . nourishing the earth. You know the Tao Te Ching . . . the words of Lao Tsu: 'It is the woman, primal mother. Her gateway is the root of heaven and earth.'"

"And you draw my essence for your ego?" Lilian exclaimed, her cheeks flushed. She was standing now, glaring defiantly into Jensen's eyes. Then at once, the two began to laugh. Jensen raised his hands to signal a truce. "Will you have dinner with me? Tomorrow? In Peking?"

"Of course," Lilian said.

◆

Jensen was waiting eagerly when the old Japanese bus lurched to a halt before the Peking railway station. Twilight was settling on the city.

Lilian emerged, wearing an old fur-lined jacket over a shining black brocade *cheongsam*. Jensen greeted her with a sweeping bow. They feasted that evening in the Pienyifang Restaurant, going to the courtyard to select a dressed duck, and within the hour accepting the bird browned and succulent, Peking style, on a spit. Afterward they took tea and cracked watermelon seeds in a malodorous theater surrounded by noisy Chinese chuckling at the buffoonery and the falsettos of the actors in the imperial costumes of Peking Opera.

At the railway station, as he bid her good-night, Jensen embraced Lilian, holding her close. She did not resist, but when he tried to kiss her, she leaned away from him. "A bit too much *yang* for tonight," she said, laughing.

◆

Jensen checked the calendar. It was the fifteenth of the month, the day the remittance from the Smith people was normally deposited in his account at the local bank. Would it be there this time? Jensen could not fathom why the Smith people had not yet made some effort to corner him, at least for questioning. Certainly they knew he was out of the Language School. Weren't they afraid he might leak something?

Ying, waiting outside the lieutenant's compound, took Jensen to Morrison Street, center of the busiest shopping district. The bank was fairly empty when Jensen entered. Two foreigners were seated at the desk of the British manager, and a half dozen Chinese were on line before the two counters. Jensen went to the Chinese teller with whom he dealt regularly and waited on line.

When he came to the counter the clerk greeted him warmly. "*Nin hao*. Your remittance is here." As the teller began to count out the dollar bills, someone behind Jensen said, "Good morning, Mr. Jensen." Jensen turned. It was the Marine major, Smith's aide. "Take your money," the major said, smiling. Jensen turned back to the teller who resumed counting out the bills. He scooped up the money impatiently and whipped about. The major was not there. Startled, he looked about the bank. But the major was gone.

Jensen climbed back into the pedicab and, as Ying threaded through the heavy traffic, he tried to sort out the meaning of the encounter. Obviously it had been a warning that he was under surveillance, that they would strike if he betrayed them. But why hadn't the major said more to him? Perhaps Smith was delaying, not having decided what was to be done with him. He could only await their next move.

◆

During the next week Jensen and Lilian saw each other every day. At Yenching the students were boycotting classes in protest of Chi's murder. His mutilated body had been found in a gutter of the Chinese City. Jensen and Lilian joined hundreds of university students at a memorial service. Afterward, the two climbed Coal Hill, where Jensen and Chi had once looked down on the Forbidden City and talked about Chi's dream of a reformed China.

"He died for the people, Eric. And he was tortured for it so terribly," Lilian said. She cupped her hands over her face and whispered: "I'll try to work as he did."

"If there's a way, I'll help," Jensen said.

One afternoon they strolled hand in hand through the Summer Palace, and in a garden pavilion Jensen put his arms about Lilian and kissed her gently. On another evening, on the shore of Kun Ming Lake, Jensen and Lilian went aboard the marble boat built by the Empress

Dowager Tsu Hsi. They sat side by side on the square bow, dropping crumbs of rice cakes to the white ducks waddling below on the thin ice.

"The Empress was a wicked old dame, but she did some good," Jensen said. "She took money from the treasury to build a navy and instead she used it to build this marble boat. She must have built it for lovers . . . like us."

"Eric, you're a dreamer out of a past age," Lilian said softly. "You're with Chuang Tzu in his Lacquer Garden two thousand years ago." She was smiling gently, her face tilted up to him.

Jensen took her hand. "May I show you how I escape into that past age?"

Lilian glanced up at him, puzzled. "Escape?"

"I have use of a small house in the compound of my friend, Wang Li, the antiques dealer. I have some precious things there. Come have dinner there with me . . . tomorrow night?"

"You make me very curious, Eric," Lilian said, as she looked out over the lake. She threw some crumbs to the ducks. "I suppose I can't refuse," she said finally, leaning against Jensen's shoulder.

Chapter Ten

Lilian lay awake in the darkness of her dormitory room at Yenching. The only sounds were the heavy breathing of her roommate asleep on the other side of the room and the ticking of the alarm clock. Returning from Kun Ming Lake there had been a message from Professor Chang asking her to come to his house at once. Lilian hurried across the campus and found him pacing his study.

"Our friend will be here on the day after tomorrow," the professor said. "What can we tell him?"

"Trust Jensen," Lilian replied.

"You are sure?"

"Yes."

"Bring him here then at four to meet our friend."

Now Lilian tossed sleeplessly on her cot. What right do I have to involve him, put him in danger? What will he think when he realizes I've manipulated him?

Chi had been her first lover. She had yielded out of affection, his insistent need, and with the freedom of a modern woman of the revolution. Yet there had been nothing of the desire she felt for Eric. How could this be? In love with an American?

Tomorrow night, she thought, I will do what Professor Chang asks. But I must also be fair to Eric . . . I must discourage his affection . . . I cannot let him be in love with me. . . .

Chapter Eleven

In the morning after his idyll with Lilian at Kun Ming Lake, Jensen went to visit Wang Li in his shop. "I have invited a woman for dinner in the little house," Jensen said. "She is a woman I respect and care for very much. I hope you approve."

Wang Li bowed. "Of course. The house is yours. Instruct my cook. He will prepare and serve dinner. You will not be disturbed."

In the afternoon Jensen went to the Wang Li compound near the Bell Tower. The gatekeeper drew open the bronze-belted portal and Jensen walked along a cobbled path through a moon gate into the courtyard. Using a worn brass key, he unlocked a small building with a sloping tile roof that stood beside the main house. During his Army days Jensen had spent some nights in this house, once the Taoist meditation abode of a mandarin family. It had been converted into a two-room dwelling place but retained its old splendor. The walls were of exquisite blackwood paneling beneath polished beams. In an alcove stood a carved rosewood table and two Ming chairs. The walls were hung with rare Taoist landscape paintings, soaring mountains amidst the clouds, gushing streams in verdant glens enfolded in morning mists. At the center of the main room was an imperial Chien Lung carpet woven to depict the emperor's cranes, symbols of longevity, fishing in a lotus pool. At the far end beyond the beaded doorway there was a bedroom in which stood a curtained four-poster wedding bed in red lacquer piled high with silk embroidered cushions.

Jensen closed the teakwood door and bolted it. After lighting a kerosene lamp, he pulled aside the Chien Lung carpet. With a thin-bladed knife he pried up the closely fitted floorboards, which came away easily, exposing a steel trapdoor with a combination lock. Jensen spun the lock, pulled open the lid, and, holding the lantern, went down a short flight of wooden steps. This brought him to a room of some twenty by thirty feet, entirely lined with cedar: Wang Li's vault. On shelves along the walls were vases, terra-cotta figurines, bronzes, gold and silver artifacts, rolled scrolls, paintings, jade carvings, and porcelains. Carpets and tapestries were folded in a corner. Jensen spent the next hour selecting pieces of the antique art, carefully carrying them up the steps, and arranging them around the rooms above. He then went to the closet where his own things were stored.

From a tray of jades Jensen took a Ching dynasty piece in the form of a pebble of gray-green nephrite with a russet skin, intricately carved. It was a piece he had reserved for the woman who would live with him forever. He put the jade in his pocket and then climbed back up the steps, closing the trapdoor carefully behind him. He then went to the kitchen of the main house to confer with the cook before setting out to the railway station to meet Lilian.

Ying, beaming and pedaling merrily in the golden light of a setting sun, brought Jensen and Lilian to the Wang Li compound. In the little house an elderly servant greeted them and then waited to serve them dinner. Lilian, dressed in a long black brocade *cheongsam* with a string of pink pearls, strolled about casually inspecting the art. She glanced through the beaded doorway at the wedding bed before going to the table, laid out for dinner in the alcove. She folded her hands and greeted the servant. Apart from compliments to be conveyed to the cook in praise of the sumptuous dishes, she said little during dinner.

When the servant vanished, Jensen put down his jade wine cup and touched Lilian's hand. "I love you very much," he said.

Lilian regarded Jensen with wide eyes. She withdrew her hand. "Do you, Eric? I'm not sure," she said softly. "Perhaps you're living in your dream of that past age." She turned away.

Jensen leaned forward. "Lilian, what do you mean?"

"Eric, you're searching for a Chinese garden. To you I'm like one of these things about the room. Something for your garden. For me . . . none of this is real. Not in these times."

Jensen fell back in his chair. The warmth of their last days had disappeared. He looked at Lilian in disbelief. "Lilian, my love for you is real. As for these things . . . art has always been my link to the culture of your people. Yes. I have been searching for a garden . . . a garden mainly of the spirit." Jensen went to Lilian's side and raised her into his arms. "I love you."

Lilian put her hands on his chest and pushed him away firmly. "No," she said. "Please."

Jensen let his arms drop. "I'm sorry," he whispered. He brushed back his hair with both hands and struggled to smile.

Lilian studied Jensen's features for a moment and then reached up and touched his cheeks with the palms of her hands. "I believe you,

Eric. But I must go now. Please come to Yenching tomorrow. It's important to me. I want you to meet Professor Chang. He's a professor of philosophy . . . my good friend. He has invited us to tea. Yes? At four?"

Jensen, abashed at having lost his composure, nodded. He reached into his gown for the jade pebble he had carried all evening. He took Lilian's hand and placed the jade in it. "Maybe this will tell you of my love," he said.

Lilian examined the jade's carving, looking for the message locked in its rebus. The carving was of melons and vines. "*Wan dai*," she said slowly. "Long life. Ten thousand generations. Many children together." Lilian closed her eyes, thinking: What about all the resolutions of the night before? She looked up. "Yes, Eric," she said quietly. "Yes, I love you, too."

Jensen felt Lilian's body bending to him. He kissed her, and, lifting her into his arms, he carried her toward the beaded doorway. Lilian struggled free. "No. No. Not like that," she said. Taking his hand, she led him to the wedding bed.

The night was rapturous. They clung to each other hungrily, tumbling and searching, uttering little cries as they made love. Hours later Jensen fell into a deep sleep. He dreamed of struggling over a rocky hill and then magically gliding down a slope through a meadow where Lilian waited. Startled awake, Jensen brushed his hair from his eyes and looked for Lilian. The bed was empty. He sprang up and ran into the other room. She was gone.

◆

Lilian, smiling and radiant, was waiting beside her bicycle at the Yenching gate as the bell on the little island of the lake pealed four o'-clock. Jensen dropped his bicycle and reached over to kiss her. Passerbys looked on as the foreigner and the Chinese woman held hands, gazing at each other.

Lilian mounted her bicycle and, signaling Jensen to follow, rode swiftly to a wooden house in a garden surrounded by tall bamboo and pines. "Professor Chang lives here," Lilian said. "He's a leader of the Democratic League and the peace movement."

Lilian knocked at the glass of the garden door. Without waiting for a response, she opened it and led Jensen into a lounge. Two Chinese men rose from a black leather couch, and one of them, an elderly man in a blue, fur-lined mandarin robe, came forward. "I am Professor Chang. Welcome," he said in English, extending a delicate hand. He gestured toward his companion, a lean man in a blue tunic. "This is my colleague, Teng Hsieh. Mr. Teng is a graduate of Yenching, like myself."

"Yes," Teng said, as he shook hands with Jensen, "We're all products of American missionary education."

Teng smiled as he spoke, but Jensen thought his eyes remained peculiarly cold. He was evidently in his thirties, his thin face and high cheekbones sun-darkened like the faces of the peasants in the fields. Jensen found something vaguely familiar about him.

"Haven't we met before?" Jensen asked.

"Perhaps at the American Library," Teng replied. "I've been there several times."

Chang interrupted. "Please be seated."

Jensen glanced around. A worn red carpet embossed with a floral design lay on the polished floor before them. The only heat came from a potbellied stove with silver handles. A servant entered with a porcelain tea service and began pouring green tea.

"Those are fine Chi Pai-shih," Jensen said looking up at the three shrimp scrolls on the wall behind the couch.

"Ah, you know our contemporary painters," Chang said. "Those scrolls were done more than ten years ago . . . in Chi Pai-shih's best pe-riod." He sipped his tea and put his cup down deliberately. "Your American ambassador in Nanking lived in this house when he was president of Yenching. Have you met him?"

Jensen shook his head.

"He's a very fine man. I was in a Japanese internment camp with him during the war. Few Americans know China as well as he does. We re-spect him very much. We don't hold him responsible for American pol-icy in China."

With a thin smile, Teng added, "He has one weakness as a diplomat. He retains the optimism of a missionary. He believes he can reform Chiang Kai-shek."

"More tea?" Lilian asked. Jensen noticed that her hand trembled as she filled his cup. He wondered why she had brought him here.

"The ambassador has written to me. He's very much concerned about Yenching," the professor said. "He has reason to be. The Army is forti-fying our campus. Yenching is near the principal highway to Peking. If the Communists attack . . . the university could be severely damaged . . . even destroyed."

"One can say the same for Peking," Teng said.

"The Communists say they are for the people," Jensen said. "It's hard to believe they would risk destroying Peking."

"The Communists are more concerned about the well-being of the people than relics of emperors," Teng said dryly.

"Peking is more than a relic," Jensen said, speaking in Chinese, his voice rising. "It's not solely your cultural heritage. It is the treasure of all mankind."

"Very poetic, Mr. Jensen," Teng said. Jensen looked at him angrily.

The professor coughed and intervened. "I think Lilian told you I'm a member of the Democratic League. We've offered to intercede with the Communists to ensure no harm comes to Peking. Chiang Kai-shek has rejected the offer. He's a politician of the south. He cares little for Peking. Fu Tso-yi has been ordered to fight street to street if the Communists breach the wall. Anything to delay the advance of Lin Piao's army to the Yangtze and Nanking."

"That's hard to believe," Jensen said, frowning and shaking his head.

Chang looked intently at Jensen. "If Fu obeys, Peking could be destroyed in the fighting. The siege will begin soon. We are working on a plan to protect Peking . . . perhaps by making it an open city."

"I have no influence," Jensen said earnestly. "But I'll be glad to help . . . do anything . . . "

Lilian stood up. "Forgive me, Professor. Eric, you must get back to Peking before dark."

"Let me walk out with you," the professor said. Jensen shook hands with Teng and went out into the garden. He paused to look at a carved marble birdbath. The professor pointed at the pedestal. "It is Ming. Taken from the old Summer Palace after the palace was destroyed by foreign troops half a century ago. We must do everything to prevent such destruction from taking place again.

"I hope we shall meet again," the professor said, shaking Jensen's hand. "We face difficult days. We need the help of foreign friends." Turning to Lilian, the professor said, "Come to see me." Lilian bowed.

Lilian led Jensen to a small hidden gate that opened on the Peking road. Under an ancient cedar whose branches extended over the wall, Jensen put his arms around her waist and drew her to him.

"Your jade. It is so precious . . . so beautiful," Lilian said. "I'll keep it close to me. I have something for you, too." She reached into the pocket of her jacket and held up a pendant of white and russet nephrite on which were coiled two dragons. "It belonged to my grandfather. See the red dragons? They are the child dragons. When my grandfather gave it to me, he said they possessed the wish-fulfilling gem. Now I want it to be yours." Jensen took the jade, examining it carefully. "Lovely," he exclaimed, "so lovely!"

"I have a proposal," Lilian said. "Do you know how to skate?"

Jensen replied expansively: "I was on my high school hockey team."

"You are indeed talented. Would you like to skate with me?"

Jensen's face spread into a wide grin. "Marvelous idea."

"Then meet me tomorrow at twelve o'clock at the front gate of the Pei Hai Park."

Jensen put his lips against her brow. "I'll be there. My love . . . "

"Don't forget to bring skates. They no longer rent them as in the old days. And I'll invite you to lunch at a special restaurant in the park." Lilian opened the gate to allow Jensen to wheel his bicycle through. She stood there waving as he went off.

Jensen pedaled down the road to Peking, happily thinking of the skating date with Lilian on the morrow. Then his thoughts turned to the meeting at Yenching with Professor Chang and the strange Teng Hsieh. Obviously he had not been invited there only for tea and chitchat. He was almost to the Peking gate when he halted abruptly. He remembered where he had met Teng Hsieh before.

Chapter Twelve

Jensen stood beside the Peking road, his hands tightening on the handlebars of his bicycle. "He was one of them," Jensen muttered as he recalled the scene: Defiant, desperate men grouped around the table. The
shock of battle still lingering in their drawn features. The room pervaded with the stench of destruction creeping in from the looted city.
Yes, it was at the end of that day, that bloody awful day, Jensen recalled,
May 21, 1946, his most hellish day on the truce team.

◆

Shortly after midnight on May 21, 1946, Jensen was awakened in the
Marine barracks, told to pack his field gear and report immediately to
Executive Headquarters. The headquarters was fully alight as Jensen's

jeep pulled up. In the briefing room more than a dozen Chinese and Americans in field uniforms were already seated before a large map. They were members of the truce team drawn from the American, Nationalist, and Communist branches of the headquarters. The team commander, an American colonel, went to the map with a pointer. He was a heavyset man, a reserve officer from Kansas who had only recently arrived in China. With Jensen translating for the Chinese, the colonel outlined the mission.

After a brief hiatus the simmering civil war had erupted once again. Millions of Nationalist and Communist troops were poised for new clashes. General Marshall, his mediation mission on the verge of collapse, had ordered Executive Headquarters to separate the two sides in Manchuria, focal point of the hostilities. The truce team was ordered to Ssuping, a strategic railway junction in Manchuria, flash point of the renewed fighting. As the briefing went forward Jensen observed the visible evidence of the breakdown in the ceasefire agreement arranged by Marshall. The Nationalist and Communist delegates sat stiffly apart with the Americans grouped in the middle. The fury in the questions of the chief Communist delegate and the venom in the rejoinders of the Nationalists told of two decades of bloodletting.

At daybreak the truce team took off for Ssuping in a bucket-seat C-47. As the plane flew over the Great Wall and headed northeast, Jensen looked about the cabin. The chief Communist delegate, in a shapeless yellow uniform without insignia, sat silently with his deputy at the rear of the cabin. Up front the American colonel chatted in English with the chief Nationalist delegate, a major who wore a natty belted brown uniform and chain smoked Camels. His deputy, a young lieutenant, absently turned the pages of a *Silver Screen* movie magazine with a picture of Lana Turner in a red bathing suit on the cover. Jensen tried with little success to pass the time by reading the second volume of

Shih Nai-an's classic novel *Water Margin*, the adventures of a Chinese Robin Hood. Opposite him, the team's other two American enlisted men, a radio operator and a driver, loudly compared notes on the brothels of Peking. Earlier Jensen had failed to draw the Communist delegates into conversation.

The plane flew low over the Manchurian plain, circled over the Liao River, and bounced to a halt on a rutted grass airstrip, bordered by green sorghum sprouts, south of Ssuping. A jeep drove up alongside the truce plane as it taxied to a halt. Seated beside the driver of the jeep was a Nationalist general in field dress, padded tunic and cloth leg wrappings, the ear flaps of his cap tied up. Jensen recognized him as Tu Yu-ming, commander of the New Sixth Army and one of Chiang Kai-shek's top generals. The general leaped out of his jeep and returned the salute of the colonel as he was coming down the plane ladder followed by Jensen. Tu shook the colonel's hand and then greeted Jensen warmly. "Ah, Sergeant Jensen, an old friend," he said in English, shaking Jensen's hand. "You translated for General Marshall at the dinner he gave for me and my officers at Executive Headquarters." He chuckled. "The Peking duck was better than the general's recipe for peace." Turning to the colonel, he said, "You're a bit late. The Communists have retreated. You're expected in the north in Changchun, where you'll meet Lin Piao."

"Yes, sir," the colonel said, glancing quickly at Jensen, who shrugged. "Can we have a look at Ssuping before we go?" asked the colonel.

"Of course," Tu Yu-ming said, smiling and motioning to his jeep.

Jensen and the colonel rode in the rear as the jeep bumped along the shell-pocked dirt road running beside the Mukden-Changchun railway. Nationalist divisions had fought their way north from Mukden toward Ssuping along the single-track railroad. In the fields adjacent to the tracks, Jensen could see blasted Japanese trucks, small tanks, and

75-millimeter guns—equipment given to the Communists by the Russians. He caught the stench of corpses in the irrigation ditches at roadside and glimpsed unburied Communist dead being torn by yapping dogs, and flocks of ravens hopping in the fields. Mao would not easily forgive the Americans for this debacle, Jensen thought. While Marshall was negotiating to bring Chiang and Mao into a coalition government, the U.S. Air Force had flown Tu Yu-ming's troops and other American-equipped Nationalist divisions north to repossess Manchuria. This had enabled Tu Yu-ming to strike at the Communists infiltrating from the north.

As Tu Yu-ming described his victory, the driver navigated past destroyed pillboxes and trenches littered with corpses into the outskirts of Ssuping. The town, now deserted, its ramshackle buildings largely demolished by Nationalist artillery fire, had been held in turn by the Japanese, the Russians who occupied Manchuria at the end of World War II, and then the Chinese Communists. The jeep passed two weapons carriers lurching over the fields dragging Communist dead to a mass grave. The bodies were tied with rope to the rear bumpers. "We've not yet counted all the dead," the general said, obviously embarrassed by what the Americans had seen. "The Communists fought bravely. We took the high ground to the east and stood off with our artillery and pounded them. They had no counterbattery except a few light Japanese guns. When they advanced we caught them in the open and cut them down. Most were green Manchurian troops with old weapons. Your 105- and 155-millimeter howitzers are very effective. We hurt them badly. But Lin Piao got away with most of his army."

The driver braked the jeep behind a truck parked on the road. As soldiers watched, peasant laborers pitched the bodies of Communist dead into the back of the truck. Jensen hopped out of the jeep and went into the sorghum field, bending to look at the crumpled bodies, faces caked with brown dust, some with features pecked by the ravens, bulky uniforms bloodied. He returned wiping his face with a red bandanna. "Most look like teenagers," Jensen said tightly. "Two or three had bullet holes in the back of their heads."

"We don't have enough medical facilities for our own wounded," the general said, as the driver wheeled the jeep about. At the airfield Tu climbed out of the jeep. "My tanks are moving toward Changchun," he said. "We'll agree to a truce only if he withdraws from Changchun. Please tell Lin Piao that."

As the C-47 took off, Jensen was thinking of the young Chinese he had seen dead on the battlefield. Tu said they fought bravely. Why? And against such odds. He thought of nights when his truce team was bivouacked in Communist camps, sitting around fires talking to the young soldiers. They were simple peasant boys, almost all of them illiterate, who, before being conscripted, had tilled the wheat and sorghum fields. They spoke reverently of the time of enlightenment when Communist political workers came into their villages. And soon, miraculously, their families were free of landlords who had extorted high rents, moneylenders who charged usurious interest when money was needed to buy seed, and Kuomintang village headmen who had squeezed them for exorbitant taxes. Mostly they told of how the Communists promised them land of their very own that would be seized from the landlords. So the young men fought gallantly, believing that Mao had entered into a compact with them. As the faces of the battlefield dead passed through his mind, Jensen prayed that the compact would be kept. He had his doubts. The Bolsheviks in Russia had sounded the same revolutionary cry—"Land to the Tillers"—but then cheated them by collectivizing.

The brilliant orange sun was already low over the flat black-earth plain when the truce plane circled over Changchun. Jensen looked down on the stately city, its large public buildings along broad avenues. The Japanese had rebuilt the city, modeling it after Washington, and proclaimed it the capital of their puppet state of Manchukuo.

The plane came down on the concrete runway of South Field and taxied past the remains of Japanese transports and Zero fighter planes to the small terminal that had somehow survived American and Soviet bombing. The control tower was dark and silent. There were no other planes on the field. The only lights came from a small bus that drove toward the truce plane to pick up its passengers.

The bus entered Changchun by its broad central boulevard, where it encountered heavy truck traffic, all heading north. The great white government buildings flanking the boulevard were dark, façades scarred, their windows smashed, lawns littered with debris. As the twilight settled, some sections of the city came alight, but others remained dark.

The Nationalist major said to the colonel: "Some parts of the city are without electricity. The Russians hauled away some of the power plant generators. From the air we've seen their trains heading for Siberia loaded with our machinery." He pointed out the window. "Look," he said. "Changchun is being looted again."

A stream of heavily loaded Japanese-made trucks and cars was moving north in the right lane. Jensen glimpsed hospital equipment aboard one truck. Beside them trudged columns of Communist troops under full field pack.

"They are leaving," the major said. "They are letting us have the cities. Then they will try to pin us down in static positions while they fight a war of maneuver. That strategy worked well for Mao in the south."

"Why do you stick to the cities? Why don't you go after the main

Communist forces as our people advise you?" the colonel asked impatiently.

The major shrugged. "The Generalissimo is employing the strategy he used against the warlords in the twenties. It may be the only one he knows."

The bus pulled up before three-story brick building. There were a half dozen shaggy Mongolian ponies grazing on its ragged lawn. "This was the Japanese military headquarters," the major said.

A soldier led the party past the sentries up a broad staircase and into a room with scarred walls. A portrait of Emperor Hirohito, its frame cracked, was on the floor in the far corner. At the head of an oblong conference table covered with maps sat a slender man whose thick black eyebrows and intense dark eyes contrasted vividly with his pale complexion. Jensen recognized him immediately as the legendary Lin Piao. He wore a black visored cap and buttoned-up tunic without insignia. Flanking him were two others in similar uniforms. Lin Piao returned salutes and motioned the truce team to seats around the table. A bulb in the ornate chandelier overhead winked incessantly. A soldier poured boiled water—the peasant "white tea"—from a tin kettle into mugs set at each place.

With Jensen translating, the colonel reviewed his orders to arrange a truce. He began to report Tu Yu-ming's ultimatum when Lin Piao interrupted: "Do not worry, Colonel. We are leaving Changchun. There will not be another Ssuping here." Lin Piao coughed, took a sip from his mug, and with a tight smile said, "But we will be back."

The Nationalist major cleared his throat nervously. "Your troops are looting the city."

For the first time, the officer on Lin Piao's left spoke. He was a young, hawk-faced man with high cheekbones. In fluent English, he said angrily, "We've taken nothing from the people. We take only what's needed to carry on the people's war."

. . .

Jensen pictured the hawk-faced officer as he began to pedal once again toward the Peking gate. It was Teng Hsieh, who he had just left on the Yenching campus.

Chapter Thirteen

It was only a short distance from the lieutenant's compound to the imperial Pei Hai Park where Jensen was to meet Lilian for their skating date. He had dressed warmly in his old Army jacket over a woolen sweater. The rusted skates he had bought in the flea market hung from the handlebars of the cook's bicycle. He turned up his collar against the frigid air sweeping down on Peking from Siberia and thought of buying one of the fox fur hats he had seen in Charlotte Horstmann's curio shop in the Wagons-lits Hotel. Pedaling along the wall of Pei Hai Park, which enclosed the North Sea lake, Jensen marveled at how much priceless space the emperors had reserved for their pleasures.

Lilian was waiting at the front gate of the park. She looked very different. She was dressed in peasant garb—padded blue tunic over black trousers, rubber-soled canvas shoes—and her hair was plaited into a pigtail. She wore no makeup. Why the change of style? Another perplexing mystery, he brooded, following upon that encounter with Teng at Yenching. She hadn't been open with him, from that night at the Language School when she silenced Chi. Jensen padlocked his bicycle in the rack beside the gate.

Lilian took his arm and led him into the Round Town Hall at the entrance to the park. "Come, let's look at the Jade Bowl. Its beauty will warm us," Lilian said. They entered a courtyard shaded by pines and in a little pavilion viewed the Black Jade Bowl, a magnificent sculpted receptacle some five feet in diameter. "Eric, look at the carvings on the bowl . . . those sea monsters. Imagine . . . once the bowl belonged to Kublai Khan. They stored wine in it. Now it belongs to the people."

"More of your propaganda," Jensen said with a forced smile. He took Lilian's arm and said, "Let's go skating," not noticing that Lilian had furtively looked back at a thin, bespectacled Chinese in a long gray robe standing behind them. The man bowed to her.

They strolled down to the lake's edge beneath the Bridge of Eternal Peace. Hand in hand they followed the footpath past the Gem Light Hall, the Hall of Sweet Dew, and the Pavilion of Calligraphy to the ferry landing on the north end of the lake. Loudspeakers were blaring the ballad "China Nights" over the ice. Sitting on a wooden bench, they put on their skates and joined the throng on the ice gliding to the rhythmic tunes popular in the Shanghai dance halls. Foreigners clustered on the ice were exchanging quips in English and French. Most skaters were students from the middle schools and universities, but there were also dowagers and elderly gentlemen in elegant dress demonstrating figure skating learned in a more gentle era. They navigated deftly among the bumps on the ice carved by the winds. When Jensen stumbled, Lilian said sympathetically, "In the time of the Manchus, they smoothed the bumps with hot irons."

Jensen crossed hands with Lilian and led her away from the other skaters. "I know Teng Hsieh," he said curtly.

"You recognized him," Lilian blurted out. "He thought you might."

"Why was he there?"

Lilian glanced uneasily at Jensen, who was skating with long, deliberate strides, gazing fixedly ahead. "I asked you to meet me here so I could explain everything. You know, of course, that Teng Hsieh is Lin Piao's aide. Lin Piao sent him to Peking to confer with Professor Chang. Leading intellectuals have asked the professor to arrange the peaceful surrender of the city. They and the professor have only one aim—to preserve Peking from a destructive battle. They've got a secret plan which has been approved by Lin Piao."

"And what's your role in all of this?" Eric interrupted, his resentment at being manipulated breaking through. "You're doing well enough with the Communists. Why draw me in? Damn it all! Is that why you slept with me last night?"

Lilian dug her skates into the ice and spun around. She confronted Jensen angrily, tears welling. "I didn't want to deceive you. And I never wanted to fall in love with you. I couldn't tell you of the plan until Teng approved of bringing you into it."

"*Me?*" Jensen said incredulously.

Lilian wiped away the tears with the back of her glove and glanced at her watch. "Come with me," she commanded. "You may be more understanding on a full stomach."

The two skated to the bench on the shore, where they put on their shoes. As they walked along a paved path, skates slung over their shoulders, Lilian stopped, turned, and pointed. "Eric, look there. That's the Hill of Ten Thousand Years. It leads to the White Dagoba. I'll explain later. Now come."

They climbed Lone Hill to the Fang Shan Restaurant. At an ancient arched gateway, they were met by an elderly waiter in a white apron. He bobbed his shaven head to Lilian seemingly not put off by her peasant dress, and escorted them through a walled courtyard. "They know you," Jensen said.

"My father brought me here during his visits. It's the best restaurant in Peking."

The waiter seated them at a small round table in a partitioned dining room, illuminated by Ching dynasty painted glass lanterns hung from polished beams.

"All the dishes are from the imperial cuisine," Lilian said as she made a show of scanning the menu of some two hundred items.

Jensen glanced around curiously. A young Chinese in a blue gown who might have been a university student was at the next table. Jensen thought it odd that a student was taking his lunch alone in such an expensive restaurant. A party of five foreign diplomats was at a neighboring table. At the far end of the room two Chinese in black tunics, who looked like government officials, were dipping silver ladles into a tureen of steaming soup as they spoke loudly in Shanghai dialect.

"All right. How do I figure in all this?" Jensen asked impatiently.

Lilian put her arms on the table, assumed a nonchalant pose, and spoke softly but rapidly. "Professor Chang has been in contact with General Fu Tso-yi. He knows his position is hopeless. He's ready to surrender the city—but he wants some kind of a signal from the central government in Nanking to justify his action. He doesn't want to lose face or be counted as a traitor. But Chiang Kai-shek will not agree to any surrender. He's ordered Fu Tso-yi to resist whatever the cost."

Lilian leaned across the table, holding up her menu as if she were pointing out a dish to Jensen, and continued: "If Fu does not surrender by January twenty-second, Lin Piao says he will bombard the city and his troops will come over the walls."

"But what do you want *me* to do?" Jensen said.

"We want you to carry a letter to the American ambassador in Nanking. The letter says Fu is ready to surrender Peking—and asks the ambassador's help to make that possible. All this must be done quickly."

"But why the American ambassador?"

"Your ambassador is close to the Vice President, Li Tsung-jen. There's panic in Nanking. Chiang Kai-shek is under great pressure in the Legislative Yuan to retire so Li Tsung-jen can make peace with the Communists. If the ambassador persuades the Vice President to authorize the surrender of Peking—that would be enough for Fu Tso-yi. He'll turn Peking over to Lin Piao before January twenty-second."

"I still don't understand. Why do you want me to deliver the letter?"

"We don't see any other way. No Chinese can enter the American embassy residence without being stopped and questioned by Chen Li-fu's secret police. It's also impossible to get one of our people on a plane to Nanking. The airports are closely watched. There are no commercial flights to Nanking or Shanghai. Now only Nationalist Air Force and government-chartered planes are permitted to land at Peking. The American consulate's courier plane is the only foreign plane still shuttling between here and Nanking. We hope you can get on it."

"Why not send the message through the radio of the American consulate?"

"Impossible. There are people in the consulate who are sympathetic to us. But most of them follow the State Department line blindly and support Chiang Kai-shek. If our plan were reported to the Foreign Ministry, Fu Tso-yi would lose his head."

"Why are you so convinced the ambassador will do what you ask? How will he know the letter is genuine?"

"The ambassador loves Peking as much as we do. He trusts Professor Chang. The ambassador worked with the professor when he was president of Yenching. You, an American, delivering the message will help convince him the letter is genuine. Eric, please. *Help us.*"

Jensen looked at Lilian's pleading expression, lowered his eyes, and tried to think through what was asked of him. Is all this possible? he wondered. I'd be sticking my neck out . . . way out. The Smith people? Going to Nanking without their permission. Chen Li-fu's secret police? Two sets of killers hunting me. God! His lips tightened. Yes . . . I'll do it. Of course, I'll do it . . . for her, for Peking, and for Chi.

"Okay," Jensen said quietly. "I'm not sure I can get on the courier plane—but I'll try." He pressed Lilian's hand. "And I'll be back for you— before Lin Piao takes the city. Now tell me: The letter. You have it?"

Lilian sighed in relief. "No. I don't have the letter. Too risky for me to carry it. The secret police have been watching me . . . and you. I think— up until now—they've been unsure about us. We've been so open in our meetings. They may have passed it off as just a flirtation. But by now they must know more." She reached for a dried melon seed and said softly, "Eat now. Before you leave the park you'll have the letter."

The waiter approached, his arm sagging under the weight of a large tray loaded with covered dishes. "I ordered in advance," Lilian said. As the steaming dishes were arrayed on the table and silver covers re-moved, Lilian said to the waiter, "One more dish, please. Peking Snow-balls. Later."

The waiter, a middle-aged man with fat round cheeks and bright inquisitive eyes, smiled broadly and bowed. He left them to go directly to the table of the young Chinese, who was signaling to him. The man paid his bill and rose hastily to leave. At the far end of the room the two Chinese in black tunics scrambled from their table as if to follow him. But their exit was blocked by the waiter. "You must pay," he shouted.

Jensen looked on, unsure as to what was happening. Lilian whis-pered, "They are Chen Li-fu's men. The waiter is trying to give the stu-dent time to escape. The student must give the signal for the letter to be put in place."

Jensen began to rise from his chair. Lilian extended a restraining hand. "Sit down," she commanded. "Pay no attention. Eat." As they dug their chopsticks into their Dragon Beard Noodles they saw the pursuing Chinese knock the waiter aside and run from the room. The diplomats were on their feet, conversing excitedly in French.

Lilian glanced at her wristwatch. "Keep eating," she said. Jensen munched obediently. "I'll tell you when we can move." They toyed with the sumptuous dishes. Lilian glanced at her watch again. "Now," she said. "Quickly. They'll be back soon. They may be after me next."

The waiter, still smiling despite a bruised lip, came back with the bill without being called. Out of her jacket Lilian took a wad of yuan and dropped it on the table. They walked briskly out of the restaurant.

"The waiter told the student I ordered Peking Snowballs," Lilian said. "That was the signal you're with us . . . and the letter should be dropped in the designated spot. If he escapes, he'll pass the signal. He was supposed to get out of the kitchen through a trapdoor. The police must have followed him from Yenching."

The wind was rising. Dried leaves swirled on the path as they hurried on. "When you reach Nanking," she said, "telephone the embassy residence. Ask for the ambassador's Chinese secretary. His name is Philip Fugh. Say you're a friend of Professor Chang. You'd like to meet the ambassador. It'll be enough. Use the American Army telephone line. It's safer. One more thing. If you can, I beg you, it's important to me: telephone my father, C. K. Yang." As they hurried along, Lilian thrust a slip of paper into the pocket of Jensen's jacket. "That's his Shanghai telephone number. The first three numbers are reversed. Convey my respects to my father and my mother. Tell them I will not go to Shanghai. Tell them I'm doing what I must."

They passed under the giant cypress trees that lined the path to the Ascending-Hill Bridge linking the isle to the East Gate of the park. At the bridge, Lilian slipped through an excited crowd milling about and looked over the rail. On the ice below a man lay spread-eagle, his robe torn open and blood oozing about his head. Beside him was a black fur hat.

"It's the student," Lilian whispered to Jensen as he came to her side. "I know his lamb's hat. They must have caught him as he tried to leave the park. Look at his robe. They searched him." Her voice came in gasps. "It's the work of Colonel Liu—the Blue-Eyed One. He's Chen Li-fu's chief agent." Lilian led Jensen away to a nearby bench and steadied herself. "Eric," she whispered, "go now. Up the stairs of the Hill of Ten Thousand Years; the hill I showed you. To the White Dagoba at the top. Few people go there this time of year. On the south side there's an alcove beneath a Sanskrit inscription. On the left of the alcove there's a flat rock. If the signal was passed, you'll find the letter beneath the rock. If it's not there, when you leave the park, tie your skates to the left handlebar of your bicycle. Understand?"

"Beneath the Sanskrit inscription," Jensen repeated. "I've got it." He grasped Lilian's hand. "Tell me where I'll find you when I return. You love me, don't you?"

"Eric . . . Yes, yes, I love you. We'll be together. *Now go!* It's the appointed time."

"Lilian . . ."

"Eric—*go!*" Lilian said fiercely.

Jensen watched Lilian push through the gossiping mob on the bridge. The student's body was being heaved onto an ambulance stretcher. As Lilian disappeared, Jensen turned in the direction of the Hill of Ten Thousand Years. Sidling through the crowd, his temples throbbing, he wondered if he would see Lilian again . . . whether she really loved him, a foreigner. Was she simply using him? Impatiently he shook his head and took control of himself. Of course she loved him.

How could he be so preoccupied with himself? He turned his mind to his mission, crossed the bridge, and strode toward the southern end of the island.

At the hill, Jensen went up the steps, two or three at a time, through a series of rock tunnels. When he reached the top there was no one at the south side of the spired White Dagoba. Drifting clouds darkened the sky, and a bitter wind whipped dust about the summit. One of the seasonal dust storms off the Gobi was approaching. Cautiously Jensen walked around the square masonry base of the onion-shaped Buddhist memorial to the north side. A lone Chinese couple was there, more entranced with each other than with the view of the Forbidden City. Behind the couple at the base of the temple stood a guard, rifle slung over his shoulder, sheltering from the wind. The guard watched indifferently as Jensen strolled by, his skates tied by their laces dangling over his shoulder. Once around the corner Jensen looked about. The south balcony was deserted. He went to the alcove and crouched down. At the left side he saw the flat rock. He needed both hands to upend it. With his right hand he reached under and groped. "Oh God," he gasped, and then felt the envelope. He let the rock fall back and thrust the envelope under his jacket.

Jensen slipped down the stairs, walked swiftly back to the marble bridge and out the gate to the bicycle rack. He unlocked his bicycle, tucked his pants legs into his socks, and draped his skates around his neck. Beside him a thin bespectacled Chinese in a long gray robe was unlocking a bicycle. "Time to go," the man said, smiling. "A storm is coming." Jensen in his haste did not reply. He didn't notice as he pedaled off that the Chinese was following him. But at the door of the lieutenant's compound, Jensen glimpsed the bespectacled man biking by.

Jensen went to his bedroom, dropped heavily into an armchair, and looked about the room for a place to hide the envelope. He shook his head. His room would be the first place Chen Li-fu's people would look. He walked out into the courtyard, nodding to Leone's cook, who was heading for the kitchen carrying a live chicken by its bound legs. He opened the latticed door to the lounge of the main house. No one was there. He looked about the room tensely. His glance fixed on the golden Tibetan Buddha, hands delicately postured in blessing, sitting at the center of the mantelpiece. He lifted the weighty sculpture, seated himself at the edge of the couch, and inverted the Buddha between his legs. He slipped the blade of his pocket knife under the bronze plate at the base and pried it off. Carefully he removed the prayer rolls inscribed on rice paper, folded the long gray envelope, and stuffed it inside the Buddha. He replaced some of the rolls of sutra scriptures and refastened the plate. After placing the Buddha precisely on the spot where it had left a slight mark on the oak mantelpiece, Jensen hastily returned to his pavilion. He stretched out on the canopied bed and prayed that Lilian had eluded the police.

Chapter Fourteen

At noon the following day Jensen was at his desk in the American Library twisting a paper clip as he pondered how he might contrive to get on the courier plane to Nanking. The library was crowded with gossiping Chinese students who had come more to escape the cold than to read. The air was rank with the odor of sweaty bodies and of fumes escaping from an old coal stove. Jensen had telephoned the consulate to inquire if he could have a seat on the next run of the courier plane. The assistant air attaché, whom Jensen knew slightly, told him he couldn't issue travel orders since he was only a locally hired employee. "Anyhow, we'll be lucky if we can bring the courier plane into Peking at all," the officer had said. "The Chicoms have knocked out West Field, and they've already lobbed a few mortar shells near our hangar on South Field."

Listening to the nervous chatter of the students in the library, Jensen could gauge the shift in mood of the city from indolence to pervasive anxiety. Many city folk had assumed the Nationalists and the Communists would not risk a battle that could scar the treasured capital. But to their dismay, the Communist radio at Mao's headquarters at Yenan was warning that Lin Piao's troops were prepared to scale the walls if Fu Tso-yi did not surrender the city.

On his way to the library Jensen had observed long lines of refugees, household possessions piled on wooden-wheeled carts, straggling into the city. Some of the rude carts were being pulled by children and women, some by the few men who had not been drafted into the army or the labor battalions. These families were fleeing artillery shelling in the outlying suburbs. Jensen also saw that sandbagged gun emplacements were already being erected at the city's major intersections in anticipation of street fighting. In the information bulletin, published by the consulate for the few American civilians who had elected to remain in Peking, Jensen read that Fu had withdrawn some 150,000 troops into Peking itself. He had evidently lost contact with his elite divisions battling the Communists in Inner Mongolia. This meant that Peking was isolated except for the vulnerable seventy-five-mile corridor to Tientsin and its nearby port at Tangku. Apart from an occasional Nationalist Air Force transport and the American courier plane there were no flights into or out of the city.

The air attaché told Jensen that only the consul general could authorize travel orders for him. Though he barely knew the consul general, a rather dour career officer who preferred the pursuit of Sinology to mingling socially in the international community, Jensen decided to approach him. He began concocting a reason for his professed need to fly urgently to Nanking. After telling another library clerk he would be back shortly, he walked to the nearby Marine barracks on Legation Street, which housed the consulate. Jensen entered the office still quite not certain what he would say. In the reception room he found Blanche Heyward, the consul general's secretary.

"Well, I told you we'd meet again," Blanche drawled as Jensen stood before her desk. Blanche didn't look quite as intimidating as when he had seen her in the Mongolian restaurant. She was wearing less mascara, her lips were not so heavily rouged. She wore a plain black wool dress with a fringed flowered shawl of Chinese silk over her shoulders. "What can I do for you, honey?" she said.

Jensen, with an uncertain smile, said, "I need some help. My dad . . . he's been killed in an automobile accident. I've got to make some arrangements for my mother. I can't get through by telephone from here. Any chance of going to Nanking on the courier plane?" As his voice trailed off, Jensen thought, Oh shit! I'm not very good at lying.

Blanche's dark eyes measured him coldly. "Sorry about your dad. But you don't have clearance for the plane. We can send an emergency message on the radio."

"Well, I guess I'll try something else," Jensen said, and he made for the door.

"Why don't you stop by for a drink tonight," Blanche called after him. "You look like you could use some cheering up."

Jensen turned around slowly, his hopes rising. "I'd like that . . . very much."

"I'm at number four Ta Tien Shui Ching. About seven?"

Jensen skipped quickly down the stairs into the courtyard. A biting wind swept down the street, and he tightened the scarf about his throat as he walked briskly back to the library. At his desk he picked up the bent paper clip and began twisting it again until it snapped. Blanche could get me those orders if she wanted to, he thought. With a start he became aware that a Chinese girl was standing before his desk shyly asking for a reference book. He led the student to the stacks, where he pulled down a copy of Walter Lippmann's *Public Opinion* and handed it to the girl with a distracted smile. Walking back to his desk, Jensen swore he would do whatever it took to get those travel orders.

◆

Jensen and Leone dined early that evening on steamed *chao tze*, a delicious dish of spiced pork dumplings, and a bottle of red Bordeaux. Leone kissed his fingertips and shouted "*très bien*" when Jensen told him he was invited to Blanche's house. "Take my jeep. Be sure to chain the wheel. You'll probably not leave until morning." Jensen looked over his wineglass at Leone with a mixture of amusement and dismay.

As he drove up to the American compound Jensen heard an explosion in the distance. A Chinese soldier emerged from a narrow sentry box beside the iron gate, shaking his head. "They are coming closer," he said, as he inspected the jeep before pointing out Blanche's house.

Blanche opened the door as Jensen pulled the bell chain, and with a low bow and a sweep of the hand she invited him to enter. In the dimly lit foyer she took his coat and threw it across an ebony chair. She led him into a lounge illuminated by lamps on matching Han bronze vessels flanking a couch facing the fireplace. On a rosewood table before the couch was a silver tray embossed with a dragon and a phoenix. A bottle of scotch stood one-third empty.

Blanche had returned to her image of the evening. Her lips were scarlet and her eyes heavily darkened with mascara. She wore a red, gold-flowered brocade *cheongsam* that fitted tightly over her full breasts. Jensen couldn't help but think of Lilian and how much better a *cheongsam* graced her figure. Blanche sank into the couch. "Glad you could come by," she said. "Have a drink. I've got a head start." She crossed her legs so that the deep slit in her skirt fell open. Jensen sat down beside her and mixed a scotch and water.

"Like this place?" Blanche asked.

"Lovely," Jensen said, glancing about. At the rear of the lounge a shaft of light from an open bedroom door fell on a row of Han clay tomb figures displayed beneath Ming landscape scrolls. On the marble fireplace mantel stood a jade wine pot, its spout in the form of a ram's head. Jensen had seen one like it in a museum. It was a very precious early Ching dynasty piece.

"Like those antiques, Eric? Worth more than a couple of hundred thousand bucks." Jensen looked again at the Han grave figures and thought Blanche was underestimating by far the worth of her treasures.

Blanche poured another drink. "Didn't pay that much for these trinkets," she said with a throaty laugh. "With dollars you can get almost anything . . . cheap."

"Will the State Department let you take the antiques with you?" Jensen asked.

"Take them with me? I'm not going anyplace."

Jensen was perplexed at the unexpected harshness of Blanche's reply and the brooding expression that settled on her features. "I'm not going to let those bloody Chicoms drive me out of all of this . . . back to sharing a crummy apartment in Washington with another State Department broad." Blanche rested her head on the back of the couch. "At home—Louisville, before I went to Washington—I was a secretary. Never thought I'd have servants . . . like my boss in the tobacco mill. Well, I've got 'em now." She flipped open a silver box and selected a cigarette. "Eric, have another drink . . . go on."

Here's yet another one who's run away to China, Jensen thought, as he leaned over to light Blanche's cigarette. She wore a musky perfume. He gulped the rest of his scotch and refilled his glass generously. He ran his eyes up Blanche's shapely silk-clad leg, to the exposed thigh. He hardly heard what she was saying.

"You know, I often think about coming out of the State Department building at night . . . in that crowd . . . going for the bus. Used to hate pushing my way in. Now I go home in a car with a chauffeur . . . looking out the window at the mob. It's all phony . . . but it makes me feel classy. Have another drink and tell me what in hell you're doing here."

Jensen accepted a cigarette from Blanche and topped his drink as he considered how he might parry Blanche's question. "I was an interpreter at Executive Headquarters. I stayed on at the Language School to study the Chinese classics. I'm working on a book."

Blanche interjected. "You live pretty fancy with that lieutenant. That Leone . . . he sure acts the cocksman."

Listening to Blanche, Jensen was becoming less sure he could persuade her to slip him unauthorized travel orders. She was tough. And she'd never risk her job. He thought about just finishing his drink and leaving.

A Chinese woman in a white tunic and black pants shuffled into the room carrying a large dish of black caviar and a bottle of vodka on a silver tray. "It's Russian caviar . . . from a can but good," Blanche said, as the servant put the tray down. "Before the Chicoms took Harbin we used to get fresh caviar in kilo glass jars. Came down from Manchuria on the railroad. Harder to get now." Blanche spread the caviar thickly on toast and sprinkled it with chopped onions. "Caviar and Russian vodka, you know it," she said, pouring the chilled spirits into small tumblers. Jensen followed Blanche in tossing back two shots of vodka in quick succession. The caviar was soon gone, but they continued to sip vodka. Blanche rose unsteadily and went to the servants' call button to order another bottle.

The fire was smoldering. Jensen rose and put a log on. He turned back to the couch and stood there looking at Blanche. She had crossed her legs, letting the skirt fall open. He felt desire rising in him. Blanche, her eyebrows arched, looked up at him. Her eyes slid down. "Well," she said. She stubbed out her cigarette and held out her arms. "Sit down, lover." Jensen dropped onto the couch beside her. She kissed him, ran her hands down over him, and then knelt before him. She reached out. "Oh, man, oh, man," she said. Jensen's head fell back and he breathed heavily. He reached down, lifted her up into his arms, and carried her through the dancing shadows into the bedroom.

Jensen awoke from a doze to find Blanche sitting on the edge of the bed wearing a black silk dressing gown, balancing a drink and a cigarette. "Not bad," she said. "Not bad at all."

Jensen sat up, propping a pillow behind his head. The room was coming into focus. "Not so bad, yourself," he said, reaching out to stroke Blanche's back. He took the proffered cigarette.

"Like a drink?" she asked.

Jensen shook his head. "No, thanks." He drew heavily on his cigarette. Blanche went into the other room to refill her glass. Returning, she leaned over to kiss Jensen and then stretched out beside him sipping her drink. "Blanche," Jensen said hesitantly. "Do something for me. Get me those travel orders to Nanking."

Blanche looked at him coldly, her eyes narrowing. She rubbed out her cigarette in the ashtray on the side table. "You bastard," she said. "That's why you came here tonight—isn't it? Well—get the hell out of here. Fast."

"Blanche, I really like you," Jensen said feebly.

"Get going," Blanche yelled, and she pitched her drink into Jensen's face. He rolled out of bed, wiping away the scotch with the back of his hand, scooped up his clothes, and stumbled into the lounge. He dressed hurriedly, not returning to the bedroom for the one sock he had left behind.

Jensen drove the jeep to the compound gate, honking the horn savagely. The guard came out rubbing his eyes. Jensen held his watch under the dashboard lights. Only twenty minutes to curfew. To the south the sky shone a dull red as if reflecting a giant fire.

Leone's compound was dark. Jensen quietly let himself in, grateful that the lieutenant was not awake to question him. He went into the bathroom and undressed as the tub filled. He soaked in the hot bath, his legs draped over the end of the tub, staring at the wall where Leone had hung a Tibetan Tantric tanka of a bull copulating with a naked woman. "What am I doing? Why am I such a fool? I thought I'd given up those games," Jensen murmured, biting off the words, as he reached for a hard brush and began to scrub. "If Lilian knew . . . how could I risk that."

The next morning Jensen went to the library wondering how he could get a message to Lilian or Professor Chang saying it was impossible to get to Nanking. There were no telephone connections to Yenching. The Communists evidently had occupied the campus. He had been at his desk less than an hour when a messenger arrived from the American consulate with a brown manila envelope addressed to him. He opened it and scrutinized a handwritten note: "See you, Lover Boy." It was signed "B." Attached was a set of round-trip air travel orders to Nanking.

Chapter Fifteen

In the early morning darkness Jensen was awakened by Leone's Number-One Boy knocking at his bedroom door. "Master, telephone for you." Jensen bolted out of bed. It must be the courier plane, he thought. The plane's arrival had been postponed repeatedly because of intermittent Communist fire on the airfield. Jensen threw on his robe and followed the servant through the courtyard to the main house where he picked up the telephone. It was the assistant air attaché. "Be at the consulate compound at four a.m. ready to travel," he shouted over the shaky telephone connection. Jensen looked uneasily at his watch. It was nearly 3 a.m.

Jensen dismissed the servant and waited until the house was still before going to the Buddha on the mantel. He turned it over on his lap and with his fingernails picked at the bronze base plate. It wouldn't give. He had jammed it back too tightly after inserting the letter. Frantically he scraped at the tarnished plate until one of his nails broke and his finger bled. Finally the plate gave and he extracted the letter. Wiping the blood from the Buddha with his sleeve, he replaced it on the mantel and stuffed the letter into his robe. It had been a good hiding place, he thought. He was certain that the pavilion had been searched and that he was under surveillance.

Two days earlier, he had escaped being run down by an Army truck. He was in Ying's pedicab returning home from the library. As Ying turned into the Yeng Yao Hutung less than a hundred yards from the lieutenant's house, Jensen heard the roar of a truck bearing down on them from behind. Ying veered sharply to the side of the alley, but the truck caught the wheel of the pedicab, turning it over and hurling Jensen onto the cobblestones. Bruised but not badly hurt, Jensen glimpsed the Army truck as it careened down the alley and vanished. Ying rose unhurt, lamenting the damage to his rented pedicab. Jensen gave him a handful of bills as compensation and walked to the lieutenant's house. He didn't doubt it had been an attempt to kill him. But by whom? The Blue-Eyed One? The Smith people? After the encounter with the Marine major in the bank, he had speculated that the Smith people hadn't decided what to do with him. Now, he knew there were killers after him. They must be working for the Blue-Eyed One or the Smith people, or perhaps both. After the truck attempt, Jensen telephoned the library to say he was ill. He no longer ventured out of the lieutenant's compound.

Picking up his duffel, Jensen went to Leone's bedroom door. Days earlier, feeling guilty about lying to his friend, he had told the lieutenant the fabricated tale of his father being killed. Leone readily offered to take him to the airfield when the courier plane arrived. Now the lieutenant came bleary-eyed to the door, tying his dressing gown. Over his shoulder Jensen could see a Chinese girl in the large canopied bed looking at him wide-eyed over a quilt held up to her bare shoulders.

"Sorry, Jean. The air attaché called. I'm to be at the consulate at four. The plane must be coming in."

"*D'accord*," the lieutenant said wearily.

As Leone drove through the Legation Quarter, Jensen could see that Fu Tso-yi was withdrawing more of the troops entrenched beyond the walls into the city. Lin Piao's Fourth Field Army was closing in. Guerrilla units, penetrating to within two miles of the West Wall, had seized the Temple of Ten Thousand Years of Longevity.

The jeep nosed through the columns of listless, disheveled infantrymen coming into the city. Some trucks towing artillery pieces were stacked with sofas and other furniture obviously belonging to officers. Within the city of two million, already overcrowded with refugees, the incoming troops were taking up bivouac in the Pei Hai Park, the Forbidden City, and in other palaces and temples.

The air attaché, Colonel Roberts, was standing with five other men near a covered military truck in the consulate compound when Leone drove in. Jensen, wearing his old Army clothes stripped of insignia and the slouch hat, yanked his duffel bag out of the jeep. The lieutenant took Jensen's hand and stuffed a roll of bills into it.

"Three hundred American dollars. You may need it, *mon ami*," Leone said.

"No thanks, Jean," Jensen said, handing back the bills. "I've got enough money." Jensen had been back to the bank, withdrawn from his personal account what he had saved from his Army service, and was carrying it in a money belt.

"*Au revoir*," Leone said. "If you don't make it back to Peking, contact me through the embassy in Nanking or the Quai d'Orsay in Paris."

"I'll be back," Jensen said.

"Don't be so sure. Lin Piao may be planning to celebrate the Chinese New Year in the Forbidden City. His forward units are within artillery range."

Leone embraced Jensen and with a wave of the hand drove out of the compound. Jensen greeted the air attaché, a middle-aged man wearing a combat jacket and pistol belt, who nodded curtly in response. Four of the other men were Marine guards of the embassy, all garbed in camouflage fatigues and armed with carbines. The fifth, a tall, youngish man with a deeply lined face, put out his hand and said with a smile, "Dirk Howard, State Department courier." He was wearing a civilian overcoat and carrying a leather dispatch bag.

"This is the deal," Roberts said, as the light from the lantern flashlight in his hand played over the tense faces of the men grouped about him. "The plane has left Nanking and will land at the South Field at the crack of dawn. The West Field already has been evacuated by the Nationalists. They still hold the South Field, but it is under mortar fire. This may be the last chance to bring the plane in. We need the medical supplies it's carrying. The Navy offered to send in a Marine rifle company to hold the South Field while we receive supplies and evacuate dependents, but the consul general turned the plan down. One company couldn't hold against what the Chicoms could throw against the field. It might have only drawn them in quicker."

The colonel glanced around at the faces. The Marines looked at each other. The courier tipped back his battered fedora. Jensen folded his arms tightly against the night frost.

"The plane won't leave the runway. We'll take the truck out to meet it and begin unloading immediately. Everyone will help. There are four Marines aboard the plane coming to reinforce the guard complement. When the plane is unloaded, Jensen and the courier will get aboard. The plane will then take off."

Turning to Jensen, the colonel said, "This won't be a hayride. The dependents and others scheduled to take this flight have canceled. You can, too."

"I'm going," Jensen said.

"Okay. By the way, Jensen, a friend of yours came by this afternoon. A Marine major. He asked me to tell you Mr. Smith will be in touch in Nanking."

Jensen, stomach muscles tightening, nodded. "Thanks, Colonel," he mumbled.

"Okay men," the colonel said. "Let's shove." The truck went down Legation Street, passing the Tung-tan glacis, a large open area bordering the Legation Quarter on three sides. Hundreds of coolies were constructing an airstrip on the old polo field. They labored in the eerie light of kerosene lamps and the headlights of trucks whose motors were kept running. The Communists had occupied the main power plant at Shih-chingshan, fifteen miles to the southwest, two days earlier.

At the Eternal Fixed Gate of the Chinese City the driver was signaled to a halt by sentries. The colonel dismounted, conferred with an officer, and came to the back of the truck where Jensen and the others sat. "There's some Communist shelling along the seven-mile run to the airfield. The Air Force has evacuated the field, but it's still held by Nationalist infantry. The Nats are laying down covering artillery to the south of the field. We're going to douse the headlights and try to make it by moonlight. If we come under fire, lie flat. The sides of the truck will give you some protection."

"This run gets more lively all the time," the courier said to Jensen as he lit a cigarette. "Bad enough when I carried the bag to the consulate in Mukden during the siege. I really don't get paid enough."

Jensen forced a polite chuckle. He reached into the breast pocket of his shirt where the letter was folded. What if I do catch it and they find the letter on my body? If it goes to Chen Li-fu, the Blue-Eyed One will grab Professor Chang. He might crack under torture. If they find Lilian they'll execute her. I should have taped the letter under my armpit.

The truck rolled quickly through the gate. Less than a mile down the Nan Yuan Road it slowed to skirt a shell hole. Jensen leaned out and saw a blasted peasant cart, beside it a swollen dead ox and the bodies of a man, a woman, and a child. Near them were sprawled the bodies of two soldiers, one of them with his head split open like a melon with the crimson flesh showing. There was the crack of artillery and a whoosh overhead. Jensen and the others fell flat on the swaying floor. "It's the Nats firing over the field," one of the Marines said.

The truck halted at the entrance to the airfield. A lone sentry with a lantern emerged from a foxhole, opened the barbed wire fence, and waved them through. There were no lights on the field, but the full moon in the starlit sky illuminated the tarmac. The truck moved to a hangar and was backed in under cover. The main runway was clear but the rest of the field was littered with the wrecks of three Nationalist air force transports and debris of all kinds. Transports had landed at the airfield on previous days to pick up Kuomintang officials and their families. When the Communists lobbed an occasional mortar shell onto the field the evacuees scrambled madly for the planes, leaving behind their baggage. Looted suitcases littered the field. A baby grand piano, one of its ebony legs shot away, sagged on the tarmac. Some high official evidently had tried to push furniture aboard one of the transports. On the far side of the field loomed the blackened exploded tanks of a fuel dump. Jensen lay back against the tailgate of the truck, stretched out his legs, and closed his eyes. The Nationalist troops, dug in along the north side of the field, were nervously sending bursts of machine-gun fire into the darkness. There was no sound or visible movement on the other side. Jensen tried to doze, pulling his overcoat over his ears to shut out the staccato of the gunfire. He turned his mind to Lilian: In her black *cheongsam,* hair flowing over her shoulders . . . going to the side of the wedding bed, unhooking her garments . . . she standing there naked . . . kissing her breasts and then kneeling before her, to kiss her flat belly . . . reaching for each other in bed.

"Put it out," the colonel snapped as the courier lit a cigarette. Then in silence they waited for the dawn and the plane from Nanking.

As the first light crept up from the east, they heard a distant hum. Soon they saw the plane, a C-47 transport, coming from the south, diving steeply to evade gunfire and leveling off sharply toward the runway. As the C-47 bounced onto the tarmac, the colonel shouted, "Let's go," and the truck roared out of the hangar to where the plane was halted. The plane wheeled around as the truck came alongside. The side door opened, a slide was dropped to the ground, and the first crates were pushed out.

"Get in line and hand the crates into the truck," the colonel shouted. A white flare unfolded over the field and the first mortar round came in. Bursts of mortar shells marched up the runway toward them and began to blossom not far from the plane. Jensen frantically tossed the crates into the truck. He grimaced, his jaw set hard, when he noticed that one crate was a case of White Horse scotch. A box fell on the runway and cans of baby food spilled out. "Where in hell are the medical supplies?" the colonel shouted at the figures silhouetted in the doorway who were pitching out the crates.

There was a blast and Jensen was lifted off his feet and hurled onto his side. He gasped in a swirl of acrid fumes. The colonel was crawling toward one of the Marines, who lay on his side screaming and clutching at his right thigh. His leg was in shreds. A mortar shell had burst and ripped him as he was pushing a crate into the truck. The rest of the group, unhurt, gathered around. The colonel shouted, "Keep unloading!"

"You'd better get him to a hospital or he'll bleed to death," Jensen shouted. There was the softer plop of another mortar shell some thirty yards behind the plane. The Nationalist troops were firing blindly toward the other side of the field. Dawn was beginning to flood the sky.

The colonel glanced up. "Put the kid in the truck. Let's get out of here."

Jensen cradled the moaning Marine in his arms and placed him in the rear of the truck while the colonel scrambled over the tailgate to tend to him. Jensen went to the open hatch of the plane and shouted, "The truck is leaving!" Four men jumped from the plane and ran to the truck. A hand reached out and pulled Jensen into the plane. "My duffel," Jensen gasped.

"Forget it. You may never need it, buddy," said the man in the plane, evidently one of the pilots, as he reached down again and pulled in the courier, who was carrying his dispatch bag. The engines of the plane coughed and the propellers turned. The pilot ran forward to the cockpit. The C-47 taxied down the runway, picking up speed, turned north into the wind for takeoff. As the plane hammered along the runway, one of the pilots shouted, "Secure those loose cases!" Jensen and the courier fell on their knees, holding the crates as they began to slide toward the tail. Jensen shoved back a crate marked SURGICAL BANDAGES, one of the medical supply cases they had failed to unload. The plane lurched, its right wing nearly grazing the ground, then straightened and gained altitude. Jensen and the courier tied down cases with loose rope. As the plane banked, Jensen glanced out the window and saw the speeding truck smash through the gate past the sentry, nearly crushing a lone cyclist.

◆

The sentry at the gate looked cautiously at the cyclist, a thin, bespectacled Chinese wearing a long gray robe. He had been warned about Communist saboteurs. "Who are you?" he called out, unslinging his rifle.

"I have come to look for my venerable father, who has not been home for fifteen days," the man answered. "His name is Liu. He works in the gasoline storage place."

"There is no one here," the soldier said. "The gasoline place is burned. The airfield is closed."

"But I just saw a plane fly away."

"It was an American plane. Now go back to Peking or you will be among your ancestors."

"Thank you. Thank you," the cyclist said. He dusted off his bicycle, hopped on, and serenely pedaled back up the road.

Chapter Sixteen

Jensen awoke from a sleep of deep exhaustion and looked drowsily at the courier, who sat beside him in a bucket seat of the throbbing transport. He reached into his breast pocket to make certain the letter was still there. He pointed at the dispatch case that the courier held between his legs. "You've still got it," he said.

Howard smiled as he ran his hand through his thinning blond hair. "You betcha. But I lost my hat. I liked that hat. Got it in Dublin. Tweed. Damn good in the rain. It's back on the airfield with my suitcase."

"It was a nice hat," Jensen said sympathetically. "Lost mine, too. Got it from an Aussie in a bet on an elephant race in Burma. And my duffel. But there wasn't much in it." The only thing he would miss, Jensen thought, was his worn copy of Lao Tsu's Tao Te Ching, whose verses and parables he often reread. "I wonder if the Marine made it back to a hospital," Jensen said.

Howard propped his feet on the crate roped down in front of him and yawned. "He was pretty torn up. Forget the duffel. By this time your shorts are probably decorating the ass of some Chinese guy. We can pick up what we need at the P.X. in the embassy hostel." He lit a limp cigarette that he had extracted from a crumpled pack. "The last time I lost a suitcase, I was in Egypt. My plane couldn't get into Cairo because of a sandstorm. So we landed in Alexandria. I picked up a whore that night in the hotel lobby. Egyptian, not too pretty, but gorgeous body. Tricky, I tell you, screwing with a courier bag chained to your wrist. She walked out of my room with the suitcase while I was sleeping."

The plane banked sharply to the southeast, and Jensen glimpsed the Yangtze River below, its turbulent murky expanse coursing through brown land dotted with villages. Nanking came into view. The city was tucked into a bend of the river and enclosed by a wall built by the Ming emperors over the hilly terrain. Chiang Kai-shek had partitioned his capital with broad tree-lined boulevards, but many cobbled side streets were still flanked by fields of stubble grass and stagnant ponds. Cargo was being unloaded at the river docks from small steamers and tall-masted junks that rocked at their moorings in the stiff wind.

The plane landed on the Ming Tomb Airfield, taxied past military transports lined up wingtip to wingtip, and wheeled to a halt before a dilapidated terminal. The building was crowded with Chinese military and civilians waiting for flights to Shanghai. Families huddled together in the corridors, bawling children and their parents sprawled on bedding spread across the rough floors. A few foreigners in the shoddy diplomats' lounge stared curiously at Jensen and Howard when they entered, faces coated with dust. Outside the terminal, the courier spotted the army sedan waiting to take him to the embassy hostel.

Jensen stared out the window as they drove through the city. Thousands of refugees had set up flimsy lean-tos against office buildings, trying to shelter themselves from the bitter wind sweeping off the Yangtze. In front of the red brick Executive Yuan, the principal government building, soldiers were pitching several corpses of civilians into the back of a sanitation truck. Soldiers in tattered yellow uniforms, stragglers from the defeated armies north of the Yangtze, wandered aimlessly through the streets. When the car slowed at an intersection pleading beggars flattened their noses against the windows.

As the car turned into the Sun Yat-sen roundabout, a black Ford sedan drew up alongside it. Two Chinese passengers in black tunics turned to look at Jensen. Police, Jensen thought, sinking lower in his seat. The Ford looked like one of the surplus U.S. Army staff cars that had been turned over to the Nationalist police and painted black. It shot away as the Army sedan reached the walled enclosure of the two-story embassy hostel.

Jensen's room was on the top floor, with a window facing out toward the river. A cast-iron bed was set against the far wall. A cane-backed chair and a low glass-topped table sat before a small sofa whose springs protruded through a frayed cushion. A dog-eared copy of *Popular Mechanics* lay beside a glass ashtray. The whitewashed walls were bare and the room overheated. Jensen locked the door, took the envelope out of his shirt pocket, and stuck it inside the magazine. Stripping down to his undershirt and shorts, he fell wearily onto the bed. The stiffly starched sheets smelled of laundry soap. After a time he looked at his watch. It was only noon. He rose with a grunt, washed and dressed, pocketed the letter, and went down to lunch.

In the clatter of the cafeteria, surrounded by Americans, his tray bearing turkey, mashed potatoes, and peas, Jensen began to relax. As he drank a second cup of coffee, he tried to sort out the recent rush of events. He rested his arms on the table, face in his hands, eyes closed. The noise in the cafeteria, after a time, seemed to recede. Everything swirled about the image of Lilian. The pain of the parting at the Pei Hai bridge . . . Oh God! Had she escaped the police? How would he find her again? Jensen shook himself, sat upright, reached into his shirt pocket, and touched the jade she had given him.

At the far end of the cafeteria there was a telephone hooked to the wall beneath a sign that read: OFFICIAL CALLS ONLY. Jensen sidled between the tables to the phone and, when no one was looking, picked it up. As Lilian had instructed him, he asked the Army switchboard operator to put him through to the Chinese secretary at the ambassador's residence.

"This is Fugh," a voice said in English.

"Good afternoon. My name is Eric Jensen. I'd like to meet with the ambassador. I'm a friend of Professor Chang. I came from Peking this morning on the American courier plane. I'm staying at the embassy's transients hostel."

What followed seemed to Jensen to be a very lengthy silence. Then: "The ambassador's car, a Cadillac, will come for you at ten o'clock tomorrow morning. No, sorry, better not the ambassador's car. It will be a black embassy Chevrolet. The chauffeur will be Chinese, but there will be an American with him, Henry Henderson, of the embassy staff. I have a meeting which makes it impossible for me to pick you up. You'd best not leave the hostel before the car comes. Good-bye."

The following morning shortly before ten, Jensen was in his room awaiting the embassy car. He lay on the sofa reading the *North China Daily News,* which he had bought in the lobby. British-owned, it was one of the few uncensored papers in Shanghai. He had already breakfasted in the cafeteria on tasteless scrambled powdered eggs and soggy toast. In the P.X., which occupied the entire basement of the large hostel, Jensen purchased civilian shirts, a tie, shoes, and a duffel. At the stall below the sign 24-HOUR TAILOR, he bought a rough tweed sport jacket off the rack and ordered slacks from a grinning Chinese who took his measurements at lightning speed. Twice he tried to telephone Lilian's father, but the Army switchboard in Shanghai refused to connect him to a Chinese number. How would he convey Lilian's message? She had said it was important. A quick trip to Shanghai on the overnight train seemed the only way. He looked out the window at the city obscured by a heavy mist drifting off the Yangtze. The faint sounds of fog whistles on tug boats came through the grayness. There was a knock at the door and a voice called out: "American waiting for you, mister."

Jensen put on his overcoat and then hesitated, thinking. After this, there's no turning back. Delivering the letter would mean he was linked to the Communists. The secret police were following him. They must know something about what he was doing. He buttoned his overcoat and went out the door.

Jensen found Henry Henderson in the lobby. He was a slim man in his thirties, blond hair in a neat crewcut, wearing a black cashmere overcoat with a velvet collar. The diplomat sniffed delicately as he shook Jensen's hand, his eyes taking in the rumpled Army overcoat and the uncombed hair. "Mr. Jensen, the ambassador expects you," he said, and led him to the door of the Chevrolet held open by the chauffeur.

"You're the ambassador's assistant?" Jensen asked.

"I manage the residence and the document traffic with the embassy chancellery," Henderson replied. "The ambassador has a personal secretary, Philip Fugh. He's not State Department. He came from Yenching with the ambassador."

"Did Mr. Fugh tell you why the ambassador is receiving me?"

"No. Philip Fugh handles the ambassador's private affairs," Henderson said, his tone prim.

A few minutes later the car was at the residence, a white vine-covered villa on a green rise. Two Chinese gendarmes with submachine guns stood before the garden gate, which was manned on the inside by a uniformed U.S. Marine guard. Henderson escorted Jensen into a cream-colored sitting room hung with Tang landscape scrolls. He left him sitting on a sofa flanked by two armchairs upholstered in blue silk damask. A servant placed a silver tea service on the teakwood table and withdrew, bowing.

A thin, spare man with gray hair receding from a high forehead entered and extended his hand. Jensen recognized him from newspaper photographs as the ambassador, Leighton Stuart. With him was a serious, bespectacled Chinese garbed in a black mandarin robe. The ambassador, in his dark blue suit, stiff white collar, and black tie, was dressed not unlike the missionaries at Sunday chapel in the Language School, Jensen thought.

"This is my secretary, Philip Fugh," the ambassador said, seating himself beside Jensen on the sofa while Fugh took the chair to his right. He accepted a cup of green tea offered by Fugh. "You have a message for us," the ambassador said, studying Jensen with a polite smile. Jensen glanced quickly at Fugh.

"You may speak before Philip just as freely as you speak to me," the ambassador said. "He's my closest adviser, as close as a son."

"I work in the American Library in Peking and I have many friends at Yenching," Jensen said, as he took out the wrinkled envelope and handed it to the ambassador. The ambassador opened the envelope and examined the letter closely, his brow creased. "Do you know the contents of this letter?" he asked softly.

"Yes. Professor Chang and the other intellectuals ask that you persuade Li Tsung-jen to arrange the peaceful hand-over of Peking . . . to save it from destruction."

"You must care a great deal about Peking," the ambassador said. "You risked flying here from South Field although it is under fire."

"I do, Mr. Ambassador. As I told Professor Chang, Peking is part of the heritage of all mankind."

"I share your feelings, Jensen," the ambassador said, his voice shaking. He studied the letter once again and then handed it to Fugh. "Yes, it's Professor Chang's calligraphy. I know it well."

"We'll do everything we can," the ambassador said to Jensen. "We've already been giving much thought to safeguarding Peking. It's our God-given duty to help the people of Peking and to preserve the city's treasures. This letter shows us a way." He sipped his tea and put down the cup with a hand that trembled slightly. "I should tell you that our consul general in Peking was contacted by an agent of Lin Piao. Lin Piao has offered to guarantee the safety and property of Americans. In return he asked that we urge Fu Tso-yi to surrender . . . and spare Peking from bombardment and fighting in the streets. On instructions from Washington, the consul general declined. He told the agent we would not give any advice to Fu Tso-yi involving surrender."

The ambassador locked the fingers of his slender hands and twisted them in agitation. "This is typical of State Department policy. We no longer work for peace in China. But I've not given up. I've not given up trying to work out something with the Communists to stop the killing. For this, Washington has reprimanded me. Even the minister-counselor of the embassy impedes me. But I'll keep trying."

Fugh glanced nervously at Jensen. "Ambassador . . ." he began hesitantly.

"I don't understand," Jensen interrupted. "I know General Marshall gave up trying to form a coalition government. But are we now opposed to any peace settlement?"

The ambassador put down his teacup and leaned forward, hands clasped between his knees. "The policy hardened last summer after Stalin expanded his control of Eastern Europe. The President is now unwilling because of domestic politics to have anything to do with the Chinese Communists. I'm forbidden to seek any understanding with Mao Tse-tung."

Fugh coughed. "Ambassador . . . there may be a way to do what Professor Chang asks." Turning to Jensen, he said, "This is the situation: Vice President Li Tsung-jen heads a faction in the Legislative Yuan that wants peace. They have no interest in a last-ditch struggle for Peking. But the Generalissimo has ordered Fu Tso-yi to hold out as long as possible. He tells him he needs time to prepare the Yangtze defense line. In truth he wants time to transfer his remaining elite divisions to Formosa—or Taiwan, as some here call it. Soon he'll go to Formosa himself and leave Li Tsung-jen to face the Communists. Our problem is one of timing." Fugh rose, refilled the teacups, and continued. "I'm sure we can persuade the Vice President to send a message to Fu Tso-yi authorizing his surrender. Everyone knows Fu's position is hopeless. But the Vice President will need time to rally political support for such a move. That may not be possible until the moment Chiang Kai-shek makes it known he's leaving Nanking."

The ambassador nodded in agreement. "It may be the only chance," he said. "I'll speak to Li Tsung-jen."

Fugh stood again. "It's best you return to your hostel, Mr. Jensen. Henderson will go with you. But don't tell him anything of our conversation. He's more loyal to the minister-counselor than to the ambassador. Do not leave the hostel until we send for you again. It wouldn't be safe. Chen Li-fu's secret police is headed by a murderous man: a Colonel Liu who people call the Blue-Eyed One. He'll soon know that you're here. He must suspect you're linked to the Communists."

"I'll do as you say. But I must go to Shanghai for a day or two," Jensen said.

The ambassador frowned. "Shanghai is in chaos. The Generalissmo has put his son, Chiang Ching-kuo, in charge. The city is now under martial law. They are executing suspected Communists, rice speculators, and the like in the streets."

"If you must go," Fugh said, "take the overnight train. The police check documents at the airport, but they've lost control at the railway station. The trains are being mobbed by people trying to get away. Even foreigners with tickets must fight their way on."

"Thanks," Jensen said. "I'll take my chances."

"Good luck," the ambassador said as he rose.

Jensen shook the ambassador's hand and followed Philip Fugh into the adjoining reception room, pausing there. "Mr. Fugh, I need your help," he said. "After Shanghai, I must get back to Peking as soon as possible."

Fugh appeared puzzled, but said, "I'll try to help. They're building a new airstrip in Peking on the old polo field within the city walls. We hope the courier plane will be able to make it in." He hesitated, as if he were about to ask a question.

"The ambassador . . ." Jensen said, shaking his head.

"Yes?" Fugh said.

"He's a diplomat. But he's not like others I've known."

Fugh peered at Jensen over his spectacles. "Not all missionaries wear the cloth, Mr. Jensen. Come now. Henderson is waiting for you." He led Jensen to an office off the entry hall. "Good-bye, Mr. Jensen. Once again, be careful. Take no chances with the Blue-Eyed One."

Part Two

THE BATTLE OF THE HUAI-HAI

淮

海

之

战

Chapter Seventeen

C. K. Yang was in his office in the Central Bank of China on the Shanghai Bund when Jensen telephoned. His secretary told him an American was on the line with a message from a member of the family. Yang picked up the phone, a frown wrinkling his fine features.

"Yes?" Yang said.

"My name is Jensen. I'm a friend of one of your children. I have a message. Can we meet?"

"You may come to my office here at the bank," Yang said.

"It's a personal matter . . . quite important."

Yang hesitated. He fiddled with a jade signature chop on his mahogany desk before replying. "You may come to my house tomorrow afternoon . . . if you like. My chauffeur can pick you up, say at four o'-clock. Where are you staying?"

"I'll be in front of the Broadway Mansions. I'm a tall man with reddish hair. I'll be wearing a U.S. Army overcoat without insignia."

Yang slammed down the telephone and stalked to the picture window at the other side of his spacious office. He stared out over the harbor at the Whangpoo River piers, where families fearing the impending Communist approach were crowding onto small ships bound for the southern ports and Formosa.

It was Lilian, of course. It could only be Lilian. She had disobeyed him again. She would not be coming to Shanghai. "She is lost," Yang muttered. He had two sons, and she was only a daughter, but he had indulged her too much. For some reason, unlike the boys, she never fully accepted his direction. There was something in her, an independence, a stubbornness, a hard core of self-affirmation, not unlike that of her mother, who did not bend before him. It would not surprise him if she had joined the Communists. Yang shook his head, his lips compressed. Still, he must see the American . . . although he could guess what the message would be.

Yang went into the bathroom and inspected his figure in the full-length mirror. He smoothed back his hair, dyed a perfect jet black, adjusted the pearl stickpin in his red-striped tie, and made a mental note to order another suit from his London tailor. He went to his desk and put the white jade signature chop into his briefcase together with the gold-framed photograph of his eldest son and a blue envelope that he had taken from the top drawer. He took one last glance about the room and then walked out without closing the door behind him. It was five-thirty. His secretaries had already been given leave to go home. He walked down three flights of stairs and nodded to the two gendarmes, who saluted as he proceeded out the bank's side door. The street was still littered with the debris of the riot.

Two days ago, more than thirty thousand people had rushed the building after the bank announced plans to support the wildly inflating currency by issuing permits to purchase gold bars from the government reserve. The market price for gold that day was thirty-eight hundred yuan an ounce. In the mad stampede of men and women desperate to buy gold bars before the paper currency became worthless, seven people were crushed to death and scores injured. Only Yang and two other senior officials of the bank knew that the offer to sell gold had been a sham; a cover while the great bulk of the reserve was being transferred to Formosa on Chiang Kai-shek's orders.

Yang walked briskly along the waterfront Bund to the Cathay Hotel. The setting sun reflected off the towers of the former foreign concessions, softening their soot-stained fronts. He went directly to the Horse and Hounds, sat up on one of the tall stools at the bar, and ordered a pink gin. It was a farewell drink. Yang intended to leave China in two days' time.

The Horse and Hounds, the most elegant bar in Shanghai, was even more crowded than usual for the cocktail hour. The voices were louder, the laughter more raucous. Drinks were being knocked back more rapidly, as if the bravado would somehow dispel the despair hanging over the city. "The buggers will have to blast me out with artillery before I leave," an English voice trumpeted over the din. Most of those in the bar were British, French, and American, among them women, all of whom were ignoring the consular warnings to leave Shanghai. There were two Marine officers from the U.S. naval transport *Bayfield*, which was lying in the Whangpoo River only several hundred yards from the Cathay, with seven hundred Marines aboard to aid Americans in case of emergency evacuation. At the tables Yang recognized British acquaintances from the Hong Kong and Shanghai Bank and the trading company Jardine Matheson, but he turned his back and bent over his gin.

Yang toyed with his glass, pondering once again his decision to go to the United States rather than follow the others at the bank to Formosa. He had savored the life in Shanghai . . . the high excitement of the currency and gold speculations that brought him millions, the two-hour tiffins gossiping with the powerful at the Shanghai Club, gambling at the racetrack, and the nights in the singsong houses. But what is there now? he thought. I am finished in China. There would be nothing for me in Formosa. He thought back on the miraculous chance that had brought him to fortune in Shanghai.

Yang had arrived in Shanghai with his family in 1945 from Chungking, the Nationalist wartime capital. As the protégé of H. H. Kung, the brother-in-law of Madame Chiang Kai-shek, the minister of finance, he was given a fine villa, which had been formerly occupied by a high Japanese official. In the early forties in Chungking, Yang had been an obscure bureaucrat in the Ministry of Finance. Then one hot summer day when Chungking was under a Japanese bombing attack and most of the populace was cowering in the air raid shelters, Yang was sent to a large house atop the high cliff bearing papers for Minister Kung to sign. The minister, dressed in a white silk shirt and holding a bamboo fan, received him beside a marble fountain in the garden shaded with blossoming plum trees.

"I see that Japanese bombs do not deter you from your work," Kung said as he handed over the signed papers. Before he dismissed him with a wave of his pudgy hand, Kung told Yang to leave his name card with the servant. After that encounter, life was magically changed. Yang was brought onto Kung's own staff. He had been living with his wife and their three children in a sagging frame house on a cliffside alley of the old walled town overlooking the Yangtze. His sons were given responsibility for clubbing the rats that swarmed through the house. When he joined Kung's staff, the family moved to a brick house on the Street of the Fairy Grotto. When the ministry was transferred to Shanghai after the Japanese defeat, Yang was made one of Kung's personal aides.

Now all was changed. Kung had been banished by the Generalissimo, who resented the notorious financial dealings that had made Kung so fabulously wealthy. At the bank Yang found himself, as a Kung man, delicately shunted aside in management decision-making. It was then that he decided not to follow the others to Formosa.

Yang drained his third gin, threw some American dollars on the bar, and edged through the crowd out of the hotel. He walked to his Jaguar coupe parked near the bank and drove down Nanking Road past the racetrack to Avenue Joffre in the center of the former French Concession. On a street lined with plane trees reminiscent of Paris he parked before an old four-story building, entered the courtyard, and rang the bell of the garden apartment. Standing in the foyer to greet him, her head bowed and hands cupped, was White Lotus, a slender Chinese woman in a flowered brocade *cheongsam*. Yang tilted back her chin and surveyed her exquisite features intently. "How are you, my flower?"

White Lotus smiled, her eyes shining. "I am well, sir, and filled with happiness." Yang glanced about the lounge furnished in French period furniture and a large ivory-and-jade screen in the far corner. He went to the bedroom and changed into the soft silk gown that was laid out on the canopied bed.

Yang took his chair near the fireplace while White Lotus sat on a black satin cushion at his feet, gently fitting his slippers. She waited for him to speak, but Yang only looked down at the jeweled comb in the bun of her glistening hair.

Yang had found White Lotus in the Lido nightclub eight months ago, choosing her from among the Chinese and White Russian sing-song girls waiting for clients. Beckoned by a waiter, she came to Yang eagerly, grateful for the attention of a Chinese gentlemen rather than a rude foreign sailor. They sipped champagne until Yang, charmed, invited her to come to his Avenue Joffre flat on the following night. That was time enough for Yang to dismiss his concubine of seven months and make space in the lacquer chests for the belongings of his new companion.

Yang had been happy with White Lotus. To signify his approval, he provided a small house with a garden patch on the edge of Shanghai for her mother and her three siblings, of whom she was the eldest. The family had been living on a sampan on the foul Soochow Creek. The father, who had hauled freight on the sampan, had died of tuberculosis two years earlier.

Yang raised White Lotus to her feet and led her to the round dining table, laid out for dinner. As the dishes were brought out by a woman servant, he ordered French champagne instead of the hot yellow wine that he usually drank when dining in the apartment. Distracted, he picked at the sesame pork dumplings, ignoring the other dishes. He took deep sips of champagne and insisted White Lotus do the same, although he knew that she disliked champagne, which reminded her of her work at the Lido. There were two empty bottles on the table when Yang stood up unsteadily and muttered "Come" to White Lotus. He led her to bed and made love to her ferociously, his body heavy upon hers, his teeth sinking into the nipples of her breasts. When his passion was spent, he turned on his back with a groan and was soon asleep.

In the morning Yang dressed again in the black cashmere suit while White Lotus watched him quietly. She followed him to the door. "White Lotus, I must leave Shanghai," he said. "You have your jewels and you may keep this apartment." He opened his briefcase and handed her the blue envelope. "Here are one thousand American dollars." The woman servant opened the door, her features immobile, as if she had not heard. As the door closed, Yang heard White Lotus cry out.

Yang drove down Nanking Road toward his villa in the Hung Chiao suburb. The avenue was clogged with early morning traffic. Military trucks and limousines of the rich, their horns honking incessantly, threaded past rickshas and carts loaded with freight, pulled by ragged coolies. The once fashionable thoroughfare was shabby with litter. Refugees camped on the sidewalks in defiance of frequent police sweeps. The metropolis of six million was becoming more unmanageable each day despite the thousands of troops enforcing martial law.

Most certainly it is time to leave, Yang thought, as he contemplated the misery around him. He could build a new life in the States. There was more than enough money. He had already transferred some of his secret funds from the numbered accounts in Zurich to the Chase Bank in New York. And H.H. had rented a house for him and his wife on Long Island. He would miss the golf club in Hung Chiao.

Yang parked the Jaguar beside the Rolls-Royce in the driveway. Like the other villas in Hung Chiao, the house was surrounded by high walls. The riffraff could not reach them. "Where is Madam?" Yang asked the servant who opened the heavy oaken door.

"Honorable Master, Madam is in her bedroom."

Yang went quickly up the broad staircase to the bedroom door, knocked, and without waiting for an invitation, entered.

Gentle Spring was reading in the peacock chair near the window overlooking the garden. She rose as Yang entered. She is still very beautiful, Yang thought, as he greeted her. "How are you?"

"Thank you. I am well."

Yang glanced around the room. He had not been in the villa for two days. "You have not packed. We must go to the airport tomorrow at three." Gentle Spring, a tall, slim woman elegant in a plain black *cheongsam* with a gold embroidered collar, returned to the peacock chair. "I will do what must be done," she said, lowering her dark eyes.

Yang took the chair opposite his wife and studied her for a moment. He wondered briefly why she had never dyed the gray streaks in her hair or bobbed it in the modern style. When she was young she had been more beautiful than White Lotus. As a lover, she had been passionate, never submissive, demanding her own satisfactions in return for her favors. They had not slept together for more than two years, not since the night he came into her bedroom and she had refused him. He had been astonished at her impudence—how she had reproached him for appearing at the racetrack gala with his latest concubine. He never felt any guilt about keeping concubines. His father kept two in his house together with his wife.

"I received a telephone message yesterday morning from a friend of our daughter," Yang said. "An American. He brings us a message from her. He is coming here this afternoon."

Gentle Spring nodded. "Good. Is there news of our second son?"

"The news is not good. The Battle of the Huai-Hai is going badly. Robert is still in Hsuchow at the headquarters of General Liu Chih. The Communists may have encircled the city." Yang paused. "There is some hope. A relief column is marching up from the south. The planes of the American Chennault are flying supplies into the city."

"And what of Fragrant Iris and the child?"

"They are with Robert."

"It must be very cold on the Huaipei Plain."

Yang shrugged. "Soon you will see your eldest son. I have asked him to visit us on Long Island as soon as he can leave Harvard. He is doing very well."

Gentle Spring did not reply. Yang rose from his chair. At the door, he turned. "The American will be here at about five o'clock."

Chapter Eighteen

Jensen spent a quiet night at the Broadway Mansions hotel and arrived at the Yang villa recovered from his exhausting journey on the Shanghai Express. He had suffered the night on the train, squeezed into a vestibule that reeked of urine. He had thought endlessly of Lilian, worrying about her safety. Now that he had delivered the letter, the ambassador would surely arrange his return to Peking. It would have to be soon. The courier plane would be making runs to the new airstrip on the city's polo field, but once Lin Piao occupied Peking all contact would be lost.

Jensen was installed in the lounge when Gentle Spring and Yang entered, followed by a servant bearing a tray of drinks.

"Welcome," Gentle Spring said in English, extending her hand. "No one is more welcome than a friend of Lilian's. Please be seated. Will you have a drink?"

"Thank you," Jensen said, his voice faltering. "You look very much like Lilian." Her figure was a bit fuller, the hair drawn back in a bun was graying, the eyes more heavily made up, but still she was nearly the image of Lilian.

"Others have told me so," Gentle Spring said. "How is my daughter?"

"What has she gotten herself into?" Yang interjected impatiently.

"Lilian was very well when I saw her in Peking not long ago. She asked me to convey her respects. She'll not be coming to Shanghai. She asks forgiveness for disobeying you," he said, his eyes on Yang.

"I'm not surprised," Gentle Spring said. "It's understandable. She doesn't want to go into exile, to lose what is most precious to her . . . her country."

Yang scowled. "Has she joined the Communists? That wouldn't surprise me."

"I don't know. She asked me to tell you that she is doing what she must. That was all." Annoyed by Yang's aggressive manner, Jensen addressed Gentle Spring. "It seems to me Lilian cares about the people, not ideology."

"She's always been for the rabble . . . and getting nothing in return." Yang said sharply. "I remember when she was thirteen I gave her a black puppy. We were living in Chungking . . . during the war with the Japanese. Our life was hard. I meant the puppy to comfort her. After a week the puppy disappeared. When I asked her if the puppy was lost, she said no, she had given it to the little girl who lived in the shack below the cliff. 'She's so poor,' she said to me. I went down to the shack. Of course, the beggars had eaten the puppy. When I told Lilian, she said, 'The little girl must have been very hungry.'" Yang folded his arms, his eyes half closed. "She's not changed. She's lost to us."

"Not to China," Gentle Spring said. "Mr. Jensen, won't you have dinner with us? You're welcome to stay the night. You've had a hard journey. The roads into the city are not safe in the late hours."

Yang glanced at Gentle Spring, barely concealing his displeasure. "Yes, of course, do," he muttered.

They dined in a gilded hall, largely bare of furniture, on a small table under a very large crystal chandelier. The best pieces of furniture, brought to the villa by Gentle Spring from her family home in Suchou, had been shipped a week earlier to Long Island, she explained. Yang complained he had only faint hope of seeing them again. The port of Shanghai was clogged, the stevedores were on strike, and thievery was rampant on the docks. Otherwise Yang was silent at dinner, tossing back many cups of yellow wine. Jensen felt compelled to keep up with him as Yang raised cups in the ritual manner. Gentle Spring questioned Jensen about his home and what had brought him to China. Jensen pressed her to speak of Lilian.

"When she was young she would sit at my feet in the garden and beg me to tell her about my father," Gentle Spring said as Yang listened sullenly. "He was a student revolutionary leader in the struggle for the republic against the Manchu rulers. I remember once Lilian came home from school in tears. She had heard a lecture about the suffering inflicted by the British on China during the Opium War. She was so young, but already a revolutionary, even then."

Jensen listened as Gentle Spring told him of her concern for her son, Robert, stranded with his wife and child in the Huai-Hai battle area. He sensed that she was looking to him for some reassurance, some suggestion as to how they could be rescued. When the maid brought orange slices at the end of the meal, Gentle Spring said: "Please forgive me. I've much to do before tomorrow. The manservant will show you to your bedroom." Jensen rose as Gentle Spring left, but Yang remained seated.

In her bedroom Gentle Spring went to her vanity table and withdrew photographs of Lilian and Robert from a drawer with pink jade handles. She leaned the photos against the mirror, viewing them from various angles. A slight smile played about her lips. She cradled her head on her right arm and remained so for a time gazing at the photographs.

Robert . . . there would be no reading of poetry with him in the garden when the magnolias bloomed. He had not become what she had hoped, but she loved him and regretted burdening him with her ambitions. Perhaps she had been selfish. He could never be like his grandfather. Her father's strength and essence was in Lilian.

Gentle Spring studied her reflection in the mirror and then replaced the photographs in the drawer. Lilian made death seem less final. She was her seed and would blossom. She would find her way. It was Robert who needed caring for. In her dressing room Gentle Spring changed into a white woolen gown. She extinguished the bedroom lights except for a small night lamp and seated herself in the peacock chair to wait for the rise of the moon over her garden.

The house was completely dark when the waning moon came into view. Gentle Spring lit the three candles of a silver candelabra and, holding it aloft, went silently down the hall to the guest bedroom. Jensen, who had been sleeping fitfully, sat bolt upright. "Lilian," he cried. Naked, he leaped out of the bed and, snatching up the linen coverlet, wrapped it about his waist. Now, he could see in the candlelight that it was Gentle Spring.

"Forgive me," Gentle Spring said. "You thought I was Lilian?" Jensen breathed heavily and nodded. "You're in love with Lilian?" Jensen nodded again.

"Yes, I saw it in your eyes when you spoke of her," Gentle Spring said.

She put the candelabra on the bedside table. "I told you at dinner of my son, Robert, who is in Hsuchow. The American planes still fly into the city. I beg you please have this sent to him." Gentle Spring took a silver amulet strung on a red cord from within her gown. "Tell him it contains the eye of the Buddha from the shrine in my father's house. He'll know it. Let him accept it as a sign of my love, my faith, and our family bond. It may give him the courage he'll need to survive." She went to Jensen, who bowed so she could drape the red cord around his neck. "Please help me," Gentle Spring said softly. "There's no one else I can turn to."

"Honorable mother," Jensen said in Chinese. "It shall be done." He lifted Gentle Spring's hands to his lips, then watched silently as she picked up the candelabra and left.

Gentle Spring walked down the curving staircase to the glass doors leading into the walled garden. She carefully placed the candelabra on a little bench and sat beside it, gazing at the rippling pond beneath the marble bridge. This had always been her retreat. Here she had planted seeds from the earth of her parents' Suchou garden. Here, together, she and Robert had read aloud the Sung and Tang poets.

Gentle Spring took a small mother-of-pearl case, the gift of her parents, from within her robe. She opened it and carefully shook four cyanide tablets into her hand. She knelt beside the pond. As the carp scurried away, she dipped her cupped hands into the water and drank, swallowing the tablets.

In the morning Yang was awakened by a wailing outside his door. Irritated, he grabbed his dressing gown and went out into the hall. It was the old nurse of his children. "Madam . . . in the garden," the woman sobbed.

Yang ran down the stairs. Gentle Spring's body lay beside the pond, doubled up, as if she had suffered great pain. Her eyes were open, fixed. Yang knelt beside her and reached out a hand but then withdrew it. He seated himself beside the candelabra on the stone bench. The candles were no longer burning. He folded his arms and with his eyes closed began to sway, side to side.

Chapter Nineteen

The night express, on which Jensen returned to Nanking, was nearly empty of passengers except for several cars filled with troops. On the bare boards of a bunk in the shabby wagon-lits car, Jensen lay awake thinking of the white-robed body beside the lotus pool. Gentle Spring was to him the very spirit of womanhood portrayed by Lao Tsu: *Giving herself to her children. Mysterious Mother of the earth.* Before falling into restive sleep, Jensen vowed he would find a way to take Gentle Spring's amulet to her son. He would help rescue Robert's family if he could.

As the train steamed into the Nanking station, wild-eyed refugees swarmed aboard. Jensen, pushing through the mob, jumped into a pedicab. At the American hostel he went straight to his room and telephoned Dirk Howard.

"Yeah," replied the groggy voice of the courier. "Who's this?"

"Jensen. I need to see you right away."

"Okay. Okay. You know my room."

The door was ajar. The courier, in flowered boxer shorts, was sitting sleepy-eyed on his bed. "Delighted to see you, old chap," he rasped as Jensen, unshaven and rumpled, stood before him. "You look in great form."

"Dirk, I need help. I've got to get to Hsuchow."

Howard sighed. "Eric, it's too early in the morning for jokes." Then he squinted at Jensen. "My God, you're serious," he said incredulously. "You know the Chicoms are moving in on the city. They could take it anytime. Only the Nat Air Force and Chennault's supply planes are going in. The place is a mess."

"I know. Dirk, please . . . if you can."

The courier swung his legs back into the bed, pulled the quilt over his shoulders, and turned to the wall. "There're more fucking things going on around here I don't want to know about," he grumbled. "I'll get back to you."

In his room, two days later, Jensen switched off the late evening news of the Armed Forces Radio Station, picked up the paperback novel he had been reading, flipped a page, and then hurled it across the room. He slouched onto the sofa and stared at the motionless overhead fan. There had been no word from Dirk Howard or from Philip Fugh at the embassy. Jensen had not left the hostel. He had done little more than read paperbacks bought in the P.X., watch a Rita Hayworth movie in the cafeteria, and peruse the *Shanghai Evening Post and Mercury*. Last night he had tossed about until daylight, unable to sleep. What had become of Lilian?

In the *Evening Post* there was a dispatch reporting on Peking under siege. The distant rattle of gunfire had become as familiar in the city as the cries of the street peddlers. The Communists had pushed to within a mile of the city walls. When the electrical power failed, loudspeaker trucks toured the darkened streets warning that looters would be shot. The jails were emptied of petty criminals to provide barracks for troops withdrawn from the outlying fortifications. The municipal government, striving to halt panic food buying, announced that there was a three-month supply of grain in the city. No one believed it.

There was a rap on the door, and Jensen went to open it, thinking it was the room boy returning to pick up the tea tray. Dirk Howard stood in the doorway, wearing a soiled trench coat and carrying his courier's bag. He grinned broadly as he tipped back his brown trilby. "May I join you for vespers, Brother Jensen?" he said as he walked in. He pulled a fifth of Johnnie Walker Black Label out of his coat, emptied the teacup that stood on a tray, and poured himself a drink. Jensen brought a glass and joined him.

"There's a press plane going up to Hsuchow tomorrow morning," Howard said. "It's a one-day trip on a Nat Air Force transport. The Foreign Ministry press office is taking foreign correspondents there for some sort of a phony press conference. There'll be a lot of bullshit about how Hsuchow is holding out and Nanking is safe. The idea is to quiet the panic here."

"Can I get on that plane?" Jensen asked tensely, pulling a cigarette from a pack offered by Howard.

"Why I'm sticking my ass out for you," Howard said, taking a sheaf of papers from his breast pocket, "I'll never know. These are travel orders in my name. I'm on the manifest. You'll go in my place. Supposedly I'm going to the compound of the American military advisers. The Americans have already been evacuated. But nobody is checking in this screwed-up situation. If anybody in Hsuchow asks, you're taking funds and instructions to the caretaker of the mission property. Shake loose long enough to visit the property to make the story convincing."

Howard tossed the orders over to Jensen. "Here, take them. Get some G.I. clothes in the P.X. Take the bag and this key. I have another. I'm going to Tokyo day after tomorrow. Pray God there's no foul-up." Howard put on his trench coat and retrieved the scotch bottle. "There're some things I won't give up for anybody, including you, Jensen," he said. "My driver will pick you up at six a.m. The plane leaves from the Ming Tomb Airfield at eight."

◆

The twin engines of the C-46 transport were already turning over when Jensen, wearing a pile Army jacket and a fur hat with the earflaps tied up, crossed the tarmac with six correspondents and two Chinese press officers. Several of the correspondents were grumbling about risking the trip just to get an official handout. Jensen was directed to a bucket seat beside a stocky, beetle-browed American, an empty ivory cigarette holder tilted in his mouth, who promptly stuck out his hand. "Henry Libman of *The New York Times*. You're the courier they told us about, aren't you? I thought all Americans were out of Hsuchow." Jensen put the courier bag between his legs. "I'm making arrangements for a Chinese caretaker at the compound of the Military Advisory Group." Libman looked at him quizzically and shrugged.

As the plane began its descent over the Huaipei Plain toward Hsuchow, the *Times* correspondent, a long ash hanging from his cigarette holder, jabbed Jensen and pointed through the window. "Nienchuang-chi, at least what's left of it. Chen Yi's columns took the city . . . destroyed ten divisions of the Nationalist Seventh Army." Jensen could see smoke still rising from the ruins. The concentric walls and moat that had shielded the ancient town for centuries had been of little use. Trenches were dotted with corpses, shattered equipment, and shreds of the parachutes used to drop supplies. "The Chicoms are isolating these towns in turn and chopping up the Nationalist garrisons," Libman said. "The Nats hold Hsuchow itself with one hundred seventy-five thousand troops, but it could be next. They'll give us a lot of crap at the briefing, but at least we'll see what's happening to the town."

What am I getting into? Jensen wondered.

The C-46 circled over Hsuchow, a sprawling market and rail center, and landed on an airfield crowded with Chennault transports and Nationalist Air Force planes. Jeeps were waiting, and the party, Jensen included, piled aboard. They were taken to the headquarters of General Liu Chih, commander of the 600,000 Nationalist troops that were still holding the principal towns on the Huaipei Plain. A small stage had been set up in the briefing room with a large map board. Liu Chih, a fleshy man in a loose-fitting brown tunic, labored up the steps of the stage and was handed a pointer by a young officer.

"I'm Lieutenant Yang, the translator for General Liu Chih," the young officer said in flawless English. Jensen stared at Yang, marveling at his luck in locating Robert so quickly. There could be no mistake. The officer's fine, rather delicate features resembled those of Gentle Spring and Lilian. He was slender, pale in complexion, and looked like a schoolboy beside the corpulent Liu Chih.

The briefing lasted less than an hour. Liu Chih stabbed at the map on which arching black arrows were shown overrunning clusters of red dots. He spoke of the impregnability of Hsuchow and of lashing out to entrap the Communist columns. Jensen noted that the correspondents took few notes. There were many yawns. As the correspondents were led away to luncheon, Jensen approached Yang.

"May I have a word with you, alone?" Jensen said.

The lieutenant looked puzzled. "You are the courier, correct? We have a jeep and a driver to take you to the military advisers' compound.

But you must return to the airfield by two o'clock, when the correspondents' plane returns to Nanking."

Jensen waited until they were alone before saying, "I have a message from your mother."

Robert moistened his lips and looked wide-eyed at Jensen. "Come with me," he said. "I won't be needed before the luncheon toasts." He led Jensen to a second-floor conference room, closed the door, and spun about. "Who are you?" he asked hoarsely.

"I'm a friend of Lilian," Jensen said. "I carried a message from Lilian, who is in Peking, to your mother and father in Shanghai. Your mother asked me to give you this," Jensen took the silver amulet from his breast pocket. "It contains the eye of the Buddha that stands at your grandfather's shrine. She said it is a sign of her love, her faith, and the family bond. She said it will give you strength."

Robert took the amulet and slipped the cord over his head, tucking the pendant beneath his shirt. "How is she?" he whispered. He looked up in alarm when Jensen hesitated.

"I'm sorry. The morning after she gave me the amulet, she took poison . . . beside the lotus pool. She's dead."

Robert turned about, lowered his head, and was quiet for a long moment. "I'm not surprised," he said bitterly. "We knew she would resist leaving China. And my father?"

"He seemed determined to go the United States . . . to join your brother."

Robert nodded. "And Lilian?"

"I'm not sure. She may be at Yenching. The Communists have occupied the campus."

"I've never worried about her," Robert said quietly. "In some ways she was always the strongest of us. She had such fierce opinions, beliefs to cling to. She believed China could be great again."

"And you?" Jensen asked.

Robert shook his head, his eyes lowered. "I'm glad Lilian has her illusion."

Jensen watched Robert's mouth working in agitation as he spoke. He studied him, the soft white hands and nervous manner, his evident vulnerability. While Robert resembled his mother, there was no manifestation of her inner strength. Little chance he or his wife and child would survive if the Communists overran Hsuchow. Jensen thought of his promise to Gentle Spring. Yes, he would fulfill it. He would find a way to help Robert.

Chapter Twenty

Except for the distant crump of artillery fire, the Hsuchow airport was strangely quiet. Only hours before, Chennault's transports had been landing in quick succession, pausing only long enough to unload supplies before thundering off. Poised on a runway amid the shells of a half dozen wrecked aircraft was a single operable transport, a C-46 with Nationalist Air Force markings.

A lone figure paced before the ramshackle air terminal. It was Robert, hands clasped behind his back. He had escorted the correspondents to the airport, all except Jensen, who had not returned from his visit to the American compound. The flight had waited for half an hour and then, on the insistence of the pilot, took off without Jensen. Robert agonized that they would blame him. As he looked about wondering what to do next, a convoy of limousines and army trucks sped onto the tarmac. Robert watched in astonishment as General Liu Chih, the commander-in-chief, descended from an antiquated Rolls-Royce and waddled to a waiting C-46. Trailing behind were his wife, his concubine, three children, and his staff carrying his baggage. At his side was Chiang Wei-kuo, commander of the Armored Corps in Hsuchow, the youngest son of Chiang Kai-shek. Robert looked on, stupefied by this bolting of the high command. What of me? he thought. Although he was a member of Liu Chih's staff, he was being left behind. Since his father had purchased his commission for ten thousand American dollars, his only Army duty had been that of interpreter for Liu Chih. He had never fired a gun.

As he watched the general board the plane, he remembered with a start that he had not yet reported Jensen's disappearance, and he ran into the terminal to telephone headquarters. A sergeant answered the adjutant's phone. "There are no officers here," the sergeant blurted. "They have gone to their quarters to pack. The garrison is leaving Hsuchow to meet a relief column coming up from the south. General Tu Yu-ming is in command. There is a staff meeting here at five o'clock." Shaken, Robert hung up the phone and walked from the terminal to watch the C-46 carrying Liu Chih take off.

Just as the transport disappeared, he saw a jeep bouncing across the tarmac. As it came closer he made out Jensen, seated beside the Chinese driver, waving cheerily. Robert ran to the side of the jeep. "You've missed the plane," he gasped.

"Sorry, we had a flat tire," Jensen lied calmly. He had bribed the Chinese driver without much difficulty to delay their return. "What's going on?" Jensen said, as he climbed out of the jeep. At that moment a series of explosions and flames spewed out of two hangars. Demolition teams were blowing up the installations. Jensen's driver shouted something unintelligible, turned the jeep about, and made off.

"Hsuchow is being evacuated," Robert said. "Liu Chih and the Gimmo's son have already left."

"My God," Jensen muttered. What a fool he had been. He had believed Liu Chih, that the Nationalists would defend Hsuchow. Bringing in the correspondents for a briefing merely hours before the planned evacuation was a more cynical propaganda ploy than he had even imagined. Jensen realized now how ill-conceived was his plan to escape Hsuchow with Robert's family. He had been planning to use some of the six thousand dollars in his money belt to bribe one of Chennault's pilots to take them out. Now he was trapped with them.

Through the smoke drifting from the burning buildings Robert led Jensen back to his jeep. During the three hours that they had been away, Hsuchow had slipped into chaos. As rumors spread that the Nationalist garrison was abandoning Hsuchow, the townspeople had flocked into the streets, joining the thousands of desperate refugees from the outlying war-shattered villages. On the main avenue, looters were smashing shop windows. The police had deserted their posts. Robert maneuvered his jeep through the crowds. A gang of peasant youths pounded on the sides of the car and two climbed onto the hood. Robert leaned out, pointed his pistol into the air, and fired. As the youths ran off, Robert looked elated. "First time I've used this," he said.

When Robert and Jensen entered the briefing room at headquarters, the new commander, General Tu Yu-ming, dressed in a tailored brown tunic, was already on the platform speaking before a map. The room was crowded with staff and unit commanders in padded field uniforms. Tu glanced at Jensen. He recognizes me, Jensen thought.

"Our immediate situation is not good," Tu Yu-ming said crisply. "There are twenty-seven Communist columns—more than six hundred thousand troops under Chen Yi—concentrated on the Huaipei Plain. Our Seventh Army Group on the east flank has been overrun except for three thousand men who have reached our lines. Our Sixteenth Army Group, which left here two days ago to open the south

road, has lost one division and is retreating to rejoin our main body."
Ignoring the buzz in the hall, Tu Yu-ming went on. "We must evacuate Hsuchow. We will march out in column formation. Our objective," he said, striking the map, "is to link up at Suhsien, forty-five miles to the south, with the Twelfth Army Group, marching north to our assistance. The Sixth and Eighth Army Groups are also coming north from Huai River to our relief. We will have cover from the Air Force."

Tu Yu-ming turned from the map, gripping the pointer with both hands. "Our column will be spearheaded by the Thirteenth and Sixteenth Army Groups. They will be followed by the Second Army Group, which is taking up wedge formation. The tanks of the Armored Corps will proceed within the wedge, reinforcing it with their firepower. Our rearguard, led by my headquarters unit, will come after the Armored Corps within the wedge. The supply trucks carrying the Army families and Hsuchow officials will follow. Other civilians can fall behind. My headquarters unit will lead the rearguard out at zero-seven hundred. The Air Force has been informed that the evacuation of Hsuchow will be completed by noon. Troops entering the town thereafter will be presumed to be Communist targets. That is all."

As Tu Yu-ming left the stage, Robert approached him and saluted. "General, this is the American courier. He was delayed and could not leave with the correspondents."

Tu Yu-ming looked at Jensen with a raised eyebrow. He does recognize me, Jensen thought. He remembers meeting me at Ssuping before the truce team went on to Changchun to meet Lin Piao.

Tu Yu-ming curtly waved Robert away. "What are you doing here, Jensen," he said gruffly in English.

"I've left the Army. I'm working as a State Department courier," Jensen said. He watched the general nervously, not expecting to be believed.

"I think you'll regret missing that plane," Tu Yu-ming said grimly. "Never mind. I don't have time to talk. You're now in it with us. We can make good use of you. When we march out, stay with the communications unit of my headquarters. We'll be getting air drops from Chennault's transports. Talk by radio with the American pilots. They may give us more information about our situation if they talk to another American. I trust the Americans more than Nanking to tell us what is happening."

As the general left with his aides, Jensen rejoined Robert, who was waiting in a corner of the briefing room. "I'll be traveling with you in the headquarters unit," Robert said. "Stay in my cottage tonight. My wife, Fragrant Iris, will prepare supper for us. In the morning we can go to the assembly area together."

◆

While Robert was at the headquarters, Fragrant Iris went as usual with other officers' wives to the central hospital, which received the wounded. The hospital was overflowing with casualties. Hundreds were lying untended on stretchers in the corridors and in the damp cold of the open courtyard. Fragrant Iris dreaded her routine task of taking water and food along the lines of moaning and bloodied men, many of whom were dying. Today she noticed that there were fewer attendants than usual. The wives were taken to the chief nurse, a young Cantonese woman in a dirty white smock.

The nurse, her eyelids sagging with fatigue, pointed to large piles of mess kits and canteens stacked behind her in the corridor. "Please take these to the kitchen. Fill each mess kit with rice and the canteens with water. Leave them beside each bed and stretcher. Hsuchow is being evacuated. It is all the men will have until the Communists arrive."

"The wounded are to be left behind?" asked a plump woman in a flowered *cheongsam* in a tremulous voice.

"Most of the doctors and nurses have already left," the nurse said stolidly. "Only two elder civilian doctors are here to treat the wounded. I am leaving with the rest of the staff tonight. So please work quickly."

Fragrant Iris picked up a gunny sack, filled it with mess kits and canteens, and went to the kitchen, where there were large vats of cold rice. She pressed the rice into the kits, filled the canteens from the water taps, and, dragging her gunny sack, went to her assigned corridor. On previous visits she always paused beside each soldier to speak comforting words, but now Fragrant Iris walked quickly down the lines smiling wanly at each of the wounded before running back to the kitchen for more supplies. Many of the wounded were young conscripts in their teens who had been in the Army only a few months. "Mother, where is my leg?" one boy cried out. Fragrant Iris turned her head and walked on.

Not long after the women had left, a band of peasants entered the hospital courtyard. Ignoring the pleas from the rows of wounded, the peasants picked up the rice-filled mess kits that had been placed beside each man and ran off.

◆

Fragrant Iris, a slight figure in a blue padded gown, was at home when Robert, accompanied by Jensen, arrived at their mud brick cottage. She was huddled with their son, Peter, on the large *kang* bed covered with a red satin quilt, reading to him from *The Legend of the White Monkey King*. As Robert and Jensen entered, the four-year-old tumbled off the bed and ran to his father.

Fragrant Iris greeted Robert with a relieved smile. "I am glad you are at home," she said as Robert put his arm about her. The harsh Huaipei climate had not blemished her porcelainlike features, which, to Fragrant Iris's embarrassment, Robert often compared to those of a lady of the court in a Five Dynasties painting.

"This is Eric Jensen," Robert said. "He is a friend of Lilian. He will stay with us tonight."

Jensen bowed, and Fragrant Iris bowed shyly in return. "You are welcome." Turning to Robert, she said anxiously: "I have heard the news. I was at the hospital. It is being evacuated. The families in the officer billets are packing their belongings. What shall we do?"

"I will explain," Robert said, glancing down at Peter.

"Go play in the courtyard," Fragrant Iris said to their son. She took his thickly padded coat from a peg on the rough plastered wall and bundled him through the door.

"You must be hungry," Fragrant Iris said. "I'll bring rice and a little cold pork. We have nothing else. There was no market today." She brought three bowls and set them down on the table.

"We will leave Hsuchow in the morning," Robert said, as he scooped rice with his chopsticks from the bowl tucked under his chin.

"Where will we go?" Fragrant Iris asked.

Robert composed himself, determined to be convincing. "We are going south to meet the Army Groups marching to help us. The families will ride in the big trucks with the supplies. We will cross the Huai River. We shall be safe there."

Fragrant Iris bowed her head. "The Huaipei Plain is cold. There is little shelter. May I bring my red quilt?"

Robert placed his hand on her shoulder. "Yes. Bring your red quilt. We should not leave our wedding gift behind. But you must begin to gather our things now."

"What shall we tell Peter?"

"Tell him he is going on a long journey. He will have adventures like the White Monkey King."

In the darkness just before dawn Robert, with Jensen at his side, drove his wife and child to the convoy assembly area. Fragrant Iris clutched little Peter more tightly as she looked over the turbulent scene. Soldiers with bayoneted rifles were holding off hundreds of civilian families trying to climb into the canvas-covered Army trucks. Only the families of officers and government officials were being permitted to board. Others were told to follow on foot or on whatever transport they could find. Some of the wealthy arrived in cars that had little chance of making it on the dirt roads across the plain.

Robert took Fragrant Iris and Peter to one of the headquarter's trucks. It was loaded with drums of fuel and sacks of grain except for a small space at the rear. Fragrant Iris and Peter squeezed in with the wife of a colonel and her three children. Robert touched Fragrant Iris on the cheek. "I will come to see you when I can," he said.

Jensen and Robert went to the communications truck to which they had been assigned for the march. It was a covered vehicle with radio equipment stacked in the rear. They sat in the cab beside the driver, a young round-faced man who wore his field cap at a rakish angle. "Chief radio operator Corporal Hu Pao-ying," the driver barked, awed at the prospect of sharing his cab with two important personages.

The column remained immobile until dawn flooded over the plain and then rumbled forward. The headquarters unit fell in behind the tanks of the Armored Corps, which moved within a wedge formed by the troops of the Second Army Group. The civilians followed, their numbers swelled to thousands, strung out on the road. The wedge crawled forward with the columns of infantry trudging over the frozen fields well out on the flanks. Clad in padded yellow uniforms, cloth leg wrappings, and caps with ear flaps tied up, the troops trod over paths between shattered villages. The fields were covered with the stubble of summer sorghum and furrows of winter wheat, which had been planted before the Battle of the Huai-Hai had engulfed the villages. Horses and mules carrying heavy mortars and ammunition plodded beside the troops, their hooves breaking through the crusted earth.

The few peasants remaining in the villages watched sullenly as the soldiers marched past, bowed under the weight of heavy field packs, their heads lowered into the cruel wind. Weeks before the battle began, Communist propaganda teams had passed through the villages, swaying the peasants with promises that the landlord holdings would be divided among them. In some Huaipei villages the Communists had already begun the ritual Turning-Over of Lands.

As reconnaissance planes from the Air Force base at Nanking circled over the Hsuchow column, their crews stared down incredulously on a pulsating procession of some two hundred thousand soldiers and civilians intermingled with trucks, cars, and bicycles forging slowly across the desolate plain. The wedge moved sporadically, making some ten miles a day. It veered to the southwest when the advance units encountered heavy Communist fire. During night halts Jensen was often jolted awake as artillery and Sherman tanks of the Armored Corps laid down interdicting fire on the tracks over which Communist guerrillas moved to harass the column.

Corporal Hu cursed and bantered during the day-long drives as he wrestled the truck over the deeply rutted tracks. Hu had been an engineering student at Chiaotung University in Shanghai before he was arrested while carrying a banner in an antigovernment demonstration. "They gave me the choice of prison or the Army," Hu explained, chuckling. "The way the war is going, I thought I would have a shorter sentence if I chose the Army."

During the nights as they lay side by side in the back of the truck,

Robert would speak of his gentle life in Shanghai. "When my father bought my lieutenant's commission, he arranged for me to be assigned to the Shanghai Garrison Headquarters. Nothing much would change, he said. But they sent me instead to Hsuchow as Liu Chih's interpreter."

"But why did you bring your family?"

"We were told Hsuchow would be safe . . . the center of an iron defense complex."

Robert spoke reluctantly about Lilian when Jensen pressed him. "We've not heard from her in almost a year," he said in an embarrassed tone. "When she came home from Yenching at the New Year holiday, she asked me to march in an antigovernment demonstration. 'You must join,' she said. 'Get off your knees and stand on two legs. We must fight against corruption, for peace and democracy.' She became very angry when I told her I couldn't do it. What if I was arrested? Fragrant Iris and little Peter would be alone. She hasn't replied to our letters."

Lilian can be hard, Jensen thought. Willing to sacrifice everything . . . even her family ties . . . for her cause. What did that mean for his own relationship with her?

Listening to Robert, Jensen began to form a plan to smuggle Robert and his family across the Huai River to Nanking once their column linked up with the Nationalist divisions coming from the south.

On the fourth day of the march, Jensen was with Hu as he manned the ground-to-air radio. An observation plane sent a message that there was unusual activity on the road ahead of the Hsuchow column. Thousands of Communist soldiers and peasants were digging wide trenches across the march route. Tu Yu-ming came to the side of the communications truck. "Tell the Center at the Defense Ministry we need air support to clear the road," he shouted. By early afternoon P-51 Mustang fighters began to wheel overhead making strafing runs along the road. The wedge moved forward for a few miles.

On the sixth day the point units of the Thirteenth and Sixteenth Army Groups came under Communist artillery fire as they halted short of the first ditches blocking the road. Tu Yu-ming again asked for air support. Twin-engine B-25 and four-motor B-24 bombers accompanied by Mustang fighters came overhead. Tu Yu-ming stood at the side of the communications truck watching through binoculars as the bombers dropped their strings of explosives. The general lowered his binoculars and spoke furiously to Jensen, who stood nearby. "How can they hit anything from those high altitudes? Why don't they go in? The Communists have no antiaircraft guns . . . nothing but fifty-caliber machine guns." He thrust his hands into the pockets of his trench coat. "Perhaps the Generalissimo is more concerned about saving the Air Force for the defense of Formosa," he said savagely.

As the planes turned toward their Nanking base, Tu Yu-ming ordered the Sixteenth Army Group forward to break the roadblock. Three divisions scrambled across the ditches under the cover of artillery fire and the guns of the Armored Corps without opposition. The long skirmish lines moved over the furrowed fields and disappeared from sight. Tu Yu-ming ordered the Hsuchow column to prepare to resume the march at daylight.

The general was warming himself at a fire of dried sorghum stalks when Jensen came with a radio message shortly after dawn. The reconnaissance aircraft were reporting that the advancing Sixteenth Army divisions had come under counterattack and surrendered. Communist columns were now enveloping the flanks of the remaining Hsuchow force. The general looked into the fire, hands clasped behind his back, features impassive. Then he turned to his staff aide. "Assemble the Army Group commanders for conference," he said heavily. "We will form a square with the Armored Corps, the artillery, and the civilians in the center. Order the troops to begin digging perimeter defenses. We will remain here until the Twelfth Army Group joins us and the Sixth and Eighth come from the south. Then we will make for the Huai River."

A cold rain began to fall.

Chapter Twenty-one

Fragrant Iris held Peter's chubby hand as they stood beside the road in the early morning, watching the Nationalist bombers circle overhead and listening to the crunch of bombs to the south. "The big birds have been summoned from the Mountain of Flowers and Fruit to strike the evil Green Demon," Fragrant Iris whispered to Peter who appeared convinced that it was all a wonderful game. Since leaving Hsuchow, Fragrant Iris had been amusing the boy with tales of giants and other creatures who cavorted in the mythical world of the Monkey King. Once during a road halt she fashioned a fan from twigs which she told Peter was as magical as the fan the Monkey King used to cool the Flaming Mountains when he traveled with the pilgrim monk Tripitaka through the Gobi Desert. When Peter was frightened at night by the gun flashes she would tell him to ward off harm by waving his magic fan. Peter would wave the fan and call for the Red Giant. Jensen had accompanied Robert on some of his brief visits to Fragrant Iris. Charmed by this physical embodiment of the good mythical giant, the boy would cry out in delight as he was carried about on Jensen's shoulders.

Suddenly, engines growled up and down the column. Fragrant Iris gathered Peter up and climbed hastily into the back of their truck. It lumbered off the road and bounced over the fields as the entire column dispersed. The truck carrying Fragrant Iris and Peter careened over a muddy track for about a half mile. It stopped in a large village of mud-brick houses with thatched straw roofs. The village was empty of people and strangely quiet. Taking Peter by the hand, Fragrant Iris climbed out of the truck and wandered past the abandoned cottages. The peasants had fled with anything they could carry, including their ducks and chickens. Hung before the cottages were fierce images of the Protective Gods of the Four Directions to frighten off the evil spirits. Long tissue scrolls inscribed with characters of good omens fluttered in the wind.

A jeep carrying Tu Yu-ming swept into the village and stopped before the largest of the houses, the only one with a tile roof. Corporal Hu parked the communications truck carrying Jensen and Robert alongside the headman's house. It was to be the new headquarters. Jensen and Hu ran inside to take messages. Tu, hatless and his tunic open, was already working over a map spread out over a rickety wooden table with two aides looking over his shoulders. As Jensen watched, Tu drew a five-mile-square perimeter. "These are the coordinates," Tu said, his finger stabbing at the map, as his aides took notes. "Here are the positions for the Second and Thirteenth Group armies along the perimeter. Order the tanks of the Armored Corps to go hulls down in the center to give supporting fire." Hu was handed radio messages by one of the aides, and the operator ran out of the house.

"What about the civilians?" one of the aides asked.

The general shrugged. "Tell them to scatter out in the villages inside the perimeter. They will have to look out for themselves. Tell the quartermaster to put them on half the rations we are giving the troops. Radio Nanking for food drops by the Chennault transports."

As the aides went out of the house, Tu looked at Jensen grimacing, and said in English, "Not so nice, my friend, is it? Remember? In Hsuchow I said you'd regret missing that plane."

At nightfall a hush fell over the encampment. The only sound came from children who sat together chattering and gazing at the winking kerosene lamps. Aside from the distant rumble of artillery fire, the night passed peacefully. Fragrant Iris and Peter lay on the earthen floor of a cottage, wrapped in the warm red quilt. Peter slept soundly, but Fragrant Iris could not block out the cries of infants and the whispers of women lying beside them.

In the morning the women went out into the fields to fetch sorghum stubble and twigs for cooking fires. A quartermaster unit doled out the scanty rations of rice. The Hsuchow column had planned to reprovision at Suhsien, the rail town, which was to have been the link-up point with the Twelfth Army Group. Listening to the radio traffic, Jensen learned that Suhsien was now in Communist hands.

Nationalist reconnaissance planes came overhead and radioed that Communist units were deployed on all sides of the perimeter. Corporal Hu intercepted messages to the Defense Ministry in Nanking from the Twelfth Army Group, dug in some thirty-five miles to the southeast, reporting that it was also encircled and that its 110th Division had defected. At noon Corporal Hu showed Jensen a message from the Generalissimo. It instructed Tu Yu-ming to hold out. The Sixth Army Group was said to be steadily advancing north from Huai River to the relief of the Twelfth Army Group, and together they would come to the aid of the Hsuchow column. It concluded with warm greetings and assurances that the general's family in Nanking would be well cared for.

Hu, his mouth twisted in a sneer, tapped the message pad. "The Gimmo is telling Tu that his family will not fare too well if he surrenders."

When the corporal took the message to Tu Yu-ming, the general studied it carefully before tearing it into bits.

Shortly after midnight Jensen awoke to the sound of gunfire along the perimeter. Tu Yu-ming, buttoning his tunic, came running out of his billet to the communications truck. Field radios were already crackling with messages from unit commanders. The Communists were probing the perimeter with ground attacks and heavy mortar fire. Tu Yu-ming ordered the tanks and artillery to respond. In the center of the encampment the civilians cowered, terrified by the gun flashes lighting up the night.

In the morning, once the artillery fire had subsided, hundreds of casualties began to arrive at the medical aid station set up near the headquarters. The first Communist fire had caught many of the infantrymen asleep in trenches along the perimeter by surprise. Jensen helped the stretcher-bearers carry the wounded to the medical station. Many young soldiers, their bleeding wounds still unbandaged, lay in rows in the drizzling rain waiting for treatment by the four doctors. Black flies speckled a pile of amputated limbs.

Monitoring the radio traffic, Corporal Hu soon figured out why the Communists were using their mortars but withholding their heavy artillery. The Communists had concentrated the bulk of their forces and all their artillery around the perimeter of the Twelfth Army Group and were pounding the trapped divisions. The commander of the encircled Twelfth was pleading for heavy air strikes. On December 15 the radios of the Twelfth fell silent. The Hsuchow column could no longer expect their help.

"They're finished. We're next," Jensen told Robert grimly. "The

Communists kept us pinned down while they finished the Twelfth. Soon they'll concentrate around us. We had better dig those foxholes behind the truck a lot deeper." Robert thought of the trench outside of Fragrant Iris's hut. It was quite shallow.

As the days passed, there was nothing for Fragrant Iris to do except hide from the cold or hunt for roots and bark to eat. Every morning she would go out into the fields with the other women to dig in the frozen ground for half-grown sweet and white potatoes. Food supplies had dwindled. She was thrilled when she could find even one potato root to add to Peter's small ration of rice. Robert would sometimes bring extra rice or a bit of meat from the column's slaughtered horses. Fragrant Iris prepared these treats in secret. She watched in horror as other women clawed and fought over the last of the twigs and dried sorghum stems that fueled their fires.

Chennault's transports dropped sacks of rice and flour, but the strong winds often blew the floating parachutes beyond reach. The Communists had tightened their lines around the perimeter and erected close-in earthen pillboxes. They machine-gunned the hungry soldiers who scrambled out to retrieve the sacks. Bodies lay in the fields, picked at by the ravens and starving village dogs. In the night Communist loudspeakers called upon the Nationalist soldiers to defect, offering them food and safety.

Jensen spoke each day by radio with the American pilots of Chennault's planes as they flew overhead. The pilot he came to know best was a certain Harry from Iowa.

"What the hell are you doing there?" Harry exclaimed on the first exchange. "Mister, you're in big trouble."

"Tell me another," Jensen replied. "For God's sake, why don't you guys make your runs lower? We're losing most of those parachute loads."

"Sorry, pal, but we have orders to stay out of the range of those Chicom fifty-calibers. We lost a couple of planes in the drops at Mukden."

On December 17 Mao Tse-tung radioed Tu Yu-ming: *"You are now at the end of your rope. For more than ten days, you have been surrounded ring upon ring and received blow upon blow, and your position has shrunk greatly. You have such a tiny place and so many people crowded together that a single shell from us can kill many of you. Your wounded soldiers and the families who have followed the Army are complaining to high heaven. Your soldiers and many of your officers have no stomach for more fighting. Hold dear the lives of your subordinates and families and find a way out for them as soon as possible. Stop sending them to a senseless death."*

Mao offered to guarantee the life and safety of everyone in the perimeter if Tu Yu-ming would surrender. The broadcast also reported what Tu Yu-ming already knew: The Sixth and Eighth Army Groups, which had been moving north to the relief of the Hsuchow column, were also under attack and had turned back to the Huai River. Tu's forces, encircled by some three hundred thousand Communist troops, made up the last island of Nationalist resistance on the Huaipei Plain.

When Corporal Hu brought the message from Mao to Tu Yu-ming, the general was in his billet drinking steaming tea from a cup that he held with both hands. There were wisps of beard on his chin, and he was wearing an overcoat draped about his shoulders. He scanned the message and waved Hu out of the house. From inside his tunic he took out an earlier radio message and reread it. *"You must resist as long as possible. We need time to prepare the Yangtze defenses. Your family is well."* It was signed by Chiang Kai-shek. Tu Yu-ming turned up the collar of his overcoat and continued to drink his tea.

That night, as if to underline Mao's warning, the perimeter was subjected to its heaviest bombardment. Jensen watched the gun flashes lighting up the night sky. He found a bare patch amid the sorghum stubble and seated himself cross-legged. There was no moon, but the heaven was studded with brilliant stars. Jensen stared upward. How could he fulfill his vow to Gentle Spring? The position of the Hsuchow garrison was hopeless. The Communists were girding for a final assault. And then what? If he and the Yang family survived and were taken prisoner, he might be able to negotiate their release. The Communists were indebted to him for carrying the Peking letter. Chen Yi commanded the encircling forces. He would remind Chen Yi of their meetings when he had served on the truce teams. There was a chance that it would work, he decided. Now more at peace, he took Lilian's jade from his pocket and held it in his hand, summoning its *ch'i*, the breath and the energy force of the dragons.

The next morning, carrying a shovel and a pickax over his shoulder, Jensen accompanied Robert to the cottage where Fragrant Iris was hiding. Holding Peter by the hand, he led the three away from the cottage to a place where they would not be overheard.

"Listen well, Fragrant Iris," he said. "When the Communists make their final assault, lie flat in the trench with Peter and wait. Robert and I will come to you as soon as we can. Do not fear the Communists. I have friends among them who will care for us."

Robert looked at Jensen with astonishment and nodded vigorously. With Robert following, Jensen climbed into the trench beside the hut. All day they worked to deepen and reinforce it. As women watched and children clapped their hands, the red giant brought boulders from nearby fields to shore up the trench. Before Jensen left, he lifted Peter high in the air as the boy squealed happily. "Take care of your mother, my little friend."

The next day, Mao repeated his surrender demand and then again two days later, this time as an ultimatum. Robert was in the radio truck when the Communist barrage began. Peering over the edge of a foxhole near the communication truck, he watched as the shell bursts stitched across the fields and through the far end of the village, where Fragrant Iris and Peter were hiding. Jensen tried to stop him, but Robert leaped up and stumbled the quarter of a mile down the track to the hut. Jensen followed. They found Fragrant Iris and Peter in the trench behind the cottage huddled under the red quilt. Fragrant Iris, gaunt, and her eyes dull, whispered, "Peter is ill." The boy's face was flushed with fever. His thin body was pressed to Fragrant Iris's breast. He was crying softly. Robert crouched beside them until the Communist artillery settled down to random shelling of the encampment.

Jensen kept up a running conversation with the American pilots of Chennault's transports as they dropped food and ammunition. He made contact with Harry from Iowa. "Say, pal, you'd better stay away from those tanks," Harry said. "I hear the Nat Air Force is going to bomb them so they won't be taken by the Chicoms."

"God! What miserable buggers," Jensen swore. Slamming down his earphones, he marched to the door of Tu's billet and asked his aide's leave to enter. Tu Yu-ming was bending over a map with the commander of the Second Army Group when Jensen walked in. The general looked up in annoyance at the interruption, but smiled tightly when he recognized Jensen. "What new disaster, old friend?" he asked grimly.

"Sir, a Chennault pilot says the Air Force will soon bomb the Armored Corps so that your tanks will not be captured by the Communists."

The Second Army commander, a burly man with shaven head, jumped to his feet. "I don't believe it," he shouted.

Tu Yu-ming stood up, resting his knuckles on the table. "Well, I believe it," he said quietly.

Shortly before dawn the encampment was struck with a devastating barrage. Jensen and Hu could hear infantry commanders along the perimeter reporting a general Communist assault. Leaping from the truck, Jensen pushed Robert into a foxhole and then ran to a nearby trench. Robert was crouching in his foxhole when the earth bulged up under the impact of a shell burst, toppling the radio truck on its side and half burying him. Stunned, he lay there motionless. When he opened his eyes, Jensen was standing over him, in the first light of dawn, his face caked with mud. The barrage had slackened. A few yards away, blasted out of his foxhole and sprawled on his back, lay Hu, blood trickling from his mouth. "He's dead," Jensen said as he lifted Robert to his feet. The general's billet was still standing but most of the rest of the village had been leveled. A light rain was falling.

Babbling incomprehensibly, Robert, followed by Jensen, staggered down the village track, strewn with bodies and wounded. The trench where Fragrant Iris and Peter lay had taken a direct hit. Its primitive reinforcements of rock and sand had not been enough to withstand the shell burst. The bodies of women and children were spewed into a heap at one end. Sobbing, Robert jumped into the trench and began groping among the human fragments. Jensen sat on the edge of the trench, his head bowed. Robert found Fragrant Iris first and then Peter beneath her, lying on the red quilt. He stood over his wife, his face buried in his hands. Jensen lowered himself into the trench and carried the two bodies out, one over each arm. Retrieving the quilt, he wrapped Fragrant Iris and Peter, then carefully spread soil over the red shroud.

As the Communist barrage resumed, Jensen led Robert to one of the foxholes near the headquarters billet. He shoved Robert down into the foxhole. "Stay there," he said roughly. "It's our only chance." He jumped into a nearby foxhole just as machine gun fire sprayed the area, tearing into the billet. Wiping mud from his face, Jensen cautiously raised up to look about. "Mother of Earth," he shouted. Robert had climbed out of the foxhole and was walking with his arms dangling toward the sound of the gunfire. Robert fumbled at his throat for the silver amulet. When the bullets struck, he jerked about before falling. Jensen didn't know whether the fire had come from the Communists or the Nationalists.

A skirmish line of Communist troops with raised bayonets was advancing across the field. When they closed in, a squad halted at a strange sight. A red-haired foreign devil was standing before them, the body of a Chinese in his arms.

◆

Pelted by the rain, Jensen lay on the battlefield where he had been hurled after wrestling with his captors. His arms and legs were bound by tent ropes. Stunned, he did not speak to the impassive soldier who squatted beside him, covered by a dripping poncho, rifle across his knees. Nearby was Robert's body, his feet stripped of the fine leather boots that his mother had given him, his eyes staring at the leaden sky where ravens were wheeling, cawing excitedly. A squad of infantrymen appeared. Wordlessly, the soldiers freed Jensen's legs and led him to a weapons carrier, where he lay on gunny sacks as the vehicle bumped to a village encircled by bivouacs and parked military trucks. Jensen was taken to a peasant hut and led into the back shed, where sacks of grain were stored on the hardened earthen floor. A burly officer, whose right cheek bore a livid scar, stood over Jensen as his hands were untied. "There are two soldiers outside," the officer said. "You will be shot if you try to leave."

Jensen remained in the shed for a day and a half, seeing only an elderly peasant who came with sorghum bread, water, and once with a bowl of rice. At night rats scurried about, at times scrambling over his face, which he tried to cover with the blanket given to him by the peasant. On the afternoon of the second day, the rumble of distant artillery fire ceased. The Battle of the Huai-Hai had ended, Jensen surmised. Yes, a tremendous Communist victory. Later, he would learn that more than a half million Nationalist troops had been killed or captured. The Communist path to the Yangtze was open. But for now the outcome left him unmoved. His caring did not extend beyond the field where Robert's bones would bleach, and the grave beneath the frozen sod where Fragrant Iris and Peter lay wrapped in the red wedding quilt.

Jensen listened silently when the scar-faced officer came with the news that his release had been ordered by Chen Yi. His money belt and identity papers, taken when he was captured, were returned and he was driven to within a half mile of the Huai River. Guided by two peasants, he crossed no-man's-land on foot into Pengpu, a river town deserted except for a small Nationalist garrison. Jensen spent the night in an Italian Jesuit mission and the next morning was taken by a priest to the railway station. He rode the one hundred miles into Nanking atop a boxcar bulging with refugees.

Chapter Twenty-two

Every day during Jensen's absence Ying visited the lieutenant's house to ask the cook when the American master would return. The fares he picked up on the street were not enough to feed his wife and four small children and the rent for his pedicab rose almost daily in the raging inflation. The refugees who crowded the city were desperate for work and ready to pay any share of their earnings to the shops that rented rickshas and pedicabs.

Peking was virtually sealed off by encircling Communist armies. Only very meager food stocks dribbled into the markets from the countryside. The well-to-do had hoarded food supplies, but the poor were living on what they could scrounge day to day. For a time Nationalist planes based at Tsingtao made airdrops of sacks of rice and flour, but most burst upon striking the ground or the ice of the lakes. When successful drops were made, mobs fought for the food and the parachute cloth.

As the weeks passed, Ying became more resentful of Jensen's absence. He had come to depend on the largesse of the foreigner. Also he no longer received the small payments from the police for reporting on the foreigner's movements, an arrangement that had been made after the demonstration at the Temple of Heaven.

Ying could hardly believe his good luck when he was first hired by Jensen. He would return home to his wife gleefully, pockets bulging with bundles of yuan notes and occasionally American dollars. The American paid three times what a Chinese paid. But now he was returning to a disappointed wife and hungry children with an empty purse. Would the foreign devil never reappear? Ying made one last visit to the house of the lieutenant. He had not eaten since the previous day, when a Russian whom he had taken to the Soviet consulate had given him a persimmon from the bagful he had bought in the market. The cook told Ying that Jensen had not come back. Ying did not beg, but the cook gave him the end of a stale loaf of bread. Ying put the bread under the cushion of the pedicab and pedaled back to his home in a dank hutung behind the Flower Market. His wife was seated on a straw mat on the floor of the unheated one-room shanty, nursing their infant at her flaccid breast. On her knee teetered a small boy with head shaven except for a pigtail. Ying called their other two children, who were playing among the shacks in the refuse-filled courtyard. He divided the bread among his wife and the children.

"Tomorrow," Ying said, as his wife looked at him with dull eyes, "you will have good food."

The next morning Ying returned his pedicab to the rental shop and walked to the square before the East Railway Station. At one corner there were several well-dressed Chinese, each surrounded by beggarly-looking men jostling for attention. Ying elbowed into one struggling knot and pressed close to the tall figure in the black fur hat at the center. "Here is a strong person who can go today," Ying shouted.

The man in the fur cap inspected him. "Two bags of flour," he said. "No more."

Ying hesitated, but as the man turned to another, he shouted: "Yes, yes."

The man in the fur hat was a *pao-chia* chief, one of those officials in charge of each neighborhood. Each *pao-chia* in the city was required under the conscription decree to provide men for the army and gang labor. However, conscripts were permitted to arrange the hiring of substitutes through their *pao-chia* chief. In these transactions it was assumed that the chief would withhold some squeeze for himself. The chief who was hiring Ying had withheld one bag of flour from the three promised by a merchant whose son was threatened with conscription. Accompanied by two of the chief's men, Ying went to his home to hand over the two bags of flour to his weeping wife. The flour would keep the family alive until he could give them his meager Army pay and whatever he could save from his rations. Ying embraced his children and then followed the *pao-chia* men to the wide courtyard extending before the Great Hall of Supreme Harmony in the Forbidden City. Several thousand conscripts were gathered under the guard of gendarmes. Ying was put among them.

In the bazaars people were grumbling about the conscription, the requisition of household goods, and the forced billeting of troops in their homes. Many were saying that it would be best to surrender the city. Perhaps the Communists are not so bad, they said, reasoning that the Communists had allowed electricity to flow into Peking from the generating plants, which they had seized outside the city.

One day, .75-millimeter artillery shells fell on Peking. The shells, most of which were intended duds, did little damage. None of the historical monuments or major buildings were hit. But it was enough to inspire terror among many refugees who stampeded out through the city gates, preferring to return to the lesser risks of life in their villages. At his headquarters in the Forbidden City, Fu Tso-yi told his deputy generals the shelling was a warning. Soon they would have to either surrender or fight.

Ten days after Ying's conscription into the Army, his unit of recruits was marched to an outpost beyond the city walls, only several hundred yards from the Communist positions.

Chapter Twenty-three

For days after his return to Nanking from the Huaipei Plain, Jensen confined himself to the Army hostel. He wrote an anguished letter to Lilian's father, hoping that his bank would forward it, telling him of the death of Robert and his family. Each morning Jensen assumed the Lotus Position, meditating for an hour or more to bring tranquillity to his mind. The meditations did not, however, erase the horror of what he had seen.

There was no message waiting for him from the ambassador's secretary when he returned. Jensen speculated that obtaining the Vice President's sanction of the surrender of Peking must be proving more difficult than Philip Fugh had foretold. On the fifth day after his return he was awakened shortly after 4 a.m. by the shrill of the telephone. The caller did not identify himself, but Jensen recognized the voice of Philip Fugh. "We're making good progress. Do not leave the hostel until you hear from us. Others are aware of your presence."

Jensen lay awake until dawn pondering the message. It wasn't surprising that he was being watched by the secret police. He had left a broad enough trail. Were the Smith people also tracking him? Jensen took breakfast and lunch in his room and then restlessly walked down to the cafeteria for dinner wondering if the warning precluded a quick stroll in the hostel garden. As he crossed the hostel lobby Jensen felt a tap on the shoulder. He turned about nervously. It was Dirk Howard, chained to his courier bag. "Back from a run to MacArthur's headquarters in Tokyo. Great Occupation over there. I occupied as many women as possible," Howard chirped. Jensen grimaced and shook Howard's hand, his dark mood dissipating. "Let's have a drink at the American Officers' Club," Howard said. "I'll drop the bag at the chancellery and pick you up in an embassy sedan at seven." Jensen hesitated. "Come on, buddy, you look as if you need a little diversion," Howard said, slapping Jensen on the shoulder.

Jensen laughed. "I'll be there."

Jensen waited in his room until seven and then walked swiftly down the stairs, the collar of his Army coat turned up and a knitted wool hat pulled down over his ears. He hurried through the lobby with his head down. The two Army sentries at the gate only glanced at him as he slipped into the embassy sedan beside Howard.

The American Officers' Club was a palatial residence with stately gardens that had once belonged to Wang Ching-wei, puppet President under the Japanese. Jensen and Howard strolled into the large dining hall, which also served as a ballroom. Apart from a half dozen couples, the men in civilian dress, dancing to the music of a White Russian orchestra, the club was deserted.

"Welcome to the Officers' Club sans officers," Howard said, grinning. "The Military Advisory Group has been pulled out. They finally gave up on Chiang Kai-shek and his generals." As they settled at a table near the orchestra, Howard said, "You know what the top guy, General Barr, said when he left? Great epitaph! 'The military debacles can all be attributed to the world's worst leadership.'" Howard whooped.

Jensen was oblivious to the yawning emptiness of the club. Cheered by Howard's company, he downed three scotch highballs in quick succession as he told Howard tersely about Hsuchow. Howard, as always, did not ask too many questions. Jensen was looking at him through a pleasant haze when the courier signaled the Chinese waiter for the chit and said, "This is dreary. It reminds of my Uncle Joe's funeral parlor on New Year's Eve. How about Fu Tze Miao?"

Jensen laughed. "Why not? I could use some action," he said.

It was drizzling and the city was swathed in smog, but Howard steered quickly and surely out of the diplomatic quarter into Fu Tze Miao, the oldest Chinese district. Jensen looked moodily through the misted windshield as they drove past scruffy houses, sidewalk food stalls, and neon signs promising everything to delight the flesh. Howard edged the car through the melee of rickshas, peddler pushcarts, and jostling pedestrians to a corner restaurant with a Phoenix-shaped neon sign. He was greeted with a smile of recognition by the proprietor, a rotund Chinese with shaven head and heavy jowls glistening with sweat, who guided them through the clatter at the dining tables to a staircase at the rear. Howard and Jensen followed him into a long narrow room lined with wooden double-decker beds on which men sprawled holding opium pipes. A heavy, cloying fragrance pervaded the room. Women were rolling and tamping opium balls into pipes and handing them to the smokers.

Jensen examined the premises in a mock studious manner. "Dirk, you disappoint me. I've seen better opium divans in Rangoon." His speech was thick.

"This isn't the place," Howard reassured him.

They walked to a beaded curtained doorway. The proprietor parted the curtain and stepped aside. As they entered, a statuesque, middle-aged blond woman greeted Howard. "Ah, Mr. Howard, you have returned just in time," the woman said in a throaty Russian accent. "Nanking is becoming unpleasant. I go to Shanghai next week with the girls to open a new house."

The woman was dressed in black silk pants and a sleeveless brocade jacket which was unbuttoned, affording a full view of her generous breasts. The six other women in the room, apparently all of them Russian, were dressed similarly.

The oblong room was furnished more in opulence than in any particular style. Six couches covered with red velvet lined the walls. At the far end there was a scroll painting of the Empress Dowager. Two men, a Chinese and a foreigner, were reclining on two of the couches, with girls kneeling on cushions beside them tending to their opium pipes.

"Natasha, this is my friend, Eric," Howard said. "He needs cheering up."

"Ah, of course. Poor man. I've someone special for him." Natasha signaled to a dark, buxom girl with fine pale features and violet eyes under long lashes. "This is Tanya. She will serve you." Jensen, swaying slightly, gazed upon this Russian beauty . . . this Tanya, who was offering unexpected escape from the harshness of the last weeks.

"Oh, you are a very big man," she said. As he followed Tanya to a couch a mood of delicious euphoria enveloped Jensen. He stretched out, his head on a silken pillow. Tanya opened his shirt and began caressing his chest as Natasha brought over a porcelain dish of yellow-brown opium paste. Tanya placed the dish on a bronze stand, lit a candle, and heated the dish until the opium congealed. Then she kneaded a bit of the warm opium into a ball and tamped the ball into a wooden pipe. "Take it in one draw," she said, as she put a burning taper to the opium.

After three pipes a pleasant lassitude overtook Jensen. After the ninth pipe, he fondled Tanya's breasts as she smiled. But he felt no surge of desire, only an all-engulfing sense of well-being. He could solve all the problems afflicting him. . . . He was drifting now . . . above Tanya's breasts rose the face of Lilian . . . then he was swimming with Lilian to the little island in the lake at Yenching, and then he was leading his father through the Temple of Heaven, showing him the magnificence of the halls as if they were his own.

Far in the distance Jensen heard a woman scream. Suddenly he was shaken roughly. His eyelids fluttered opened and he looked into the contorted features of a Chinese with shaven head. Jensen struggled to rise, but the Chinese clutched him by the hair and two others flipped him over and bound his hands behind his back. Jensen was lifted from the couch and dragged down into the street, where he was pushed into the rear seat of a black Ford sedan. Seconds later Howard was pitched in beside him. From the front seat, the Chinese with the shaven head pointed a pistol at them. The car pulled away from the restaurant, preceded by another sedan whose siren parted the early morning traffic. Jensen shook his head, trying to dispel the fog of alcohol and opium.

"Untie me," he mumbled as Howard, swaying beside him, gasped, "What in hell is going on?" The car jolted to a halt. They were in front of the American hostel. The car door opened and Howard was pushed out onto the sidewalk. With a squeal of brakes, Howard's sedan, which the police had seized, stopped behind them. The driver climbed out, hurled the car keys at Howard, and, pistol in hand, slipped in beside Jensen in the police car. Howard looked in shock after the vanishing Ford.

Jensen felt a pistol muzzle against the side of his head. The car bumped over pocked streets and careened around corners before making an abrupt halt. They had parked in the courtyard of a large red brick government building. Chinese laborers were at work packing documents into cases. They looked up indifferently as Jensen was hustled out of the police car and half-dragged down stone steps into a dark corridor. Pistol muzzle in his back, Jensen was searched and then pushed sprawling into a cell. An iron door clanged shut behind him. The cell was perhaps six feet by twelve feet, with rough mortared walls and no window. A torn mattress, its straw poking out, lay on the cement floor, and in the corner stood two wooden buckets, one half-filled with water. Jensen fumbled in his breast pocket. Lilian's jade was still there. The light from the bulb overhead went out. Jensen felt blindly for the mattress and sat on it, back against the wall, knees drawn up under his chin, arms folded against the damp cold. He lost all sense of how many hours elapsed. What a fool he had been not to heed Philip Fugh's warning. His throat was so dry. He thought of the foul water in the bucket and measured his burning thirst against his fear of dysentery. He crawled to the buckets and drank from his cupped hand.

Jensen was dozing when the light snapped on. He stood up, blinking as the iron door opened and three gendarmes entered. As one held a long-nosed pistol on him, the others turned him around and tied a blindfold over his eyes. Held by his arms with the pistol snout prodding into his back, he was led stumbling along a corridor. There was no sound except the thud of the gendarmes' boots. Struggling up a flight of stairs, he slipped and a boot slammed into his buttocks as he was jerked upright. When the blindfold was removed he was facing a small table, bare except for an American .45-caliber pistol. Behind the table sat a powerfully built man with piercing blue eyes under dark bold eyebrows. He wore a black tunic unbuttoned at the throat. On the wall behind him were photographs of Chiang Kai-shek and Sun Yat-sen. In one corner of the room stood a gendarme wearing a visored cap and armed with a Luger pistol on his leather belt. A bespectacled Chinese in a blue robe was seated beside the table. He held a notebook and pen.

"I am Colonel Liu," the man behind the table said in Chinese. Jensen guessed he was not a Han Chinese . . . the strange blue eyes . . . the accent that suggested he might be from one of the far western provinces. So this was the Blue-Eyed One. "Your whore, Li-nan has told us everything. So answer my questions if you want to live. You are a Communist spy, and we execute spies."

Throttled by apprehension at the mention of Lilian, Jensen replied hoarsely: "She has done nothing."

The colonel gestured angrily. "You are wasting time. Li-nan confessed to being a Communist agent. We may let her live if you cooperate. Now quickly, what was the message you carried to the American ambassador? We know of the letter Li-nan handed you in the restaurant in the Pei Hai Park."

Jensen lowered his eyes. She is alive, he thought gratefully. He collected himself. This beast does not know everything. The colonel was glaring at him, his blue eyes slits, waiting for a reply.

It's all like a bad Hollywood movie, Jensen thought, and this somehow gave him reassurance. "I demand to see an official of the American embassy," he said.

The colonel leaped up and slapped Jensen across the face. "You turtle shit," he shouted. "You will answer. You will learn how we treat spies." His spittle sprayed over the desk. The bespectacled man beside him taking notes wiped his pad with his elbow. "You will know a slow death, like your friend Chi."

A deep roar welled up within Jensen. "Chi . . ." he shouted. "You murderers." Shaking off the hands pinning his arms, Jensen lashed out with his right foot and sent the table crashing against Liu. A trio of gendarmes descended, holding him face down against the floor. Liu stood up unhurt, righted the table, and restored the .45 to its place. The bespectacled Chinese had not moved and was still writing.

"Thank you for confirming your connection to Comrade Chi," Liu said calmly but with rage in his eyes. "Take him back to the cell." The gendarmes pulled Jensen to his feet. He faced Liu, still defiant. "No food," the colonel snapped. As he was being blindfolded, Jensen glanced quickly at the only window in the room, savoring the faint glow of sunshine. It's been one day, he calculated. He was led shuffling back to his cell.

Jensen was lying on his side asleep, his wrists bound behind him with the blindfold askew, when the cell door banged open again and the light came on. The colonel stood over him with two gendarmes at his back. He reached down and roughly pulled Jensen to his feet. "This will be your last chance," the colonel said. He went out of the cell leaving behind the gendarmes, one of them holding a pistol. The other gendarme pulled off the blindfold, looped a rope in a slipknot around Jensen's neck and led him out. They walked down a dimly lit basement corridor past a row of cells, each with a small solid metal door and a peephole. The rope reminded Jensen of the executions he had seen on the square before the Peking railway station. The doomed prisoner was led with a rope around his neck through the press of onlookers into the square and forced to his knees as a soldier with a pistol stepped up to fire a bullet into the back of his bowed head.

At the end of the hallway Jensen was yanked by the rope into a large cell brilliantly lit by two overhead flood lamps. The colonel was seated in a chair resting against a water-stained wall. In the center of the room stood a tall gendarme holding a Luger pistol pointed down. As Jensen was brought before him, the colonel raised his fist and said, "Now, what message did you bring to the ambassador? Answer. If you don't answer, you die here and your whore in Peking will go the same way—after we have played with her."

Jensen looked down at the colonel: the unshaven chin, the twisted mouth, the scar over the cheek now livid. He won't kill me, Jensen thought, measuring the man. He needs to know what I know. "I demand to see an official of the American embassy," Jensen said coolly.

The colonel tipped forward in his chair. "No one knows you are here. You are alone. Once more . . . the last time. What was the message?" The colonel sprang to his feet as Jensen shook his head. "Take him," he said. Jensen was jerked by the rope across the room to the gendarme with the Luger and forced to his knees. Jensen tried to breathe. His thoughts were tumbling. He felt the muzzle of the Luger at the back of his head. The hammer of the gun fell. He heard a click, but then there was nothing. The gendarme put his boot in Jensen's back and pushed him face down onto the wet stone floor. Jensen lay there, his eyes closed. "This was a rehearsal for what will happen when I come for you next," the colonel said.

Having performed the purifying *Ch'i Kung* breathing exercise, Jensen sat on the floor of the cell in the Lotus Position, meditating. He thought of Liu's threat. He had not visibly buckled before Liu. But there had been fear in him, deep fear of death, more so than in the worst days of combat in Burma. Perhaps it stemmed from what was new in his life, from contemplation of what life could offer if he survived and lived with Lilian. No, he was not free of the fear of death, even though he had thought himself wedded to the teachings of Chuang Tzu: *Welcome death as relief from the burdens of earthly existence, of return of the spirit to the body of the cosmos ever-changing, union with the God Force.* I am not yet at one with the Master, Jensen thought.

Jensen was squatting over the bucket, suffering from diarrhea, when the door opened and a gendarme entered, carrying a tray of food, chop-sticks, and a teapot.

He went out and returned with a basin of steaming water and tow-els. He untied Jensen's wrists. "Wash and eat," the gendarme said. "You are being released." Jensen looked at him in disbelief.

Jensen was drinking the last of his tea when the gendarme returned. "Come with me," he said. They went up stairs to a reception alcove where a male clerk sat behind a desk. The clerk opened the door to an inner room. Jensen entered alone. It was a study furnished elegantly with Ming furniture and a blue Sinkiang carpet embossed with white cranes. Dynastic scrolls hung on the yellow walls. Behind a teak desk sat a silver-haired man whose fine features seemed chiseled out of ivory. "Please sit down," he said in unaccented English. "I am Chen Li-fu. I'm sorry you've been inconvenienced." His dark intense eyes took in Jensen's soiled figure. "Our security people are sometimes overzealous."

Jensen looked at him incredulously. "'Inconvenienced,'" he said. "Your Colonel Liu is a savage. What have you done with Li-nan Yang?"

"Li-nan Yang?" Chen said with a puzzled expression. "I do not know of any such person. Please understand, Mr. Jensen, I do not be-come deeply involved in the work of the security police. I'm too busy with Party affairs. Colonel Liu may be able to help you."

Jensen regarded Chen with undisguised fury. "Your Colonel Liu has already stated his price. You'll get no confession from me."

"Do not be so hard on the colonel," Chen said. "You must under-stand why he is such an angry man; why he has such antipathy for Communists. His father was an Amur Cossack officer chased by the So-viets across the Manchurian border. After his father's death, the Colonel took the name of his Chinese mother. He fought courageously against the Japanese. When we returned to Nanking he was given a good house and fine furniture as a reward. Now, like his father, with the Communists approaching, he may be forced to leave everything . . . all that fine furniture. He hates the Communists and anyone who helps them," Chen said, humor in his eyes.

"Li-nan and I . . . we have done nothing to harm China," Jensen said grimly, resenting the way Chen was toying with him. "Also, I don't feel responsible for what may happen to Colonel Liu's furniture."

"Outlooks vary, Mr. Jensen. The colonel has his values. I have mine. And I'm familiar with yours."

A servant entered carrying a tray with a silver teapot which he placed on the glass-topped desk. Chen poured the tea into blue rice china cups. "Lung-ching tea," he said. "Our best green tea . . . from a farm in the West Lake country near Hangchow."

Chen sniffed the tea appreciatively. "You've been consorting with Communist agents," he said between sips. "I don't know precisely your role. But I'm sure," he added, with a slight smile, "that you've been act- ing out of good motives. You often told students in the American Li- brary in Peking that you are devoted to China." Chen sighed. "That's what is so infuriating about you Americans. When we deal with the British or the French or the Japanese they make no secret they act out of self-interest. But you Americans wrap yourselves in your morality and insist you are befriending us . . . that you know what's best for China."

Chen picked up a red jade chop and leaned back in his chair, turning the chop between his palms. "Please understand I'm not anti-American as such. I should tell you I earned a master's degree at the University of Pittsburgh School of Mines. I lived among your people. I found their in- nocence about China charming."

Jensen was startled when Chen suddenly pitched forward in his chair and slammed the chop down on his desk. "But suffering the naïveté of your government has been too high a price to pay for your guns. You've weakened us rather than strengthened us. At first you tied our hands by demanding we negotiate peace with the Communists. Now you abandon us as the Communists exploit the opportunity you gave them."

Jensen shifted in his chair as he felt sharp diarrhea pains in his bowels. What a time to talk politics and ideology, he agonized. Yearning for an end to the meeting, he kept silent.

"The Generalissimo has ordered us to release you," Chen said. "Ambassador Stuart requested it of him. Chinese do not forget to serve old friends, even when they become aged and childlike. Also," Chen said, grimacing, "the two are Christians. You know, of course, that the Generalissimo is a Methodist. He was converted by Madame Chiang at the time of their marriage. He finds it useful to bring his Christianity to the notice of Americans."

Chen rose. "Mr. Jensen, a car is waiting for you in the courtyard." Chen's features hardened. "It would be better if you returned to the United States very soon. You are in some ways typical of your countrymen. Blundering about China . . . full of goodwill, but not quite understanding us. These are difficult days, Mr. Jensen. At times, to survive, we resort to desperate measures."

Chapter Twenty-four

Jensen found the door of his room at the hostel unlocked. Philip Fugh was seated in the armchair reading the paperback that Jensen had left on the bed two days earlier. The ambassador's secretary glanced up as Jensen entered. "Good morning," he said, and then he resumed reading.

Jensen wearily slipped the overcoat from his aching shoulders and hurried into the bathroom. He showered, shaved, and put on the slacks and shirt hanging behind the door. He emerged in stocking feet and stretched out on the bed, muffling a groan. After a few minutes he opened his eyes, swung about, and sat cross-legged with his head bowed. He raised his right hand in a fist and pounded it into the palm of the other.

As Jensen let his hands fall and closed his eyes, Fugh managed a polite little cough. "I'm sorry you've had a difficult time," he said. "Forgive me, but I must ask. Did they compel you to reveal what was in Professor Chang's letter?"

"No," Jensen said, as he planted his feet on the floor and rubbed his bruised knees. "But they know some things. They assume I delivered a message. They knew about my contact at Yenching. To make me talk they put me on my knees . . . with a pistol to the head . . . as if they were going to blow out my brains. I didn't tell them anything."

"You were very courageous, Mr. Jensen. Fortunately they didn't torture you physically in the usual ways. Colonel Liu guessed we might obtain your release. He knew your courier friend would raise the alarm. They didn't want to leave the evidence of scars on your body. But you showed, my friend, that you were ready to sacrifice your life for China."

Jensen rubbed his knees again. "China, Mr. Fugh? On my knees all I thought about was staying alive. And about Lilian."

Fugh adjusted his glasses, his brow wrinkled. "Lilian?"

Jensen began to pace the room. His voice was strained when he replied. "She's a student at Yenching. She was my contact with the professor. She arranged for the letter to be passed to me." Looking to Fugh for understanding, Jensen said softly: "I'm in love with her. Liu, that filthy animal, said they have her . . . that she confessed. I don't believe it."

"I hope you'll meet her again," Fugh said. "This war will not go on forever. But for now it's best you return to the United States. To obtain your release we pledged you would leave China soon."

Jensen wheeled about. "No," he said tautly. "I'm going back to Peking. I've delivered the letter. Now I'm going to back to find Lilian. She needs me."

Fugh's face hardened. "That would be senseless. If the police have the woman, you won't be able to see her. If not, she'll be in the Communist-held areas. Chen Li-fu's agents will never allow you to enter there."

"I'll find her," Jensen said.

"You'll be in great danger. You are easy to track. People will remember you . . . the tall red one. You could end up on some garbage heap . . . with dogs tearing at your body. You wouldn't be the first foreigner to disappear."

"I'll risk it."

Fugh went to the radio in the corner, found a Chinese music program, turned the volume up, and drew Jensen down on the couch beside him. "Jensen, listen to me. The situation in Peking is critical. The Nationalist troops are dug in for street-to-street fighting. They've positioned their gun emplacements in the shelter of the monuments. If they draw Communist fire many people will be killed. Many of the palaces and temples in the Imperial City will be destroyed. Food supplies in the city are running out. The people may riot and begin looting. But there's hope. The ambassador has persuaded the Vice President to send a secret envoy to Peking. He'll carry a letter authorizing Fu Tso-yi to surrender the city. But if you return to Peking it's possible you'll draw Chen Li-fu's agents upon us and endanger the plan."

"I won't get in the way," Jensen said. "You owe this to me."

The two men looked steadily at each other without speaking. Fugh sighed, openly dismayed. The radio was crackling with a commercial for Tiger Balm Lotion. *Try it. It will stop any pain . . . cure any . . .* When the music resumed, Fugh said in a low urgent voice: "All right. Listen. Tomorrow morning go to the China National Aviation office on Nanking Road. Make a reservation for the plane that leaves for Shanghai on Sunday, January second. Make another reservation on the Pan American plane that leaves Shanghai the following Monday for San Francisco. They'll say you're on the waiting list. Return to the office two days before the flight and pick up your ticket. Chen Li-fu's men will have instructed the airline to issue it. The embassy will have paid for it. This was agreed to last night." Leaning closer to Jensen, Fugh whispered, "But I'll be making other arrangements. On New Year's

Day, come at four o'clock to the diplomatic reception at the ambassador's residence. Do not bring any baggage with you. Do not expect to return to this hostel. Do you understand?"

Jensen nodded. As Fugh rose to go, Jensen put out his hand, but Fugh ignored it. "Perhaps you've forgotten. Tonight is Christmas Eve," he said. "The ambassador thought you should not be left alone. He also wants to brief you. We'll come for you at eight." He turned and walked out the door without saying good-bye.

◆

Precisely at eight, the ambassador's Cadillac parked before the hostel. "Merry Christmas," Jensen said wryly, as he eased his bruised body onto the soft cushions. Fugh, who was sitting on the other side of the ambassador, sniffed irritably.

"We're going to the Song of Victory Church, Mr. Jensen," the ambassador said. "It's a Methodist Church. It was built for Chinese officials at the request of Madame Chiang. The Generalissimo invited me to the Christmas service."

The car went along Pei-ching Boulevard through the Great Peace Gate in the eastern wall, past Lotus Lake to the slopes of Purple Mountain. At the church, Nationalist sentries armed with Thompson submachine guns stood beside the festive Christmas trees that flanked the entrance.

The ambassador led the way into one of the wooden pews already crowded with uniformed Chinese Army officers, officials in black tunics, and their wives in silk *cheongsams*. The walls of the church were hung with scrolls bearing religious texts in Chinese characters. Arranged about the pulpit were vases filled with white chrysanthemums, the Chinese flower of immortality. Jensen was thumbing through one of the Chinese-language Bibles when the Generalissimo entered, inclining his shaven head to the congregation. He was dressed in the black jacket and long blue robe of a Chinese gentleman. As he walked to the front pew he smiled at the ambassador, uttering his usual greeting: "*Hao, hao.*"

"Where's Madame?" Jensen asked the ambassador in a whisper.

"In Washington. She went to ask for more aid."

A Chinese pastor in clerical garb opened the service with a Christmas carol. The Generalissimo joined in with his strong Chekiang accent. Father would be very much at home here, Jensen thought.

Driving back down the mountain after the service in a procession of limousines, Jensen remarked: "Up there, the Gimmo didn't seem to be such a monster."

The ambassador glanced sharply at him. "The President is an upright man, not corrupt like many about him. He leads an austere life dedicated to his country."

"Then why are we conspiring against him?" Jensen said, bridling at the rebuke.

Fugh touched the glass partition separating them from the chauffeur, making sure it was tightly shut.

"One must understand," the ambassador replied, "the President is a Confucian more than a Christian or a modern man. He sees the Communists as destroyers of the traditional fabric of Chinese society. He was bred in the warlord era. The death and destruction of civil war does not weaken his resolve. Nanking has been his capital. He's not very concerned about imperial Peking. He believes if he prolongs the civil war the United States will eventually join him in a holy crusade against the Communists. I oppose what he's doing. But one cannot say he is an unprincipled man."

When the car reached the Great Peace Gate, the ambassador cleared his throat and said, "The Generalissimo called me to his office last night to tell me he's going to resign as President. He will make the announcement on New Year's Day. Li Tsung-jen will be named Acting President."

"An act of Confucian humility in the face of national adversity," Fugh said in a challenging tone that surprised Jensen. "It's a tactic. He'll keep command of the Army and the secret police while he builds his Formosa fortress. Li Tsung-jen will have little power."

"But sufficient for our immediate purpose," the ambassador said firmly. "When Fu Tso-yi receives the letter signed by Li Tsung-jen as Acting President, it will convince him to surrender Peking. No one will be able to charge him with being a coward or a traitor."

"But how . . ." Jensen began, but was interrupted by Fugh.

"Not now," Fugh snapped. The car was at Jensen's hostel. "We'll see you at four at the ambassador's residence on New Year's Day."

"Merry Christmas," the ambassador called after Jensen.

◆

On Christmas Day, Jensen went to the airline office as Fugh had instructed and made his bookings for Shanghai and San Francisco. He took a ricksha back to the hostel. It was raining. He settled back under the canvas top as the coolie trotted past squalid houses and open lots where chickens pecked at garbage strewn beside frozen puddles. "Christmas," Jensen muttered. Time was dragging miserably. So many uncertainties. What had happened to Lilian? Could he rely on Fugh to arrange his return to Peking? Arriving at the hostel, the ricksha man, a gaunt refugee in a soiled soldier's shirt, asked: "You likee girlie?" Jensen shook his head curtly. "You likee suckee?" Jensen threw a handful of yuan at the coolie and went to his room.

Chapter Twenty-five

Jensen was awakened early New Year's Day by Fugh, telephoning to confirm their rendezvous. "Ambassador Stuart wishes to invite you to his New Year's diplomatic reception," he said perfunctorily, words meant for those who might be listening. "Please join us at the residence at five thirty. And the ambassador also suggests," Fugh added dryly, "you attend the ceremony today at noon at the Sun Yat-sen Memorial. A propos your conversation with him, the ambassador suggests you see another side of the President."

Jensen telephoned Howard, proposing they view the ceremony and enjoy an outing in the countryside. In an embassy jeep they drove up Purple Mountain to the white and blue-tiled mausoleum of Sun Yat-sen. They joined a large crowd of Chinese officials in formal attire, officers in dress uniform and diplomats awaiting the arrival of the Generalissimo. The officials were grouped at the foot of the Spirit Way, white stone steps ascending to the Memorial Hall. In keeping with tradition, the President would mount the Spirit Way to honor the memory of the founder of the Republic who had led the 1911 revolution against the Manchus. The annual ritual was a symbolic celebration of eternal Nationalist rule. As Jensen strolled through the crowd with Howard he heard talk that belied the pretense of the ceremony. Farewells were being exchanged. "The passing of yet another dynasty," Jensen heard a British diplomat remark.

The Generalissimo arrived in a black Cadillac. From his office in the Tai Ping Palace he had already broadcast his intention to retire as president. He greeted the assemblage with smiles and small bows. Over his brown-belted uniform he wore a cloak against the morning chill. Approaching the Spirit Way through a corridor of great deodar cedars, he swept the cloak from his shoulders and handed it to an aide. He mounted the one hundred steps to the Memorial Hall between rows of soldiers standing rigidly at attention. At the top of the monument he bowed three times before the white marble statue of Sun Yat-sen and then paused, gazing beyond the hills at his capital.

Jensen could imagine what the Generalissimo was thinking: This had been his capital since 1928. Leading the Northern Expedition, he had marched from the southern province of Kwangtung to seize this center of power on the banks of the Yangtze. He battled and intrigued with the warlords along the way in the savage politics of that time seeking fulfillment of the Sun Yat-sen dream of a united republic. Yes, he had succeeded in this endeavor and had gained the recognition of the great foreign powers. Yet one unrelenting challenge to his authority remained: the Communists. Even in the struggle against Japan, when there was an American-imposed truce, he had maneuvered against Mao Tse-tung, knowing that the ultimate contest for power would come after the end of World War II. Now, with the core of his army annihilated in the Battle of the Huai-Hai and in Manchuria, the Communists would soon be at the gates of Nanking. It was time to leave. His Formosa refuge was being fortified. It was from there that he would prepare to recapture the mainland.

The Generalissimo saluted and walked down the Spirit Way, smiling and bowing before he entered his limousine.

"He's saying good-bye to the mainland . . . everyone knows it," Jensen said, not without a tinge of sympathy.

"And it's bye-bye for me too," Howard said cheerfully. "Let's go. I'm leaving for Canton. Then out to Hong Kong and Washington. This party is over. You're lucky to be getting out tomorrow."

"You never know until you're on that airplane," Jensen said.

◆

Jensen was at the hostel desk asking for his room key when a familiar voice said: "Good afternoon, Mr. Jensen." Turning, he came face to face with a man in the uniform of an American Army colonel. It was Smith, one hand thrust into a pocket of his trench coat, leaning on a cane. A chill enveloped Jensen.

"I've been waiting for you, Mr. Jensen. For quite some time." Smith smiled. "You've been busy. Can we chat?"

"Good afternoon," Jensen said. "In my room?"

"Better in the cafeteria. Noisy. More secure . . . you understand . . . yes? You've become more expert in these matters since I saw you last. How about a cup of a tea?

"You've been into a lot of things," Smith said as they settled themselves at a corner table. "Colonel Liu has kept us apprised of your activities. We cooperate with the colonel on occasion. Incidentally, we had nothing to do with that collision you had with a truck in Peking," Smith added dryly. He sipped his tea and made a sour face. "I prefer

Chinese tea. So. You've chatted with the Blue-Eyed One. Nasty fellow, but usually quite efficient. Unlike the colonel, we've had no objections to your association with Professor Chang. In fact, we approved of the contact. We tracked your friendship with Chi from the start. And later with that charming girl, Li-nan. Your relations with them, and presumably with the Communists, made you even more valuable to us than we'd hoped." Smith beamed. "That's why we let you coast after you left the Language School. We always knew we could regain control. Chen Li-fu and his colonel, of course, haven't been players in our game."

"And where are we now?" Jensen said.

"Unfortunately, the game is over," Smith said with a sigh. "There's been a leak. Distressing. Truly distressing. Very unfortunate for our country's future relations with China."

"What does it have to do with me?" Jensen asked impatiently.

"A lot, my friend. At this moment the House Committee on Un-American Activities is grubbing for proof that there's been a conspiracy involving the CIA, the State Department, and the White House to hand China over to Mao. 'Who lost China?' is the war cry. The witch hunters have burned some State Department types at the stake, accusing them of being friendly to the Chinese Communists. Now they're hunting for a link to the White House. The Committee has gotten wind of Wagging Pipit . . . to them, prima facie evidence of a Communist plot. The leak came from a talkative officer of the agency. He didn't like what we were doing. Fortunately, he was never fully briefed on the operation. But he did give the committee the names of three American agents who he said were in China developing close ties to the Communists." Smith cocked his head and regarded Jensen with a smile. "Yes," he said, "the director of the agency has testified under oath that Wagging Pipit was considered but never launched. And he denied any knowledge of the three agents. The committee doesn't believe him. Two staffers of the Committee are in Nanking—*here, now*—trying to locate those agents. All they have are three names. They are spreading quite a net. If any one of those three people should talk . . . any one of them . . . all those involved, directly or indirectly, in the plan to open lines to Mao could be destroyed. With anti-Communist fever gripping the whole country, it could sink the administration. People in high places are worried . . . in a great sweat, I'd say." Smith refilled his teacup. "And especially my people."

"So," Jensen said uneasily.

"Yes," Smith said. "Only three names. One of those people is out of reach. "You're one of the other two."

Jensen emptied his cup. "Go on," he said, bracing himself.

"We have a way out. You're scheduled to fly to Shanghai tomorrow. At the Shanghai airfield Liu's agents will be watching to make sure you get on the plane for San Francisco. But as you walk across the tarmac to the plane, a half dozen men in U.S. Army uniforms will join the line waiting to board the plane. There'll be a lot of jostling and you'll be hustled by my people into a fuel truck under the wing of the plane. Don't resist. Later you'll be on a plane for Australia. You'll be enrolled under another identity as a graduate student at the University of Melbourne. We'll supply your academic documentation. Stay there for two years, maybe less, until the congressional investigations blow over . . . and the politicos turn to some other stunt. We'll pay your expenses . . . and more."

Jensen looked at Smith stunned. "I need time to think this over."

"There isn't time. *Do it, Eric*. I'd like to see you stay healthy and happy." Smith's lips curled. "And yes, *I'd* like to stay healthy and happy, too." A soldier walking by the table glanced curiously at the two men, one leaning toward the other.

Jensen toyed with his teacup and looked into it. "All right," he said. His thoughts were already turning on escape to Peking. Disappear in China. Somewhere . . . with Lilian. Away from all this.

"Excellent," Smith said. "Incidentally, Eric, the University of Melbourne has an outstanding department of Chinese philosophy. I should mention one other thing. Do you know Sanford McCormack, professor of history at Sun Yat-sen University in Canton?"

Jensen shook his head.

"He's been one of your colleagues in our enterprise. Young American, not much older than you, very talented, beloved by his students. Like you, he made some very interesting and useful contacts. Regrettably he's one of the three. For a time, he disappointed us by being reluctant to leave China. Then, however, he had quite a fright. He's been working for years on a biography of the first emperor of China. You know Chin Shih Huang Ti, of course. Very mysteriously, his manuscript, his notes, and all his other research materials disappeared. Just disappeared," Smith said, arching his eyebrows. "It could have been worse. He might have disappeared himself. However, it's all ended happily. We were able to help the professor find his papers. He's now comfortably continuing his work in another country. And with an excellent East Asian library very near by!" Smith exclaimed.

Jensen averted his eyes from Smith's taunting smile, thinking of his own treasured manuscripts in Peking. "You said there were two others. Who's the third?"

"Yes, we'll be looking for you tomorrow," Smith said rising. "Happy New Year, Eric."

Jensen went to his room, weighing the chances of survival. If he escaped to Peking, Smith would team up with Liu to track him down. Jensen began considering the possibility of sheltering with the Communists. But first, he must find Lilian.

Thrusting the meeting with Smith out of his mind, Jensen dressed for the embassy reception. He carefully left his few possessions in their customary places, went down to the lobby, and asked the clerk to get him a pedicab. When he arrived at the ambassador's residence, the street was blocked with limousines bearing official license plates. Jensen made his way through a knot of gossiping Chinese chauffeurs to the gate, where he was admitted by a Marine in blue dress uniform. In the foyer of the residence, Jensen encountered Henderson. The ambassador's aide hailed him with outstretched arms. Jensen struggled to smile.

"Come, Mr. Jensen, I'd like you to meet our minister-counselor," Henderson said, as a servant took Jensen's overcoat. Henderson escorted him into an adjoining reception room away from the receiving line where the ambassador was greeting guests. "The minister really runs the embassy, you know," he whispered, as they entered the cream-colored drawing room. Heads turned, and there was a buzz from the Chinese and foreign guests conversing in knots. Everyone seemed to be turning to stare at the unfamiliar tall man in the tweed jacket. The minister, a heavyset man with elegantly coiffed steel-gray hair, was chatting with two bemedaled Nationalist generals, but he turned expectantly as Henderson arrived with Jensen.

"Ah, you're the young man who has had so many adventures," the minister said. "You've become very friendly with our ambassador."

"He's been very kind to me," Jensen said.

"Yes, the ambassador is a marvelous old man. We all adore him. A great symbol of our friendship with China. Keeps struggling for a compromise with the Communists . . . hopeless, of course." The minister smiled. "I'm sure you understand that, Mr. Jensen?"

"So I've been told," Jensen said.

"Have you been able to contact your family about that terrible accident?"

Jensen was caught off guard. He had almost forgotten the excuse he had given Blanche in pleading for travel orders to Nanking. "Yes, thank you," he muttered.

"Well," the minister said, patting Jensen on the arm. "I'm delighted you're leaving for the States tomorrow to be with your family. By the way, before you leave we'd like you to meet two of our officials. They're from Washington. By coincidence they are returning to the States on your plane. They could be helpful in arranging for you to sail through customs and get transportation home. Would that be convenient?"

"Fine," Jensen said.

"Then you'll meet them tomorrow morning. Henderson will make the arrangements. Have a good trip," the minister said, turning back to the generals.

Jensen felt a tap on his shoulder. It was the ambassador, who had left the receiving line.

"I've done my duty as host," the ambassador said, grasping Jensen's hand. "Now come, let me introduce you to my very good friend, K. M. Pannikar, the Indian ambassador. He's the best-informed diplomat in Nanking. I confide in him." With Jensen trailing him, the ambassador threaded through the throng and hailed a short, dark man with a Vandyke beard. "Mr. Ambassador, this is Eric Jensen. Now, pardon me, I must have a word with the Russian ambassador."

"I know about you," the Indian said, his brows lifted over dark, mischievous eyes. He extended a limp hand to Jensen while he watched with an amused expression as the American ambassador hurried across the room to a stocky, jovial man wearing the uniform of a Soviet general. The Russian was laughing loudly and gesturing before the group pressing about him.

"General Roshchin has reason to smile. He's doing very well," the Indian said, substituting his empty glass for a gin and tonic offered by a servant. Jensen selected a glass of white wine. "Look at that crowd around him," the ambassador said, pointing with his drink. Clustered about the Russian were several diplomats, a Chinese Catholic bishop in white pontifical robes, a government official, and two Nationalist generals.

"The Russian is playing them off against each other," Pannikar said. "He teased your ambassador by offering to set up negotiations with the Communists. The ambassador, poor man, got his knuckles rapped by Washington simply for communicating the offer. The Soviets must be enjoying it all." The Indian continued to chat with Jensen, but his eyes were on the ambassador, who was now in earnest conversation with the Russian near a bay window overlooking the garden.

Pannikar chuckled. "Great play," he said. "Our Nationalist friends offering mining and trade rights in Sinkiang to the Soviets if they'll persuade Mao Tse-tung not to go south of the Yangtze. All this in addition to those concessions in Manchuria at Dairen and Port Arthur . . . the gift to Stalin at Yalta. And once Mao takes control he'll have no one to turn to except the Russians for aid." The Indian chuckled again, his beard twitching. "Diplomatic roulette— and the Russian wins no matter how the wheel spins."

Jensen reached for another glass of wine from a passing tray. He was irritated by the Indian's smug tone. "And the Chinese people, Mr. Ambassador, how will it play out for them?"

The Indian shrugged. "Victims. But only for a time. Eventually, as in the past, the Chinese will find a way to wring out the foreigners . . . the Russians as well . . . and pitch us out when we're no longer useful. As a matter of fact," he said, his manner becoming stiff, "they are starting with you, the Americans."

Jensen was joined by Philip Fugh as the Indian strolled away with a wave of his hand. "You've had a chat with the American minister-counselor?" Fugh asked. "Despicable man. A true representative of the new

American policy." He sighed. "I suppose I should cultivate him. I'll be needing an American visa soon."

Jensen evinced surprise. "You'll be leaving China?"

"Certainly. Under the Communists there'll be no place for people like me." Fugh took off his horn-rimmed glasses and polished them with a white silk handkerchief. He smiled sardonically. "We're class enemies, corrupted by the West. They'll never trust us, no matter how much we've done for China. People like me are being crushed between Chiang Kai-shek and Mao." He looked away. "You've met the exiled White Russians? Well, I'm about to become a White Chinese." He replaced his glasses. "Enough. Come with me."

"Wait," Jensen said, his hand on Fugh's arm. Across the room he could see Smith in Army dress uniform chatting with a Chinese official. Smith returned his gaze and bowed, a slight mocking bow.

Jensen inclined his head. "That man. The one in the American uniform. You know him?"

"Of course . . . Colonel Richardson, the assistant military attaché. He's a specialist on the Chinese Communist leadership. Come, we don't have much time." He led Jensen into a library alcove that was free of the crowd. "The ambassador's courier plane leaves for Peking at daybreak to evacuate some of the women and children of the consulate," Fugh said. "It will land on the new airstrip on the glacis near the Legation Quarter. Colonel Carson, our air attaché, will be the pilot. He's here tonight with his crew. You'll be on his plane."

Jensen attempted a question, but Fugh silenced him. "Everything will be explained." He glanced about. "Remain in the residence. At five thirty go into the kitchen. There's the door. A servant will be waiting to guide you." Fugh strolled out of the alcove.

Jensen returned to the party, which already was thinning. He approached a young couple who were laughing uproariously and introduced himself. The woman, a beautiful, dark-haired girl, let her wide green eyes run up and down Jensen's figure, the shaggy hair, the combat boots, the sports jacket and the overly long slacks purchased from the Twenty Four-Hour Tailor. Shaking her head in astonishment, she extended her hand with a gay smile. Her companion shook hands with Jensen cordially. They had been speaking in French but slipped easily into English for Jensen. She was the daughter of the Italian ambassador. He was the third secretary of the French embassy.

"Louis was telling me," the girl said laughing, "how he went around to the quarters of the Military Advisory Group just after they flew off. He picked over what the servants hadn't looted . . . and liberated a case of Listerine. The Chinese tasted only one bottle, found it was not scotch, and left the case. No one quarreled with Louis when he carried it off. What a coup! Mouthwash is unobtainable in Nanking."

Jensen joined in the general titter while observing the couple enviously, thinking of how long it had been since he and Lilian had laughed together.

It was six forty-five. The White Russian orchestra was playing "The Surrey with the Fringe on Top." Jensen slipped away and followed one of the servants who was carrying an empty tray into the kitchen. Another servant was waiting for him just inside the swinging door. Jensen was quickly led up the back stairs. When he entered the bedroom on the first landing he found five men already there. Fugh was seated on a white sofa beside an American colonel in a brown dress uniform, evidently the air attaché. Standing in a corner were a captain and two enlisted men. Jensen noticed that his overcoat was lying on the large double bed together with the coats and hats of the airmen. Fugh did not bother to introduce Jensen. "The ambassador will be here soon," he said. They waited in unbroken silence, the military men exchanging puzzled glances.

Stuart entered a few minutes later. In a thin but firm voice, the ambassador addressed the air attaché: "Colonel Carson, there's been a change of plans for your flight to Peking. You'll be accompanied by this gentleman, Eric Jensen, who is on a special mission, and also by a Chinese government representative, Ho Ssu-yuan, the former mayor of Peking."

The colonel, a tall, middle-aged man with a lean jutting jaw, protested. "But, Ambassador, I can't transport them without orders."

"Colonel, Mr. Jensen has travel orders issued by the consulate in Peking, as you'll see," the ambassador said, raising his voice slightly and adopting a commanding manner that Jensen had not witnessed before. "The mayor will be carrying a letter from me authorizing his transportation. He'll join you at the airfield shortly before daybreak. The mayor will also be carrying a pass from the office of the Vice President that will admit him at the gate."

The colonel, his lips compressed, nodded.

"One other detail, Colonel. It is imperative for the security of his mission that Mr. Jensen not be recognized as he leaves the residence. Therefore, you'll take him in your car from the garage area. Mr. Jensen will stay with you tonight in your quarters and go to the airfield with you in the morning."

The colonel's jaw went slack and his eyes darted to Jensen and back to the ambassador. "I can't do this without checking with the chancellery."

"You're forgetting, Colonel . . . you and your plane are assigned to me . . . personally. That's all the checking you need to do."

The colonel turned to the taller of the two enlisted men. "All right, McPherson, give your hat to this guy. He'll need it in the car when we go past the guards by the gate."

The sergeant hesitated. "But, Colonel . . . "

Carson reddened. "Damn it, sergeant, you heard what the ambassador said."

Jensen was trying on the hat, pressing it down hard to make it fit, as Fugh said, "Very becoming, Mr. Jensen. May I have a word with you?" Jensen followed Fugh into an adjoining room.

"As you've probably guessed, the mayor has the letter for Fu Tso-yi authorizing surrender of Peking," Fugh said. "Li Tsung-jen has signed it as Acting President. Everything depends on that letter being delivered."

"I understand," Jensen said. "I'll do everything I can to help."

"Also, Jensen, you must be aware you'll be in great danger. The embassy plane will arrive in Peking at about eleven o'clock tomorrow morning. You'll have only a few hours to go underground. The airline flight to Shanghai departs tomorrow at two o'clock. When you fail to appear, Liu's agents will be after you." With his hand on the doorknob, Fugh paused. "Take my advice, Eric. Stay underground until the Communists occupy Peking. Then you can begin looking for Lilian."

Chapter Twenty-six

As the first light of dawn filtered through the mist on Shanghai's South Field, Jensen boarded the embassy plane with the air attaché, the copilot, and the crew sergeant. A car drew alongside and the former mayor, a slender, hollow-cheeked man dressed in a black Western business suit, hurried up the steps carrying a small suitcase and a leather briefcase. Jensen greeted him in Chinese and took him to the cockpit to meet the colonel and his copilot. The colonel switched on the twin engines as soon as introductions were made. The plane thundered down the runway, swung over the smog-covered city, crossed the Yangtze, and settled into a course for Peking.

"I am happy to be returning to Peking," the mayor said to Jensen conversationally, as the engines subsided into a steady drone. "I was born there, educated at Pei-ta University. My family still lives there. I am not going to Formosa like the others. It would be safe . . . and comfortable. But I would find it unbearable to be away from Peking. I want my grave to be near those of my ancestors."

"I can understand why the Vice President selected you for the mission," Jensen said.

"It is more difficult, Mr. Jensen, for me to understand why you risk so much for us."

Jensen looked for a moment at the cockpit door on which was pasted a photograph of Franklin D. Roosevelt and then said quietly, "When I was a boy my father asked me to put coins in our church offering box . . . to help the Chinese people. Perhaps I am still doing that."

The mayor closed his eyes and folded his hands over the briefcase on his lap. "I hope, Mr. Jensen, you will find your coins well spent. It may take some time before you receive interest on your investment."

Shortly before eleven o'clock the sergeant poked his head out of the cockpit. "Fasten your seat belts. We'll be landing soon. We're going in steep to dodge any groundfire from the Chicoms."

The plane began to circle. Jensen looked out through the small cabin window relishing the sun-burnished splendor of Peking. He quickly located the new airstrip, a gash in the field where foreign garrisons once played polo. The plane passed over the airstrip twice but did not descend.

Finally the colonel entered the cabin, his jaw set tautly. "There's a problem. We've been in contact with the air controller. He tells us the airstrip is surrounded by gendarmes, not the regular police or troops. I asked the controller to have the consulate send a car for us. But the gendarmes are barring all cars from the field. They're aware the mayor is on the plane. No mention made of you, Jensen. Whatever the problem, we'll have to land soon. Our fuel is low."

The mayor stiffened, clutching his briefcase more tightly. "Mr.

Jensen, I must speak to you alone before we land. It is very important."

As the colonel returned to the cockpit, Jensen turned to the mayor: "You understood?"

"Yes," the mayor said. "There is something I must tell you. Before we left Nanking, I was told Fu Tso-yi's troops would be in control of the airfield. If Chen Li-fu's gendarmes have taken over the airfield, it means there was a leak from the Vice President's office. Chen Li-fu is still loyal to Chiang Kai-shek. Chen's secret police must be waiting for me on the airstrip. The chief of his secret police, the Blue-Eyed One, must suspect that I am carrying word to Fu Tso-yi about the surrender of Peking. But, Mr. Jensen, they do not know you are on the plane." With trembling hands he opened his briefcase and took out a long rice-paper envelope. "Here, Mr. Jensen, you are the only one who can deliver the letter to Fu Tso-yi."

Jensen looked in consternation into the mayor's ashen face and then at the envelope in his extended hand. "Mr. Jensen," the mayor begged. "I was instructed to pass the letter to you if I was trapped by Chen Li-fu's agents."

Jensen hesitated. I'm in for it, he thought. Two sets of killers would be after him when he didn't show at the Nanking airfield, either to get on the plane as Liu expected, or on the flight with the Smith people. How could he dodge them, deliver the letter, and at the same time search for Lilian?

As the plane nosed into its descent Jensen reluctantly accepted the envelope. The mayor fell back in his seat and sighed. "Thank you, Mr. Jensen, thank you for this last coin."

The plane went into its steep landing approach and flattened out hard on the runway. Once they came to a full stop, the sergeant opened the hatch and let down the steps. The mayor stood up, blocking the aisle, as the colonel emerged from the cockpit. "I suggest you let me go out first and alone. It will be less troublesome for you," the mayor said calmly.

Jensen translated: "There's a good reason, Colonel. I suggest you do what he asks."

"Okay, okay," the colonel barked in exasperation.

The mayor picked up his suitcase and briefcase. "Good-bye, Mr. Jensen," he said. "Thank you." He walked down the steps onto the tarmac. A black Ford whipped across the field to the plane. Two Chinese in black tunics scrambled out, seized the mayor, and pushed him roughly into the backseat. The car wheeled about at high speed and raced away, jolting over the rough field.

Jensen waited, sweating. He's leading them away from me, Jensen thought. They don't know I'm on the plane. My God, what will they do to him? As he waited, Jensen recalled what Philip Fugh had told him: "You'll have only a few hours to go underground before Chen Li-fu's men begin looking for you."

"All right, let's go," the colonel shouted. Jensen went down the steps followed by the crew. The gendarmes were leaving, climbing into large trucks. From the Legation Quarter bouncing across the field came three Chevrolet sedans that Jensen recognized as cars of the consulate. Then, amazed, he saw a jeep careen in front of them. It was the French lieutenant.

Jensen ran to the jeep as it veered close to the plane. "Jean, am I glad to see you." Leone swung out of the jeep and embraced Jensen.

"*Mon ami*, I'm happy to see you, too. I heard the embassy plane was coming from Nanking. Thought you might be on it. Where's your baggage?"

"I've got no baggage. I'll explain later," Jensen said hurriedly. "Let's go. Fast." The driver of one of the consulate sedans shouted. Jensen pretended not to hear. "Go, Jean," he said urgently.

As the lieutenant sped toward the Legation Quarter, Jensen quickly repeated the story of Lilian and the letter. He made no mention of the Smith people.

"*Mon Dieu*, what a tale!" Leone said, shaking his head. "Eric, you are something else. But how can you deliver this letter? Every gendarme in Peking will be after you."

"I'll find a way," Jensen said, his face drawn. "I'll also find Lilian."

Leone laughed mockingly. "*Bien sur. Ah, ha*. The woman. That explains everything."

Jensen, not amused, bit his lip. "I care enough for Peking to risk my skin," he said. "But I'm not going to be just a tool. The Communists can have Peking without a fight. Fu Tso-yi can have the deal he wants. But they'd better take me to Lilian."

The lieutenant maneuvered around the sandbagged gun emplacements at street intersections. He pulled the jeep over to the curb when a truck filled with gendarmes, some of them holding broadswords, sped by. "One of the new discipline squads," the lieutenant said. "Nice boys. They have the power to execute violators of the martial law on the spot. You'll see some beheading."

The lieutenant drove along Wai Chao Pu Street and turned down the hutung to his house. "Eric, you're right," he said. "It'll be too dangerous for you in my house. I'll arrange for you to stay in the home of a friend on Hatamen Street. But there's time for you to pick up a few things." Leone grinned and plucked the Army cap resting askew on Jensen's head. "I've even got a fur hat for you."

The Frenchman drew up before his house. As he parked against the compound wall, a shabby gray sedan came speeding down the hutung toward them and halted with a jerk alongside the jeep. A tall, thin, bespectacled Chinese in a long gray gown vaulted out of the backseat. In his hand was a long-nosed Japanese pistol that he pointed at Leone.

"Don't move, Lieutenant. I do not wish to shoot you," the Chinese said calmly in English. "Now turn off your engine. Throw the keys to me." As the lieutenant tossed the key onto the street, the Chinese said "Come with me, Mr. Jensen. We are from Lilian and Teng Hsieh. Please get into our car."

Jensen climbed eagerly out of the jeep. "Jean, it's okay. They'll take me to Lilian."

"It may be a trick," the lieutenant said, motioning toward the gun.

"It's my only chance. I've got to go with them," Jensen said, and he ducked into the backseat of the sedan.

"Don't move . . . do not fear for your friend," the Chinese said, still waving his pistol at the Frenchman as he eased into the sedan beside Jensen. He threw the jeep keys out of the window. As the sedan went back down the hutung, two pedicabs parked against the opposite compound wall suddenly swung out in front of the lieutenant's jeep, blocking the way.

◆

The sedan was being driven expertly by a woman. Her hair was square-cut short, and she was dressed in a blue peasant tunic. In the backseat the Chinese leaned back smiling jovially as he tucked the pistol into his robe.

"My name is Han," the Chinese said. "Recognize me? No? Think back to the Pei Hai Park. After picking up the letter at the White Dagoba you went to the rack at the gate to get your bicycle. There was a man unlocking a bicycle who said to you: 'It is a good time to go. A storm is coming.' That was I." He smiled. "It was not a chance encounter. I'm a member of the political section of the People's Liberation Army."

"I remember you," Jensen said. "But Lilian . . . what's happened to Lilian? Do the police have her?"

"No. After the student messenger was killed on the bridge in the Pei Hai, the police agents went back to the Fang Shan Restaurant. They arrested the waiter who had delayed them as they were running after the student. We believe they beat him until he confessed that he had passed Lilian's signal to the student. But by that time Lilian had already left the park. She is with us. She's safe."

"When can I see her?"

"It can be arranged. You've been away from Peking for many days. The situation is critical. Lin Piao must soon bring the siege to an end. His army is needed in the south. You have a message for Fu Tso-yi?"

Jensen hesitated. Should he withhold the letter until they let him see Lilian? But then, what was the use of trying to bargain with this character holding a gun? "Yes, a letter," Jensen said, feeling inside his coat for the envelope. "It authorizes Fu Tso-yi to surrender the city."

"Ai ya," Han exclaimed and clapped the driver on the shoulder. The woman bobbed her head but said nothing.

"Let me tell you what's happened," Jensen said. He recounted quickly the events in Nanking and the seizure of the mayor at the airfield. "Here's the letter."

"A thousand thanks," Han said, eagerly examining the envelope. "We must report to our leaders. They'll honor you. Now we must take you to a safe place. Chen Li-fu's agents will torture the mayor . . . threaten his family. Soon they'll know you're here and carrying the letter."

Jensen nodded. "Yes, but tell me. Where's Lilian?"

"You must rest now. Our leaders can arrange a meeting with Lilian."

Jensen looked out the window. Han was obviously not being entirely open with him. Were they using Lilian and him simply as pawns?

As the car entered the Chinese City through Hatamen Gate a large flock of pigeons fluttered down from its towering pagoda and shied before the car. They drove on to an outlying district and halted beside a furrowed field. Jensen thought he recognized the area as being near the city's abandoned military arsenal.

"We walk from here," Han said.

The driver turned to speak to Han, and as she did, Jensen shrank back. The left side of her face was a welt of red-and-purple scar tissue. Just below her short-cut hair her left ear had been sliced away. "This is my comrade. Her name is Dark Jade," Han said. Jensen extended his hand awkwardly. Dark Jade acknowledged the introduction with a curt bow but did not take his hand. "Put the car in the usual place and meet us at the house," Han said. "Come, Mr. Jensen. We're going to a village up ahead. It's less than a mile." The two began walking down a dirt track.

"You were shocked at Dark Jade's appearance?" Han asked.

"Yes, I'm sorry."

"She's accustomed to it. She was a leader of the peace activists at Tsinghua University. The Thought Control Police arrested her after a demonstration. She was turned over to Colonel Liu of the secret police. She was tortured. Her face was burned with a hot poker and her ear was cut away. But we know she didn't speak. She's not like the others. She's made of steel."

"What do you mean?"

Han shrugged. "Most of the students come from bourgeois families. They're not bred to revolution. Dark Jade is a peasant."

Jensen looked curiously at Han's sensitive features, the inquisitive eyes behind the horn-rimmed glasses, which gave him the air of a scholar. What sort of a man was he?

"Are you married?" Jensen asked.

"Yes. My wife is in Shensi Province in the Liberated Areas. But I haven't seen her or our two children for three years."

Jensen murmured sympathetically.

"It's not such a great sacrifice. Some comrades who have fought against the Japanese and the Kuomintang haven't seen their families for ten years or more."

Two ravens flapped out of a nearby field and flew low overhead. Inexplicably Jensen felt relieved at seeing the ravens . . . something that was alive and natural along the desolate road. He stumbled on a clump of frozen earth. Han steadied him.

"It may amuse you to know I graduated from Yenching in the same class as Fugh, your ambassador's secretary," Han said. "Fugh's father is a wealthy merchant. He paid for his son's education. I'm from a peasant family. After my parents were lost in a flood of the Yangtze, an American missionary school in Hankow took me in. The school arranged for me to enter Yenching. After graduation Fugh worked as a secretary for your ambassador, who was then president of Yenching. I went to the Liberated Areas."

Han laughed and tucked his hands into the sleeves of his robe as he walked with long measured strides. "Fugh and I had many debates at Yenching."

"Do you think of Philip as a traitor because he works for the Americans?"

"No. Fugh loves China as much as I. But we differ on the central question. He believes China must depend on Western aid for salvation. We Communists believe salvation lies in our own efforts."

"You speak like a missionary."

Han chuckled. "I've not yet purged myself of the rhetoric of the missionary schools. It's one of my shortcomings."

"I gather you don't think highly of missionaries."

"On the contrary. I'm indebted to them. The mission in Hankow took me in when I was twelve. My parents lived in a poor mud house when the waters of the Yangtze began to rise. They refused to abandon their things. They told my sister and me to run to the nearby city. The next day we stood on the city wall and saw the water all around. We knew we were orphans. So we followed others to the mission to beg for food. The missionary gave us shelter. My sister was taken into the school for girls. It was tended by the wife of the missionary, who was very kind and rescued many abandoned baby girls."

Han stopped and took off one of his felt shoes to shake out a pebble. "I'm indebted for still another reason. We were taught about America and its history. I learned life could be better than what we know in China. That may explain why so many Chinese revolutionaries come from missionary schools. Do you think of your Declaration of Independence as a revolutionary document?"

"Yes. But you must know that it also has words in it like *freedom* and *democracy*."

"Those are attractive words for me, too. But we cannot afford your luxuries. We carry the burden of thousands of years of backwardness and poverty. We are an ossified society. The revolution must smash the old mold so that a new China can arise."

Jensen abruptly stopped walking and confronted Han. "Yes, but why build it in Stalin's mold. Why not a more humane society?"

Han searched Jensen's features, surprised at his vehemence. "We learn from the Russians. But we do not parrot them. Revolution destroys the old system. It does not always dictate what will rise on the ruins. There will be many changes before the coming of the new China."

The two men walked on, not speaking, as if there was nothing further that could be said.

As they approached the village a pack of dogs, ribs protruding under mange-ridden hides, came out to sniff at them. The village was only a scattering of crumbled mud-brick houses. In the doorways, men in thickly padded cotton jackets and women holding children watched them pass. They returned Han's greeting as he waved.

"These houses were built for workers of the arsenal when it was operated by the Japanese puppet government," Han said. "Only a few poor vegetable farmers remain. They know me as a teacher and a friend. We'll be safe here."

Han led the way to a house with a tiled roof that was slightly larger than the others and set back from the road. They entered by an unlocked door into a room with a pressed earthen floor and rough-plastered walls. One side was taken up with a brick *kang* bed covered with matting and brightly checkered quilts. In the center there was a crude wooden table and some stools. A shrine for ancestor worship stood in a corner. When Jensen glanced at it, Han said with a smile: "It belongs to the owner. You'll sleep in this room. Dark Jade and I will stay in the back room. Now we're going out to get food."

Jensen lay down on the bed, speculating about where Lilian might be. It had been weeks now since their parting in the Pei Hai Park after the handing over of the letter. It was an enormous relief to think she was safe . . . that is, if Han was to be believed. If Lilian was with the Communists, she must have escaped from Peking. Was she at Yenching? The Communists had already occupied the Yenching campus before he left Peking for Nanking.

Jensen was dozing when Dark Jade returned carrying a basket of charcoal balls. He woke as she lit the fire in the heating oven under the bed. She didn't say a word or glance in his direction. On the table was a large bottle of beer, a dish of white rice, pewter bowls, and chopsticks for two. Han entered holding a platter with a steamed fish sprinkled with red peppers. "I'm quite a good cook," he said, forsaking the customary Chinese humility.

Jensen sat on the edge of the bed. "How long will I be here?" he asked. "When can I see Lilian?"

"Your questions will be answered at an auspicious time. Come. Let us eat. Tonight there's good food and drink on the table. Tomorrow will be its own master."

Chapter Twenty-seven

Jensen was stoking the stove in the village house shortly after dark when he heard a car drive up. For two days Jensen had been alone with Dark Jade. As he ran to the window, Han tramped into the house accompanied by Professor Chang, who had discarded his mandarin attire for a gray padded coat, fur hat, and heavy boots. Jensen and Professor Chang greeted each other as old friends, although their sole encounter had been the meeting at Yenching with Lilian and Teng Hsieh, Lin Piao's aide.

"Have you seen Lilian, Professor?" Jensen asked eagerly.

"No. Not since she left Yenching to meet you at the Pei Hai Park. Have you heard anything from her?"

Jensen glanced at Han in fierce indignation. "No. Every day I beg to see her, to have some word from her."

Han shrugged. "There's an opportunity now," he said, as he invited Jensen and the professor to the table. "Please bring tea," he said to Dark Jade, who had emerged from the rear room.

"Eric, I've met with General Fu Tso-yi in the Forbidden City," the professor said. "He's ready to negotiate the surrender of Peking. The city is now completely isolated. The Communists have taken Tientsin and the port of Tangku. Much of Tientsin was destroyed. More than one hundred thousand Nationalist troops were killed or captured."

"Has the letter from the Vice President been delivered?" Jensen interjected.

"Not yet. But Fu knows about Li Tsung-jen's letter. We must deliver it to him. He needs it. The letter will save his face. He'll publish it after he surrenders the city. But his deputy generals say that is not enough. They want Lin Piao to guarantee they will be free after the occupation to return to Nanking and their families. Fu cannot move without their agreement. They control most of the troops in Peking." The professor reached out and touched Jensen's hand. "You and I must go tonight to meet Lin Piao . . . to make the final arrangements for the peaceful turnover of the city."

Jensen drew back, frowning. "But why me? I've done my part. You've got the letter."

"Lin Piao insists on it," Chang said imploringly. "Before going any further he wants to know directly what the American ambassador told you about his contacts with the Vice President."

"Yes," Han said. "And then we can arrange for you to see Lilian."

Jensen regarded Han contemptuously. This was absurd. He was being manipulated. It was all so blatant . . . so damn blatant. But still, maybe it was the only chance to see Lilian . . . "All right," he said curtly. "What's the plan?"

"There's a colonel of Fu Tso-yi's personal guard waiting for us on the road in his staff car. He'll guide us," said the professor.

Jensen put on his overcoat and followed the professor outside to where the colonel waited, seated beside the driver. The sedan jostled down the road to the first highway junction and waited until a weapons carrier loaded with a squad of soldiers fell in behind it. "If we are stopped for a search by Chen Li-fu's gendarmes, my soldiers will deal with them," the colonel said.

The sedan crossed the Pai River on the road to the North Airfield. After less than a quarter of a mile it turned past the Russian Cemetery and halted at a Nationalist pillbox near the abandoned military drill grounds. The driver blinked the headlights three times. "The Yellow Temple is just up the road. Please walk toward it," the colonel said. "You will be met. I will be here on your return."

Trudging up the mud-crusted road, Jensen and the professor peered at the darkness ahead. They were within sight of the Yellow Temple when the headlights of a vehicle hidden in the shadows of the Buddhist shrine flashed on. A battered Japanese Army car followed by a weapons carrier came toward them. Jensen immediately recognized the man who got out of the staff car and opened the rear door for them. It was Teng Hsieh. His baggy uniform bore no insignia and his thin features were darkly sun-burnt, as if he had spent much time in the field.

"It's good you have come," Teng said, as the car turned back toward the main north road. "There's not much time. Mao is impatient. Lin Piao must lead his Fourth Field Army south for the Yangtze crossing. Only Peking stands in his way."

"Where are you taking us?" Chang asked.

"Twenty miles north, to the Hot Hills."

The morning light was glinting off the frozen ponds along the road as they drove into Tang Shan, a small modern town on the shore of a lake near the three peaks of the Hot Hills. Chang had dozed during the drive, but Jensen remained awake, gazing at the bleak countryside dotted with villages, wondering if he was on a quest without end. The sedan pulled up before a foreign-style hotel.

Lin Piao and his political commissar were seated at a long table set with tea, rice gruel, boiled eggs, and hot sorghum bread. The general, dressed in a wrinkled fatigue uniform and black peaked cap, rose to greet them. "Welcome," he said, and then, addressing Jensen: "So we meet again." A little smile played about his lips. "Our fortunes have changed since Changchun," he said. "I recall telling you we would not repeat our mistakes at Ssuping. We learn from experience. Fortunately, Chiang Kai-shek does not. Come now. Share our food."

As the visitors breakfasted, Lin Piao asked: "Is Li Tsung-jen honest in his letter? Does he truly authorize the surrender of Peking? Or is this another maneuver to delay our occupation of the city? What did your ambassador tell you?"

Jensen put down his teacup. "The ambassador loves Peking. He will do whatever he can to protect the city and its people. He vouches for Li Tsung-jen's letter."

"We do not always agree with the ambassador. But we know he is a friend of China," Lin Piao said. "I accept his word and yours. We will ask you to perform one more important service for us . . . there is no one else we can turn to. But first, you and Professor Chang must know the terms for the surrender of Peking." He nodded to the political commissar.

The commissar picked up a rice-paper document and began to read as Chang took notes. "All troops must surrender with their weapons. In keeping with our policy for occupation of cities, private property will be protected but enterprises controlled by the Kuomintang officials will be confiscated. Apart from war criminals, all officials and police will be pardoned. If Fu Tso-yi does not surrender by January twenty-second, we will break into Peking."

Lin Piao leaned back in his chair. "Are we understood?"

Lin Piao's dark eyes scrutinized Professor Chang, who sipped from his porcelain mug and then said nervously, "General Fu Tso-yi will be agreeable to those terms. He asks that he be permitted to live in Peking after the occupation in a manner befitting his rank."

Lin Piao glanced at the political commissar, who said, "Agreed. Fu Tso-yi can be removed from the list of war criminals."

"To surrender the city," Chang said, "Fu Tso-yi must have the agreement of his two deputies. They ask for a guarantee that they will be permitted to leave Peking after the occupation. The Li Tsung-jen letter approving the surrender will be enough to spare them from being shot as traitors when they return to Nanking."

The commissar, a man whose soft hands suggested that he had spent more time with documents than with guns, leaned across the table, his voice firm. "No. One cannot be removed from the war criminal list. He commanded a division at Shanghai in 1927 when Chiang Kai-shek violated his alliance with us and attacked us. Five thousand in the worker brigades were slaughtered—and many of our closest comrades. Even Chou En-lai barely escaped. We cannot forgive that."

The professor shifted uncomfortably in his chair, his eyes flicking nervously from the commissar to Lin Piao. He put his tea mug on the table. "The deputies control one hundred forty thousand of the central government troops," he said. "The general can count only on his own troops—the 35,000 men he brought from Inner Mongolia—to obey him. He must also deal with Chen Li-fu's gendarmes."

Lin Piao stood up. "You will have our answer tomorrow," he said, cutting off the commissar, who had started to reply.

The next day Teng Hsieh summoned Jensen and the professor to his hotel room. Chain-smoking British cigarettes, Lin Piao's aide strode about the room speaking in rapid English: "The deputy generals will be allowed to leave Peking. We have a radio message from Chairman Mao approving the concession. Punishment of the war criminal is not as important as preservation of Peking and the start of the Yangtze offensive." He went to a briefcase, extracted two envelopes, and placed them on the table before the couch where Jensen was seated.

"You'll recognize one of these envelopes. It's the letter which you brought to us. The other is a letter from Lin Piao to Fu Tso-yi. It contains the terms of surrender and the guarantee his deputies will be free to leave Peking. We ask that you personally deliver these letters to Fu Tso-yi."

Jensen, startled and confused, stood up silently and walked to the window. For several minutes he looked out at the jagged rocks breaking the surface of the lake. Would there be no end to this? Turning about, he said, "Haven't I done enough? Why put me in such a spot? The Blue-Eyed One now knows that I've been your agent. He'll never give up tracking me. Professor Chang, did you know about this?"

The professor nodded. "We are asking you to deliver the letters because only you, an American, can convince the generals that the Li Tsung-jen letter is not a forgery . . . that all this is not a Communist trick. They will trust you. They remember you as a member of General Marshall's truce teams. You can tell them of your meetings with the American ambassador and with Lin Piao. Please, you must deliver the letters before the ultimatum expires."

Jensen folded his arms. "No," he said firmly. "I've done enough."

The professor put his hand on Jensen's arm. "Eric, have you forgotten what you said that day at Yenching? You told us Peking is not only a Chinese city . . . that it is the heritage of every civilized man. It was those words that convinced us we could rely on you to see us through."

Jensen shrugged. "Yes. I'm no less devoted to the city. But not at the price of being used as a tool."

Teng studied Jensen's features and in a measured tone said, "That's not what you said to Lilian."

"My pact was with Lilian . . . not with you."

"If you deliver the letters," Teng said, "we'll make arrangements for you to see Lilian after the liberation of Peking."

Jensen leaped up shouting, "'Can be arranged' . . . 'can be arranged.'" He glared at Teng. "That's all I've been told from the day I started as your messenger boy. All right. I'll deliver the letters. But first, I want your word that I will be able to see Lilian alone right after you occupy Peking. And before that, I want a letter from Lilian. I want to know if she's alive, if she's well . . . that she knows we'll be together again."

Teng stood directly in front of Jensen, anger in his eyes. "You have my word, and you'll have your letter . . ." Teng stalked from the room.

The professor grasped Eric's hand. "Thank you. Thank you. But you shouldn't have spoken in such a manner to Teng. It doesn't serve us well."

"I'm being manipulated, Professor," Jensen said, his manner suddenly calm and deliberate. "I've got only one card to play . . . the letters. I have to know what's happened to Lilian."

"Eric," the professor said with a sad smile. "You're not the only one being manipulated. Do you think I have any illusions as to what the Communists intend for the Democratic League and me? Not long after their victory we shall be devoured. There will be no place for us in their world except as tokens."

"Why do you allow yourselves to be used?"

The professor smiled wearily. "To lift China up from the depths to which it has fallen will be a hard struggle. Only the Communists have the discipline to do it. If there's a chance that they may succeed, it is enough for me. But it will be a long night," the professor said heavily, as he rose to go. "I do not expect to see the dawn of a democratic China."

Part Three

THE FALL OF PEKING

北平之沦陷

Chapter Twenty-eight

When Lilian left the Pei Hai Park after her meeting with Jensen she followed the escape plan to be used if there was a police raid during the handing over of the letter. She did not return to her bicycle but took a pedicab to Furniture Street. She walked past shops filled with Ming and Ching dynasty furniture sold by wealthy families who had fled Peking. In front of a very small shop, an old bearded man sat smoking a long-stemmed water pipe. Lilian spoke while looking into the shop window.

"Venerable One, I am told you have a Ming sandalwood chest for sale." The old man beckoned and Lilian followed him. They entered living quarters at the rear of the shop, where a woman was cooking on an iron stove and a girl was milking a long-haired goat tethered in the corner. "My wife and daughter," the old man said. "You are welcome." The women greeted her with smiles. There were no questions.

Lilian remained in the shop for days waiting for a prearranged contact. Once she suggested going out for a stroll, but the old man advised her against it. Police surveillance had tightened, he told her. It was forbidden to admit a stranger to a home or to hold meetings without informing the police. Listening to Communist broadcasts invited arrest, sometimes even public execution.

On the seventh day Han came, identifying himself as the contact by saying, "Jensen took the letter from under the flat rock at the White Dagoba." Lilian recalled him as the Chinese who had stood behind her as she and Eric inspected the Jade Bowl at the entrance to the Pei Hai Park.

Relieved, tears welling in her eyes, Lilian asked, "Eric . . . where is he?"

"He left Peking on the American plane for Nanking. Now, come with me," Han said gently, before she could question him further. He handed the furniture seller some money and bowed to each member of the family. Lilian followed Han to where the Japanese sedan was waiting, Dark Jade at the wheel. In the darkness they drove to the village house near the abandoned arsenal.

"You will not be here too long," Han told Lilian as they came into the house. "Have patience."

Three days passed in boredom for Lilian. Han would leave in the morning and return at nightfall. Her questions about Jensen and the progress of his mission went unanswered. She thought back over her parting with Jensen in the Pei Hai Park, regretting there had not been time for tenderness, no time to speak of her love except in a fleeting, unconvincing way. Had she made him doubt her? She often touched the carved jade hidden deep in her pocket.

Lilian slept on the *kang* bed beside Dark Jade but she was not able to draw the woman into conversation. Dark Jade's replies were always curt gestures or grunts. One morning as the three breakfasted on a rice gruel there was only hot water on the table. "Is there tea?" Lilian asked.

Dark Jade's face contorted in fury. "The oppressed peasants do not have tea to drink . . . only white tea like this," she shouted. "The rich like you do not know how the peasants live. But all this will change with the revolution. The class enemies will disappear."

Han reached over and clutched Dark Jade's arm. "Be still. Remember Chairman Mao's teachings. The revolution must employ democratic personages of every class. Lilian is working to preserve Peking."

Dark Jade leaped up from her stool, rattling the bowls on the table, and stomped into the back room.

"You must forgive Dark Jade," Han said. "She is full of bitterness. We have many people who are so. Perhaps it is for the best. It strengthens their will to fight for the revolution."

During the evenings Han would sometimes chat with Lilian. He showed an endless curiosity about her family life in Shanghai and especially the banking activities of her father. One evening Han gave her a pamphlet printed on the yellow grass paper manufactured in the Communist areas. Inside were printed Mao Tse-tung's Yenan Forum lectures on Literature and Art from May 1942. The next day when Han asked her what she thought of the lectures, Lilian replied hesitantly that she had had difficulty understanding Mao's thesis that there could be no worthy art and literature other than propaganda serving the revolution. "People of your class do not understand that the revolution demands every sacrifice . . . but you will learn," Han said brusquely.

One afternoon, as Dark Jade was washing clothes at the well, Lilian wandered into the rear room where Han slept. On the floor beside his bed was an English paperback of Hemingway's *For Whom the Bell Tolls*. She picked up the novel and was scanning it when Han walked in. "It's a good piece of revolutionary literature," he said.

.   .   .

Lilian had been in the village house for one week when Han returned after an unusually long absence. "Our comrades in the city have
received a radio message. You will leave tomorrow for Yenching," he
told Lilian. This was her first word of where she was to go.

"Have you had any news of Eric Jensen?" she asked anxiously.

Han brushed aside her question. "To cross the lines into the Liberated Area will not be difficult," he said. "For almost two weeks there
has been no major fighting on the approaches to the city. The People's
Liberation Army is in full occupation of the outlying suburbs. We will
disguise you as a peasant. Both sides are letting the peasants move quite
freely across the lines between the farms and the city markets. I will
bring you clothes tonight. Dark Jade will fix your hair."

Lilian looked at him in distress. "My hair?" she said, reaching back
to pat her long tresses.

Han smiled sympathetically. "It is necessary."

That night Lilian wiped away the last traces of her makeup. She discarded the lipstick that she had tucked in her coat pocket before her
meeting with Eric at the Pei Hai. She winced as she sat on a stool while
Dark Jade hacked at her hair with a long knife and pulled the short-
ened tresses into a peasant back-knot. Han brought a heavily padded
peasant jacket, baggy trousers, scuffed cloth sandals, and a broad-
brimmed straw hat. He showed her a yo-stick with buckets at each end.
"You know how the peasants use this for carrying?" Lilian nodded.

At ten the next morning they drove into the Tartar City. "We will
drop you near the west gate," Han said. "At the gate tell the Nationalist
guards you brought eggs and two ducks to the morning market from
your husband's farm beyond the Great Bell Temple. They may demand
squeeze before they allow you to pass. Protest, but then give them this

money if you must. Beyond the gate, go to the temple, one mile beyond the last Nationalist checkpoint. On the west side of the temple you will see a two-wheeled cart and mule driven by a man wearing a sheepskin hat. He will take you to Yenching. At our checkpoint yet another mile down the road he will know what to say to the sentries of the People's Liberation Army. There is no danger except for robbers who sometimes roam between the lines. By nightfall you should be on the campus. Say nothing to the other students of what has happened to you . . . say only you were tending a sick aunt in Peking and got stranded there by the fighting."

Lilian fingered the yo-stick nervously. "Will I be able to see Eric when he returns from the south?"

"It can be arranged."

Lilian crouched out of sight as Dark Jade drove the sedan toward the West Straight Gate. Near the abandoned Military University, Dark Jade steered the sedan to the side of the road and kept the engine running as Lilian got out. Han passed the yo-stick and buckets to her.

"At Yenching do not try to find Professor Chang," Han said. "He is not there. Our people will give you instructions. Good-bye." Lilian pushed the broad-brimmed hat down on her head. Dark Jade had smudged her face with charcoal. She heaved the yo-stick over her right shoulder and began walking at the side of the road toward the gate.

Bracing herself against the cold north wind Lilian trudged to the west gate, trying to hide her nervousness. The gate in the looming city wall was open, but there was no longer a stream of vehicles coming and going from the Summer Palace. The few peasants entering the city for the morning markets were being inspected casually by the guards. Except for an Army truck with a load of cabbages there was no military traffic.

"Woman, what are you carrying?" one of the Nationalist guards asked, leaning on his rifle as Lilian approached with her head bowed.

"Nothing. I have sold my eggs and two ducks in the market."

"You still must have an egg or two for a hungry soldier?"

"No. An accursed one already took one when I came through this morning."

The soldier laughed and waved her through the barbed-wire barrier. Outside the wall, Lilian followed the west road past a network of artillery and machine gun emplacements. After about one mile she came to the last Nationalist checkpoint, which was covered by machine gunners in slit trenches. The checkpoint guards gathered around a fire of twigs and dried sorghum stalks hardly glanced at her as she passed.

The pale sun was already low over the fields when she reached the Great Bell Temple, a huge six-sided tower topped by crimson eaves. Lilian remembered coming here with other students to picnic. In imperial times the bell tower was known as the Temple Where They Understand the Secret of Existence. I am no closer to knowing the secret than I was then, she thought, as she walked on, buckets swinging at the ends of the yo-stick. Finally she spotted the two-wheeled cart and the driver in his sheepskin hat.

"I am Lilian," she said to the driver, who grinned and helped her into the cart. He cracked a long whip over the mule, and the cart lumbered slowly along the rutted road. The driver grabbed a burlap bag, which he placed between his legs. As he fumbled inside the bag, Lilian could see there was a Japanese machine pistol tucked under his coat. He took out a loaf of black sorghum bread and a chunk of goat's cheese and handed the food to Lilian, who tore into it thankfully.

The cart crossed ripped-up railroad tracks, and some hours later they came onto the main road curving to the Summer Palace. At the Communist checkpoint, which in appearance was not unlike the Nationalist post, the driver spoke to an officer, who looked at Lilian curiously. He waved them on, and they resumed the journey. Dusk was yielding to night when the cart finally halted before the main gate of Yenching. Lilian dismounted, leaving the yo-stick, the buckets, and the peasant hat in the back of the cart. She walked to her dormitory across the grass lawns, avoiding the students on the paved walks.

◆

It had been little more than two weeks since the Communists occupied the Yenching campus, but the university was already transformed. The first troops to enter the gates had been greeted by the students with cheers and banners hailing Chairman Mao and the People's Liberation Army. A few days later, political workers in uniform arrived from the Liberated Areas. Now, except for the guards at the gates, there were no troops on the campus. The university administration remained in place, but control had passed to the political commissars. Academic studies were suspended. Students and faculty were organized into forty-member study groups for indoctrination. They were told they must learn the thought of Mao Tse-tung and purge themselves of their bourgeois past to qualify as citizens of the New Democracy.

Lilian returned to her old room but found the dormitory changed. The easy ways had been replaced by a military orderliness of rooms and halls. The dormitory was supervised by a Youth League activist from the Liberated Areas. Lilian was assigned to a study group. It met in the gymnasium, where she heard day-long lectures on Maoist doctrine by a political officer.

At the lunch break Lilian would stroll along the campus walks, grappling with the doubts that were seeping into her mind. She had looked to the Communist Party as the engine of the revolution without knowing much of its inner workings. Now she was being disciplined to accept a rigid doctrine that did not accord with her vision of a more compassionate China. She walked along the frozen lake beneath the gaunt willows that bent before the stubborn winds sweeping down from Siberia. She listened for the temple bell on the islet. It clanged softly in reassurance that not everything of the gentle past was dying. Lilian often thought of how she and Eric had bicycled along these campus walks. Once she returned to the bench where they had picnicked and, holding his jade in her cupped hands, cried quietly. She thought of his dream of a Chinese garden. Though it was only a fantasy, she allowed herself to indulge in it—an escape from the oppressive harshness closing about her.

One week after her return, Lilian was summoned to the dormitory office. The Youth League activist was waiting for her with a stocky, middle-aged woman in a rumpled uniform without insignia. "My name is Wu," the woman said. "I am a Party political cadre. I will be your leader in a study group. We will meet every night. As your first task you must write a report on your past life. Every important detail about your childhood must be included: your education, your family life, your feelings about your parents, their class, and you must confess to errors you have made in your thinking. You have two nights to prepare the report. Leave it on this desk. We will meet at seven o'clock in the evening. Understood?" Lilian nodded. Wu dismissed her by standing up.

Lilian went to the first meeting of the study group full of apprehension, fearing that her résumé would be found wanting. The meeting was in a classroom with the students seated on stools arranged in a semicircle facing an armchair before a blackboard. Lilian felt reassured when she saw her roommate and close friend, Sweet Blossom, among the six students. The classroom walls bore photographs of Mao and posters picturing heroic figures of soldiers and workers struggling against the Kuomintang and the American imperialists. There were caricatured figures, blood dripping from their fingers, of the Four Rich Families: those of Chiang Kai-shek; Chen Li-fu; T. V. Soong, the brother of Madame Chiang Kai-shek; and her banker brother-in-law, H. H. Kung.

Wu entered carrying a sheaf of papers. She stood before the students, her darkly sunburnt features stern, holding their reports aloft. "All of your family histories are most unsatisfactory," she said, her voice rising shrilly. "Only by true self-criticism will you rid yourself of bourgeois influence and the sins of the past. There is no place in the revolutionary universities for slaves to the old thinking."

Wu paced before the group. "You will criticize each other's family histories. You will rewrite them until we can judge whether you are fit to serve the New Democracy or if you are hopeless class enemies." Wu broke off her pacing in front of Lilian. "Yours was the least satisfactory," she said, glaring at her. "You have confessed to the evil ways of your family . . . how they lived in luxury while surrounded by the starving masses. But you did not write of the crimes of your father. He is an important official in the Central Bank of China, an organ of the reactionary Kuomintang regime. He joined in the bandit schemes of Chiang Kai-shek and the blood-sucking of the Four Rich Families. He is a criminal," Wu shouted. "Do you not agree?"

Lilian replied softly: "I have not thought of him as a criminal. He was always kind to me."

Wu's lips twisted in a sneer. "And you did not know while he was kind to you he was serving foreign capitalists who are draining China of its wealth? You knew, of course, he traveled often to New York and to London?" Lilian nodded. "And yet you did not know he was a lackey for American and British imperialism?"

Lilian sat speechless, her eyes darting between Wu and the others in the semicircle of chairs.

"Rewrite your family history," Wu said, and went on to the other students.

It was already midnight when Wu dismissed the group. As the students filed out, Sweet Blossom said to Lilian: "I am frightened." She was a shy, slender girl, the daughter of a Shanghai physician, who often came to Lilian with her problems. As they walked down the corridor Lilian put an arm around her shoulders.

Two nights later Wu strode into the study room and hurled Lilian's rewritten report into her lap with the command: "Again." In a rasping voice Wu called on Sweet Blossom: "Tell us what you think of your roommate Lilian."

Sweet Blossom rose, visibly trembling, her eyes riveted on Wu. "Lilian still shrinks before the truth and her duty to the masses," Sweet Blossom said. "She has not yet denounced her father for what he is, a criminal and a traitor to China."

Lilian walked out of the meeting alone. In her room she stretched out on her cot, burying her face in the pillow. Questions flooded into her mind. Was her father so guilty? What must she do? She lay awake on her cot for hours, forcing herself to think clearly and deliberately. She thought of Chi, of their hopes for a China reborn. Chi had died believing in the revolution. She must have faith, like Chi, that there would be a better China. Her roommates were already asleep when Lilian went to her desk to rewrite her family history.

Weeks later Lilian was summoned again to the dormitory office. Alone in the room and leaning against the desk with his arms folded was Teng Hsieh. Lilian had not seen Teng since the meeting in Professor Chang's house. He was in Army uniform. He extended his hand, and Lilian shook it firmly. "You are changed," Teng said.

Lilian lowered her eyes. She had cut her hair very short and was wearing a worn blue jacket and baggy trousers. She wore no makeup, her features were pale, and there were lines under her eyes.

"Comrade Wu tells me she is satisfied that you are dedicated to the revolution," Teng said.

"There was no reason to doubt it," Lilian said quietly.

Teng shrugged. "The party must be sure. You are to be given an important post. You are to organize and lead a unit of Army nurses. We have so few people with any medical training."

"I am ready to serve the people," Lilian said.

"There is one question Comrade Wu did not put to you. The American . . . Eric Jensen. He is helping us. But he is an American. He was your lover. Do you still feel for him?"

"Yes," Lilian said without hesitation.

"More than for the revolution?"

Lilian closed her eyes for a few moments and gathered herself. "I know that this is not a time for us. I accept that. But I must see Eric Jensen once more. I owe it to him."

"It can be arranged," Teng said. "Jensen has returned to Peking from Nanking. He brought a letter from Li Tsung-jen addressed to Fu Tso-yi. It authorizes the surrender of Peking. Unless Fu and his generals receive the letter from Jensen's hands they may not think it authentic. But he will not deliver it until he has a letter from you. He wants to know if you are well. He demands some word from you." Teng folded his arms. "You understand what must be done?"

At this first news of Jensen, the dullness in Lilian's eyes vanished. She clasped her hands tightly behind her back, trying to restrain herself from crying out. In a hushed voice she asked, "Is Jensen in good health?"

"Yes," Teng replied, handing her a sheet of writing paper and an envelope. "You will see him again. Write at the desk." He walked to the other side of the room where he studied a wall newspaper. At the desk

Lilian began to write:

Yenching, Jan. 18

Dear Eric,

    I am at Yenching and well. I am learning how to do my part in building a new China. The comrades tell me you have a letter from Li Tsung-jen that can spare Peking from destruction. Please deliver it, for me and for my people.

    Here, on the campus walks the willows are now bare. But soon they will become fountains of green. The acacias will be dressed in yellow blossoms. Yenching is very beautiful in the spring. We have never shared a spring together. We shall meet again. I long to be with you.

Lilian

Teng walked to the desk. "May I see your note?" Lilian handed it to him. He read the note, sealed it in the envelope, and raised his eyes to Lilian's face. Her features seemed graven in clay. Silently he went from the room, leaving Lilian alone behind the desk.

Chapter Twenty-nine

Shortly before midnight on January 18—four days before the deadline set by Lin Piao for the surrender of Peking—Han returned to the village house after an absence of two days. His shoes were encrusted with mud and he was obviously exhausted. Jensen was sitting on the *kang* bed, a blanket around his shoulders.

"Here's Lilian's letter," Han said coldly, reaching into his robe for the envelope. Jensen snatched it from Han's hand and went into the rear room where Dark Jade was dozing. She awoke startled and reached for the Japanese pistol beside her. When she saw it was Jensen, she buttoned her jacket over her cotton jersey, picked up the pistol, and silently walked past him. Jensen sat on Han's rumpled cot and tore open the envelope. In the dim light of the kerosene lamp he scanned the letter eagerly, then read it over slowly.

When Han came into the room the next morning he found Jensen asleep on the cot fully dressed, the kerosene lamp still burning, and the letter lying beside him. He shook Jensen's shoulder. "Fu Tso-yi will receive you tonight," Han said. "You'll meet at the former Austrian legation rather than at his headquarters in the Forbidden City. Safer. Less chance of being spotted by Chen Li-fu's men."

"I'll be ready," Jensen said.

Han and Jensen set out in the late afternoon, walking briskly along the road. Dark Jade had gone ahead to fetch the car. It had begun to snow. "This is good," Han said, looking at the snowflakes eddying in the gusts of wind. "The snow will help hide us until we reach the legation." Han had changed into the garb of a ricksha coolie: tattered padded jacket, black cotton trousers, straw sandals, and a dirty towel wrapped about his head. Before leaving the village house Dark Jade had sewn the letters from Li Tsung-jen and Lin Piao under the lining of Jensen's overcoat. She also gave him a rabbit fur hat.

Han turned to Jensen as Dark Jade drove through the thickening snowfall. "We're going to the Tungsze Bazaar," he explained. "I'll get out there. Follow me to a shop in the bazaar where I'll rent a pedicab. Wait outside. When I leave, act as if you've just hired me and get into the pedicab. The Austrian legation is on Hart Hutung, about three hundred fifty yards from Marco Polo Street. The sentries at the legation will let me take you to the front gate, but I won't be permitted to stay there. I'll wait for you on Marco Polo Street."

The car passed Coal Hill, whose pagoda was already obscured by the snow. Han continued: "The bazaar is not far. One other thing. After you've met with Fu Tso-yi, walk as quickly as you can from the legation gate to Marco Polo Street. If Chen Li-fu's agents have learned of your visit, they're most likely to be waiting for you somewhere along those three hundred fifty yards. If they come after you, run to Marco Polo Street. We've arranged for a crowd of people to close in about you and shield you. Dark Jade and I will be in the car nearby."

"Can't you bring the car to the gate?" Jensen asked hoarsely.

"No." Han said sharply, as the car jolted to a halt. "We get out here."

With Jensen following at a short distance Han walked into the open Tungze Bazaar, lined with shabby shops and peddlers' stands. There was a power failure and shopkeepers had set out kerosene lamps, lending the scene a ghostly cast. Undeterred by the snow, people waited at the doors of the flour, rice, and cooking-oil shops. Long lines of shoppers curled around the square. In a ridiculous race against the spiraling currency inflation, people shuttled between money-changing shops and the queues before the food stands. Gendarmes, rifles slung over their shoulders, patrolled the square. There had been food riots in the last days. Scores of starving refugees had been shot. Beggars, some with snow covering their open straw sandals, were gathered before the Mohammedan Restaurant, where mutton was being grilled over open fires. Customers threw them scraps. Passersby turned to stare at the tall foreigner strolling about the marketplace.

When Han emerged from the pedicab rental shop, Jensen signaled to him and mounted the pedicab. Han buttoned up the foot cover apparently to protect his customer from the snow. Jensen slid down in the seat so that he was barely visible. His thoughts drifted back to Lilian's letter, to its tenderness and its promise of reunion. Would they know a spring together? The pedicab bumped over the cobblestones of the Hart Hutung. Jensen dismounted before the Austrian legation gate. Two sentries were stamping in the snow to keep warm. An officer came out of a sentry box to lead Jensen through the garden to the mansion. Han was waved off, and he pedaled back to Marco Polo Street.

Jensen entered a hall whose moldings still bore traces of Hapsburg gilding. The building evidently had its own power generator since the hall was brilliantly lit. The servant at the door looked puzzled when Jensen refused to surrender his overcoat. He ushered Jensen into a narrow green-carpeted reception room illuminated by crystal chandeliers. At the far end stood a rose damask couch and above it hung a large painting of peacocks in a garden. Seated there was a heavyset man, moon-faced, with a high forehead and thinning hair. The man wore a black civilian tunic, its high collar unbuttoned, black trousers, and cloth-topped military boots. From his work with the truce team Jensen recognized the man as Fu Tso-yi. Two officers with webbed pistol belts sat in armchairs flanking the couch. Evidently they were the deputy commanders.

Fu Tso-yi greeted Jensen warmly and introduced him to his deputies, a lean erect officer on his right and an older balding officer, whose cheek twitched, on his left. Jensen assumed the older man was the deputy accused of war crimes by Lin Piao's political commissar.

"I remember you, Mr. Jensen," Fu said. "You translated for General Marshall when he gave a dinner for General Tu Yu-ming and me. Yes, I wish we had taken the general's advice." He laughed. "Certainly Tu Yu-ming must have regretted that when he was trapped on the Huaipei Plain. Come now, Mr. Jensen, you have something for us."

Jensen took off his overcoat and spread it out on the carpet. As Fu watched with amusement, he ripped open the lining and took out the two letters. Fu accepted them with both hands and a short bow. "Please have wine," he said, pouring hot *shaohsing* from a white flask into a small jade cup. Jensen sipped the yellow wine as the general scanned the letters.

Fu Tso-yi handed the Li Tsung-jen letter to the general on his right. The letter from Lin Piao, he handed to the general on his left, adding sardonically, "You will be more concerned with this one." The general's cheek twitched even more violently.

"Now, Mr. Jensen, tell us how you came into possession of these letters."

The generals listened intently as Jensen sketched his journey to Nanking, the meeting with the American ambassador, his return to Peking, and the encounter with Lin Piao. For the better part of an hour he answered their questions.

"Not long after you returned from Nanking, the body of the former mayor was dumped before his family house," Fu said regretfully. "He had been tortured. We can assume the secret police know he passed the Li Tsung-jen letter on to you."

Jensen nodded and emptied his wine cup.

"Thank you for bringing the letters." Fu said. "You have endured much for the people of Peking." The general leaned back in his chair, folding his hands over his paunch. "It is not easy for us to turn our backs on the Generalissimo. We stood by him through the war with Japan and against the Communists. And now he tells us, 'Resist. . . . Give me time to strengthen the Yangtze defenses.' But we know the mainland is lost. The Gimmo will go to Formosa soon. If we continue to resist," Fu said, rising, "Peking will be devastated. I cannot allow that. The letters let us do what we must . . . without sacrificing our honor."

The general shook Jensen's hand, holding it as he looked fixedly into his eyes. "I must tell you, Mr. Jensen, there is an agreement between the Nanking authorities and my headquarters. I command the Army. Chen Li-fu controls the gendarmes and the secret police. I cannot vouch for your safety after you leave this compound. The secret police are everywhere, even in our army ranks. They may know you are here."

Jensen was going out the door when the general raised his hand and called out: "Peaceful journey."

Jensen paused outside the legation gate and peered down at his watch. He could just make out the time in the gloom. It was 7:25. There were no lights in the old Customs House on the other side of the hutung. Marco Polo Street lay in darkness. Apprehensively, Jensen drew his overcoat more tightly and walked rapidly through the thickly falling snow. Heavy snowfalls were infrequent in Peking and he was grateful for the concealment. He walked faster. Suddenly he sensed some other presence, and remembering Han's instructions, he began to run toward Marco Polo Street. He slipped in the snow and scrambled back up, encumbered by the heavy overcoat. At that moment the lights on Marco Polo Street came on again and he glimpsed the people waiting for him at the end of the narrow hutung.

Just some fifty yards from the mouth of the hutung, the first great blow fell on his back, driving him to his knees. A second blow followed to the back of his head, knocking him face down into the snow. He was jerked to his feet, spun around, and thrown against a compound wall, where he slumped helpless. Hands seized his throat. A flashlight switched on and Jensen looked groggily into the face of the Blue-Eyed One.

"Yes, once again, and for the last time," Liu said, his face contorted with rage. The man beside Liu holding the flashlight ran his hands through Jensen's clothes. "Nothing," he said. Liu wrenched Jensen from where he sagged against the wall, held his throat with one hand, and drove a fist twice into his groin. "Tell us, you turtle shit, what was in the letter you brought to Fu Tso-yi?" Liu hissed.

Jensen shook his head. The colonel drove his fist into his groin again and then into his mouth. Jensen tasted a rush of blood as his head snapped against the wall. Then he heard a shot. And another shot. The hands on his throat loosened. As Jensen slid down, his back scraping against the wall, he saw Han and Dark Jade, pistol in hand, standing over two bodies. The one lying at his feet groaned. Han bent over him. "The Blue-Eyed One," Han exclaimed. Through blurred eyes Jensen saw Dark Jade put her pistol to Liu's head and fire.

At the legation gate the sentries had turned their backs, pretending not to notice what was happening in the alleyway. Han shouted, and the crowd on Marco Polo Street parted to let a ricksha man run through. With Dark Jade's help, Han lifted Jensen into the ricksha, leaning him against the backrest. At the fringe of the crowd gendarmes were shouting vainly for the people to make way. Standing shoulder to shoulder, the people, some well dressed and others ragged, opened an avenue for Han and Dark Jade who were running in front of the ricksha. The sedan was parked on the other side of Marco Polo Street. Han lifted Jensen into the backseat and held a cloth to his bleeding mouth as Dark Jade gunned the car away.

"Drive to the house of the French lieutenant," Han shouted. At the lieutenant's door, Han pulled the bell cord in hard jerks until a grumbling servant came out.

"Hurry," Han said. "Help me with Mr. Jensen. He is in the car . . . seriously wounded." Jensen was carried into the courtyard as Jean Leone emerged from the house.

"*Merde*," he said, as he bent over Jensen's unconscious figure.

"The secret police . . ." Han said. "They caught him in the hutung outside the Austrian legation . . . after he met Fu Tso-yi."

Jensen was carried to his room. Jean sponged his bleeding face and sent a servant for his medicine kit. "He needs a doctor," Han said. "He was very badly beaten. But do not take him to a hospital. Chen Li-fu's agents will find him. They now have a blood score to settle. Keep him here. Do not leave him alone."

Han went to the door and as he opened it, he said, "I'm sorry. Eric has done a great service for China. We shall not forget it."

Chapter Thirty

Jensen was unconscious for two days. When he awoke he looked through a haze at a woman seated at his bedside. "Lilian," he mumbled. He shut his eyes as he felt a sharp throbbing at the back of his head. He reached up and touched a heavy bandage. When he opened his eyes again Leone stood by the bed, smiling down at him. "The hero awakes," the lieutenant said.

"What happened?" Jensen whispered.

"Quite an adventure, *mon ami*. The secret police ambushed you in the Hart Hutung after you delivered the letter to Fu Tso-yi. You were brought here by that Chinese who took you from my jeep. You'll survive. Your mouth is badly cut. You suffered a concussion. You have some internal injuries. My doctor is looking after you. He says you must stay in bed for a week or so."

Jensen ran his tongue over his swollen lips and winced.

"This woman will serve you," Leone said, inclining to the Chinese woman beside him. "Recognize her?"

Eagerly, Jensen raised his head but then let it drop back. "No," he said.

"It's Little Flower," Leone said, smiling. "It's the girl you met in Madame Loh's company house. She came here more than a month ago. She works in the kitchen."

Little Flower bowed. As Jensen closed his eyes again in pain, the lieutenant said, "I must go. You'll be safe. There are two Sikhs armed with rifles at the door. I brought them over from the security detail at my consulate. Fu Tso-yi has put soldiers of his personal guard around the compound."

◆

The following morning Leone returned, flipped his cap onto the bed, and pulled up a chair. "There's a ceasefire," he said excitedly. "It's connected with developments in Nanking. We have a cable from the embassy. Chiang Kai-shek has left Nanking. And he did it in elegant mandarin style."

Leone grinned and went on. "He summoned all the foreign ambassadors to the audience room in the Tai Ping Palace . . . received them in a black jacket and long blue gown. And with deep Confucian humility." Leone offered a bow and a graceful wave of his arm. "The Generalissimo informed their excellencies he was retiring for meditation to his birthplace. Then he flew off to Fenghua in Chekiang. To live, of course, as a country squire."

Leone stood up and laughed uproariously, arms akimbo, shaking his head. "No one believes the retirement story. He still controls most of the Army and the Party. He's shipped art treasures and gold to Formosa.

He'll go there soon. Li Tsung-Jen . . . poor man . . . is Acting President. He's left to face the Communists."

The lieutenant patted Jensen's shoulder. "I must go. I must tour the city and cable the embassy. There are rumors Fu Tso-yi is about to sign a surrender agreement. As he rose to leave, Leone said, "Oh yes. An officer from your consulate, a Marine major, came by yesterday to ask how you were getting on. He said there wasn't any need to see you. He said that your friend, Mr. Smith, will be in touch."

After Leone departed, Jensen lay quietly thinking: Smith would not let go. There was sure to be another run-in. He was not certain he would survive it. He wondered if it was wise to hold to his vow of secrecy, if he shouldn't just tell Jean about the Smith people.

Little Flower entered with a tea tray. She approached Jensen with eyes lowered and he looked at her more closely. There was not much resemblance to the beautiful girl with the exotic makeup in the clinging silk *cheongsam*. She was thin and pale. But there were still those luminous eyes which she raised to peek at him shyly. Her long hair, which once flowed so gracefully over her shoulders, was tied back in a thick pigtail. She wore a blue peasant jacket, baggy pants, and wooden clogs.

"Put the tray on the table and sit beside me," Jensen said. Little Flower perched nervously. "How did you get here?"

"It is a sad tale, Mr. Jensen."

"I would like to know."

"When the fighting came close to the house of Madame Loh . . . you remember it was just outside of Peking—she took me and the other five girls into the city. Madame Loh wanted to take us to her new house in Formosa. But she found it too expensive. The airline was asking more than three thousand American dollars for each seat on the plane. She gave us each a little money and left."

Little Flower bowed her head. "You should rest," she said. "May I give you tea?"

Jensen shifted with a grimace and pulled his quilt up. "No. Please go on."

"Soon, there was no more money for the hotel or food. We went out and begged. We slept on the street. We fought with other beggars and dogs for the garbage from the restaurants. We went to the Peitang Cathedral where the Catholics were giving flour to the poor. We waited on the long line but could not reach the doors before they closed. We were full of despair when a well-dressed Chinese man walked along the line and looked carefully at each of us. He offered us food if we would work. We followed him to the brothel district."

Jensen shook his head. He knew the brothel district in the Chinese City near the Front Gate. There were more than two hundred brothels on about eight hutungs of the district, all licensed by the municipality. "Go on," Jensen said.

"I worked at first in a rich brothel for Army officers and merchants. But it was not like the house of Madame Loh. The girls were treated cruelly. We were beaten when we complained of entertaining too many men. When I became sick, I was put into another brothel for common soldiers. When I could not go on I was thrown into the street."

"How did you come here?" Jensen asked.

"I was sick and no one would care for me. You were kind when you came to the house of Madame Loh. You told me where you lived." She gazed at Jensen, her eyes moist, her lips pressed tightly together. "Please let me be your slave, Mr. Jensen," she said, and ran from the bedroom sobbing.

Jensen propped himself up when Leone burst into the room the next morning. It was another date that he would not forget—January 22, 1949. "The siege is ended," the French lieutenant exclaimed. "Fu Tso-yi has signed a surrender agreement. He's turning over two hundred fifty thousand troops and all of North China to the Communists. The agreement was broadcast on the radio together with the text of the Li Tsung-jen letter you delivered to him.

"And now," Leone said, falling into the armchair and propping his feet on the bed, "tell me, if you are well enough . . . tell me what happened after you were taken from my jeep."

The lieutenant listened in wonder to Jensen's story. "*Mon cher*, you've served everyone very well except yourself."

Jensen shrugged. "Now I care for only one thing. Do you think they'll let me see Lilian?"

"Yes. Teng Hsieh promised you, didn't he? Chinese keep their word. They are in debt to you. But I don't think they'll let Lilian go with you. She's now one of them."

Jensen turned his cheek to the pillow. "I'll find a way. I won't give her up," he said.

Little Flower came to carry away the tea tray. When she left Jensen said, "Tell me about her."

"Not much to tell. When she came here from a brothel she was sick with a venereal disease. My doctor treated her with sulfa drugs. When he told me she was well I put her to work in the kitchen. She's a good woman."

◆

Jensen's recovery was slow. He had suffered more serious internal injuries than had been first diagnosed. Little Flower tended to his every need. As she was carrying in his breakfast tray one morning, Jensen heard her sing. In the evening when she came to put out the lights Jensen beckoned to her. She stood silently at his bedside. He reached for her hand. Without a word, she turned out the lights, undressed, and slipped into the bed beside him. She slowly unbuttoned his pajamas and gently ran her fingers over his bruised body. As he fell asleep she heard him softly whisper, "Lilian."

After the announcement of the surrender, a strange hiatus settled over Peking. The airports reopened. Planes arrived from Nationalist cities and departed with evacuees, among them Fu Tso-yi's deputy commanders. The Communists were fulfilling their bargain. Nationalist army units moved to designated areas outside the city to be disarmed. Communist agents emerged from the underground and joined with sympathizers to make preparations for the entry of Communist troops. Wall posters went up hailing the People's Liberation Army and exhorting the people to protect public property for the New China. Students daubed Down with American Imperialism on the U.S. consulate wall. On January 29 firecrackers popped throughout Peking. It was Chinese New Year, the Year of the Ox, the year when evil spirits disturb the rivers. People joked that soon the People's Liberation Army would cross the Yangtze to take Nanking, the Nationalist capital, and Shanghai.

It was nine days after the ceasefire when Leone brought the news to Jensen that Communist troops had entered Peking. "They marched through the west gate, only an infantry regiment . . . not the best troops. Lin Piao's crack units must be getting ready to move south," Leone said in a disappointed tone as if he had hoped for a more dramatic scene. "Some students and city employees holding pictures of Mao rushed out to greet them . . . not much excitement. The people are glad it's over."

The morning after the Communist entry into the city Leone came into Jensen's room agitated and angry. Jensen was reading in an arm-chair, a bandage still wrapped about his lacerated scalp. It was his first day out of bed. "There are Communist soldiers posted at the gate," Leone said. "No one can enter or leave the compound. They won't tell me what is happening." The doorbell jangled in the courtyard, and a few moments later a servant knocked at the bedroom door. "There is a Communist officer at the gate. He wishes to see Mr. Jensen," the servant said in a quivering voice.

"Bring him here, you fool," Leone shouted.

The servant, cringing, ushered the officer in. It was Teng Hsieh in Army uniform. Lin Piao's aide shook Jensen's hand warmly and ac-knowledged the introduction to the lieutenant with a nod. The lieu-tenant started to leave, but Teng protested. "Please stay. I would like you to hear what I have come to say."

Teng took off his field cap. "I hope you are recovering satisfactorily," he said.

"Thank you. I'll be getting about Peking soon."

"You have rendered an important service to China," Teng said, switching from English to Chinese and adopting a formal tone. "I speak now as head of the Alien Affairs Bureau for Peking. You not only helped us spare Peking from a full assault by Lin Piao's troops, but you also hastened the liberation of all China. Lin Piao's Fourth Field Army can now march south to join the columns of Chen Yi and Liu Po-cheng for the crossing of the Yangtze. Nanking and Shanghai will soon be lib-erated and then the rest of the mainland."

"How is Lilian?" Jensen interrupted.

"She is well. She is still at Yenching."

"May I see her?"

"Of course," Teng said. "We will arrange a meeting. I will send you a message as to the time and place. Americans will be leaving Peking soon. But, if you wish, you may remain here for a time to complete the research for your book. We will give you access to the Taoist archives—though we will be closing the Taoist monasteries. They are centers of antirevolutionary activity. Taoism is a reactionary philosophy, a relic religion. We will ban all study of it in our schools. Taoism has no place in the new China."

Teng grasped Jensen's hand. "Now you must have a rest," he said. He turned to the lieutenant. "I've put sentries at the gate to make sure you're not disturbed. You and Mr. Jensen may, of course, come and go as you like. You've nothing to fear in the Liberated Areas."

Chapter Thirty-one

Joan Taylor mashed her cigarette into the ashtray beside the phone, waiting for it to ring. It had been two and a half months since she had said good-bye to Jensen at the Language School and moved to a house which she shared with Ted Burke and his Chinese mistress. She was paying rent to Burke from what she earned working for Chris Harris in the Universal Press office. The office was a stuffy ground-floor room in the house where Harris also lived. In the two hours Joan had waited for Harris to telephone, she had filled the ashtray with cigarette butts smudged with her pink lipstick. Harris had learned at noon that a delegation of municipal officials, accompanied by students carrying a huge portrait of Mao, were at the West Straight Gate to welcome the entry of Communist troops into Peking. He quickly wrote a bulletin and, before leaving for the gate, instructed Joan to rush the dispatch to the post office as soon as he telephoned confirmation of the entry. He was fairly confident it would get out. Fu Tso-yi's surrender agreement stipulated that wireless services were to be maintained.

When the telephone rang Joan picked up the receiver and mumbled hello. It was Harris. He had watched Communist troops march into the city preceded by a municipal sound truck loudly proclaiming the liberation of Peking.

"Get your ass to the post office with that bulletin and fast," Harris shouted. Joan hung up, lit another cigarette, went to the coffee pot on the hot plate in the corner of the room for another cup, then leisurely put on her raccoon coat and ambled out to one of the office jeeps. At the cavernous post office, which smelled of mold and urine, there was a queue at the telegraph counter. When she reached the counter the clerk laboriously counted the words of the dispatch and then thumbed the yuan which Joan emptied in bundles from a shopping bag to pay for the message to the U.P. desk in Tokyo.

When she returned to the office. Harris was already at his typewriter banging out a lead to his bulletin. Joan looked over his shoulder and her eyebrows shot up. "Mister, that's going to get you into big trouble," she said. Harris was describing the reaction of the population to the Communist entry as similar to the welcome given in the past to the Japanese invaders, the American Marines, the Nationalists, and hundreds of years earlier to the Manchu conquerors. Harris, hunched over the typewriter and punching at the keys, ignored her. He had thought up this angle even before the Communists arrived. Joan took the next take of Harris's story to the post office.

It was dusk when Joan arrived home in a pedicab. The portly amah, wife of the cook boy who served meals, brought a basin of steaming water to her small house in the compound. She washed, put on a red Chinese jacket lined with sheepskin wool, and went across the cobbled courtyard to Burke's house, where they customarily dined together. She found Burke stretched out on the couch in an open white silk shirt. Already drunk, he was oblivious to the chill in the house.

"Come in. Come in," Burke called. "I'm celebrating the liberation of our cozy little town. Have a drink." Joan went to the sideboard and poured a brandy into a whiskey shot glass. "When are you going to stop drinking that local poison?" Burke said, sitting up unsteadily on the couch.

Joan settled into a frayed brocaded armchair. "Why don't you mind your own damn business?" she said. "You're not doing all that well slurping scotch every night. Let's eat. I'm starved."

"Okay, okay," Burke mumbled. "Don't get mad." He coughed. "I'm going to knock off the booze. Starting tomorrow. Really. I've been to the doc. He says my liver is shot." He stood up and bellowed: "Silver Pearl!" A young Chinese woman peered timidly into the lounge. She brushed back a lock of hair that had strayed over the brow of her exquisite features. She was pregnant, and her figure bulged in the flowered silk *cheongsam*.

"Get us dinner," Burke said roughly. Silver Pearl bowed and shuffled out.

Joan frowned angrily. "You shouldn't treat her like that. She's not a servant."

"You're right, Joan. I'm sorry. You know I still love her . . . even now when she looks like a cow. God, she was beautiful when I first saw her in that jade shop."

It would be so nice to get away from this drunk, Joan thought, as they went in to dinner. Perhaps she should move in with Henry Sung, even though his room was so tiny. Her life had become more bearable since she had taken up with Henry, a lean, handsome Chinese bachelor with a twinkling sense of humor. A professor of geology at Pei-ta University, he had been a schoolmate of her husband, John, at Georgetown.

When they lived in Taiyuan, John had read Sung's letters to her, laughing at his clever antigovernment quips. Last night in Sung's small room in the Chinese City they sipped red wine by candlelight, emptying the two bottles that Joan had bought at the Benedictine Monastery, and feasted on a carp that Henry had cooked with ginger and hot spices. They slept on a mattress on the floor of the unheated room, under a quilt filled with goose down.

In the days after the Communist occupation of the city, Joan found scant work at the U.P. office. Peking was drying up as a news center. While consolidating their control of the city, the Communists avoided all contact with foreigners. The consulates were not recognized. Foreign correspondents were ignored, except for ferocious press attacks on Harris and other reporters, citing their disparaging dispatches on the way the populace greeted the entry of Communist troops. Finally, *The People's Daily* published a list of foreign correspondents together with an edict of the Military Control Commission, forbidding them to function as journalists and ordering their deportation. Joan was on the list together with other foreign employees.

That afternoon Joan went to Harris's house to help Tamara, his White Russian mistress, prepare a farewell dinner for the correspondents. She found Tamara in the upstairs bedroom, pacing about and nervously twisting a lace handkerchief around her fingers. Tamara began to weep as Joan entered. "What should I do, Joan?" she cried. "Harris will leave now because he cannot send news. I'm stateless. I have no passport. I won't be able to go with him. What will happen to me?"

Tamara was an extraordinarily beautiful woman, in her mid-twenties, with thick black hair and dark eyes heightened by her pale skin. During lazy afternoons, when Harris was away, Joan had taken to long chats with her. Tamara told Joan how she and Harris had met in Manchuria. Tamara was the daughter of a Russian officer who fought against the Bolsheviks in Siberia with Admiral Kolchak's White forces and later escaped across the border to Harbin. In the White Russian community, he had chanced upon and married a beautiful Jewish woman. While he gambled at the Railway Officers' Club, she managed a restaurant in his name until he succumbed to vodka. Harris had discovered Tamara behind the bar in her mother's restaurant. The restaurant was shabby, like most of the Russian quarter since the takeover by the Chinese Communists. Tamara yearned to leave Harbin. She gladly introduced Harris to the city, taking him in a horse-drawn droshky down snow-covered winding streets past old wooden houses and the red onion-domed Orthodox churches, into cabarets where they feasted on borscht, smoked salmon, and caviar, and drank toasts in vodka and Georgian wine, before frolicking in bed. Harris, who had never experienced such a woman in his native Michigan—and certainly not in the conjugal bed that he had left behind in Grand Rapids—was entranced. He smuggled Tamara to Peking on an Executive Headquarters truce plane in return for a case of Armenian cognac divided among the crew.

Now things had changed. "What shall I do?" Tamara sobbed.

"Go back to your own," Joan said curtly. "There are lots of White Russians in Shanghai. There's nothing in Harris's world for you."

As Joan turned to leave, Tamara said, "And what about you, my Joan?"

Joan shrugged. "My party is over, too." Leaving Tamara staring after her, Joan went downstairs to say good-bye to the others.

Harris, in shirtsleeves and a loosely knotted tie, was sitting morosely in a corner of the lounge, already plotting how to leave Peking without Tamara in his baggage.

Joan walked over to him. "I suppose, Mr. Harris, there's no point in coming into the office tomorrow," she drawled.

Harris belched. "That's right," he replied stonily.

As Joan was walking out the door to her pedicab, Harris's Chinese translator came running after her. "A man telephoned when you were out, Miss Taylor," he said. "Mr. Jensen like you go see him tomorrow afternoon. He is at the lieutenant's house."

"Terrific," Joan exclaimed, her spirits rising.

◆

Jensen was in his wheelchair reading when Little Flower knocked and announced that Joan was at the door. "Really," he said. "Wonderful. Bring her in."

Joan entered smiling and kissed Jensen. "My God, honey, what happened to you?"

"Just a little jeep accident," Jensen said, grinning. "I'll be fine in a few days. You're looking great," he said, as Joan took off her racoon coat and mink hat. He noticed that Joan's hair was no longer done in a tight bun. It fell over her shoulders in crinkled waves. "Glad you telephoned," Joan said as she pulled up a chair.

"I didn't telephone, Joan," Jensen said, puzzled. "Maybe it was Jean. Anyhow, great to see you. What are you up to?"

"I've been working in the U.P. office. But I'm getting ready to leave. The Chicoms are throwing out all the correspondents, and me. So I'm going. I'm not sorry. I've had enough."

"Where you headed?"

Joan tilted back her head, a slow smile breaking on her lips. "Louisiana."

"Louisiana?" Jensen exclaimed.

"Yeah . . . Nice, Louisiana. I'm going home to put it all together . . . before moving on. I can do it now. What about you?"

"I'm going to hang around a while."

"Can't leave China, huh? You're like Ted Burke. China's got its claws into you. The only difference is, he's got a Chinese girlfriend."

Jensen settled back in the wheelchair uneasily. "You're still living in Burke's house?"

"Yeah. With him and Silver Pearl. You know Silver Pearl?"

"Yes. I met her a couple of times in the shop of her uncle, Wang Li, the antiques dealer. She's very beautiful," Jensen said, remembering how he had once been tempted by her.

Joan put her hands in her lap and, with a mischievous expression, leaned closer to Jensen. "The rarest rose quartz," she said.

Jensen's eyes widened and he looked at her incredulously. "In my Suchou garden," he replied.

Joan threw back her head, laughing. "I guessed you were one of them."

"You . . . you're the other one?"

"No, John, my husband. I visited him in the prison before those crazies in Taiyuan killed him. He told me everything. I knew John lived in Washington for a year. I didn't know he was being trained by the CIA. He was made an American citizen before he left Washington, but they had him travel on a Chinese passport." Joan lit a cigarette and inhaled deeply. "At the end, John couldn't have been more bitter. Couldn't understand why the CIA wasn't trying to get him out. I guess they figured he was better dead because he'd lost his cover. Then the spooks came after me. They guessed John might have told me what was going on. My passport and local residence permit disappeared from my bedroom one night. They had the Chinese police put me on one of Chennault's planes heading for Shanghai. The plane was diverted to Tsingtao. I was taken off the plane by a Marine major, a Chinese-American. He took me aboard a Navy transport in the bay where I met this guy, Smith."

Jensen nodded.

"You know him. Nice-spoken feller, isn't he," Joan said, grimacing. "Offered me a deal I couldn't turn down. Life in Peking. They'd arrange a job with the U.P. They thought the Chicoms would let the correspondents stay . . . so I could hang on. I was to get real friendly with John's old university chums. The big target was Henry Sung, John's classmate at Georgetown. Sung was in contact with the Communists. He was in a group trying to make Peking an open city. Smith said his people would be in touch. I played along. There wasn't much choice. I came out of Taiyuan without a dime. Smith said he'd have me booted out of China if I didn't cooperate. Maybe they'd do something worse, he kind of hinted. They gave me back my passport and put me on a Navy plane going to Manchuria to pick up missionary refugees. I was mixed in with them. We put down in Peking."

"Did you see Smith again?"

"No. But before the Chicoms came into Peking, the Marine major showed up. Told me some crazy story. Asked me to go to South America for a couple of years. Hide out. Would you believe it? I said shit, no. He got real nasty. But I told him to shove off. I also told him I'd never forget how they let John die . . . and someday I'd stick it to them."

Jensen scrutinized Joan's upturned face. "Not scared? They're dangerous."

"I've known worse types in Louisiana," Joan said, throwing back her head and laughing. Joan stood up, kissed Jensen on the cheek. "I've got to go . . . pack and everything. I'll come by to see you before I leave. Okay? Bye, honey." She scooped up her coat and went out the door. Jensen looked after her admiringly, thinking: The lady from Nice is going to make it.

He had just picked up his book when he heard shouting in the compound. The door was thrown open and a Sikh guard rushed in. "Mr.

Jensen, Mr. Jensen, your friend, the lady . . . she's been killed . . . in the hutung. A truck hit her pedicab. The truck didn't stop. What should we do?"

Jensen propelled the wheelchair out of the room into the courtyard. The Smith people, he thought as he lunged into the hutung. Joan lay face down in the center of the alley, several feet from the crushed pedicab, a widening pool of dark blood about her black tresses. Jensen pounded the arms of the wheelchair with both fists, tears in his eyes. Those murdering buggers. They'd pay for this somehow. He wheeled closer to Joan's body and shouted for a blanket. Later, as he reentered the compound, the thought occurred to him: Now there's only one. Me.

Chapter Thirty-two

Ted Burke woke as the first glimmers of dawn made patterns on the floor of the lounge. He lay on the couch, an almost empty scotch bottle beside him. He groaned, sat up, and went to the bathroom. He returned to the couch and sat there with hands clasped, his head throbbing.

He had been sober yesterday morning at Joan's burial service and had not started drinking again until after the visit of the Communist officer, who came to his door accompanied by two soldiers.

"I am from the Alien Affairs Bureau," the officer said in English. "Your residence permit, please." Burke went to his bedroom and returned with his passport and city residence permit. The officer handed back the passport. "We do not recognize this document. Your residence permit has expired. Where are you employed?"

"I don't have a job. I used to work at the American consulate. I was discharged for medical reasons."

"There is no American consulate in Peking," the officer replied.

"You are living here as a parasite. Therefore, in keeping with the peoples' new regulations, you will be deported."

Burke breathed heavily. "I can't leave Peking," he said. "My wife is here."

"What is her nationality?"

"Chinese."

"Do you have marriage documents?"

Burke shook his head.

"In two days our police will come here to carry out the deportation order. I am posting a guard at the entrance to the compound. The Chinese woman will remain here," the officer said. Ignoring Burke's pleas, he turned and left.

Burke picked up the scotch bottle, but then he threw it across the room and stretched out on the couch. "What am I going to do?" he muttered. "What'll happen to Silver Pearl? The baby?"

He went to the bedroom, put on fresh clothing, and then seated himself in an armchair, arms folded and eyes closed.

Burke, the dashing former Marine captain who had won the Purple Heart and Silver Star in combat in the Pacific islands, had been a popular figure at parties. Few knew that before the war he had been a salesman in a clothing shop in Des Moines. In Peking, the diplomatic whirl was at the center of Burke's life. Only in his passion for jade did he become deeply interested in things Chinese. He spent hours shopping on Jade Street for precious pieces. His favorite shop was that of Wang Li, who laid out the rarest Stone of Heaven pieces for his covetous inspection. On an afternoon visit Burke found Silver Pearl behind a gem showcase. She was Wang Li's niece, a war orphan. Burke's visits became increasingly frequent, more to chat with Silver Pearl than to look over Wang Li's treasures. When he asked Silver Pearl to dine with him she replied with lowered eyes that he would have to speak to Wang Li.

Over tea and baked watermelon seeds Burke found himself bargaining for the company of Silver Pearl as if he were buying jade. "Do you have a large house?" Wang Li inquired.

"Yes," replied Burke, puzzled.

"Silver Pearl could be happy there, but very sad if you left Peking."

"I'm not planning to leave."

"A small security would be helpful. Who knows what will happen when the Communists come."

Burke then understood. Silver Pearl was being sold to him as a concubine. When he next came to the shop he handed fifteen hundred American dollars to Wang Li. Silver Pearl went home with him.

Burke rose from the armchair and looked out the window at the dew-cloaked garden and then pressed the call button summoning Yu, the Number-One Boy.

"We must have a special dinner tonight," Burke said. "Silver Pearl and I shall celebrate the coming of our child." Yu withdrew, smiling broadly.

That night, Silver Pearl donned the festive red-and-gold silk *cheongsam* that Burke had brought her from Shanghai, and she twined a matching ribbon through her pigtail. Burke wore a shining black silk mandarin robe. He did not tell Silver Pearl of the visit of the Communist officer. Silver Pearl had not been so happy in many weeks. At Burke's gentle urging she joined in toasts of yellow wine to happiness and the child to be born to them. Burke picked up Silver Pearl and carried her gently to the bedroom. He cradled her in his arms under the quilt stitched of furs, and he whispered of his love until she was asleep.

In the morning Burke told Silver Pearl it was time to buy clothes for their child, and he sent her with American dollars to Morrison Street to shop. After watching her go out the gate past the sentry, he went to the camphor chest in their bedroom and took out the brocaded boxes in which he kept his jade collection. He opened them and lovingly picked out the ornamental jade, the green Mandarin necklace, the white belt buckles and pendants, and the archer's ring. He laid them out on the bed together with the jadeite vases, figurines, and the pink jade cup. Beside the rattan peacock chair facing the foot of the bed he placed the mortuary jade, vessels, and corpse shields. From the tall oxblood vase atop the yellow rosewood armoire he fetched a bundle of American dollars and piled them on the bed beside the slender white Kuan Yin. On a folded paper, addressed to the American Consul General, he scribbled: "I leave all to Silver Pearl." He signed it: "Captain Theodore M. Burke."

From the camphorwood wardrobe he took out his Marine dress uniform. He dressed meticulously, straightening the ribbon decorations. He seated himself in the peacock chair, placed the jade pendant of resurrection in the shape of a cicada into his mouth, picked up his .45-caliber service pistol from the side table, put it to his temple, and pulled the trigger.

Chapter Thirty-three

The days went by slowly for Jensen as he waited for word from Teng Hsieh as to when he could see Lilian. When he was well enough he drove in the jeep to the American cemetery where Joan had been buried. He knelt in the snow and put a brandy bottle filled with artifical flowers at the foot of the grave. The Chinese pastor of St. Michel's Church had officiated at the funeral. Joan lay not far from where missionaries slain during the Boxer Rebellion were buried.

On another day he went to the shop of Wang Li. He was alarmed to find the shop barred and a Communist sentry standing at the door. Quickly he drove to a hutung near Wang Li's home, parked the jeep, and walked to the compound gate. A Communist guard was seated on a stool with a rifle across his lap beside the great oaken door. The soldier rose as Jensen approached.

"Comrade, I am looking for Wang Li, the antiques dealer," Jensen said. "I left my mother's jade necklace with him for repair. His shop has been closed for two days."

The soldier, a young, rosy-cheeked peasant lad, slung his rifle over his shoulder and laughed. "You will have to look for Wang Li in another world. He was tried by a People's Court and executed. He was a black marketeer. Many precious things belonging to the People's China were found under the floor of his house."

Jensen gazed at the soldier in shock, his temples throbbing. Lao Tsu's words of caution lept into his mind: *When gold and jade fill your hall, you will not be able to keep them safe.*

"Now move on," the soldier said. "No one is permitted to stay here."

When he returned to the lieutenant's house he did not venture out for two days. For hours he sat on the floor of his bedroom in meditation, struggling to quiet his mind. Was this how the Communists would rule?

Over the next days Jensen observed that the Communists were adhering to the surrender terms outlined when he and Professor Chang met Lin Piao. The disbanded Nationalist troops were given the option of joining the Communist Army or returning to their homes as civilians. The Communists took over publicly-owned enterprises and seized the holdings of Kuomintang officials, but allowed private companies to function as before. The police remained on duty under a new Bureau of Public Security. They imposed strict controls to halt speculation and black marketing in money and goods. Violators were dealt harsh summary punishment. Wang Li had evidently been a victim of this purge.

Jensen roamed the city, examining the faces of women students who passed by, hoping to come upon Lilian.

Three weeks after Teng's visit, a soldier brought a letter to the gate asking Jensen to come to the Military Control Commission the following morning. Soon after sunrise, unable to conceal his excitement,

Jensen was up and pacing the courtyard under the skeletal branches of the great linden tree. Little Flower watched him through a window of the servants quarters. She did not ask any questions. She had not shared his bed since he was well enough to sit up. When it was time to go, Jensen donned his padded Mandarin gown and blue scarf. Leone ceremoniously popped a long-haired red fox fur hat on his head.

"An old friend of yours is waiting at the door," the lieutenant said with an enigmatic smile. In the hutung, reclining in the seat of a pedicab, somewhat thinner but still wearing the battered fedora at a rakish tilt, was Ying. The pedicab man leaped up grinning. "Are you well, Master?" he said.

Jensen grasped Ying's hand. "Where have you been?"

"After you left, Master, I was drafted into the fascist Kuomintang army. When Peking was liberated, my platoon was allowed to go home . . . and we were indeed fortunate. We were given a little money."

"And your family?"

"They have food now."

"Good. Take me to the Municipal Hall."

As the pedicab wheeled through the streets of the Tartar City, Jensen noticed the streets had been scrubbed. Huge pictures of Mao Tse-tung were hung together with placards denouncing the Kuomintang and the United States. On many public buildings there were portraits side by side of Marx, Lenin, and Stalin. At the Municipal Hall, which now housed the Military Control Commission, Jensen dismounted. Not knowing what awaited him, he told Ying to return to the French lieutenant's compound. At the gate an officer of the guard examined Jensen's identification and escorted him to a third-floor office. Teng Hsieh sat behind a worn teak desk piled high with documents. He greeted Jensen with a firm handshake and inclined his head with a smile to a side door: "She's waiting for you."

Jensen entered a large room dominated by a conference table centered under a rusted brass chandelier. Leather couches were set against the peeling plaster walls. On one of the couches, hands folded in her lap, was Lilian. She was dressed in an ill-fitting baggy uniform without insignia. She was alone.

Jensen, his hands clasped tightly, walked slowly to her. He reached down, took her hands, and raised her into his arms. She came to him shyly. And then he felt her arms press more tightly about him. She leaned back to look up at him, touching his lips with her fingers. "Eric, Eric," she whispered.

He stroked her hair, loosening it where it was tucked under her field cap. "Lilian," he said. "I love you. Do you still love me?"

She rested her head against his shoulder. "Yes, Eric . . . yes, I love you. Here, look! Your jade." She took the carved pebble from her breast pocket and poised it on the palm of her hand. "When I was in great need . . . it comforted me."

Jensen produced in turn the jade of the entwined dragons. "Remember. Your grandfather said it was wish-fulfilling. Let it be so now." He drew her to the couch and they sat close, hands entwined.

"Your mother . . ." Eric began.

"Yes, I know," Lilian said. "My father stayed on in Shanghai for her funeral. A university student brought me a letter from him. My father told me what you did for Robert and Fragrant Iris on the Huaipei. Our family is indebted to you, Eric. And you saved Peking from destruction. You performed a great deed for China."

"Lilian . . . that's past. Now it's our turn. I want you to marry me. We'll live here in Peking."

Lilian folded her hands in her lap, her lips trembling. The rumble of traffic on the road outside the building penetrated the room. "Eric, I can't. It wouldn't be permitted. I'm now in the People's Liberation

Army. I'm a nurse in the South Going Corps. We'll cross the Yangtze with Lin Piao's army in Central China. My mission is to set up a school for nurses in the south."

Eric shook his head slowly. "Not without me. I'll go with you. Why not? I'll become a teacher of English in the Liberated Areas. There'll be plenty of work for me."

Lilian looked at him silently for several moments, clasping her hands more tightly. "Eric, this is not a time for us. There's no place for you in this China. It's best you return to your own people. Finish the research for your book quickly and go home."

"I won't let you go without me," Jensen said, his voice choked. "I will go to Teng. I've helped his people. This is something he can do for us. Wait for me, Lilian."

Jensen strode to Teng's office. Teng was at his desk writing. Jensen seated himself in front of the desk, pulled the chair close, and leaned across. "I want to go with Lilian," he said in Chinese. "Live with her in the south, in the Liberated Areas. I'll work as a teacher of English."

Teng continued to write. He made brushstrokes on the document before him and then on another before he leaned back and examined Jensen's strained features. "I'm sorry, Mr. Jensen," Teng said deliberately in English. "But the answer must be no."

Jensen frowned at Teng. "I don't understand."

"In revolutionary China there is no place in our schools for teachers who do not share our ideology."

"I can work as a translator," Jensen interrupted.

"Yes, Mr. Jensen, we do have Americans and other foreigners working for us as translators. They translate our propaganda. Some broadcast it to the world. I've watched these people . . . guided them. They're not happy. Even the ones who marry Chinese women are never fully accepted by our people. Some are denounced as traitors in their own countries. They live stranded between two worlds. They become wooden men. No, I'll spare you that. As for Lilian, she has her duties."

"But you owe this to me," Jensen said, his voice rising.

Teng stood up. "I'm serving you as well as ourselves. Perhaps it's better that you return home at once. You can return to China at another time. We'll not forget our debt to you. We will welcome you. But now you're out of step with us."

"You'll not take Lilian from me," Jensen said fiercely. "She's not one of your robots." Jensen ran back to the conference room and jerked the door open. Lilian was not there. At the table a meeting of military officers was in progress. They looked at Jensen in puzzlement. Jensen turned back to Teng. "Where is she?" he asked savagely.

"She's returning to Yenching. That was her intention before meeting with you."

Jensen spun about, knocking over a chair. He ran out of Teng's office, shouldered through the crowded hallway, and rushed down the stairs to the ground floor. There he calmed himself and approached the guard who had escorted him to Teng. "Has the woman student left?" he asked.

"You mean the tall woman who was in Comrade Teng's office?"

Jensen nodded impatiently.

"She left a few minutes ago in a truck, sitting beside the driver."

Jensen walked slowly out the gate. He motioned to a pedicab and directed the coolie to the lieutenant's house. There, Jensen went to his room. Leone had not yet returned from his office for lunch. Head bowed, Jensen paced the room. Cheated . . . cheated, he thought. They had given him so little time with Lilian. Not even time to talk of a future when they could be together. Jensen went to the window and gazed at the linden tree. He had opened the gates of Peking for them. They had repaid him with a gesture, fulfilling their promise by allowing him only a glimpse of Lilian . . . a glimpse that had left him with more pain than happiness. *"No! No!"* he said, slamming his hand on the window frame. He would not accept their lies. Lilian had spoken under duress. She needed him. He picked up his scarf and went to the kitchen, where he asked the cook for the loan of his bicycle. As he pedaled away from the compound the sentry saluted him and went to the telephone in the neighboring house. Jensen pedaled toward the West Straight Gate, toward Yenching.

Chapter Thirty-four

With the siege ended, Jensen found that the West Straight Gate had once again become a bustling thoroughfare. On the city side there were pedestrians, peasant carts, and civilian cars waiting to be checked by the Communist guards. Jensen pedaled around the long line but was waved to a halt by a sentry. An officer approached him.

"Where are you going?"

"To Yenching."

"Your pass, please."

Jensen set his jaw. "I have gone to Yenching many times without a pass."

"Foreigners cannot leave the city without a pass from the Alien Affairs Bureau."

"You don't understand. I must go. It is urgent."

The young officer looked uneasily at Jensen and hitched his pistol belt. The sentry beside him unslung his rifle. "Please get a pass."

Angrily Jensen remounted his bicycle, twisted it about, and, head down, pedaled furiously toward the gate. An alarmed sentry ran alongside and seized the handlebars, toppling Jensen to the ground. He rose, covered with dust, and pushed the sentry from the bicycle. "Get away, you fool!" he shouted, his eyes wild in frustration. A squad of soldiers was already running toward him. Jensen was seized from behind, his arms pinned. He was dragged into the guardhouse, shoved into a chair, and his arms were bound. A soldier stood over him with rifle at the ready until a small covered truck arrived outside. Jensen was untied and hustled into the back of the truck. An officer climbed in beside him and the truck drove back into the city.

Jensen saw he was being taken to the prison west of the Temple of Agriculture near the city wall. Subdued, he walked into the prison between two guards and was led into a cell. He sat down on the moldering straw mattress that lay on the damp stone floor. Several hours later the iron door was pulled open and an Army officer entered. He handed Jensen the wallet that had been taken from him.

"I am from the Alien Affairs Bureau," the officer said in English. "Mr. Jensen, you've committed a serious offense. You attacked and insulted a soldier of the People's Liberation Army. The time is past when foreigners can mistreat Chinese without punishment. Now come with me."

Jensen was put into a creaking Japanese sedan with the officer at his side and driven to the Peking Hotel. The hotel, not far from the Imperial City, had been occupied by the military after the Communist entry into Peking. Jensen was taken to the third floor and led into a large, high-ceilinged suite whose furnishings were of worn Victorian elegance. "You are known to our leaders," said the officer. "They want you to be comfortable until a decision is made in your case."

When he was alone Jensen went into the lounge and parted the heavy brocade curtains to reveal a double glass door. It opened on a north-facing balcony and a view of the yellow-tiled roofs of the Forbidden City. In the bathroom Jensen found an array of toilet articles. The ancient plumbing wheezed but performed.

A white-gowned waiter appeared and served an elaborate lunch. He was the only human contact Jensen would have over the next few days. In he would come with a beaming smile and a wheeled cart, uncovering special delicacies with a ceremonial flourish. Each day the waiter brought Jensen a copy of the Communist party organ, *People's Daily*. Jensen took little pleasure from these gestures. He knew he was a prisoner.

Jensen wandered restlessly through the suite. He was consumed with both yearning for Lilian and resentment at her flight from him. Meditation did not calm him. He stood for hours on the balcony, gazing at the panorama of the Imperial City, churning over the happenings of the last months. Where was the reward for all that he had done?

On February 10, several days into his confinement, there was a mass meeting before the Tienanmen of the Imperial City. Jensen heard the speeches booming out from loudspeakers, each repeating the same themes: The Kuomintang regime was collapsing; the era of the New Democracy was at hand; China would join the Soviet Union in resisting United States imperialism. As the crowds chanted their approval, Jensen felt suffocated by hostility. He saw himself suddenly like the United States: a well-intentioned giant, blundering about the Middle Kingdom and suffering from unrequited love. Lilian was right, there was no longer any place for him in China.

The next day the sentry opened the door and Leone, in a mink fur hat and a belted black overcoat, entered. He carried a large suitcase and a straw picnic basket. Jensen, who had been napping on the sofa, leaped up to hug the Frenchman.

"Ah, my dear Eric, I thought you might like to share a bottle of wine with me," the lieutenant said, as he shed his coat.

Jensen nodded happily. "How did you find me, Jean?"

Leone busied himself with the picnic basket. "All that later, my dear friend. Let's have our lunch first." Triumphantly he held up a bottle of Chante-Alouette and laid out on the table a lunch of cold chicken, cabbage salad, French cheese, and bread.

Leone was addressing himself to the Camembert when Jensen asked, "What do they intend to do with me?"

Leone continued to pat cheese on a bit of French bread and drained the last of the wine in his glass. "Excellent wine, a Hermitage vintage. *Mon cher*, you will be deported," he said. Jensen rubbed his brow and leaned back in his chair. Leone went to Jensen's side and put a hand on his shoulder. "They asked me to bring your manuscripts and clothes."

"How will I leave?"

"A Polish oil tanker is unloading at Taku Bar off Tangku. It's bound for Hong Kong. You'll be on it. I'm sorry."

Jensen shrugged. "No matter, now."

"Blanche sends good wishes," Leon exclaimed brightly. "She asked me to give you this." He reached into the basket and came up with a bottle of Russian vodka. Tied around the bottle was the brown sock Jensen had left behind when he had fled her bedroom. "She's going home." Leone said. "The minister-counselor of your embassy ordered her dismissed. She gave you those air travel orders without permission."

Jensen sighed. "I'm sorry."

"She didn't seem too upset," Leone said cheerfully. "All she said was: 'Louisville is looking better.' Eric, it makes little difference. The other Americans are packing too. The consulate expects to be shut down before long. Your government has taken a tough, uncompromising line toward Mao. The Communists are retaliating."

"And the Language School?"

"The Communists are closing the school. The missionaries have been told to leave the country.

"I must go," the lieutenant said, standing up. "They gave me only one hour with you. It's not for always. We'll meet again, in Paris or maybe in China."

Embracing his friend in farewell, Jensen shook his head. "This new China is not for me."

The next day, an officer from the Alien Affairs Bureau entered Jensen's suite. "Please pack, Mr. Jensen, we are leaving by train for the port of Tientsin. You are being deported." A jeep was waiting outside and drove them toward the Front Gate en route to the East Railway Station. Jensen strained to capture a last sight of the crimson ramparts of the Imperial City. Maybe, it was worthwhile, he thought. I helped preserve all that . . . helped these people. As they passed through the Front Gate he looked up at the city wall, remembering the spring days when he strolled with Chi atop its broad expanse. Would Chi's dream of a better China come about? What did Han say? "Revolution destroys the old system. It does not always dictate what will arise on the ruins. There will be many changes before the coming of the new China."

Jensen and his guards arrived at the railway station in the late afternoon. Tientsin had been badly damaged in the Communist assault, but already some of the textile mills were reopened, spewing smoke over the sprawling metropolis. Jensen was confined to his wagon-lits compartment. After a half hour the train steamed out on its thirty-mile run to the Tangku river port. A jeep was waiting at Tangku, and Jensen was taken quickly to the customs quay. A customs officer still wearing his white Nationalist uniform questioned him as he searched his baggage. "Do you have any valuable antiques in your baggage? Foreigners are no longer permitted to carry away China's treasures." Jensen thought of his precious things left and lost in Wang Li's vault.

Jensen was put aboard a launch flying the new red flag that bore the yellow hammer and sickle. It chugged slowly down the Pei Ho. As they emerged from the mouth of the river, a searchlight near the ruins of the old Taku forts scanned the launch. It was already dusk. Off Taku Bar lay the rusted Polish tanker, its lights aglow. The launch bumped the ship's accommodation ladder and a sailor leaped out to secure the lines. A crewman led Jensen to a small stateroom.

As he was unpacking there was a rap at the door. Jensen opened it and gasped. It was Lilian, smiling, dressed in a baggy officers' uniform. Jensen enfolded her in his arms. "Come," she said, taking his hand. "We've only a few minutes." They sat close on the bunk.

"I couldn't let you leave so embittered," Lilian said. "The comrades let me come. They've not forgotten their debt to you."

Jensen held Lilian's hand more tightly. "But Lilian . . . "

"Eric, listen to me," Lilian interrupted firmly. "I love you. But I couldn't encourage you to remain in China. Not the way things are. No American can stay here unless he condemns his country. It won't always be like that. Believe me. Some day you'll be welcomed back."

"Welcomed back? But to what?" Jensen said. "You've chosen your road. . . . Without you, there's nothing here for me. No lacquer garden," he said with a wry smile. "But I haven't lost everything. I know that, Lilian. You gave me your love. I'll treasure that always. And I did something for Peking. Chi would not be disappointed in me."

The ship's whistle sounded. Jensen drew Lilian closer to him and kissed her. "My love . . . good-bye."

"Not good-bye. Eric, please. Let's say only *tsai chien* . . . until we meet again."

Jensen nodded.

"*Tsai chien . . . tsai chien . . .* " Lilian cried, as she turned about and ran out the door.

Jensen stretched out on the bunk, his right arm flung over his brow. He lay there for a few minutes. Then he assumed the Lotus Position on the cabin deck. Through his nostrils he inhaled the breath of the Nine Heavens, and in total concentration guided *ch'i*, his breath, through the passages of his body, bringing energy to the Palace of the Brain. For one hundred and twenty heartbeats he let the *ch'i* cleanse his being and then meditated.

Lilian lost. My love. Now emptiness. Seek the Way of Chuang Tzu. In emptiness find illumination . . . Accept life as only a time of cultivation of spirit in a vortex of love, evil, pain, and contradiction. Rise above misfortune and transitory values. Thus become free and know the Tao.

Jensen bowed. He looked upward. Bowed again.

No. The wisdom of Chuang Tzu had not bestowed peace. The pain was no less. The longing for Lilian. The vanished garden. I am not at one with the Master.

The tanker shuddered as the engines started up. Jensen rose and went up on deck. It was raining lightly. He stood at the rail until the lights of Tangku disappeared. He thought about what had brought him to China, about his search. He had learned the catechisms of Taoism, but he had not encompassed its inner meaning, nor had he found solace in the words of the Master. The Tao, the Way, origin of all being, sum of the Universe, remained for him indefinable. He had been impelled to search for the essence by the timeless promise of Chuang Tzu: *Free yourself, if you would know the Way and the God Force.* But he had not been able to summon the mystical intuition or the faith demanded, any more than he had for the teachings of Luther. Better, perhaps, as he continued to search, to abide by the humility of Lao Tsu: *The Tao that can be told is not the eternal Tao.*

.   .   .

Just after dawn, Jensen snapped awake. The ship's engines were no longer throbbing. He rolled out of his bunk and went to the porthole. The ship was dead in the water. Jensen could see a destroyer standing several hundred yards off. He was dressing when there was a sudden hammering on the door. When Jensen opened it, a young Chinese in the uniform of an officer of the Nationalist navy elbowed into the room waving a pistol. He was followed by two sailors carrying Thompson submachine guns. Jensen backed away.

"You are Eric Jensen?" the officer asked.

"Yes."

"Your passport."

Jensen picked up his passport, which was lying on a table, and handed it over as the officer sheathed his pistol in the holster on his hip. "You are under arrest. We have proof you are a Communist spy. Now come with us."

"I am not a spy," Jensen said calmly. "This is a mistake."

"Come." The two sailors pointed their guns.

"I must pack."

"We will bring your belongings."

Jensen followed the officer to the upper deck and was prodded down the ship's ladder to a naval motor launch. Jensen sat in the rear of the launch and watched with foreboding as it made for the destroyer. He thought of Hsi Kang, the Taoist poet, going to his execution strumming his lute. No lute for Jensen to ease the passage, he reflected.

The launch came alongside the Nationalist destroyer and was hoisted aboard. Jensen was lifted over the side of the launch onto the deck. As he was led away, he caught a glimpse of Smith in a trench coat standing at the rail watching.

. . .

Smith was leaning against a steel desk in the wardroom when Jensen was brought in by two armed sailors. He looked haggard. The collar of his white shirt was undone and he was unshaven. He motioned the sailors out of the room and examined Jensen with a slight smile.

"Welcome aboard," Smith said. "Do sit down. Coffee? Brandy?" Jensen did not reply and remained standing, breathing heavily, unconcealed animosity in his eyes.

"I brought you here because those Congress investigators were waiting for you in Hong Kong. The embassy told them you were on the tanker."

"I could have handled them," Jensen said.

"Perhaps. And perhaps not. Not if you were threatened with prison for contempt of Congress if you refused to tell the Committee on Un-American Activities about Wagging Pipit. We couldn't risk it."

"You murdered Joan Taylor," Jensen spat out.

"She did it to herself," Smith said, as he picked up his cane and walked heavily to a side table on which there was a bottle of brandy. He poured a drink, looked into it, and said bitterly. 'I'll stick it to you,' she said to us. She made us into something we didn't want to be."

Smith gulped his drink. "Listen, Jensen. There's a lot involved here. Not only for my people. The testimony of any one of the three—McCormack, Taylor, or you—would have given the worst extremists in Congress what they wanted. Those witch hunters would hold up Wagging Pipit as a plot against the security of the United States. The administration would be hurt . . . badly. And get this: Those people are the most deadly enemies of your Chinese friends. They'd like to kill any chance of our coexistence with China."

"You're only trying to save your own hide," Jensen said stubbornly.

Smith shrugged. "For your own good, Jensen. For your country and China. Do as we ask. Go to Melbourne. Stay out of sight. It'll only be about two years."

His mind churning, Jensen did not reply.

Smith slammed down his glass. "There are police agents on this ship who know you only as a Communist spy. My word would be enough to have you dead . . . overboard." Smith reached into his inside breast pocket. "Your passport," he said, holding it aloft. He slowly ripped it to shreds and threw it at Jensen's feet. "That tanker was diverted from Hong Kong. Its passenger log was confiscated. There'll be no trace of you."

Smith reached again into his breast pocket and pulled out another green passport.

"Your new identity: Peter Svensson. The residence visa says scholar at Melbourne University." He placed the passport on the desk and stepped closer to Jensen. "Pick it up," he said quietly. Jensen did not move. "For God's sake, pick it up, Eric," Smith shouted, his features convulsed. "Let's end this."

Jensen went to a porthole and looked out at the sea, thinking, . . . Sick of it all. Joan murdered . . . For what. . . I'm trapped. Not only by what they can do to me, but by everything Smith said. What he said about hurting my country and China. Melbourne. . . . Time to heal. Sort things out.

Jensen went to the desk and picked up the passport.

Smith sighed with undisguised relief. He pressed a call button twice. "You're free to go, Eric," he said. "Our people will care for you until you return home."

Jensen walked out of the cabin, past the two guards, and up to the stern of the vessel. The destroyer was steaming down the China coast. Jensen held on to the rail and gazed out over the turbulent wake. He reached inside his jacket and took out the jade of the entwined dragons that Lilian had given him. He held it out over the rail. But then, he paused. He rested the jade on the palm of his hand, looked at it once again, and thought of Lilian. More than anyone or anything else, she had given meaning to his life. He gathered himself. He glanced toward China and deliberately put the jade back into his breast pocket. "*Tsai chien*," he said softly. "Until then."

PUBLICAFFAIRS is a new publishing house and a tribute to the standards, values, and flair of three persons who have served as mentors to countless reporters, writers, editors, and book people of all kinds, including me.

I. F. STONE, proprietor of *I. F. Stone's Weekly*, combined a commitment to the First Amendment with entrepreneurial zeal and reporting skill and became one of the great independent journalists in American history. At the age of eighty, Izzy published *The Trial of Socrates*, which was a national bestseller. He wrote the book after he taught himself ancient Greek.

BENJAMIN C. BRADLEE was for nearly thirty years the charismatic editorial leader of *The Washington Post*. It was Ben who gave the *Post* the range and courage to pursue such historic issues as Watergate. He supported his reporters with a tenacity that made them fearless, and it is no accident that so many became authors of influential, best-selling books.

ROBERT L. BERNSTEIN, the chief executive of Random House for more than a quarter century, guided one of the nation's premier publishing houses. Bob was personally responsible for many books of political dissent and argument that challenged tyranny around the globe. He is also the founder and was the longtime chair of Human Rights Watch, one of the most respected human rights organizations in the world.

. . .

For fifty years, the banner of Public Affairs Press was carried by its owner Morris B. Schnapper, who published Gandhi, Nasser, Toynbee, Truman, and about 1,500 other authors. In 1983 Schnapper was described by *The Washington Post* as "a redoubtable gadfly." His legacy will endure in the books to come.

Peter Osnos, *Publisher*

28 ~~14~~ DAYS

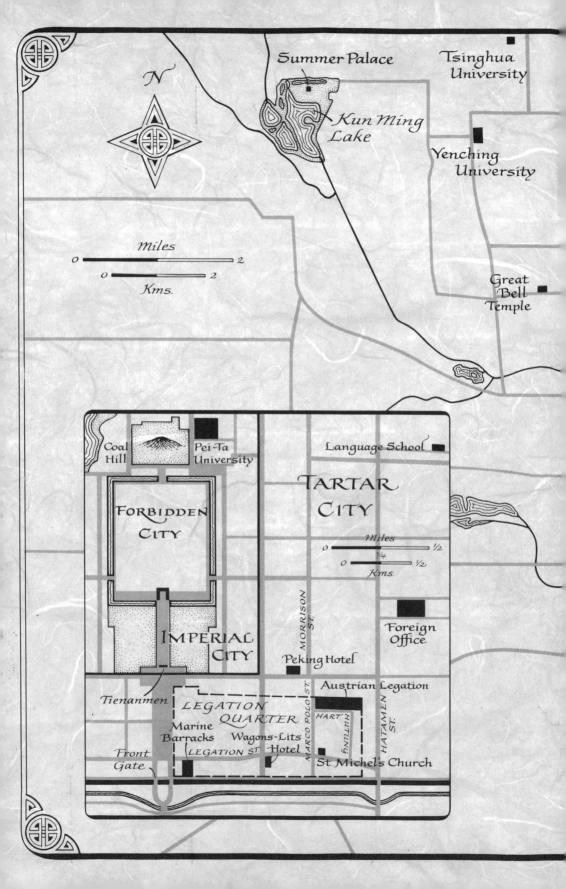